Heir to Power

The Healing Crystal

Heir to Power

Book One

MICHELE POAGUE

iUniverse, Inc.
Bloomington

Heir to Power: The Healing Crystal
Book One

iUniverse books may be ordered through booksellers or by contacting:

iUniverse
1663 Liberty Drive
Bloomington, IN 47403
www.iuniverse.com
1-800-Authors (1-800-288-4677)

ISBN: 978-1-4502-7880-5 (sc)
ISBN: 978-1-4502-7881-2 (dj)
ISBN: 978-1-4502-7882-9 (ebk)

Library of Congress Control Number: 2010918460

Printed in the United States of America

iUniverse rev. date: 02/04/2011

To Bette Rose Ryan and Lois Deveneau for believing.

Acknowledgments

The book you hold in your hand is not the one I wrote, and for that I'd like to thank my friends and family members who took the time to read and critique the various incarnations of this story: Nilajean Croonquist, Belinda Grush. Patricia Jeffryes, David Lassiter, Monte Poague, Tony Ryan, Lauren Stadler, and a special thank you to Reggie Rivers whose critique led to the most sweeping changes.

Prologue

The sound of snowmelt dripping off the clay tiles of the roof and splashing into muddy puddles woke Isontra well before dawn that early spring morning. She was drenched with sweat from a torrent of nightmares that had distressed her for the fifth night in a row. Surrealistic images, never clear enough to understand, haunted her. She never considered herself precognitive as her great grandmother had been, but the dreams seemed significant in some alien way she couldn't grasp.

Rubbing the grains of sleep from her eyes, she listened to the stillness enveloping the Chancery. Unlike herself, her extended family slept peacefully. Sitting up in her bed, her steel gray eyes heavy with sleep, she stared into the blackness of her suite, the smell of pine and clover tickling her nose. She shivered. The room was cold; the embers of last night's fire only a memory in the hearth.

While listening to the mournful cry of a snowy owl, the old woman tried to make sense of the latest dream. Images of her granddaughter's pale blue eyes, wide with fear, distressed Isontra. The dreams were likely based on her apprehension concerning the stranger currently housed in the small colony she ruled. Shaking off her anxiety, she reached for the rabbit-fur robe on the chair beside her feather bed. Wrapping the heavy garment around her thin body, she got up to light a taper. The howling of a lone wolf reminded her she needed to send out hunters to ensure her people wouldn't be overrun with predators by this time next spring,

1

and feared this might be an omen of an even greater danger, a danger to the granddaughter who must be prepared to assume the role of Vice Miral at the harvest Seridar.

At sixteen annums, Kairma was little more than a child, and a child with the handicap of being very different from the rest of her people. Isontra sighed, knowing that being different was only one of many difficulties she would face as heir to the Healing Crystal.

The colony of Survin was once strong and healthy, but a deadly plague had decimated the small village several annums earlier, reducing the total number of inhabitants to just over one hundred and thirty. Isontra worried the colony wouldn't have a sufficient genetic pool to continue, but religious law forbade the introduction of strangers.

Isontra's nights had grown uneasy since the stranger, Trep, had arrived. She knew it was a sign of change, and felt it was the one she had been awaiting her entire life, but it carried with it some unfathomable terror. *This stranger could be the answer to our prayers or the end of the life we know. Then again, maybe these are one and the same.*

Laws had been broken in the past—sometimes to the benefit of the colony and sometimes to its detriment. Now it was up to Isontra to decide which, if any, laws would be broken today, and which unpopular decisions she would lay on Kairma's shoulders to be defended time and time again. The young girl who was being groomed to become the colony's leader could not divorce herself from the decisions of the thirty Mirals who had served as Healers before her.

The candlelight threw heavy shadows on the rich bur-oak paneled walls as Isontra made her way to the finely carved pine table and began to write. She usually put off writing in the daily Ogs until she had drunk several cups of terrid, but there was no way she could go back to sleep now. She didn't want to wake the rest of the household, so like many Mirals before her, she quietly recorded the events of the previous day as the sun crept into the narrow mountain canyon.

ATD 797-3-21. How can I tell my people how different our lives will be, that is, if we survive?

Chapter 1

It was seventeen days past the spring equinox and the late morning sun felt warm on Kairma's back as she was loading baskets of food onto a battered pine cart. She was looking forward to making the long trip to the Godstones. Of her many responsibilities, taking the religious offerings to the altar was the one duty she felt most competent executing, while the Crystal, lying heavy between her breasts, reminded her of the many she did not.

She straightened up to her full six feet five inches and stretched her back. At sixteen, she wasn't particularly tall for a Survinees, whose women were on average six feet six inches and whose men were often over seven feet. Like a newborn fawn, she had long legs that never seemed to go in the right direction, and like a fawn, she was just a little clumsy.

Looking toward the east, she saw the sun rising above the deep green pines, cresting the gray granite wall of the canyon she called home. Winter snow still covered the hills around the valley and the nights were cold, but the sun rose in a cloudless sky, hinting at the warm day to come. Around her, the mountain was coming to life so different from the long, snowbound winter.

Kairma greeted two dark-haired boys of eight and ten. The boys shyly put their right hands to their right eyebrows in a formal greeting as they offered her their family tribute basket. In a low melodic voice Kairma said, "North, east, south, and west. May Nor bring them home safely." The children repeated the prayer and then ran off to help their mothers and fathers prepare for the first hunt of the spring.

Villagers scattered about in preparation for an extended hunting trip on this, the first full moon of the spring. Kairma arranged the woven hemp baskets in the cart while she watched brawny men of varying ages pack their hunting gear. Bows, slings, bedrolls, and cookware littered the ground. Women aired musty blankets and swept out storerooms. Dark-haired children darted about with excitement while the scent of baking bread drifted on the morning breeze.

Three muscular young men passed by talking excitedly. As usual, they didn't look at Kairma. She recognized Efram, a mean-spirited boy who often made rude remarks about Kairma and her family. He was one of the boys who'd most recently passed his Seridar, so this would be Efram's first hunt. Her older brother, Zedic, had also passed his Seridar on the last Harvest Moon—the beginning of the new annum. She smiled, remembering how proud Zedic had been when he took first place in the sling competition.

Thinking about her brother, she searched the small groups of men to see if she could find him. As a member of the Healing family, Zedic wouldn't be required to hunt until he took a mate, but Kairma thought it was unusual for him not to be among the animated young men preparing for their first real adult adventure.

As she watched the men stringing bows and packing gear, she noticed Collin wasn't among them either. *That's odd,* she thought. *Collin loves adventure. I wonder where they are.*

A formal greeting was offered as Kairma accepted another basket from a small girl with dark auburn hair. The color was unusual for the people of Survin, whose hair was generally deep brown to black. Taking the small basket, Kairma placed it with the rest; the cart now precariously close to overflowing. The little girl smiled widely, her blue eyes sparkling. Kairma smiled back at the pretty child, who quickly ran away.

Realizing she would have to leave soon, Kairma looked again for her brother, hoping he would join her today. Zedic was nowhere to be seen, but she saw three young boys, all identical, come running from the Chancery. They squealed loudly as they each fought to carry the bedroll to her father, Tamron. She laughed as they ran by. *Well, I guess Zedic isn't helping Mother with the boys. And if he's somewhere with Collin, that somewhere could be anywhere. I wish he had told me where they were going. It's not like Zedic to keep secrets from me.*

The morning had been hectic and her braids were beginning to unravel, so Kairma sat down on a three-legged wooden stool and began to re-braid her ivory hair. As she combed her slender fingers through her waist-length hair, she thought about the many times Zedic and Collin had walked with her to the Godstones in the past. The three of them were rarely separated with the exception of when she attended her lessons.

Zedic was already looking more like a man than a boy. At six feet eleven inches, he was already an inch taller than his best friend, Collin. She knew Zedic would mate soon, and their childhood adventures together would come to an end.

She watched her father pack his gear and talk enthusiastically with the other men. Most of the men of Survin liked to hunt, and her father was no different. She found herself thinking how much easier life would have been if she had been born male.

Like Zedic, Comad Tamron of the Survinees wasn't required to hunt. As members of the Healing family, the village provided for the needs of the Comad and the Miral. Kairma suspected her father always went on the hunts because he had never truly been comfortable with the position into which he'd married. Tamron didn't like receiving gifts he hadn't earned.

Kairma was proud of her father. He went out of his way to help others and contributed greatly to the success of the colony. As a baby, Tamron had come to Survin with a group of strangers, and although the group was allowed to join the community, he was still an outsider, and several people were openly bitter about his marriage to the Vice Miral.

Kairma finished twisting her hair into its customary braids and called to her little sister. Kinter could try her patience sometimes and today would be no exception, she was sure. However, she couldn't go to the Godstones alone and she had few choices for assistance. Some little time passed and Kairma still hadn't seen Kinter. Curling her tongue against her teeth, Kairma let out a long, low whistle followed by two short notes. Tying her braids up in a muted umber scarf that completely covered her hair, she watched Kinter slowly ambling down the center of the canyon, clearly upset to have her playtime interrupted.

"Have you seen Zedic?" Kairma's voice even more husky than usual. She laid a blanket over the baskets of food. "I can't find him, and Mother will be angry if I go to the altar alone."

"He's already *at* the Godstones…" Kinter sneered, flipping a long dark braid over her shoulder. "*With Collin.* I saw them sneak off just after breakfast."

"Why did they leave so early?" Kairma asked, ignoring her sister's taunt. "Zedic should have waited for me."

Kinter busied herself by pulling new green buds off the limb of a briar bush. "Zedic told Mother he was going to help Collin get blooding rods for tomorrow night."

"So what makes you think they went to the Godstones?"

Kinter screwed up her pretty face. "I followed them down to the lake and saw them head toward the mountain. Where else would they be going?"

"You know, they might actually be going to find blooding rods." Kairma wouldn't admit it, but she thought Kinter was probably right. She took her little sister by the hand, knowing Kinter dreaded the four-mile walk to the altar. "Well, I guess that means you'll have to go with me then."

Kinter frowned. "Why can't you go alone? Zedic and Collin can walk you home, Mother will never know."

"Well, just in case I can't find them, you had better come with me." Kairma headed purposely toward the road with Kinter in tow. "And I don't want to be all day at it, so come on." Grabbing the cart by the handle, Kairma began to walk down the path. "You have your sling with you? Gramme heard a wolf a few days ago."

Nodding assent, Kinter kicked a rock and fell grudgingly in behind Kairma.

The two girls walked along the winding path down the northern slope of the mountain, toward a small lake. Kinter was in no hurry and Kairma had to prod her along at every turn. "Kinter, do you have to walk so slow? I really would like to get back home sometime before dark."

Kinter made a face but began walking a little faster, and the old cart creaked and rattled in steady rhythm as they made their way through a thick forest of ponderosa pine and scrub oak. The natural path twisted and turned following a small creek, winding its way down to the northwest. The narrow creek spilled into a pretty lake surrounded by large conifers, mountain mahoganies, and aspens. At the edge of the lake, the trail widened and made a sharp turn to the left. Here large granite boulders lined the roadway, and sunlight glistened off the mica like newly fallen snow. Fox squirrels and yellow-bellied marmots darted for cover as the girls approached.

Kairma pointed to a large golden eagle making lazy, graceful circles in a deep azure sky. "Of all the birds I have ever seen, that one is my favorite. It must be wonderful to have that kind of freedom."

Kinter looked up, shielding her eyes from the bright sunshine. "I like the hawk myself. The other day I saw one pick up a snake that was at least a meter long. It was amazing." In an imitation of the great bird, she circled around Kairma, swooping up a stick and pretending to fight with it. "The hawk has it all: beauty, grace, power, speed—what more could you want?"

The two young women chattered as they walked uphill the last mile and a half to the Godstones. Here the road wasn't as steep and didn't wind as severely as the narrow path that led from the canyon. Kairma's long bronze skirt tangled around her legs as she walked. Picking it up, she cursed to herself. *I hate skirts. I wish Mother would let me wear leggers. Who cares if people can tell if I'm in my moontime? It's not like they look at me anyway.* She looked at Kinter, who was dancing gracefully up the road in a skirt that swirled gently about her knees. *Ugh. The girl just annoys me. Like Mother, she's always worrying about what someone is thinking. I would bet my life that if I weren't heir to the Crystal, the rest of the Survinees wouldn't even know I existed.* Annoyed, she blew out a soft sigh and bit down on her lower lip.

The responsibility of the Crystal frustrated Kairma. She couldn't imagine herself capable of being the Vice Miral in ten harvests, let alone in one. It seemed to Kairma that the older she became, the more unanswered questions she had.

The girls approached the temples from the southeast. A wide grassy area measuring three hundred by sixty feet across lay in front of the great monument. The young girls crossed this grassy field and walked up a ruined stairway to another field as large and flat as the first one. A wide path led to two majestic temple buildings of pale gray granite and soft pink quartzite. Between the two once-elegant buildings ran an aisle twelve feet wide. The aisle led to the crest of a huge amphitheater, which could easily seat several thousand people. The great temple ruins were hundreds of annums old. Turning back to the southeast, the mountains rolled out below them for as far as the eye could see and faded into a malachite haze in the distance.

Zedic and Collin were making slow progress on their recent discovery. The morning waxed as they removed layer after layer of dirt from a large golden rectangle that was embedded in the side of the mountain. Zedic brushed his hands on his brown leggers to wipe off the dirt. It didn't help much, and Collin was as dirty as he was. Collin's once curly black hair now took on the appearance of dun-colored weeds, and the emerald charm that hung from a leather thong at his neck was now the color of the oak-eagle claw that held it. Zedic laughed, and said, "We come home covered in dirt or mud more often than not, but you never seemed to notice."

Zedic ran a hand through his dark, shoulder-length hair and stood back. "What do you think it is?"

"I'd about bet," said Collin while absentmindedly twirling a lock of dark hair around his finger, "it's meant to block some kind of passage."

"Like a door of some kind. I thought the same thing. Whoever built this cave could sure do some fancy work with alloy."

Collin looked sideways at Zedic in feigned horror. "You don't believe it was the Whitish, do you?"

"Oh, sure it was," Zedic said with a laugh, "and they made that alloy cart we found last summer, then buried it in dirt till you couldn't even tell what it was."

Collin thought about the massive cart that sat in front of one of the White Ones' caves. It was a monument to their diligence. He and Zedic spent days digging away the dirt that encased the cart only to find it too heavy to move once freed. The caves around the mountain often held surprising treasures from a long-dead world where gods had once ruled—a world of magic the Survinees couldn't begin to understand. When Collin was nine, he found a large cache of brightly colored stones. The charm he wore was fashioned from one of these stones. Although the Healers began to use the gold stones because they were malleable, the rest of the village found his collection interesting but useless. They had no need for pretty rocks. Sometimes Collin liked to sit on the cart and contemplate who had once acquired all those stones and why.

Zedic playfully hit his friend's arm, breaking him out of his reverie. "Hey, Mr. Rogue, we still have work here." Zedic's mother referred to Collin as *that rogue boy,* and Zedic teased him about it regularly. It wasn't just Zedic's mother who felt this way; many of the Survinees believed Collin was a troublemaker and a renegade. They never hesitated to tell him he should apply himself to the Words of the Ogs. However, the young man had wild fantasies, and far too many questions—questions that could not be answered by the simple teachings of the Healers. Collin vowed that one day he would know the truth. With the appearance of the strange traveler who had recently come to their mountain and this latest discovery, Collin was sure he would find his answers.

"Stones! I need a drink. You look like you could use one too." Collin reached for one of the waterskins by their meager tools.

"You look like you need a dip in the lake," Zedic said as he shook gray dust from his own straight black hair.

After their short break, they returned to moving dirt away from the huge rectangular object they recently discovered. It was covered with carvings made by a method totally unfamiliar to the boys. The large brass-colored rectangle was held in place by a darker gold frame and set in the solid silver-gray granite of the mountain. They could make out faint lines around the outer edges and a line dividing the form in half, from top to bottom. Clearing the dirt from the base, they could see that it sat on a large gray rock.

Collin stood up and stretched his back. "With a little leverage, we might be able to pry the block out of its stone frame." He wedged his knife in between the inner alloy rectangle and the stone of the mountain. "Stones! My knife is stuck. Zedic, give me a hand here."

Zedic tried to chip the rock around the knife with his alloy hammer. The frame didn't budge and neither did the knife.

When Kairma and Kinter reached the Godstones, the sun was at its zenith and the morning's chill was a memory. Now the sky was a clear and brilliant blue that almost hurt their eyes. After carrying the cart up the wide stairway to the great temples, the girls pushed it through the long passage that led to their place of worship. On the mountain crest, four carved granite faces stood majestically against the broad sweep of sapphire sky, looking to the east. Observing the Godstones, she shuddered. They were magnificent, and each head was more than sixty feet tall. Kairma couldn't fathom how they came to be.

The girls emptied the cart and set the baskets of food on the altar. The tribute food was divided into four sections: meat to the north; bread to the east; cheese to the south; and fruit to the west.

Kairma untied the leather thong that secured the multifaceted crystal in its soft suede sack. The palm-sized crystal only weighed a few grams in her hand, but the weight of the responsibility was something that could not be measured. She gingerly took the artifact out and placed it in the center of the wide granite and quartzite block. Brilliant rainbows danced across the altar.

Kairma and Kinter knelt at the base of the altar and with two fingers of their right hands they touched their foreheads and said, "Remember." Touching each of the four corners of the altar they said, "North, east, south, and west. Father Nor, please accept these sacred offerings of your humble Survinees." Bringing their fingers to their lips they said, "Thank you. May we always be worthy of your grace." It was an abbreviated version of the religious ceremony. Kairma knew it really bothered Kinter when she didn't say the entire twenty-minute sermon.

"Kairma, we have to say the whole thing. What's the point of coming all the way down here if we're not going to do it right?"

It wasn't like Kairma to renege on her duties, but right now she was more interested in finding Collin and Zedic. She blew out a sigh. "Okay. We'll do the whole sermon." Touching her forehead, Kairma began again. "Remember. North, east ..." Kairma had relented, not because she felt it was that important, but because she knew Kinter would tell her grandmother, and Kairma hated disappointing Isontra.

As she said the words she'd repeated more than a hundred times before, she wondered what Collin and Zedic were doing.

When they finished the sermon Kinter went to sit on the large block wall that separated the temple landing from the hundreds of seats of the majestic amphitheater. "How long do we have to stay here?"

"I want to find Collin and Zedic and see what they're doing." Kairma looked around, searching for a sign of the boys.

Pulling out the small set of pipes she liked to play, Kinter began blowing a soft melody. "Don't get lost," she said. "I have better things to do than sit here all day, you know."

"Yes, I know. I won't be long."

Kairma wandered down the steps toward the base of the great monument. She gingerly stepped over broken stairs and weed-infested seats. *Look at all the grasses and shrubs growing in the cracks of the rock walls. With care, the temples could be returned to their original splendor. I wonder why we let it fall to such disrepair.* She decided, as she walked, that when she became the Miral she would rebuild the Temples of the Godstones. She looked up at the gods of the mountain. *Is that why I am heir to the Healing Crystal? So your altar will once again be a place of beauty and splendor? The Crystal is such a great responsibility for someone like me. I just don't understand sometimes.*

There, to the right of the amphitheater, she saw Collin's favorite walking stick leaning against a boulder beside a discarded pathway. She glanced up at Kinter, who was still daydreaming by the altar. Walking cautiously to the right side of the monumental godheads, she felt her stomach tighten. Warnings about the power of the gods and the penalties of blasphemous acts were a part of her upbringing and not taken lightly. She stood at the base of a long, steep, granite stairway she had never seen before. The construction of the stairs was another mystery among so many at the Temples of the Godstones.

Although she could feel the presence of the two boys just above her, she didn't feel like testing fate outright. So she called from the landing of the third set of steps, "Zedic? Collin? Are you up there?"

Zedic ran to the opening of the crevice while still carrying his alloy hammer, nearly tumbling down the first step in his hurry. Zedic adored his younger sister. Kairma reminded him of their grandmother in many ways. She was at once quiet and maybe a little shy, but with a temper and tenacity that assured she'd get what she wanted. He knew he had taken a chance by not telling Kairma he was coming here with Collin this morning. Her feelings would be hurt, but Collin had insisted on absolute secrecy. He hurried down the first four levels of stairs, stopping a few steps above his little sister.

"What are you doing up there?" Kairma asked, peering past Zedic.

"Nothing," Zedic said, striving to regain his breath as he leaned against an iron railing that moved slightly from his weight. He was excited but tried to act nonchalant.

"Is Collin with you?" Kairma stared into Zedic's dark gray eyes.

"Yes. How did you know we were here?"

"Kinter told me."

"Great Stones!" Zedic exclaimed as he straightened his back. "How did *she* know we were here?"

"She followed you to the lake this morning and saw you turn up the trail. Where else would you be going? When I got here, I just looked around and I saw Collin's walking stick." She handed the staff to Zedic. "For wanting to keep a secret, you sure leave a lot of clues."

Zedic flinched. "She followed us this morning, huh? That sounds like Kinter. Now she'll tell Gramme, and I'll never hear the end of it."

Kairma hesitated. "What *are* you doing up there, Zedic?"

"It's not important." Zedic moved protectively to the center of the stairway. "How are we going to keep Kinter quiet?"

"*We?* Does this mean I've been invited to see what you're hiding?" Kairma flashed a mischievous smile.

Zedic flushed. "I have to talk to Collin first, but what about Kinter?"

Kairma deliberated and then a narrow smile crossed her lips. "I might know a way to keep her quiet."

"How?" He walked down the remaining steps and stood beside her. "If I know Kinter, she'll tell Gramme just for the pleasure of watching us squirm. You know how many times I would have gladly choked Kinter for tattling. She's a sly one and if you don't watch your step around her, you'll fall into one of her little traps, and then you will really owe her, not unlike now."

"I have my ways, and Kinter has a price." Kairma grinned. "Can I come up now?"

"Wait here." Zedic trusted Kairma not to say anything but he still needed to ask Collin. It was Collin's claim since he was the one who had first found the half-buried stairway. Zedic hurried back up the long stairway.

Kairma sat on the steps and waited. She constantly had to remind herself that Kinter would eventually grow out of this horrible tattletale stage, but in the meantime her little sister would strike a hard bargain. Kairma knew what Kinter wanted most, but it wouldn't be easy to convince Zedic. She watched Kinter from the vantage of the stairs as the pretty, young girl braided a strand of beads into her long chestnut hair. Kinter looked restless. It wouldn't be long before she would come looking for Kairma.

After what seemed to Kairma like a very long time, Zedic returned, out of breath from running up and down the long staircase. "Okay, Collin said he doesn't care if you know about our discovery as long as you swear not to tell *anybody* else."

"Your discovery? What's up there?" Kairma had a puzzled look on her face.

"Swear on the Godstones you won't tell anyone?"

"On the Godstones?" Kairma's large horizon-blue eyes widened, her pink lips making an *O*.

"On the Godstones!"

"Well, okay," she relented. "I swear," she said, putting her left hand to her right shoulder, "on the Godstones, I won't tell a soul ..." She smiled deviously. "What foolishness my brother has found behind the Godstones."

Zedic grinned hugely. "We think we found a passageway," he said proudly. "There's a large piece of alloy blocking it. Collin is trying to free it now."

Kairma, caught up in his excitement, momentarily forgot her fear of the gods and scrambled past Zedic. "Can I help? Is it another building, a new temple? Why hasn't anyone found it before?"

Zedic hurried to her side. "There is a large boulder that blocks the opening at the top of the eight hundred stairs. We couldn't move it so we'll have to climb over it. The path is overgrown with shrub, you might get a little scratched up."

"Climb over, huh? This will be fun." Her voice held a hint of sarcasm, but Zedic knew she wouldn't hesitate to make the climb. Collin was the only person in Survin who liked rock climbing and exploring caves more than Kairma.

Zedic frowned and reached out to stop her ascent. "Wait. What are we going to do about Kinter?"

"Oh yeah." She bit on her lip thinking. "Well," she said with a grimace, "you know how she's always wanted to wear the Crystal."

"No!" Zedic turned white. "You can't give her the Crystal!"

"I'll just let her wear it awhile." She looked down into the valley where she had left Kinter. "I don't think she can make it work, although I've never let her try." I *can't even make it do anything, and I'm the heir.*

Zedic shook his head. "I don't think that's the answer. There has to be another way to keep her quiet."

"I can't think of anything else that little brat would settle for."

"But the Crystal?" Zedic said nervously as he ran his hand along the handle of his hammer. "I don't like it. Maybe I could carve a new doll for her."

Kairma paused, her upper lip curled. "Zedic, she doesn't play with dolls anymore."

"You're probably right, but I don't feel good about letting her wear the Crystal."

"It's just for a while, and you know it's what she wants most."

Due to a critical illness which almost took Kairma's life, Kinter had briefly been in line to inherit the Crystal and wasn't at all happy when her older sister was restored to health. Kairma thought how strange life was. Kinter wanted the Crystal more than anything, and Kairma would like nothing more than to let her have it. In the short annum and a half that Kairma was ill, Kinter attended the Healing lessons, learning more than Kairma had learned in three annums. Kinter often suggested that she was more qualified than Kairma to become the Vice Miral, and at times Kairma believed her.

Zedic turned and headed back down the stairs. "We had better take care of her now. Not that I think there is much more one could give her, but if she comes looking for us and sees the passage, even the Crystal may not be enough."

Kinter didn't feel like sitting at the Godstones all day. Zedic and Kairma had just reached the bottom of the stairs when Kinter came walking toward them in a hurry to get back home. Kairma offered to let Kinter wear the Crystal for a week if she would be willing to wait at the temple for them to return and not tell anyone what they were doing. Kinter thought her silence was worth much more.

Kairma's eyes rolled at Kinter's demands, but she said, "Okay! You can wear this for the next three weeks. But if someone gets sick, you'll give it back. You promise?" She untied the cord and handed it to Kinter with the sworn promise of silence, adding, "I'll have to have it on Nor Day too. Gramme expects me to do the benediction."

Kinter felt a surge of jealousy as she tied the cord about her neck, but she laughed meanly. "I won't have to tell anyone because the gods will send Whitish to eat you for nosing around up there!" She stroked the soft, tan bag that held the Crystal "And then they'll have to make *me* the Healer. People think you're strange anyway." She leered at Kairma. Kairma didn't reply.

Zedic scowled. "Don't be silly. Whitish don't eat people. Collin and I have been near the caves lots of times and they've never bothered us."

"If Collin was with you, it's no wonder." Kinter looked toward the stairs to see if he was within earshot. "Collin's not like us. He's eerie. I think he's friends with them. People say he has the devil in him."

Kairma quickly came to Collin's defense. "He does not! And he's not *friends* with the Whitish either. He's just not afraid of them. That's not so peculiar."

"You mean…" Kinter hesitated, and then looked directly at Kairma, "like *you're* not peculiar?"

Kairma flinched at Kinter's accusation. "Just because he doesn't always do or say what people think he should, doesn't mean there's something wrong with him."

"Oh, you don't think Collin's weird, huh?" Kinter said. "I don't know what the two of you see in him. He drags you up here to do *who knows what*, and he runs around with that stranger, Trep. He's always sneaking off somewhere. He even tries to talk like Trep. You'll see. Collin has strange ideas and he's going to hook you two into them." She looked up the long stairway. "I'd never ask my friends to climb on the Godstones."

Before Zedic or Kairma could react, Kinter abruptly turned away and headed off to fondle her newly won prize. Making her way across the valley floor, she was angry. *Let them climb on the Godstones if they want. Someday the Crystal will be mine for good. They never should have made me give it back in the first place. In the end, people will see the truth; Kairma isn't the right person to rule Survin.*

Sitting by the altar, Kinter pulled the Crystal out of its protective sack. She held it up in the air above her head, watching the sunlight dance across the many colored facets, and daydreamed about being the next Vice Miral.

After a few minutes of amusement, Kinter took out the small pipe from her skirt pocket and began to play a tune that had been running through her mind the last several weeks. It was going to be a love song. The object of her desire had not acknowledged her yet, but in time she was sure he would. He was refined, well-respected and handsome beyond belief. Her song was written for the most charming man in

Survin, Naturi. Her feet dangled gracefully as she sat on the worn block wall, the wind playing in her long chestnut hair. The melody from the pipe drifted on a gentle breeze, reaching the others on the mountain like a soft birdsong.

☙

Kairma hurried back to the long stairway, eager to see what Collin had uncovered.

"That child!" Kairma exclaimed. "Sometimes I wonder how we can be sisters."

"You shouldn't have given her the Crystal," Zedic said nervously. "I don't trust her to have the sense to take care of it." Zedic moved ahead of Kairma, leading the way up the narrow stairway.

Kairma shook her head. "She prizes it far too much to let something happen to it and I know she'll give it back if I need it. She did promise. Her promises are expensive, but she's always been good to her word." Then under her breath, almost as a second thought, she added, "I don't know what she thinks is so wonderful about wearing it anyway. The way people treat me, you'd think I was poison ivy." But Kairma knew it was her pale hair and skin that caused people to shun her.

Most Survinees were in awe of the Crystal and respected its power. Kairma was learning about medicine and the supposed nature of the Crystal, but didn't believe her other abilities were related to it. After all, Kinter was wearing the Crystal now, but Kairma could still see Zedic's pale yellow aura as plainly as the dark green spruce that encroached on the ancient stairway. As long as she could remember, no one had ever mentioned having this ability. Maybe the Survinees had good reason to fear her. Maybe she really was peculiar.

Zedic climbed quickly to the top of the boulder blocking the passage and offered Kairma his hand. Reaching the clearing in front of the block, they saw Collin had freed his knife and was clearing the remaining debris from the base of an intricately carved alloy rectangle.

Kairma tripped over a rock and stumbled into Collin, her eyes fastened to the mountainside. He caught her before she could fall, grinning with self-satisfaction. Kairma was stunned.

The ancient shrine wall was about one hundred and fifty feet high. Her pale fingers caressed the white granite columns cut into the mountain itself. They flanked the entrance to what appeared to be a long-forgotten temple. Tilting her head back, she scrutinized the great bronze-colored rectangle. Etched in the hard stone above the massive entry was the script Kairma had learned as a child. Each letter was more than three feet tall and perfectly formed. The great bronze rectangle was divided down the center, each side nearly four feet wide and almost fourteen feet high. There were two jet-black ball-shaped objects the size of Kairma's fist jutting out from the center division about waist high. Just below the balls were large swirls of black alloy arching away from the portal. She was breathless. "Oh, my Stones!"

Collin beamed. "Hey, Boo! It's really something, isn't it?" His voice was soft and comforting, like warm summer rain. She turned to see a crooked but endearing smile play across his lips.

Collin absentmindedly played with a lock of hair as he watched her. He loved the sound of her slightly husky voice when she was moved by something. He held back the urge to giggle at her awestruck face.

Collin started calling Kairma *Boo* when she was six annums old. Zedic, Collin, and Kairma were playing in one of the many caves in the area. Zedic and Collin stood outside the opening where they'd left Kairma several yards behind in the dark. As she came running out of the cave, Zedic jumped at her from the side of the opening and yelled, "Boo!" Momentary fright crossed Kairma's face, to be quickly replaced by fury when she saw Zedic. She went at him with both fists in tight balls, knocking him down the hill. Collin fell to his knees laughing at the startled look on Zedic's face as he tumbled head over heels down the grassy incline. After that, Collin called her *Boo* when she tagged along with Zedic. Kairma would get so mad that she would try to wrestle Collin to the ground. Collin, being two annums older than Kairma, had no trouble keeping her contained. By the time Kairma turned nine the name was permanent, and she no longer got angry about it. That's not to say she wasn't willing to tumble with Collin for other reasons, but over the last few annums Kairma had learned to control her temper and the scuffling was kept to a minimum. This had more to do with Collin not teasing her as often than Kairma's willingness to back down from a challenge. She never backed down from a fight with anyone.

Kairma walked to the side of the immense rectangle and, using the hem of her supple suede skirt, she brushed away more dirt from a cylindrical ornament on the left side where it was embedded between the wall and the deep golden rectangle. "Look at this," she cried, "and there's another one up here!" Evenly spaced along the left side of the rectangle were four cylinders about the size of the handle of Zedic's hammer.

Collin was momentarily torn between looking at what Kairma had uncovered and the pale thigh she so innocently showed by raising her skirt. Although he'd known her all his life, recently she had had a different effect on him. Somehow, now she seemed more interesting than when she first began to tag along with Zedic. He used to tease Kairma unmercifully in hopes that she would leave them alone. Now he was glad she had found them here today, but wasn't quite sure why.

Hoping Zedic hadn't noticed his brief hesitation, he quickly brushed the dirt from the remaining cylinders. "I've got something like this in my pack," he said as he pulled out a small piece of alloy. "See, it looks like a butterfly with holes where the color should be." Folding the wings together he held it up to one of the cylinders on the wall. "I don't understand why someone would wedge this in the wall."

Zedic walked up to look closer. "Must be to hold the block in tight."

"Can I see it?" Kairma reached between Collin and Zedic, who were studying the artifact. As she brushed against him, Collin felt a strange tingle in his lower belly. Thinking it must be coming from the Crystal, he looked down, but the space between the upper curves of her breasts was bare. The tingling increased as he noticed the beads of sweat mixing with the dust from the mountain. Trying not to stare, he stammered, "Where's the Crystal?"

"I let Kinter wear it so she wouldn't tell anyone where we are."

He handed her the alloy butterfly. "Kinter? My Stones, Kairma! Do you think that's a good idea? What if she loses it or something?"

Kairma rolled her eyes. "Kinter losing the Crystal is the least of my worries. Getting it back at the end of the three weeks might be a larger problem. She values it far too much to lose it. She's young, but she's not stupid."

Collin looked at her, shaking his head incredulously. "Kinter?"

Kairma ignored him as she ran her fingers around the smooth edges of the alloy butterfly, poking her fingers through the holes and working its wings back and forth. With what appeared to be uncanny insight Kairma said, "Look!" She closed the wings between her hands. "If this side is attached to the wall," suggesting her left hand, "and this side is attached to the inner block," referring to her right hand, "it would open like this!" Putting her fingers in the holes, she opened her hands to demonstrate.

"Collin, I think she's right!" Zedic grabbed the ball on the right side and pulled on it.

They pulled and pushed on the vast block but nothing happened. Exhausted they sat back and stared at the slab of alloy.

Collin went to his pack and pulled out a piece of fatty meat and a cup. "I'm glad I didn't eat all of my lunch." He smiled at the others. "Maybe if we grease it up a bit, it'll come loose. That's how I got that one to move." He motioned to the object Kairma was holding.

Collin built a small fire and placed his uneaten meat in an alloy cup. Once held over the flame, the fat melted into a shiny pool around the meat. "Zedic, pick the largest leaf you can find and curl it into a funnel."

The afternoon passed to early evening as the three companions worked intently on the remarkably created block. They poured the grease on the cylinders and watched it disappear into the crevice of the block. Again they pulled on the block to no avail. They poured more grease over the ball and it turned back and forth slightly. Zedic turned it with all his strength and pulled. There was an audible *click*, and then the sound of rocks grinding together. The huge slab moved ever so slightly, engulfing them in dust and foul air.

At just that moment, the shadow of a large cloud passed over them. They looked at one another and shuddered. It was hard to discount all the tales they'd heard about the powers of the gods.

Suddenly Kairma said, "Zedic! We have to go! The sun will be down before we can get home again! I can't believe Kinter hasn't come looking for us."

As Collin brushed the dust from his leggings and looked longingly at the block, he said, "We don't have to go right away. The moon will be full. It won't be difficult to see our way home. Don't you want to see what's in there?"

Zedic looked thoughtfully at the door and then up at the sky, and once more at the door. Collin and Kairma waited for Zedic to reply. They knew Zedic was considering the situation from every conceivable angle.

Collin blew out a sigh. "Come on, Zedic. Stop chewing on it and spit it out."

When Zedic finally spoke, his tone was methodical. "We don't have any torches. Even if we did go inside today, we wouldn't be able to see anything. I am also surprised Kinter hasn't come to find us. She must be too afraid of offending the gods to climb the stairway. That's the only thing I can think of that would keep her away."

Kairma sighed.

Sounding disappointed, Collin said, "Well, I guess you're right. We can always come back tomorrow." He looked slightly hurt as he gathered his daypack and staff.

Kairma had already climbed to the top of the boulder. "Come on, you two. We still have to find Kinter, and making her happy now might not be easy."

Collin and Zedic joined Kairma on the narrow path. Wasting no time, they hurried down the stairs and across the narrow valley that separated the Godstones from the amphitheater. Quickly climbing up the tiers of seats, they reached the two large temple buildings where they found Kinter sitting by the altar.

Chapter 2

Kinter stood up, placing her clenched fists on her hips. "It's about time you came back! I was beginning to think the Whitish really had eaten you. I was just about to leave you for dead." Her anger didn't fool the others; she looked frightened.

"You don't believe that nonsense that the Whitish eat people, do you?" Collin said, winking at Kairma and then raising his eyebrows at Kinter.

Real anger flashed across Kinter's face. "*You* think it's funny!"

Suppressing a grin, Collin's cheeks dimpled at her reaction. Sobering, he whispered to Kinter, "You can leave all this food here if you want, but I'm taking this with me." As he picked up a small loaf of bread from the altar he added, "Did you know, on the night of the last full moon, I left some bread by one of the caves, and when I went back the next day," he looked around in mock anxiousness, "something, or *someone*, had eaten all of it."

Kinter fought back tears, and Kairma felt her skin crawl.

Grabbing Zedic's arm, Kairma said, "Come on. Let's go."

Zedic pushed her hand away and turned to Collin. "Why aren't you leaving your tributes here?"

Collin explained. "Whitish don't eat people. They eat the food we leave here. There won't be any great stone gods eating dinner here tonight, just a bunch of hungry White Ones. One of these days I'll show you. I'll prove it to everyone."

Kinter's cobalt blue eyes flashed as she gave Kairma an *I told you so* look.

Kairma wondered if there might be some truth in what Kinter had said about Collin, and then quickly decided she was just being ill tempered. "Zedic," she pleaded, "let's go. I don't feel good about being in here as it is, and I don't want to test the gods tonight."

Zedic turned back to Collin. "Are you coming?"

Collin smiled, as if daring the gods to stop him. "I'm coming, but I'm not leaving all this food to be wasted." Collin tossed a few more loaves of bread into his pack. "I don't feel like feeding the White Ones. One night I'll sit here and watch." In defiance, Collin chomped on a piece of bread. "Actually I do think the tributes protect the hunting party from White Ones. After all, once they have been fed they don't need to attack anyone, right? Or maybe Whitish don't come out during the day because of the light, and they don't come out under a full moon for the same reason."

"Come on, Collin." Zedic's voice was stern now. Collin often had elaborate theories for things they didn't understand. *Because the Word says it is so* didn't usually cut it with *The Rogue*. Zedic tugged on his friend's arm. "It's getting late. People will worry."

Closing his pack, Collin looked wistfully at the great Godstones. "Well, I guess there's always tomorrow."

Kairma walked behind the two boys. Collin wasn't quite as tall as her brother, but was slightly wider in the shoulders. His unruly hair curled haphazardly about the collar of his cloak. She loved his boyish charm and his quick smile. When he laughed, his eyes, the color of spring clover, crinkled, and his cheeks dimpled. Collin was interested in everything and everyone. Although he teased her unmercifully at times, of all the boys she knew, he was the most fun to be around.

Other than her family, it was only with Collin and Zedic that

Kairma felt comfortable taking off the scarf that hid her snow-white hair. Naturi had once said he liked her hair, but it had embarrassed her. Kairma liked Naturi, though she often felt very young and simple around him. Naturi was older, exceptionally refined, and very handsome. She watched Collin's broad shoulders as he walked in front of her, wondering if he ever saw her as more than Boo, the pesky little sister of his best friend.

As she watched, Collin seized a branch and wrapped the end of it with dried vines. "Just in case the sun's gone before we get back to the village." He flashed *that smile* at Kairma. Feeling her cheeks flush warmly, she started walking faster. The last thing she wanted to see was another White One.

It was four annums ago when she wandered too far from her brother, and she still bore the scar on her right shoulder where a White One had bitten her. It had run out from the woods hunched over like a very old man. Its pale skin was covered with sores oozing pus, and the thin wisps of white hair on its head were tangled and wet. She screamed as the White One wrapped its arms around her waist as it attempted to carry her away. Zedic came to her rescue. The first rock from his sling just missed the monster's head, but the next rock hit it square in the back. The beast screamed in pain, biting down on her shoulder as it dropped her and ran into the woods. She stumbled and fell at Zedic's feet.

Kairma was ill for many weeks. At first she developed headaches and the only relief was cold packs over her eyes. Then the fever came, lasting for weeks, giving her the most horrendous nightmares. Her grandmother rubbed the painful cysts with eucalyptus and lavender oil to keep the sores from opening and spreading. When word spread that her hair had turned white, many Survinees told her family it was hopeless to try to save her. Diakus and Grimly had suggested taking her to the Godstones, as was usually done with others who suffered from the white fever. There she could die in peace, close to the gods, as her time neared.

Isontra insisted on continuing her ministrations until Kairma either lived or died, and after ten weeks of sitting with her constantly and feeding her broth, Kairma began getting stronger. Isontra removed the bandages from her eyes, but it was another three weeks before Kairma could sit up and feed herself.

It was then that Kairma discovered her strange abilities. At first she noticed the clouds that appeared around her grandmother. They were a soft blue like a summer sky, mixed with streaks of yellow and white. Although the halos were beautiful, Kairma didn't mention it for fear it was another, far worse, stage of the illness. When she finally confided in Zedic, he suggested she keep this secret because people often feared what they didn't understand. It would be hard enough for people to accept that the white fever had changed her appearance so radically. This new ability would undoubtedly make their bigotry far worse. Kairma was intensely grateful for Zedic's understanding and friendship.

Because she looked white as a ghost, Collin had stopped calling her Boo. Whenever he called her Kairma, she would ask him if she had done something wrong or if he was mad at her. Eventually the nickname returned.

Several people were outraged by the unorthodox decision to keep Kairma home instead of taking her to the altar of the Godstones; a few members even refused to attend the weekly services at the Nor monument. Grimly and Diakus never relented their position and so there remained an obvious split in the Church. About twenty members regularly sat together at the meetings, raising questions about the decisions the Healers made.

Collin led the way as the young people reached the end of the wide roadway and turned to the south. The path here was tight and the forest closed around them. Kinter was feeling better now that they were more than halfway home. To no one in particular she said, "Wrote a new song today. I think I'll play it at the Spring Celebration."

Zedic encouraged her. "What's it about?"

She felt her cheeks warm. "Oh, it's nothing, really. " She couldn't tell them it was for the man she dreamed of mating. They would just laugh at her.

They headed down the narrow path with Collin in front, Kairma leading Kinter by the hand, and Zedic right behind them, pulling the small wooden cart. It was comforting when Collin began to talk casually about the strange man who had come to their secluded village. "Did you know they can make clothes in hundreds of different colors in the city? Trep says that they have huge buildings where all they do all day is make cloth."

Kinter found the idea interesting but didn't want to encourage Collin's interest in the stranger, while Kairma, thinking about how long it was taking Isontra to make her ritual mating dress, couldn't help asking, "What do they make the cloth from?"

"I don't know. He didn't say. I asked him about the tee and leggers he wears, and he told me about the place where they make them. He called them a shirt and pants. Funny names, huh?" The stranger's clothes were also made very different from the suede, leather, and fur the Survinees wore. Kairma had to admit Trep's clothes looked more comfortable than her own.

Collin continued. "Trep has funny names for lots of things. I didn't tell you this before, but I spent three days trying to figure out what he was saying. He's learned how we talk to some degree, but sometimes when he talks fast, I don't understand a thing." Trep's accent was rapid with an odd lilt on the second syllable of most words.

Kinter interjected, "I don't think you should be talking to him at all. The scrolls tell us not to befriend strangers."

"That might be, but we could learn some things from him. Like riding horses. How much better would our hunts be if all the men had horses?"

Kairma didn't say it, but Trep fascinated her. He was an olive-toned man standing at least an inch shorter than Kinter. He came to their canyon village six weeks ago riding on a horse, causing quite a stir in their sleepy little community. Of course, Collin befriended him at once.

As the darkness gained on them, Kairma began to have the uneasy feeling they weren't alone. She asked Collin to light the torch and pulled Kinter closer to her, but the feeling continued to grow stronger.

They walked down one side of the small gully where the path followed the stream for a while. Collin and Zedic lifted the cart as they stepped across the stones rising out of the swift water. Kinter was shaking because she had never been out this late and Kairma knew her sister was a firm believer of the horrible stories about the White Ones. As they walked, Kairma was sure she heard voices, very sad voices. Before she could say anything to the others, several small White Ones surrounded them. Kairma could sense as many as twenty of them hiding in the woods, about ten feet away, their almost colorless eyes watching as the four young people made their way up the steep slope of the ravine.

Kairma felt a distant pain, more in her mind than her body. "Why aren't they attacking? There's only four of us and so many of them." She stopped momentarily to see what the White Ones would do.

Zedic put his arm around her shoulder, easing her fear, and possibly his own. Collin raised the torch higher. "They won't come near our fire. Whitish don't like the light."

The path narrowed further as they reached the more heavily wooded area, making them walk in single file. Collin led the way with their only source of light. Kairma's sense of pain grew stronger with each step, making it harder to breathe. Her head ached and her eyes burned. She shielded her eyes from the torch as the pain began to overtake her. No one spoke until they came to the bottom of the cliff. Here the road doubled back on itself several times, winding up the cliff face. Collin said, "Let's climb up the cliff. It's a lot shorter. If we stick to the road, it's at least four times as far. We'll leave the cart here. We can come back tomorrow and get it."

The wall before them was terraced with clumps of bushes, good for holding onto while climbing. The north entrance of the village was no more than sixty feet from the top edge of the cliff. Although they had climbed up and down the face of the cliff many times during the day, the meager light from the torch made the cliff look ominous. When they reached the first level, where the road crossed the cliff face, Kairma turned toward the woods. She could make out the shadows of several hunched-over figures making their way down the mountain, along the sides of the trail. She began climbing to the next level of the cliff, when her foot caught an outcropping of stone and she tumbled down the steep embankment. Kinter screamed, "Zedic, catch Kairma! She slipped!"

Catching Kairma by the wrist, Zedic stopped her fall. A branch caught on her scarf, pulling it off, and her snow-white braids glowed brightly under the torchlight. One of the White Ones reached out to her and Zedic kicked at it. It drew back as Zedic lifted Kairma to his side with an unexpected surge of strength. Collin handed him the torch and he waved it frantically at the White Ones.

Some of the creatures stood just beyond the light of the torch and watched the young people scramble up the steep cliff, while the others continued on their way down the mountainside. Kinter raced ahead, passing Collin in her hurry to reach the top. Streams of tears were flowing down her cheeks.

Kairma regained her footing and climbed as quickly as she could. Zedic was right behind her, and Collin brought up the rear. Kairma was so frightened she hardly noticed the easing of the pain that she had felt so strongly only moments before. As she reached the top of the cliff, she could see the shadow of Kinter against the light of the north door. Kinter's hands were clasped tightly around the Crystal as she prayed for their safety.

Running past the heavy wooden doors of the hospital, Kairma grasped Kinter's hand and thanked the gods for protecting them. They didn't stop running until they were safely inside the canyon walls.

Collin and Zedic were a breath behind them. Dropping to his knees just outside the Chancery, Collin almost laughed. "Well, that's the second time you've rescued Boo from the White Ones."

"I know one thing," Zedic said as he glanced at his sisters, who were as pale as the full moon. "If she keeps this up, I'm going to be very old, very soon."

Collin stood up. "We'd better get inside. The adults will be thinking we're bait for the White Ones."

Zedic rubbed his head. "We were!"

Kairma didn't say anything as she huddled Kinter close to her, wondering if Zedic or Collin had felt the same incredible pain. She didn't think so.

Collin headed up the canyon toward his home. Holding hands, the other three walked into the Chancery, the grand home belonging to the Miral and Comad of Survin.

As they came through the doorway, their mother Jettena shouted, "Where have you been? You've been gone for hours. Your father's hunting and here I was, trapped with four little ones. I couldn't even go look for you!"

They all hung their heads as Jettena angrily ladled stew from a blackened pot into wooden bowls. "Your supper is cold. Serves you right, worrying me like this. Isontra's gone to bed, but I'm sure she isn't sleeping."

Still ranting, Jettena set down bowls of cold stew for each of her children. "Zedic, I thought you would have more sense than this. You said you were getting blooding rods to dress the meat from the hunt. Does that take you all day and half the night?"

Zedic turned to Kairma, looking panicked. They hadn't picked up any rods.

Jettena poured them each a cup of lukewarm terrid. Shaking her head, she directed her last outburst to Kairma. "I don't even know what to say to you, *young lady*. You're supposed to be a leader of Survin by this time next annum. Do you have any idea what that means. Any idea at all? Sometimes I think Nor gave the goats better sense."

As Jettena turned to leave the dining hall, she sounded less angry, almost relieved. "Now eat your supper and go to bed!"

Looking back at her siblings, Kairma watched a smile blossom on Kinter's crimson lips. Now that they were safe, Kinter enjoyed seeing her celebrated sister get in trouble.

Chapter 3

Zedic was an early riser by nature and tried hard to please his mother. Not only did he do his own chores, he often helped dress and feed his three younger brothers as well. The four-annum old triplets could be a handful at times, and Jettena liked to keep their home clean. Zedic didn't understand why his mother always wanted fresh flowers in the Grand Hall meeting space and enough terrid brewing for twenty people when they seldom had visitors. But that was his mother's way, and Zedic was a good son. He dusted off the Grand Hall table and brought in another armful of wood. His mother would still be mad about last night and he wanted to make sure he did everything he could to help her today.

After placing the logs by the hearth, he went to the dining area to see if there was anything else she needed. He could see Kairma and their mother in deep conversation about one of her lessons. It was obvious Kairma wouldn't be going to the Godstones with him this morning.

Lost in thought, Zedic quietly slipped back out of the warm kitchen. *Mother never lets Kairma do anything fun anymore. Sometimes I wish she wouldn't push her so hard—it's not like Kairma has to know everything today. After all, Gramme will probably be around for at least another fifty annums. In fact, I wouldn't be surprised if we all went to the Great Stones before Gramme.* Pulling his tan cloak from the rack by the door, Zedic walked out the back of the Chancery and through the Grand Hall and hospital that made up the north entrance to the sleepy little village of Survin. There was a chill in the air as he looked up at a clear sky. *Maybe it's better if Kairma doesn't come along. No telling what we'll find behind those doors. It could be dangerous.*

Zedic headed down the northwest trail toward the Godstones. *Like last night wasn't dangerous! Mother was right, I should have known better. I could never let anything happen to Kairma, or Kinter for that matter. I would die for either of my sisters.* He looked around suspiciously. *She had better not be following me again today. No, I think Kinter was too scared last night. How do I let Collin talk me into these things anyway? We could have all been killed.* He shuddered. *I wonder what that Whitey would have done to Kairma if I hadn't kicked him.*

As he walked, he searched for small elms and aspens that, when stripped of branches, would make good poles to mount the game the hunters would bring home today.

"Kairma, finish your breakfast. A growing girl needs to eat," Jettena said as she pushed a plate of oatmeal toward Kairma. A moment later she turned to scold the three little boys who were throwing food at each other. "I don't know why you boys waste your food like this." Catching a piece of sausage in one hand and the perpetrator with the other, Jettena's stance spoke louder than her words. "It's a good thing the men are hunting today!" She set the meat down. "If you're not going to eat, then go clean your room." She watched the three boys settle down and begin picking at their food once more.

Satisfied that she had the boys under control, Jettena turned Kairma. Her daughter grimaced and said, "I'm really not hungry, Mother."

Jettena looked thoughtfully at Kairma and then started peeling knotwood tubers for the noon meal. "You need to eat, dear. You have a long session with Gramme today and a good breakfast will help you think." Rinsing off a tuber, she thought about her daughter. *Kairma*

*seems distant lately. Maybe it's just her age. She's growing up fast. Even
with her colorless hair and those pale eyes, she's truly becoming a stunning
woman. Maybe I should ask Mother to talk to Kairma about mating. I've
noticed the way Naturi has been looking at her lately and I wouldn't want
Kairma to make the same mistake I made when I was her age.*

Kairma looked imploringly at Jettena. "But Mother, I wanted to go
with Zedic and Collin today." Kairma's eyes momentarily darted away.
"They're going fishing down at the lake."

Jettena sighed loudly. "I really wish your brother wouldn't spend so
much time with that rogue boy. He's trouble sure as a Tribute Moon
shines. He was with you yesterday too, wasn't he?" Before Kairma could
answer, Jettena shook her head. She smiled softly, taking a different
tact. "What do you need to know about fishing anyway? You'll be of
age in a few moons and I know Naturi has thoughts of contending for
you. I'm sure if you have a fancy for fish, he would find a way to catch
all you might want."

"Yes, I'm sure he would, Mother." Disappointment crossed Kairma's
face, and Jettena worried Kairma might not be ready for her Seridar.

Kairma's lower lip pushed out. "Can't I go? Just for a little while?
Please, Mother."

Jettena shook her head slowly, and her long dark braid wriggled
with the motion. Flipping the braid back over her shoulder, Jettena said,
"Gramme's expecting you soon. You have responsibilities and much to
learn. I don't understand you, Kairma. You should be honored to be heir
to the Crystal. Now finish up here and get on your way."

Kairma nodded as she picked at the last of her breakfast. Watching
her mother peeling roots, Kairma suddenly asked, "Why does Gramme
teach my lessons and not you? According to Gramme, the Crystal is
supposed to be passed from mother to daughter. Why don't you wear
the Crystal anymore?"

Not breaking the rhythm of her work, Jettena sat down on a nearby
chair. "When you were attacked by that terrible White One, it was
Gramme who healed you. She's older and knows much more about

Healing than I do, and for that I am very thankful." Jettena touched Kairma on the cheek. "We surely would have lost you if it hadn't been for Gramme." Jettena picked up another knotwood root to peal and continued. "With you so awfully sick and Zedic helping your father most of the day, I really had my hands full with Kinter and your little brothers."

Silently, Jettena reflected on that long annum. The triplets had been born just before Kairma fell ill. Their history had mentioned twins, but the triplets' birth was seen as a sign of great blessing. Everyone in the village had brought gifts, and the celebration lasted for several days. Some people even said Jettena was destined to be the greatest Miral of all. They sang songs about her children and even seemed to fully accept Tamron, the outsider, at long last.

Shortly afterward, the White Ones attacked Kairma, and Jettena's world came crashing down. Now, no one speaks of multiple births and few people come to visit. Because of Kairma's similarity to the White Ones, among others things, the community clearly avoided her child, and the resentment of the village forced Jettena to question her own status.

"It made good sense to give the Crystal back to Gramme until the boys were older and I would have more time to study," Jettena said as she let out a soft sigh. "And then baby Sonty was born."

Kairma giggled. "Father keeps you busy, doesn't he? With seven of us to chase around, I guess you never had much time to be a Healer."

"No, I never did." Jettena cursed under her breath. *I might have enjoyed the honor of being the Healer if things had been different—if I had been stronger.*

Lost in the reflection of how things might have been, Jettena got up from the table and put the chopped roots in the large black pot on the fire. She was only fifteen when Zedic was born and it wasn't long before Kairma and Kinter were born. Isontra's aunts, Madison and Isabella, had passed away, and Isontra had no siblings to foster Jettena's young children in those early annums, making it difficult for Jettena to concentrate on her lessons. As the annums began to slip away, she tried hard to keep up her studies, until that dreadful day she fought with her mother over the fate of Kairma.

Sonty woke up from her brief nap and Jettena went into the sitting room where the small child lay on a thick fur coverlet. Looking down at her youngest child, a sad smile came to her. *Would being the Healer have given me as much happiness as my children have? Would I have missed watching my children grow up? Did mother regret not being there when I learned to talk and play games?* Picking Sonty up from the fur cover pad, Jettena noticed the deep gray of her eyes, so like Tamron's. If she had gone through the full Mating Rite, would she have been mated to Tamron at all? Life didn't seem fair to her, but she was not unhappy.

Jettena watched Kairma head down the long hall lined with ancestral portraits. In the next annum, Kairma's own portrait would hang there, but whose face would be there next to the white-haired girl?

Collin sat in front of the rectangular doors of the unexplored site, going through his pack to see if he had everything they would need today. Zedic and Kairma would arrive soon and with their help he was sure they would be able to move the large door from its position. While he waited, he thought about the events of the previous night. He had been right—the White Ones *were* on their way to the Godstones to take the tribute food. He was intensely curious about them. *How can we share a mountain with someone, or something, for that many annums and know so little about them? Maybe if we understood everything that was written on the tablet of Nor or in the oldest scrolls we would know. If Nor promised this land to his children and his children's children, why didn't He ever mention the White Ones? It's too bad much of the script is missing.*

He walked to the boulder that sat at the top of the stairway. *White Ones are ugly and mean-looking, but they're much too weak to be the ones who built these temples.* He climbed to the top of the massive rock and looked out over the valley, hoping to see a sign of Zedic and Kairma. *Even though they outnumbered us last night, they didn't really attack. Maybe the one that tried to touch Boo was curious about her. Was he trying to help her or did he really mean to hurt her?* Collin looked back at the golden doors and sighed. *Maybe the answers are in there. If there's some kind of passage behind those doors, I'm sure we'll find something interesting. I'm really glad she came up here yesterday.* He shook his head, wondering where that last thought had come from. *Where are they? Zedic knew I'd be here early.*

While Zedic made his way to the temples to meet Collin, Kairma made her way down the long hallway that led to her grandmother's suite of rooms. This section of the Chancery had been recently enlarged to include a separate seating area and a private cleansing room. The Chancery was the largest structure in the small mountain community, and now it was the only one with a private waste and shower room.

At the northern end of the canyon was a square passageway through the thick granite cliff. From inside the tunnel, the heads of the Godstones could be wholly viewed. This was smaller and easier to keep warm than the similar channel at the south end of the canyon so the Survinees chose this as their hospital area. Naturally, the Healing family built their home adjacent to it. Over the centuries, generations of Healers had built additions and enlarged the original grounds, and the Chancery now was a stately manor covering some three thousand square feet.

Kairma rapped on the exquisitely carved archway leading to Isontra's rooms. Walking through the doorway while putting her right hand to her right eyebrow, Kairma offered grandmother a formal greeting. No matter who Kairma was, Isontra was the Miral, and one always greeted the Miral formally.

From the bedside where she sat, Isontra said, "Come in dear. I have been waiting for you." Kairma's grandmother was a tall, wiry woman of nearly sixty annums, immaculately dressed with almost perfect posture. She nodded to the writing desk by the window. "I was up early today. The dreams are back, but not to worry—I got it out of my system with a heavy dose of writing this morning."

As Kairma took her usual seat in a tall, wooden chair by the table, she noticed the odd inflection in her grandmother's voice. *Gramme is usually such a happy person. Something's bothering her. I hope she isn't too mad about last night.* "I'm sorry to keep you waiting," Kairma said. "Mother and I were talking about the Crystal."

Giving her that searching look that made Kairma believe her grandmother could read minds, Isontra asked, "Where *is* the Crystal, Kairma?" The old woman laid down the long white veil she was embroidering and walked to the table where Kairma stood nervously chewing her lip.

Kairma put her hand to her breast. *Stones! What can I tell her? I can't say I gave it to Kinter to keep her quiet.* She looked away, not wanting her grandmother to see the apprehension in her eyes.

"It seems to me I remember seeing Kinter wearing it this morning," Isontra said knowingly as she sat in the chair across the table from Kairma.

"I let her wear it because she helped me take the tribute to the temples yesterday," Kairma lied. In added defense, Kairma stressed that Kinter would take good care of the Crystal and that it was only to be for a little while.

Isontra's steel gray eyes blazed furiously. "My dear Kairma, the Crystal is not to be used for bribe or gift; it is not yours to barter away. I'm not sure if I should be more angry with you or with myself. Perhaps I've not made your lessons clear enough. The Crystal belongs to the world. *You* are only the trustee. Surely, by now you must realize its value. I want you to keep it with you, *always.*"

Kairma felt her face warm. "I'm sorry. I'll get it back from her right away."

"Please do!" Isontra looked into Kairma's pale eyes. "The Crystal has been entrusted to *you*, Kairma." She slowly shook her head. "These aren't games we play. It's time for you to grow up. You'll be mated come this Harvest Moon. You must adjust to your new way of life while your mother and I are here to help you. The Crystal is a constant reminder of who and what you are. Never forget that."

Isontra looked resigned. "Have I not acquainted you with the history of the Crystal? Yes? Well, I must have left something out of your lessons. Maybe if you understood more about it, you would then truly appreciate your responsibilities." Her smile slowly returned as she reached across the table and patted Kairma's hand. The thin woman's hands were small and cool. "Sometimes I don't know what gets into you, dear. You should be proud of your ancestry." Leaning back in her chair, Isontra fussed with her hair, now almost as white as her granddaughter's. "I wasn't going to give you a history lesson today, but it looks like that will have to change." Replacing the finely carved sticks that held her long hair on top of her head, Isontra considered where to begin today's lesson. "In the beginning, the Great Amanda of pure Efpec blood was entrusted with the Healing Crystal by the angel. She was told to safeguard the Crystal until it could be returned to its place of origin. Once placed in Nor Mountain, the Crystal will make all life peaceful and profitable; it will end all pain and sorrow."

Kairma sighed loudly. She had heard this story many times before, but Isontra's words were stern. "Many of our people have died protecting the crystal and its secret. In the wrong hands, Kairma, the Crystal could do great damage."

Isontra went to the heavy tapestry that hung across the door to the archives room. Bringing back an armful of rolled-up scrolls, she gingerly laid them on the table in front of her granddaughter. Kairma could see that they were some of the very oldest records. The writing had faded and the animal skins had become brittle. Isontra explained. "There have been many recorded battles in our history, Kairma. Some of them were quite bitter." Isontra unrolled a tattered scroll and gingerly placed it on the table. Like the Mirals before her, she had to fill in words that were faded or missing as she read.

ATD 107-3-23. Some men surprised us at sunrise. I don't know if they were from Charles' original band but it seems quite likely. We lost twenty-one men in the ensuing battle and Belendra was severely wounded. We managed to fend them off with arrows for the time being, but I am sure they will be back soon with reinforcements.

She set that scroll down and picked up another worn scroll that she read.

ATD 107-5-17. The latest battle has lasted two days and we lost three more men. I had thought we were well-hidden and have since banned the use of fire. The colony is weak from travel and our supplies are low. They are unhappy about eating cold and uncooked food but are willing to start moving west across the plains at sundown. Belendra is very ill. I don't think she will survive another move. It truly pains my heart to lose my mother. She has been a strong Miral and has given us all much hope. As the new Miral, I will continue in her place and do my best to lead the survivors to Nor. Daebra is reaching maturity and the time has come to make her Vice Miral. I am hoping to be able to spend the needed time with her. Until then, my first concern must be the safe keeping of the Crystal and my colony.

The fire began to wane so Kairma got up and put more wood on the receding flames while thinking about the many times she'd been told these same stories. *The ending was always the same. We fight, and then we run and hide because we are the chosen people—the keepers of the sacred Crystal.* After refilling their cups with steaming terrid, the kettle was nearly empty. She set it aside and returned to the tall, wooden chair at the table while Isontra unrolled another scroll and read from it.

ATD 108-12-12. It has been more than six moons since we have seen any sign of the strangers. We seem to be relatively safe here and hopefully we can rebuild our strength. The bluffs of the river have helped to conceal our temporary winter shelters and the time has done much to improve the colony's morale. We will construct more permanent structures over the summer and stay through the coming annum. We will consider further search for NOR once our supplies and health are improved.

Daebra has given birth to her first daughter, Ellanda. She is a strong and healthy child. I regret that Belendra did not live long enough to see her. I am teaching Daebra the script and will soon be turning the Ogs over to her. She has a natural gift for medicine, but the loss of many of Amanda's records is disturbing. We are having great difficulty with the inconsistency of botanical data and history.

The rest of the page had faded beyond legibility and Isontra identified with Crysten's distress over the loss of such important documents.

Standing beside the table, Isontra laid the scroll aside and gazed into Kairma's eyes. "It is of the utmost importance that you understand the hardships our ancestors incurred protecting the Crystal. These documents are all we have on which to base our current decisions. The fact that our ancestors pledged their lives to the safe keeping of the Crystal is reason enough to do the same. I know you have questions. We must continue to study if we hope to learn why." Isontra gently rolled the scroll and tied it with a leather strap. "The medicinal data is important for the well-being of the colony, but it is because we can read and write the script that we can pass our knowledge to future generations. The script is absolutely necessary to continue our duty. If keeping the Crystal safe is our first priority, it is the keeping and continuing of the Ogs that is our second greatest responsibility." She walked to the window and looked down the canyon. "If we forget our past, we will not be able to make informed decisions in our future, and if we lose our ability to understand the medical records, we will lose the colony."

Kairma began to fidget. She wasn't good at sitting still for long stretches. Isontra noticed and smiled. She motioned for Kairma to get up and join her at the window. The day was sunny and from where they stood, they could see six other homes constructed of knotted pine logs and gray stone. Spring was the time for airing out feather mattresses and opening the wooden shutters that kept out the cold and snow. Isontra loved the spring, but Kairma preferred the late summer when the nights were warm and there was fresh fruit to eat.

Isontra patted her hand. "You understand how important it is to find ways to keep essential data safe, don't you? Things like recopying the damaged scrolls. To ensure the script would never be forgotten, the ritual of naming all future generations by the Script Key began. You see, you were not named Kairma as a fleeting afterthought. *You* are the next trustee."

Kairma's eyes widened as she mentally listed her maternal heritage: *Amanda, Belendra, Crysten, Daebra, Ellanda.* Excitedly she said, "The Script Key! *A B C D E.* Oh, now I know why it was important to learn all thirty-six names in order." She unconsciously bit her lower lip, puzzled. "I know I'm the first born, but Kinter starts with a *K* too."

In a soft and reassuring tone Isontra replied, "Surely you remember, her name is Lakinter, we dropped the *La* when you became ill. We were afraid we were going to lose you." She reached out and took Kairma's hand. "When you were well enough to continue the lessons, we returned the Crystal to its proper trustee. By then, we'd gotten into the habit of calling your little sister Kinter."

Kairma felt a little better. She wasn't bothered purely by the general attitude of the community toward her, but Kairma couldn't help thinking how much faster Kinter learned things. Returning to the table, she vowed to apply herself more in her lessons. She helped unroll another scroll for her grandmother.

Isontra nodded solemnly. "Yes, we must *never* forget our heritage. Many of our greatest people have died fighting adversaries who had evil designs on the power of the Crystal. This brings me to another important consideration. How should we deal with this stranger who has come to Survin?"

Zedic had reached the front entrance that led to the Temples of the Godstones above the amphitheater. The neatly stacked square stones of the temples' walls amazed him. They seemed as old and as solid as the earth itself. Walking through the passageway, he gazed at the workmanship. *Gods must have built these.*

Stepping through the temple passageway and walking across the wide terrace, he looked down the tiers of a great amphitheater, which led to the base of the huge mountain from which the great monument was carved. Looking up at the Godstones, he felt minute and insignificant. He walked down the stairs wondering if the gods would understand what he and Collin were about to do.

He saw Collin sitting on a rock near the bottom of the stairway that led to their secret hideaway. Standing and mimicking his newest friend, Trep, Collin shouted, "Come on, Zedic! The sun'll be gone before you ever get here! Hey, where's Boo? I thought she'd be right on your heels. Don't tell me that little scare last night is gonna keep her away?"

"No, she couldn't come this morning," Zedic said as he adjusted the pack he was carrying. "When I was bringing in the firewood, I heard Mother tell her Gramme was expecting her for a lesson today."

Collin nodded appreciatively. Everyone knew Kairma's responsibilities took precedence above all.

"Well," Zedic said slowly as he stared up the long stairway. "I guess I'm ready to see what's behind that barricade."

Collin's light laugh made Zedic turn toward him. "Don't tell me you're spooked too."

Zedic grimaced. "Not really, but they are sure ugly things, aren't they?"

"Yeah." Collin straightened his shoulders in an act of gathering courage and headed up the stairs. "They sure are."

Collin wasn't easily daunted, but being that close to the dreaded White Ones the night before had given even the self-possessed Collin second thoughts about dark places. "Well, they've never bothered us in the daylight before and I sure want to know what's in that mountain. Are you coming?"

Zedic shrugged his broad shoulders but smiled. "Sure," he said. And then the boys eagerly climbed eight hundred stairs to find out what was in the unknown recesses of the mountain.

The stale air had cleared from the previous day's work and the narrow crack in the passage stood ominously before them. They tried to widen the opening, but the golden slab stood fast. Using flat rocks for shovels, they cleared away more dirt and tried again to move the obstruction from its position. They melted more fat and oiled the hinges on the left side again. No luck. There was still too much dirt at the base.

They continued to work through the morning but still hadn't succeeded in moving the obstinate block.

Zedic looked up at the sun just past its apex. "Let's have something to eat. All this digging has really made me hungry."

Collin nodded in agreement and the young explorers sat down to take a well-deserved break.

Kairma went to the dining room where her little brothers were arguing over a game of stacking sticks. Jettena, busy cleaning berries and arbitrating the skirmish, looked up as Kairma came into the room. "How is the session going?"

"Good," Kairma replied. "We talked about history mostly."

The girl took the stoneware pan from the low-burning fire and refilled the terrid kettle from Isontra's room. "Now I know why my name is Kairma." The dining area smelled of freshly baked bread. There was a large pot of bean soup on the fire, and Kairma realized she should have eaten more breakfast.

Jettena set down the barely ripe berries. "You must be studying the Script Key."

"Yes, Gramme reminded me that Kinter's name is really Lakinter."

A small line formed between Jettena's brows, and Kairma knew she was about to be lectured. "Careful," Jettena warned. "I wouldn't take to calling her that now. She's pretty attached to the name Kinter."

"Well, I'd better get back." Kairma smiled, envisioning the look on her sister's face if she called her by her given name, and left the room.

When Kairma returned, the Miral was sitting at her large pine table, a pile of old leather scrolls stacked in front of her. She was thumbing through the scrolls, looking at each of the titles.

"Thank you for refilling the terrid kettle," her grandmother said. "Please sit down." Isontra paused and took a long sip of the hot drink. "I don't know who first discovered this wonderful drink, but I am forever in his or her debt."

Kairma nodded in agreement and took her place again at the large table.

Picking up another scroll, Isontra examined it. "The last strangers to join our village were of the Efpec blood and good people. In fact, your Grampe was of the blood, as is your Father." Isontra shook her head. "This was not always so. Even now there are those who believe we are wrong to let any newcomers stay."

Kairma nodded, thinking of how Grimly had successfully split off a small faction of the church. The old man never confronted Isontra openly, but Kairma had heard the whispers of the disenfranchised.

"Ah, here it is." Finding the record she had been searching, for Isontra began to read.

ATD 174-6-28. I take a moment to record the last few days though we flee for our lives. On ATD 174-6-17 several unknown persons from a nearby settlement attacked us from the south. We were unprepared, and the long battle cost us thirty-one men, eight women and four small children. I, Fontas, have taken the Ogs as Ellanda has fallen and we are forced from our home of more than sixty annums. We are weak, and only 283 of us go from here. I believe our error was in trusting two men who had come upon us during a hunt thirty-six days past. They had shared our meals and services for five days before moving on toward the south. I cannot help but conclude that word of the Crystal had reached outsiders by way of these men. It is distressing to lose so much due to an act of kindness. We shall not be foolish again. It shall be law from this day on: all strangers the Survinees encounter shall be put to death immediately.

A chill ran down Kairma's back as she thought about those angry words.

Isontra smiled appreciatively at Kairma. "This is the first known record concerning the Law of Fontus, named after the Miral who instituted the law."

The older woman glanced at another scroll. "Let's see, this would have been just over five hundred annums ago. This is when Kitru ordered the deaths of a small family of Madics that had been discovered living in one of the Temples of the Godstones."

Setting that scroll aside, she took a sip of terrid and opened another. "According to this, we allowed someone to join our community. The Miral says that a woman who had recently given birth was found in the low hills to the east. The woman's husband and child died. The stranger promised to stay in Survin until her natural death, and after much debate she was allowed to join us."

Isontra studied Kairma a moment. "As you will see, we haven't always been this generous. In this Og, written sixty-four annums later, Miral Quensi says that while on an extended hunt, our men met six outsiders from the east. They did not allow the outsiders to escape." She sorted through a few more scrolls. "And here, Rosella ordered the death of a Madic who refused to say why he had come to Survin."

Isontra was silent a long while, and then looked deep into Kairma's ice-blue eyes. "It can never be easy to order someone to die. By weighing the consequences of our actions, and understanding that no one life can be more important than the whole of our people, you can make very difficult decisions. We are the Mirals of Survin, the guardians of the Crystal, and hence the decision must be ours alone to make."

"I hadn't realized so many strangers had been put to death," Kairma whispered.

"There were fewer strangers put to death than members of our own family, who were killed because we didn't take action."

Isontra leafed through more records while Kairma refilled the cups with fresh terrid. When Kairma settled, Isontra unrolled another recording. "Sometimes the decisions are more pleasant. This is one of my personal favorites. My mother Hestra wrote."

ATD 759-4-24. The hunting party discovered a small group of strangers living in a cave to the east of Survin. It was only by sheer luck that our hunting party had taken refuge from the rain in the small hold. The strangers are all quite ill-nourished. I do not believe they had been equipped to last through a winter as bitter as this one has been.

Isontra paused. "I remember. That was a tough annum for all of us." Unrolling the fragile scroll further, she continued.

Their bronze skin coloring and large stature leads me to believe they must be of almost pure Efpec blood. People of the smaller and weaker Madic blood would not have fared as well under such harsh conditions. The two older men have given me a little data concerning why they were holed up in our mountains. It appears that they are searching for the Mountain of Nor. They are looking for the city of the angel. I cannot recall ever having encountered another people who worshipped Nor. It may be a trick and I feel uneasy about their presence. I will consult the records to establish the proper course of action.

"Two days later she wrote."

ATD 779-4-26. I do not think the woman will last through the night. She is feverish and weak. Her son seems to be stable as of this recording. She tells me his name is Tamron. Sabra has recently given birth and has offered to milk feed the baby. Isontra has been very helpful. I think she favors the young man, Petar.

Isontra's face flushed a soft pink and it made Kairma smile. Isontra opened a new scroll and Kairma rested her chin on the palm of her hand, listening intently to the records her great grandmother had written long before her birth. She had heard the stories and even read many of the hundreds of Ogs herself, but each time her grandmother emphasized a different meaning from the ancient words and Kairma learned something new.

ATD 779-4-29. The woman died two days past. The remaining three strangers are improving quickly. I am amazed at the resilience of the Efpec blood. It is understandable how the great Amanda was able to survive and keep safe the great healing power.

Setting the fragile scroll on the table, Isontra went on to explain how the small band of outsiders had generally integrated well with the Survinees. Petar had been allowed to mate with her and had served as a strong Comad until an accident had taken his life. Petar was not of the original colony, although that fact had not been a major issue until Tamron and Jettena had found themselves in trouble.

Kairma was always uncomfortable when discussing her parents' rushed Seridar. It was a major source of contention among the elders. Kairma glanced away, but Isontra drew back her attention. "As you can see, strangers are not dealt with lightly. There is much at risk."

Kairma straightened in her chair. "There hasn't been a real war since Giannia held the Crystal more than five hundred annums ago, and it's been over three hundred annums since we've been forced to put a stranger to death. Maybe the Crystal's been forgotten?"

Isontra got up from the table. "No," she said slowly. "I think it's been very well-hidden." She walked to the small dark room to put away the bundle of scrolls.

Coming back to the table, she held a piece of slate and some chalk in her long fingers. Isontra always used these when she wanted to draw or write something that she didn't need to keep. Sitting close to her granddaughter, she began to sketch. Kairma could tell quickly that it was a picture of their canyon.

"When we came here almost five hundred annums ago, we knew this was our home because of the statue of the god Nor to the south." She drew a square marking their place of weekly worship where the smaller monument stood.

"Everything was perfect, not only because the Monument of Nor tells us this is where we belong, but because the canyon is the perfect place to hide from our enemies. Here, at the south end of the canyon, are the two square tunnels through the rock placed closely together. There is just enough room between the two passageways to let the smoke from the great center fire pit escape. Those two channels make up the Gathering House. You see there is no way to come into the canyon without going through the Gathering House or scaling that granite mountain."

Kairma's eyes flashed. "And to get in from the north you have to go through the hospital! It makes sense. For someone to attack us they would have to climb over the mountains or come through one of the passageways."

Isontra folded her fingers in front of her. "Yes, and even to find their way here, they would have to go through thick forest. We're pretty well hidden—with the minor exception that you can see the Godstones for twenty kilometers or more." Isontra blew out a gentle sigh. "I suspect that is what has drawn many of the strangers who have crossed our path over the annums. There may have been some who've seen the Godstones and its temples, but never found us here in this hidden canyon."

Kairma ran her fingers over the chalk drawing. "So we have a defendable home that has kept us safe for five hundred annums. We have the Healing Crystal that is designed to heal the world. We're here at the Mountain of Nor, and we pay our tributes to the gods annum after annum." Kairma looked up, her eyes searching her grandmother's. "Why doesn't the Crystal do everything it's supposed to do? Why do people still get sick and die? Six annums ago, we lost more than sixty people to the coughing fever." Kairma chewed her lower lip in frustration.

Isontra looked long at the pale girl. "I don't have an answer. All my life, I have searched these records trying to answer that very question. I do believe we will be given a sign when the time has come to change what has always been. Now, what can you tell me about this man they call Trep?"

Kairma hesitated. She really didn't know Trep, but the thought of having him killed tightened her throat and made her ill. "Well," she began slowly, "Collin says he comes from the east, from a place he calls Peireson's Landing. He's looking for something called *artifacts,* things made by the gods. Only he calls them the *Ancient Ones.*" Kairma fidgeted with her braid. "Collin also said he has really interesting things to trade with us. Things like clothing and alloy tools." It frightened her that Collin seemed so powerfully drawn to the stranger.

Isontra was also frightened upon hearing Trep was looking for ancient artifacts. Her first instinct was to terminate the stranger, but she knew the colony had been gradually waning, and the very oldest Ogs warned her that if she didn't safeguard something called a *genetic pool,* her people would die. Isontra didn't truly understand what this pool was, but the message was clear. Her greatest ancestors insisted the number of people in the colony should never drop below one hundred and fifty. After the most recent illness, there were only one hundred and thirty people in the village, and many of those were too closely related to mate. Trep was of breeding age, but the colony really needed ten strangers to rebuild its numbers. She didn't know where to find their kind of people—people of the Efpec blood. Trep was taller than the White Ones, but he had facial hair he kept cut very short. Isontra had never seen a true Madic, but she knew by the descriptions in the Ogs that the male Madics were small with thick chest and facial hair. Madic people frightened her, but time was running out. "Kairma, I want you to find out what you can about this man. I don't want you talking to him directly. Do you understand?" Isontra sighed heavily. "As you mentioned, we lost several people to the illness that swept through here six annums ago. We need to find a way to augment our genetic pool."

"By genetic pool, do you mean the number of people in Survin?"

"Not only the number, but the number of *unrelated* people. You see, for the past two or three generations, most families have had only one or two children. Women don't have very many children anymore, and over the last three or four generations, the infant mortality rate has risen dramatically. Now, after the last great fever, we have only six unrelated families left, and it isn't safe to mate with someone who is too close to you."

"I didn't notice it before, but why *is* our family so large?"

Isontra cocked her head to the side. "Great Stones! It never occurred to me. Jettena has seven healthy children—one of whom survived the White Fever. I'm going to see if I can find any records that might explain that."

Kairma stared out the small window across the room. "I was surprised when you let Collin bring Trep into the village. It's because of this pool that we need to make larger, isn't it?"

"Yes, I broke a rather strong law to allow that."

"I can hear people talk. Many of the elders are afraid of Trep. Do you think they will accept him in time?"

Isontra smiled. "Funny thing about time—as often as it proves us right, it proves us wrong."

Looking deep into Kairma's eyes, Isontra added solemnly, "Remember, your first duty is to the safe keeping of the colony. Until we know if we can trust this man, guard our secrets well."

Chapter 4

A moment later Jettena called them for lunch. Kairma was famished and Isontra agreed to continue the lesson later. Laying down the ancient records, the two women joined Jettena at the long dining table. Her little brothers were at the table already playing with their food, but Zedic was nowhere to be seen. Kairma was sure he was at the temples with Collin. She was envious and wondered how far they had gotten. A bubbly Kinter came bounding in to the room, giggling as she sat at the table. "So why aren't you with Zedic today? Did last night scare you?"

Kairma glanced at her but ignored the question.

Hearing Kinter's question, Isontra asked, "What happened last night?"

Kinter looked at Kairma, who was giving a sign to keep quiet. "Oh, nothing, Gramme. We just got home kind of late from the Godstones, that's all."

Isontra knew her granddaughters well and knew there was more to the story than Kinter was saying. Kairma was buying the talkative Kinter's silence with the Crystal. She nudged Kairma, and asked, "Was there not something you promised to do for me?"

Kairma cringed, not knowing how Kinter would react to the request. Resigned, she looked earnestly at Kinter with a promise to make amends clearly etched on her face, and said, "I have to ask you to give the Crystal back."

Kinter frowned, but when Isontra scrutinized her she handed the prized possession to Kairma. Slowly a sly smile tickled the corners of her mouth. It was apparent Kinter felt like telling Kairma's secret, but thought she could work this to her benefit by waiting until they were alone to exact her due pay.

Kairma sat quiet for a long time, eating her lunch. "Gramme, do you think we covered enough today? I was hoping I could go with Zedic this afternoon. He's down at the lake and most everything is ready for the feast day after tomorrow. Please?"

She saw Kinter's face light up, and Kairma knew her sister's silence would be expensive.

Isontra thought for a moment. "Well, I suppose. We did cover quite a bit this morning. I suppose it wouldn't hurt for you to spend some time playing." She held Kairma's hand tightly in her own. "We will continue our discussion about the stranger tomorrow. In the meantime, I want you to think about the past decisions that have been made on the subject."

Kairma finished the meal quickly. She would have to come up with something to keep Kinter quiet, and it wasn't going to be easy. After helping their mother clean up the dishes, the two girls went outside. Kairma took Kinter by the arm and led her away from the house. "I had to have the Crystal back. Gramme had a real seizure this morning. She went on and on about it."

Unflinching, Kinter looked straight into Kairma's eyes. "And why should I keep your secret?" She looked longingly at the Crystal, now safely around Kairma's neck, waiting for the answer.

Kairma let out an exasperated sigh, "You could just do it because I'm your sister, and because telling wouldn't be nice."

Kinter laughed heartily. "You think I should just *be nice*?" Smiling mischievously, she sat down on a log usually used for bow practice and waited for Kairma to make an offer. When no offer came, she said, "The deal is, I'll wear the Crystal whenever we aren't around Gramme, and I'll wear it at night too, after Gramme's gone to bed. But, instead of three weeks, it will be for three *annums*."

Kairma cringed and numbly sat down on the log next to her sister. *Three annums! How can I keep up this charade for three annums? If it was up to me, she could have the Crystal and everything that goes with it. No. I promised Gramme.* "Kinter, do you really think we could hide this from Gramme that long? She isn't dumb. She'd catch on before the end of the week."

"Well, if she does, I'll have to tell her what you did yesterday, *and* where you're going today."

Kairma thought about her options and concluded there was no way she could let Kinter wear the Crystal for that long. She would have to come up with another plan. "What if I ask Gramme to let you attend the lessons with me? After all, the Crystal isn't much good if you don't have the knowledge that goes with it."

The look in her eyes told Kairma her sister hadn't thought of this. Kinter's face was radiant, and Kairma knew she had struck the right cord. Kinter was fascinated by medicine and, although her training had ceased when Kairma recovered from the fever, she had a natural aptitude for recognizing herbs. "I'll have to ask Gramme. Wait here."

It was a long time before she returned, and Kairma couldn't hide the fact she'd been lectured again. Kairma knew the reprimand tickled Kinter and gave her sister a sense of power. Kinter often suggested Kairma was not Miral material, feeling herself to be the true Healer, and Kairma only having the Crystal by default.

"Gramme says it is all right with her if you start coming to the lessons. She won't go back over what we've already covered, but you'll have access to all the records to study on your own."

Kinter beamed with delight. Her script reading wasn't very good so there was little she could actually understand of the ancient documents, but Kairma knew just touching them gave Kinter pleasure.

Kinter gave Kairma a triumphant look before whirling around and racing off to play. Kairma shook her head. *Why do I let her get to me?* When Kinter was out of sight, Kairma hurried toward the temples.

Jettena walked into her mother's suite of rooms carrying a small vase filled with purple coneflowers. With her right hand touching her forehead in greeting, she asked, "Can we talk for a moment? It's about Kairma."

Isontra rolled up the last of the scrolls. "Of course, Jett. What lovely flowers! By the way, that soup you made for lunch was exquisite," she said as she walked to the storage room to put the scrolls away.

"Thank you. I guess cooking is a useful talent."

Isontra's forehead crinkled. "You have many talents. Don't berate yourself. It isn't becoming."

"Old habits die hard." She set the flowers on the large table in the center of the room. "I'm worried about Kairma. She seems preoccupied and flighty lately. Do you realize she went fishing today with Zedic and that rogue boy, Collin?"

"Yes, I'm aware." Isontra sat at the table, and Jettena joined her. "Tell me something. If you didn't have four little babies to take care of today, what would you be doing?"

"Well, I wouldn't be fishing with boys!"

"No, I expect you would be experimenting with a new recipe to fatten us up."

Jettena's face grew hot. "That's not the point really. It's that she's with those boys again."

Isontra held back a knowing smile. "I'm guessing there's a reason you don't want her running around with them."

Jettena looked down. Her hands were damp, and she rubbed them on her thighs. "It's just that I worry she'll make the same mistake her father and I made. Tamron was such a striking young man."

"Yes, he was, and you were a beautiful girl who had matured early. I know you blame yourself for this, but the fault belongs to me. To be honest with you, I was too interested in my own study of the Ogs. I never gave you enough time." She leaned across the table and held

Jettena's hand. "I had become used to my aunts, Madison and Isabella, taking care of you while I studied. I just didn't pay attention. I am so sorry."

Jettena fidgeted in her chair, not meeting her mother's eyes. "I didn't know what it was to be a woman. I was fourteen. I only remember how he made me feel. How could I have known what the consequences would be?"

"You didn't know very much about nature, or procreation. Again, the fault is mine. I should have let you have household pets. A child learns amazing things watching the lifecycle of an animal. As a member of the Healing family, you were never required to help in the fields or pens so you never spent much time around the goats." Isontra's smile was wry. "I would have thought Tamron would have known better. He was fifteen and most young men are well aware of nature by then. I realize now he hadn't passed his Seridar. He never saw the mating rites."

Isontra had called for a change in the laws, and young men were now allowed to attempt the Seridar as early as fourteen. "He really was too young to be a Comad. If tradition had been followed, you probably would have been mated to a much more mature man."

Jettena gazed off, saying wistfully, "To this day, his touch still sends shivers down my spine." She sighed and then added, "I want Kairma to be happy, but Collin is uncontrollable."

"Although the Mating Rites had been altered for the two of you, and any would-be contenders for your hand surrendered their claims, it outraged several people." Her steel-gray eyes crinkled at the corners. "I don't usually have to be hit over the head to learn something. This is why I began teaching Kairma medicine before she was ten. I had hoped to instill the weight of her responsibility in her before her hormones had the chance to tangle up her emotions. I don't see her making the same mistakes. Naturi is quite mature and has made his intentions clear."

"Yes, but does she see it?"

"She does. Kairma is all too aware of how much depends on her.

Deep down, she's scared witless." Isontra lips curled into a knowing smile. "But a little fear can be healthy."

Jettena got up, kissed her mother on the forehead, and said, "Thank you, Mother, for everything."

She left the room with vivid memories creeping into her thoughts. She heard the whispers of how the Healing family had strayed from tradition, the gossip about how outsiders had corrupted the royal line, and how the great family had brought the wrath of the gods down on the village in the form of the coughing fever. Jettena tried to shut out the gossip, but it cut her deeper than anyone could know. After what she had done, allowing her oldest daughter and the heir to the Crystal to be attacked inside the walls of the canyon, Jettena gave the Crystal to Isontra and lost herself in raising her children.

Chapter 5

Kairma was feeling a little uneasy about probing around the Godstones as she climbed up the stairs on the left side of the fourth head and walked through the narrow crevice that led to the opening of the newly discovered shrine. Seeing Collin and Zedic just finishing their lunch, she smiled brightly.

"Hey, Boo, glad to see you could get away from your studies," Collin said as he smiled back at her. "What are you learning about anyway?" He jabbed an elbow at Zedic and winked. "Has Isontra told you about the Mating Rites?" Everyone knew that for Kairma the rites would be different. Not only was she a Healer, and hence her mate would become the new Comad, Kairma was different.

Kairma grinned, though she felt the blood rise to her cheeks. "I *wish* she'd tell me about the Mating Rites. All she does is keep making white veils. And she says …" Kairma began mimicking her grandmother. *"Don't worry about it, dear. You will know soon enough. Besides, men are fools and so much trouble, you'll wish you had never found out."* Zedic looked almost hurt, and Kairma laughed. "No, honestly, she's teaching me about history."

Collin swallowed the bite of bread he was chewing. "So Gramme's gonna keep you in the dark until the fatal day, huh?"

Kairma sat down next to Collin. "You both passed your Seridar and attended Salina's mating last Harvest Celebration. Why don't *you* tell me about the rites?" She watched Collin turn away. *Oh, my stones! Did Collin actually blush? Maybe I don't want to know what happens.*

Zedic chided, "Collin, let her be."

"It's okay, Zedic," she said, removing her scarf and unraveling the long braids. "That's a long walk. I'm really warm. Do you have anything to drink?" She ran her slim fingers through her hair, gently scratching her scalp, letting the cool breeze dry her sweating head.

Handing her his water pouch, Zedic said, "You know, Gramme isn't going to let you do this kind of carousing when you're the Vice Miral."

Kairma took a drink of water and gave her brother a sly smile. "Gramme wouldn't let me do this now, if she knew!"

Zedic laughed lightly and shook his head in agreement.

She crossed her legs and leaned back against the rock wall. "Today we talked about strangers and how we should deal with them." Kairma took a deep breath. "Did you know most outsiders who have found us have been put to death? Gramme was reading from the Ogs this morning, and until recently we have always killed outsiders and those of the colony who have tried to leave the mountain."

Collin obviously didn't like the sound of this conversation, and his dark green eyes flashed at her. "What about your father and Grampe? They were both outsiders."

Kairma picked up a rock and tossed it from hand to hand. "I know. Gramme says that was the initial cause of the split in the church. That helps explain why people shy away from me, but I think she brought up the subject for another reason. We have to make a decision about the stranger. There are many things to consider, and we really don't know why he's here."

Collin got up and started putting the remainder of his lunch back in his pack. "He's here to study the *Ancient Ones*—the people he said really built these monuments." He looked squarely at Kairma, all raillery gone. "Kairma, I'll defend him, you understand that. I won't let you, or anyone else, kill him because of some stupid law written hundreds of annums ago."

Kairma understood and was slightly startled when she suddenly realized Collin spoke as a man, not as the teasing boy who was her friend. It was obvious this discussion was over.

Feeling slightly disheartened, she quietly helped them put away the remains of their lunch and then began to move handfuls of dirt away from the golden doors that guarded unknown secrets. The sun beat down on them, and the smell of sweat and dust filled their noses.

With a little more effort, they were able to move the immense obstacle far enough to pass behind it. For an intense moment, they looked at each other, grinning broadly.

Zedic walked to their packs and took out the ceramic jar that held his coal. Grabbing one of the torches Collin had thought to bring and lighting it, he moved cautiously up to the gaping slit of the entrance and handed the torch to Collin. For a few moments, they stood before the great doors and stared excitedly, unsure of what possible danger may be awaiting them.

It was Collin who made the first move. Leading with the torch, he stuck his head through the opening. "Great Stones!" he whispered.

The room beyond the door was completely free of dirt. The light of his torch threw cryptic shadows, and Collin could make out the shape of a table and various chairs. He quickly stepped back and handed the torch to Zedic, motioning for him to have a look.

Zedic peeked through the opening. "By the Crystal, Collin, what do you make of this? I'll bet it's as old as the mountain itself!" He turned to Collin, who was lighting the other torch. "It looks even bigger than the Gathering House. Do you think two torches will be enough?"

"It'll have to be enough. It's too late to go back for more. Come on, let's go in." Collin's eyes blazed excitedly as he disappeared through the narrow opening.

Kairma looked at Zedic, shrugged, and stepped through the opening. In her haste, she ran into Collin, who had stopped short, gaping at the sight before him.

Zedic squeezed past Kairma. As he held the second torch high above his sister's head, lighting the whole room, he said, "Stars and stones! It's unbelievable."

The entrance to the shrine was covered with a mosaic of opaque blue lapis and gold that framed bronze pictures of gods, birds, flags, and a myriad of things the three Survinees had never seen before. The immense, rectangular room was at least eighty feet long and sixty feet wide. Its massive walls arched gracefully to a white marble ceiling, thirty feet above the polished marble floor. Around the outer walls, about three feet below the arch of the ceiling, was a finely carved frieze depicting more mysterious objects. Some were battle scenes with men on horses. Other scenes looked like gods or men in strange wheeled carts. The floor was made of the same fine marble stone and felt slick under their soft leather footwear.

Recesses, cut into the stone of the walls to the right and the left of them, were filled with cabinets of an unfamiliar transparent material, framed by the same golden alloy as the outer doors. Inside the cabinets were hundreds of silver cylindrical canisters. Between each recessed bank of cabinets stood statues of gods. Some of them they recognized as the gods of the Godstones while others were unfamiliar. Although the faces of the gods carved into the mountain were male, inside the tomb they found female gods as well.

On the back wall was a large picture that was mostly white with patches of green and smaller spots of blue. The white spaces were divided into smaller sections by dotted lines. The center of white lay between borders of blue and had strange words written all over it. There were red and blue squiggly lines running everywhere. Kairma tried to read the words written across the huge picture. She recognized a few, like *north, south, new,* and *lake,* but the rest made no sense to her at all.

A mahogany leather chair sat behind an immense table that dominated the back half of the room, and dozens of smaller chairs lined up in front. Set on the massive table were four of the strange silver canisters that filled the clear cases.

Zedic caught his breath in awe. "How strange and wonderful these gods must have been."

For a long time the three of them stared around the room, not daring to touch anything but drinking in the reverence of a tomb untouched for countless annums. They could feel, in their heart of hearts, that they were embarking on a wondrous journey of knowledge untold. And while they were wildly excited, they were just a little scared.

Collin walked over to study one of the many statues that lined the walls. "Maybe the Ancient Ones that Trep speaks of built this shrine to honor their gods. Maybe these are their rulers or even the Ancient Ones themselves. These aren't great giants like those of the mountain. Maybe the Ancient Ones were no bigger than us. Other than the clothes they wore and the things they could build, they seem very much like us."

Zedic's tone was sardonic. "Oh, yeah," he snickered, "other than being able to do magical things, hey, they're just like us."

He moved cautiously toward one of the silver cylinders lying on the table and sat down in the broad leather chair. It was comfortable. He studied the construction, wondering if he could reproduce it, and almost fell out of it when the chair seemingly turned by itself. Recovering, he turned his attention to the objects on the table.

With effort he managed to twist the top off of one of the cylinders. "What a strange way to close a container." He twisted the top on and off a few times and then dumped the contents. His eyes lit up as he appraised all the things on the smooth table in front of him. "Look at this! It's a girl and a boy, but it's not a drawing! And look at the colorful clothes they are wearing!" Zedic picked up the picture and turned it toward Collin. "They look real! Like they're alive in there!" He quickly set it down at that thought.

"At least we know they weren't White Ones!" Collin joked as he picked up the picture and stuck it in his pack.

Collin walked over to a smaller table in the corner to examine a rectangular box covered with small squares. Most of the squares were embossed with a script symbol. He called to Kairma, "Hey, Boo, come look at this. Can you read it?"

Kairma came to stand beside him. Pointing to a row of squares, she said, "These are numbers. This one says *tab.*" She didn't know the meaning of the strange word. "And this says *control.* Maybe it's the main square, you know, one to control the other ones." She pressed on it. Nothing happened. She pressed a few more squares, but still nothing happened.

Collin pondered that thought. "That would make sense because it's longer than most of the others."

Kairma looked puzzled. "But this one is longer. It says *shi ... shift.* And the longest one doesn't have any script on it at all. I don't know, I've never seen anything like this before." She shrugged and left Collin to puzzle over the mystery.

Going back to study the large picture on the wall behind the chair where Zedic was sitting, Kairma asked, "What is this drawn on? It's not leather. It's too smooth." But no one was really listening to her because they were caught up in their own investigations.

Collin had been inspecting a strange box he found mounted on the wall above the mysterious cubes of script. It was about four feet square with a greenish-gray surface. The frame looked like a black alloy, but the center, made of a substance similar to Isontra's herb jars, reflected the light of his torch. He could almost see through the first layer and on closer inspection he could see himself staring with a puzzled look on his face. It wasn't as clear as his reflection in the pond, but it was definitely his face.

While Collin puzzled over the large wall mounted square, Zedic busied himself with the contents of another cylinder. Inside were thin sheets of silver covered with writing. "Kairma, look. They kept records the same way we do only on a different kind of alloy. It's silver not yellow, and it's really thin."

The Survinees had discovered the soft golden stone from the caves near their canyon. Once the gold was pounded flat on a smooth piece of granite, the thin sheets could be written on. These were more durable than the hides they usually used for recording information so over the past hundred annums they began the arduous task of copying all of their most important records.

Kairma joined Zedic at the table, and while she examined the silver pages he went on to discover a large drawer that slid out from the table when he pulled on it. Inside he found very thin sheets of hide with script notations all over them. They were very fragile and some crumbled when he picked them up. "Kairma, look at these! I'll bet you can read this!"

Kairma took hides from Zedic and on the top of the first one she read aloud. *"Ma-i-den, e-ar-li-est, beg-in-ing ...* Oh, beginning, I know those words!" She studied the next word, but it was totally foreign to her. She closed the neatly bound hides and set them in her pack. "I have more script lessons tomorrow. Gramme can read this!"

Collin whirled around. "Boo, you can't show that to Isontra! Where are you gonna say you found it? We're not supposed to be here!"

Kairma frowned. "It will take annums for me to know enough script to understand this. There must be hundreds of cylinders in these cabinets."

She looked so stressed that Collin walked over to her and put his arm around her shoulders, inhaling the scent of her hair. "I have an idea," he said. "Why don't you teach us the script too, then we can help you read all of this." He made a sweeping motion around the room.

"Yeah," Zedic piped in, "we'll help you read them."

"I don't know the script very well," Kairma said hesitantly. "This could take a long, long time." She went back to puzzling over the silver pages before her.

Dropping his arm, Collin found another drawer and began to investigate its contents. He picked up a small gold band from the treasures and studied it. "This is nice." Collin put the ring on his little finger.

Zedic looked up. "I think it's made of the same yellow rock we use for recording the Ogs, but harder. Do you think it's a different kind of alloy? Like what they used on the door?"

Collin looked around the room thoughtfully at the brass-encased cabinets. "I don't know. Looks a lot like it, but it's shinier." He walked over to a cabinet and opened the door. It swung open easily. Fascinated, he opened and closed the door several times. "Kairma's right. There is too much here to study. Maybe we should show this to Trep. He knows a lot and could probably figure out what all this is much better than we can."

Kairma looked up at Collin. "Do you think that's wise? Mother and Gramme have forbidden me from talking to the man. And what if ..."

"They don't want you here either." Collin reminded her.

"I know, but what do we really know about him?" Kairma shifted her gaze to Zedic as Collin's stare had become icy. "Maybe I spend too much time around Gramme, but I'm not sure if we can really trust him."

Collin shrugged and picked a few more things from the drawer and put them in his pack. He opened another drawer. Inside was a small brightly colored box. He lifted the top and gasped as music began to play. "Look! It plays a song. And there's a little girl on top spinning around in circles." The sound was high, faint, and tinny. It didn't sound like any instrument they had ever heard before.

The tune was light and lively but very strange. Kairma gasped. "Is there something alive inside the box playing the music? Maybe the gods are very tiny." Looking from Collin to Zedic and back to Collin, fear clearly etched in every line of her face, she put a hand over her mouth, and swallowed loudly. As if reading each other's thoughts, they put down the objects in their hands and quickly walked out the door. Things would be clearer once they were outside.

The three young friends stood there at the opening for some time before Zedic spoke. "We need to get back. It's late. The hunters will be home soon and I still have to set up the blooding rods."

Collin nodded as he began to pack his tools. "We need some time to think this through. Maybe I can bring Naturi up here tomorrow." He glanced at Kairma and saw that she was relieved. "And I'll see if I can't find out a little more about Trep before I say anything to him."

Collin and Zedic pushed the heavy door back into place before heading silently down the stairway, and as they walked Kairma began to braid her long hair into its customary style. A cool spring breeze whistled through the pines, drying the sweat from their dirt-covered bodies. They looked forward to a well-deserved trip to the cleansing station.

Taking the scarf she usually wore over her hair, Kairma wrapped it about her shoulders. "I can't believe no one has ever found the vault before. What if we were supposed to find it when we first came to Nor. What if it has valuable data concerning the reason for being here?"

Collin reached over and flipped one of her long, now very dirty, white braids at her before she could fend him off. "You mean to tell me, with all the studying you do, you still question why we're here."

She tried to punch him in the arm, but he was too quick for her. Sighing, she gave up the chase and said, "Well, I know what the Ogs say, but don't you think there should be more to our lives than this?"

"Holy Nor, Zedic. I think your little sister has actually heard what I've been saying for the last—oh, I don't know how many annums now."

Zedic stared ahead but murmured, "It began the day we dug out the huge alloy cart we never could move."

"Yeah, I think you're right. I still wonder what that was ever used for." Collin headed a little way into the forest. "Here's another good sapling we can use for a rod."

The three of them worked quickly to strip the small branches, adding it to the rods they'd already collected. Zedic adjusted his pack of rods and they began to walk again. "How do you think Naturi will react when we tell him? He's pretty cautious."

Collin laughed. "Yeah! I'd say almost virtuous."

Zedic matched Collin's pace. "He's just more serious than most people our age. Don't you think Naturi'll be upset if we tell him we were up here?"

"Absolutely! I can't wait." Then, in a more serious tone, he added, "He'll know what to do though. We sure can't tell the elders where we were."

Kairma agreed. "He's older. I'm sure he would talk to Trep if we ask him. He would never reveal anything about us that Trep shouldn't know." *But Naturi's still going to be really mad we were here.*

Turning up the narrow path that led to the canyon, they stopped and picked up three rods Zedic had set aside earlier that morning. Collin said, "I think Trep's safe. We already know he's here to study the Godstones. He told me that he first heard about the temples from another traveler who came through here a few annums ago. He didn't even know we were here before he met me. He seems more interested in our language and the way we dress than anything else. He's never mentioned the Crystal."

Handing Collin another rod, Zedic said, "That might mean he just doesn't want us to know he knows."

"Maybe, but I don't get that feeling at all."

Kairma stopped suddenly.

"What's wrong?" Zedic asked.

"I think I saw a wolf over there," she said. "By that old stone wall."

"Are you sure? Could it have been a coyote?" Collin asked.

Pulling out her sling, Kairma searched the ground for a hefty stone. "Wasn't a coyote. Too big." Finding one, she handed it to Zedic. "You're a better shot."

After staring into the trees for several minutes, Kairma walked quickly. "I don't see anything now. If it's one wolf, she probably ran off. We'll hear her call if there are more wolves in her pack."

Suddenly the two boys had to hurry to catch up. When Zedic reached her side, he asked, "Do you think that's a new one? I thought Toric and Canton ran off the one Gramme heard a few days ago." Zedic never questioned Kairma when she named an animal. She seemed to have an affinity for living creatures, often knowing their sex and their whereabouts without ever really seeing them.

Kairma turned toward the forest. "They looked for several days, but never found her trail. If she has pups, she'll stay close by them. We'll tell Gramme where we saw her and maybe the men will run her off for good this time."

Zedic shook his head. "All the men are hunting."

Kairma said, "Naturi didn't go. I think Hiram and Diakus may have stayed behind as well. You and Collin are pretty good with a sling too, but you obviously found a reason not to go."

Collin shrugged, but his cheeks flushed slightly. "Yeah, we probably should have gone. Maybe Zedic and I will go wolf hunting later."

At the north end of the canyon, several wide stone steps led to the entrance of the hospital. The stones had been appropriated from the temples hundreds of annums before and now seemed a natural part of the cliff face. They didn't see anyone as they passed through the ground-level exit of the great hall. The original openings to the stone tunnels were about twenty feet across and eighteen feet high. Shortly after the Survinees had come to the canyon, they enclosed the face of the openings with thick wooden walls and put smaller doors in the center. Most of the doors in Survin were made of heavy fur and leather, but here and at the Gathering House they had hung wooden doors, attaching them with leather hinges that had to be replaced often. This week, Collin and Kaiden had drawn that particular duty.

When the tired, amateur archeologists reached the village center, they found Naturi preparing the fields for spring planting. He smiled and put his right hand to his forehead in greeting as the three of them came up the path. Naturi was a striking man with a square jaw and well-defined cheekbones. His hair was cut shorter than most of the Survinees. It was thick and curled much like Collin's hair, but was slightly lighter in color. The biggest difference between the two young men was that Collin's hair and clothing were usually a mess, and no matter what Naturi was doing, he was never a mess.

Naturi stood up, taking a rag from the waistband of his leggers, and brushing the dirt from his large hands he said, "You three look as though you have had a pretty rough day."

Zedic looked at Collin and Kairma and laughed. In the bright sunlight, he could see that they were covered with dirt. "Yeah, we've been discovering things!"

Naturi bent down and gave Kairma a light kiss on her forehead, making her blush a deep pink. "And what have you discovered, beside the fact that Kairma is the prettiest girl on the mountain?" His voice was deep and smooth like black velvet.

Kairma smiled shyly and looked down at her feet.

Seeing Kairma blush gave Collin a feeling of anxiety. Even when hearing the most ribald jokes, Kairma rarely blushed. Something in Naturi's conduct embarrassed Kairma, and Collin had the urge to pull her away. Forcing the unsolicited feelings to the side, he said, "We found another temple behind the Godstones. There is a long staircase leading to a narrow canyon behind the rightmost head. The tomb is huge and it's full of really mysterious stuff."

Naturi was taken off guard. Kairma was still standing by his side, and he lifted her face up toward him. "You were *climbing* around the Godstones?" His chocolate eyes searched hers. "I do not think you should be playing there. You will soon become the Vice Miral of this community and many people's lives will be in your hands. You know what the Word says about defacing the temples."

"We didn't deface anything!" Collin interjected, now angry. "I told you, we were discovering things, important things."

Although they had grown up together as friends, Naturi was being groomed to become the next Comad and took every opportunity to express his intention. Collin was far too excitable to dedicate himself to anything for too long and found Naturi's attitude irritating. Naturi was only three annums older than Collin, but his judiciousness and self-assurance often made Collin feel young and defensive.

Naturi didn't look away from Kairma. His left eye twitched as it often did when he was bothered by something. "Collin, what *is* it with you and these foolish explorations? What could be *that* important that you would risk Kairma? She is the future of this colony. Have you no sense at all?"

Collin's eyes darkened to a shade resembling fresh spinach. Who was Naturi to scold him like that? He also didn't like the way Naturi was touching Kairma; it was almost possessive. The crack in his voice betrayed him, making him sound young and anxious. "Lots of things. Really important things, like tombs the Ancient Ones made and huge statues they built."

Now Naturi faced Collin, his own dark eyes curious. "The Ancient Ones?"

"Yeah, you know, the ones from before us. They built another temple. Only this one is a cave carved into the side of the mountain. It's filled with all sorts of things. Things like this." Collin quickly pulled out Zedic's picture of the girl and boy in the strange clothes and handed it to Naturi.

Naturi straightened, his forehead furrowing when he looked at the picture. He brushed an annoying, silky curl from his broad forehead. "Where did you say you found this? They look alive—it's as if you could reach in and touch them. The paints and the colors are fascinating. Look at the way it changes in the sunlight."

Reaching for the picture, Collin said, "We found it in the secret vault behind the Godstones." He took his prize back and handed it to Zedic. "We were hoping Trep could tell us how it was made. Here, look at this." Collin showed the ring to Naturi. "There are statues of strange men and huge cases filled with these odd silver containers and more drawings and carvings on the walls too."

Although he sounded dour, Naturi looked intrigued. "Interesting. I would love to see them. The gods must have used some form of magic to create this." He turned in the direction of the Godstones as if he could see them through the cliff walls. "But I do not feel good about this. Exploring the temples has been forbidden for countless centuries. There could be a curse on these things. You really should have thought this through, Collin. It may prove to be very bad for the colony—and to endanger Kairma like that. Where would we be without our Healer?"

Hesitantly, Zedic agreed. "Maybe we should put these things back, Collin."

Collin snapped, "Don't be so superstitious, and Boo is just fine." It was obvious Naturi was too conservative to allow his curiosity to get the best of him. "Trep would be the one to ask. He knows about a lot of things we don't understand. He says that there's no such thing as magic; that there are just ways of doing things that we haven't figured out yet."

"It is quite possible he is searching for the Crystal. This is not a risk we should take at this time. No, you will not tell him about this. He is a stranger." It sounded like a command.

Collin bristled. "To us, they are *all* strangers, Naturi."

Naturi ignored his comment. "Undoubtedly this new discovery will pique the stranger's interest and if he starts asking questions, we would find it difficult to hide the Crystal from him for very long."

Zedic nodded in agreement. "Collin, Naturi's right. I think we need to know why he's come here before we tell him anything about the vault."

Collin lamented, "Why don't we just *ask* him?" He glanced at Kairma and added flippantly, "If he *is* searching for the Crystal, you can have him killed, right Boo?"

Kairma blanched and looked away.

Naturi grimaced, and his left eye twitched. He grabbed Collin roughly by the shoulder. "The Law of Fontas is not something to make light of." He paused, and the deep furrows returned to his forehead. "I do not believe that it is necessary to invoke the law at this time, but we should not take unnecessary risks either."

Collin shrugged off the grip. "So what do you suggest? Should we wait until he comes and asks us for the Crystal? Or do you actually have a plan?"

"As it is, I am meeting with the stranger tomorrow evening. He has asked to see my drawings. Let me see if I can ascertain why he is here, and if it is safe to tell him about this discovery of yours."

"Trep. His name is Trep!" Collin said frowning. Then slowly shaking his head, he relented. "Okay, find out what you can." He knew Naturi was right for being cautious, but sometimes he enjoyed pushing Naturi's arrogance right to the edge. "He's really hard to understand.

He pronounces his words differently, and he uses lots words I've never heard before."

Kairma nervously touched Naturi on the arm, and he instantly gave her all of his attention, making her blush again.

His dark brown eyes searched her pale blue ones and his perfect mouth said, "Yes, Miss Kairma?"

Kairma looked away, confused, like she had suddenly forgotten her question. Seeing the glower on Collin's face, it must have come back to her. She looked back up at Naturi, who had never looked away, and said, "Isontra and I would like to know more about his city and its people. Could you please ask him for us? She doesn't want me to talk to him."

The corners of Naturi's mouth lifted. "Of course I will ask him for you. I agree with Miral Isontra. You should not associate with the stranger."

Collin snapped, "TREP, Naturi, his name is *Trep*!" Then, giving up the dispute, Collin looked at the sun dropping behind the trees on the mountain peak and said, "We better get home. Pa needs me to get the blooding rods together. I'm sure it will be a good hunt and you know how much I like to celebrate a good hunt." He jabbed Zedic in the ribs, making his friend smile. "There aren't many things I like more than lots of food and mulberry wine."

Zedic agreed, "The only thing that beats the Awakening Celebration is the Harvest Celebration. Put wheels on my chair and let me roll from dish to dish." They all laughed as Zedic mimicked gliding around a table eating continuously. Then, in a more sober tone, Zedic said, "I'd best be off too. Father will skin me if the rods aren't up when the hunters get back, and then I won't be allowed to eat myself sick at the feast." He looked at Naturi. "You're one of the best marksmen we have. Why didn't you go on the hunt?"

Naturi went back to pulling weeds from the field, avoiding Zedic's eyes. Forlornly he said, "I really needed to tend the fields today. Since Mother disappeared four annums ago, I have learned a lot about growing things and someone has to oversee the gardens."

Kairma adjusted her scarf, mumbling something about helping Gramme with preparations for the Awakening feast.

Naturi looked up at her, his smile returning. "I am looking forward to the celebration. Will you save at least one dance for me?"

She blushed again and stammered, "Of ... of ... course I will."

Collin felt an uncomfortable twinge in his gut and his words came out harsher than he meant them. "Come on, Zedic, we better go." Taking Kairma by the hand, he said, "Let's go, Boo," and pulled her toward the Chancery.

Zedic looked at Collin, then back at Naturi kneeling in the field. He could feel the tension build between the two friends whenever Kairma was around. He thought he understood the cause even if Collin and Naturi didn't. He thought Naturi would be a fine mate for his younger sister. He was responsible and always had the colony's interests in mind. Collin was his best friend, and although he loved him like a brother, he knew Collin had a reckless, adventuresome streak. Kairma was nearly as uncontrollable as Collin. She would need stability and a strong mate when she became the Vice Miral.

Once Zedic and his sister reached home, she looked in the pantry for something to eat. She saw Jettena carrying clothes down the stairs to be washed and said, "Mother, we saw a wolf just north of the hospital."

"That's all I need to worry about now. Go speak with Hiram in the morning and tell him where you saw it."

"I think she has pups."

"All the more reason to catch her now. The winter left the area pretty low on small game. Best you children stay inside the village until we know she's run off."

Zedic and Kairma gave each other that *Why did we say anything?* look, knowing there would be no exploring the tomb for a while. They wouldn't have been able to go tomorrow because preparations for the hunters' return and the Awakening Celebration would take all day, but with any luck Hiram could convince the wolf to move on the day after the feast.

Chapter 6

Naturi watched them walk away, thinking he'd love to give Collin a lesson in manners. He hated when Collin called Kairma *Boo*. It was undignified, and far too intimate. Collin was seventeen now, old enough to take a mate, and Naturi thought he should be more respectful. He bristled at the thought of Collin taking Kairma exploring. Despite himself, he sighed, thinking it would have been fun to unearth something like the vault. He couldn't remember ever being a child. From a very early age, his father had wanted him to take Kairma as a mate. Toric had coached him on the fine art of being a Comad, insisting Naturi be the best at everything. There was never time for playing games or climbing mountains. Naturi was taught to be responsible above everything. Day after day Naturi studied the history that led to the laws of the community until one day he found himself facing his manhood rites and wondering what had happened to the boy who wanted to draw pictures.

Life was very different now. His father had changed with the loss of his wife, but it was more than that. It was as if Toric blamed Kairma for Devon's disappearance even though a White One had attacked Kairma herself only a week later. Toric was sure the White Ones had stolen his wife and was determined to find her. Isontra reminded the Survinees of the bitter conflicts they had with the cave dwellers over the centuries. In the end, in the name of peace, Isontra had forbidden them to search the caves for Devon, or the White One who had attacked Kairma. Toric tried to raise enough interest to go against Isontra's wishes, but when he could find no backers he shut himself away from the community and his son.

Toric was a great hunter, and Zedic's casual question reminded Naturi why he chose not to hunt and of the rift that existed between his father and himself. A moment of sadness engulfed him as he thought of the great stag he had killed with his bow four annums ago. The large brown eyes of the beast had looked right at him as he let go of the string that sent an arrow into its heart. He knew how much the colony depended on the men for food, but he felt an odd sense of guilt watching the life bleed from the majestic animal. His father had been very proud, telling everyone how it had been a clean kill. With six horns, it was the largest kill of the hunt.

Shaking the memory from his mind, Naturi continued to work the garden, and began planning the questions he'd ask the stranger. He was a little nervous. This would be the first formal meeting he'd had since the stranger had come to their mountain and there were a lot of people depending on him to do well.

The following day, while Kairma and Kinter studied, Zedic constructed racks to bleed the game in preparation for the returning hunting party. Trep spent the day exploring the ancient monument south of the village. Collin had gone with him, but couldn't answer many of his questions. He was sure the structure was nearly a thousand annums old. Cryptic writing covered the front of a massive bronze plaque imbedded in a granite block almost as tall as Trep himself.

The sounds of people preparing for a feast and the smell of baking bread drifted into the cabin where Trep finished recording the day's events on a rough piece of hemp paper. The room was a trifle musty from being unused for several annums, but it felt warm and had the homey smell of wood smoke. It had been a long day and he was tired from the trip to the Monument of Nor. Getting up from the table to stoke the fire, he pondered the meaning of the things he'd seen.

He was preparing hot water for terrid when he heard a rap at the entrance of the small wood and stone cabin. He turned to see Naturi struggling with the heavy hide that hung across the opening to keep out the evening chill. Limping to the door and pulling the heavy leather back to allow Naturi to pass, Trep drawled. "I say, gotcha hands full, doncha?" He offered the greeting Collin had taught him and Naturi returned it easily.

"See ya braight chour skaetches. Goodnuf. Jate?"

Naturi's eyes darted around the room nervously. "I beg your pardon, Sir."

Trep pointed to the drawing in Naturi's hands. "Chour shaetches."

"Oh. My *drawings,*" Naturi said.

Trep's forehead crinkled, and the deep lines of a man who spent long days in the sun formed around his eyes when he smiled. He asked again, "Jate yet?"

Naturi looked confused and a little wary. Trep pointed to some bread and cheese. "Jate?"

Slowly understanding dawned on Naturi's face. "Oh! Did I eat? No, I am fine. I will eat with my father later."

Trep held up a mug of steaming liquid. "Caire fur a cup o terrid ta warm ya bones? Don't know what this drank is, but ate shore is good."

Naturi laid down his bundle on the knotted pine table by the fireplace. Naturi stared at him for a while, and Trep wondered if he should repeat himself. But before he could, Naturi said, "It is made from ground rose hips, dried blackberries, and dandelion. I believe the Healers add a few more things to the terrid they make. It is a little sweeter than mine."

Trep thought Naturi looked a little tense as he handed him an oiled wooden cup full of steaming terrid. "Jess finished this brew. Come in, have a sit down." Trep ran a hand through his shaggy hair, and his congenial smile did much to relax Naturi.

Sitting at the small table where the drawings were lying, Trep said, "It's gonna get cold 'night. Really wish I hade some whiskey." He offered Naturi some biscuits anyway. "I was jess finishin' my supper. Collin has taken sache good care of me. I must thank the boy proper."

Naturi was still standing there with a puzzled look on his face, and Trep began to speak more slowly.

Getting up, Trep pulled out a chair and said, "Please sit. Late's see whacha have."

Unrolling the drawings, Naturi said, "I tried to bring a large selection of drawings. You did not specify what you were interested in viewing. I am flattered you asked to see my work."

"Cole told me ya did good work." He lifted a hide. "My, my, Nate. Y'all are pretty talented, very accurate, and so much detail. Think these jess might be some of the best pieces I've seen in—oh, I don't know how long. A good while anyway." As he poured over sketches of birds and wild animals, Trep noticed most of the creatures Naturi drew appeared gentle, which seemed a contradiction of the austere attitude Naturi presented.

Many of the young man's drawings were of the local people and plant life, but the one that intrigued Trep the most was of the Godstones. For several minutes Trep puzzled over the drawing as he and Naturi sipped their drinks.

"Is there something wrong with my copy?" Naturi asked, sounding a little uncomfortable.

"Oh no, Nate, it's fine." By habit, Trep shortened most names to one or two syllables. His own given name was Trepard, though he hadn't used it since he was a boy of ten. "It's very accurate. I jess wish I understood more about these Godstones of y'all's. This is what brought me here in the first place. Very strange, they are. Cain't say that I've ever seen anythin' quite like 'em before. In all my travels, I've never come across such magnificent stone carvings." From what Collin had told him, Trep understood the Survinees believed the god Nor had carved the great heads out of the side of the mountain.

Trep got up from the table, limping slightly as he went to a cupboard holding a skin of apple wine. "Ya know, this is one of the best things the Surv's have going for y'all." He took two fresh cups off the shelf and filled them with the sweet, fragrant wine. Naturi accepted the cup with a nod, and Trep said, "Things are different down in the city. Ya know, we have several different spirits we store in glass containers. Some of 'em very good."

Naturi's face had gone blank again, and Trep cursed the differences in their language under his breath. The friendliness never left his voice as he explained what *spirits* were and, when Naturi still looked confused, he tried to find an example of glass as well. There was none to be found. With an exasperated shake of his head, he said, "Someday I'll show ya what I mean."

The next few drawings were of hunting parties and the game they brought home. Trep examined the drawing of a particularly large bear obviously in no condition to hurt anyone again. "This is interestin'. Is this the usual game the men bring home?"

"No, this was kind of an accident." An amused light came to Naturi's eyes. "Hiram and Drew stumbled in between her and her cub. It is really not the kind of thing a smart man does. It took the entire hunting party to bring her down. My father still has a couple deep scars from the encounter. They felt bad for the orphaned cub and Mother fed it through the spring." Naturi took a sip of wine and stared into the fire. "Sometimes, I think I still see that little black bear down by the lake."

"I'd been meanin' to ask about somethin'. I saw most of the men and older boys leave yesterday to go huntin'. Don't y'all keep any cattle for food?"

This drew another blank look from Naturi, and a longer swig of wine from Trep.

"Okay, so the people in Peireson Landin'—well, not really in the city, but folks outside the city, those on ranches, keep animals in pens. They feed 'em until they're fully grow'd. Then they butcher 'em for the meat. The ranchers trade this meat for other things they need. Men usually hunt for sport."

Naturi looked appalled. "The idea of raising animals to eat makes sense, but I do not understand hunting for sport. I would never kill an animal unless I needed to."

Trep shrugged. "So, as I was sayin', people come from miles around to trade their herds and grains for cloth, metal, and other supplies. They have some wonderful things at the market." Noting the perplexed look on Naturi's face, Trep explained what the market was.

Naturi said, "I find it difficult to imagine a building with so many different wares in it. Do they have this market all the time, or is it like our Awakening or Harvest Celebrations?"

"The market is open every weekend. There's music, with lots of singin' and dancin', and lots of different wines." He motioned for the cup in Naturi's hand and refilled it. "The wine there isn't quite like this here, but very good all the same." Trep took an appreciative sip and then refilled his cup with more wine. "And the women there! Ahh, the women, all dressed in their finest clothes. The fabric is made of such a fine weave it shimmers in the sunlight and is jess made for touching." He gave Naturi a roguish grin. "And the beautiful jewels they wear in their hair, if only y'all could see 'em!" He quickly added, "Not that y'all don't have fine women here, ya certainly do. City women are jess a little more—acceptin' of my kind."

Fascinated, Naturi looked directly at Trep. "What is metal? You said people traded for it at the market."

Trep looked around the room and then pointed to a pan sitting by the hearth. "That's made of metal, and my knife, and that pail. They're all made of metal."

Naturi's dark eyes sparkled. "You mean *alloy*. That's what we call it."

Trep shook his head, unrolling another picture. "Collin spent a long time with me trying to teach me y'all's language, but I guess there is still a lot of ground left to cover." From his extensive travels, Trep had learned how to interpret body language and hand signals. The Survinees' language was similar to his and obviously derived from the same root language. The well-traveled man wondered when and why people split into separate tribes. Scratching his scruffy two-day-old beard, he suggested, "If ya go to the city, y'all will have to learn to speak their language. I don't think too many folks would take the time to learn yours. It won't be too hard. It's a lot like yours."

Naturi's face whitened. "I could never go to the city. It is against the law to leave the mountain."

Trep studied Naturi's face. "Your hunters leave. Don't they ever go down to the plains? Haven't they ever gone to the city or another village?"

"Sometimes they go near the plains, but contact with outsiders is expressly forbidden. It is, in fact, very unusual that you are here." Naturi suddenly looked a little uncomfortable when he asked, "How is it that you decided to come to our mountain? Do the city people know we are here?"

Trep leaned his chair back on two legs to study the young man. "I heard a tale about y'all's mountain. No one mentioned a village. I think y'all can be assured no one knows 'bout it—and I always travel alone."

Naturi was visibly relieved. "This is good. We like our privacy."

"Yep." Trep nodded in agreement. "Y'all are a *very* private folk." The attitudes of this strange culture puzzled him. He knew they were hiding for some reason and he was determined to learn why.

Trep took a long drink, wiped his mouth with the back of his hand, and looked conspiringly at Naturi. "I think maybe ya jess need a *good* enough reason to go to the city." He handed the skin of wine to Naturi, who foolishly refilled his own cup again.

"It is all very interesting, but I guess it does not really have an effect on us here." Naturi took another long drink, feeling the warmth spread through his chest. "Curiosity will only lead to trouble and unhappiness. We have everything we could want right here."

"Now, *that*—is what I call a poor attitude. Really, where would y'all be if ya never tried to learn the truth of things? Many modern conveniences have been invented 'cause someone was curious or—jess plain lazy." He grinned. Then he looked about the room, noticing its gray stone walls and heavy hide door. He couldn't understand why these people hadn't developed the same conveniences they had in the city.

"If there was something in the city that y'all really wanted, surely *someone* would be willing to make the trip." Trep jumped up so quickly it startled Naturi. "I may have jess the thing, right here!" He ran back to the bedroom and reached under his meager cot, pulling out an odd-shaped piece of metal.

Returning to the great room, he flourished his prize. "This is a karrack and it's about to change y'all life, my boy!" He gently handed it to Naturi. "It demands the greatest amount of respect, but it's the most wonderful invention y'all ever laid eyes on." Trep could feel the effects of the wine and almost stumbled while reaching for the hollow horn filled with fine black powder. Laughing, he ran his hand through his thick hair. "Yes, Sir, that's some mighty fine wine ya folks make!"

Naturi held the karrack and ran his fingers over the smooth cylinder that extended from the odd-shaped handle. "What is it for?"

"Here, I'll show ya." Trep took the karrack and poured some powder into the cylinder. With a long rod he tamped the powder in tight. Then he pulled a small round ball of metal from his pocket, packed it in the cylinder, and followed that with a piece of cloth. "Now come with me. I'll show you what we do with it."

As they left the dwelling, the cool evening air felt good on Naturi's face. He didn't drink wine often and was feeling flushed and a touch off balance.

The sun was almost gone and he could just make out a patch of crocus by the pathway as he followed the traveler to the edge of the wooded area east of the homes. Trep tiptoed quietly along the edge of the woods and Naturi followed suit. The traveler was searching for something in the tall grasses. Just as Naturi was about to ask Trep what he was looking for, a fat turkey skittered through the grass before them. Trep quickly pointed the cylinder at the bird and *karraaackk!* Feathers flew and the bird fell lifeless to the ground.

The loud noise caused Naturi to stumble backward into a thorny rabbit bush. Looking back, Trep guffawed loudly. Trep walked over and picked up the bird, saying, "Damn, I missed the head. Now I gotta eat shredded meat. If there'd been jess a bit more daylight, I'd a been a better shot."

Brandishing his kill, he proudly said, "*That's* what we do with a karrack."

Brushing the leaves and dirt from his clothes, Naturi fell in behind Trep. The awe in Naturi's voice was barely concealed. "Can that thing kill big game too?"

"Ya could kill a man, or even one of y'all's White Ones at a hundred feet. That is …" He winked at Naturi, "That is if ya can see him."

Naturi looked puzzled as he looked down at Trep's feet. "A hundred feet?"

Now it was Trep's turn to be puzzled. He thought for a moment, and then drew a line in the dirt. Walking off several paces, he turned to Naturi, who was intent on watching, and said, "There! That's 'bout ten feet."

Naturi's face lit up. "About three meters!"

Trep laughed and slapped Naturi on the back. "Yeah! Meters are kind of like what we call yards."

"You have very strange names for things in the city. I think it would be hard to learn your language."

When they returned to the cabin, Naturi moved the drawings from the table onto a nearby chair so he could help Trep pluck the feathers from the freshly killed bird. "The karrack could be a very useful tool. I can see how my people could benefit from it. Could we have that one?"

Trep's eyebrows shot up. "I think not! There's no way I'd part with my Mojo. She's been by my side for the best part of twenty years."

"How could I attain one? I think we would like to have several."

"That sure don't surprise me. *I thought it'd get your attention.*"

Smiling to himself, Trep grabbed a pot and filled it with water from a large wooden barrel by the hearth. "Well, y'all would have to go to the plains. That's where they make 'em." He hung the pot over the fire and sat back down at the table.

Naturi looked wide-eyed at Trep. "They *make* them? But that's solid alloy, except the handle."

"Sure, they make lots of things of metal, I mean, *alloy*. They jess heat it up and shape it into anythin' they need." He carefully slit the bird open and removed the entrails. "All ya need is somethin' to trade and y'all can have jess about whatever you want."

As much to himself as to Trep, Naturi said, "What could I find to trade? I have some skins and a nice bow, but I do not think that the plains people would have use for anything like bows and drawings, not if they have all the things you say they have."

Trep took another drink of wine. "The way I see it, y'all gonna have to trade somethin' they don't have, or cain't get, like this apple wine or your sketches. I know some people would surely like to have ya draw their picture too. Some folk are quite vain, I suppose." He put the clean bird on a skewer and placed it over the fire, and then walked over to the chair and found one of the larger sketches. "This here's a nice one. Someone would be willin' to trade for some of these drawin's, I'm sure."

Naturi laid the feathers out to dry by the hearth. There was almost enough down to fill a small pillow, and the longer feathers could be used as quills for sketching. "Do you think my sketches are that good?" Naturi grinned, intoxicated with pride and wine. "I never thought anyone else would enjoy them. I make them for myself."

Trep held up a picture of a very old man and studied it carefully. "Yep, these are as good as any I've seen in the ancient books. I know a man in Peireson Landin', has a collection of very old books with fascinatin' pictures and fancy writin'." He winked at Naturi. "He won't let *jess anyone* touch 'em. I guess I understand. They're very fragile."

Laying the drawing on the table, Trep went to the hearth to rotate the bird. "I saw them once. Cain't read a lick of the old writing myself—don't know anyone who can." He settled back into his chair. "I sure would like to know what they say, though! There is a museum in the city with some fine artifacts, Narvin's personal collection."

"Healers can read the script." The words were out before Naturi could stop himself. He grimaced and quickly added, "Well, at least I *think* they might know."

"Really!" Trep almost dropped his cup in delight. "You mean there might be someone here who understands the ancient writings? Oh, this *is* my lucky day!" His eyes blazed enthusiastically as he held up his cup in a toast to Naturi. "Nate, my good man, I've traveled this land for many years lookin' for clues about the Ancient Ones. Yes, Sir! If I could find out what they wrote about, and I tell ya, they wrote a lot in their time, I know I could find out what happened to 'em."

Naturi was truly frightened by Trep's excitement and he worried the traveler's quest for information would lead him to the Crystal. His blunder about the Healing family reading script weighed heavily on his mind. Naturi asked timidly, "The Ancient Ones? Do you mean the gods of Nor?" He busied himself with the drawing on the rough-hewn table, trying desperately not to meet Trep's gaze. His head was spinning and not just from Trep's enthusiasm.

"Yes, yes, whatever y'all call 'em, I've always believed there were others that come before us who might not have been *gods*." Then he added with a mischievous smirk, "It's got me in more than a few scrapes, ya know. Not everyone agrees with me." He picked up the drawing of the Godstones again. "There's jess too many things in this world that lead me to believe that we cain't be the first folks to walk these lands. I heard a lotta strange legends, most of which I think I can safely ignore, but, ya know, some jess stick with you."

If Trep was searching for the Crystal, he would most likely mention it now. Looking into his cup of wine, Naturi asked, "What legends are you interested in?"

"Oh, the list is long. To believe that some god put us here to serve him, with no kind of plan, well, that's jess hard to swallow, for me anyway. Lotta folk believe that, though. Or, that we fell from the sky. Some folk really believe we came from the stars!" He chortled. "Now, don't that beat all? Oh, and the legends that speak of magical powers? No, there's no such thing as magic, jess things we don't understand, yet."

Naturi pressed on. "You mean you do not believe in the power of the Godstones or any magical powers?"

Trep glanced curiously at Naturi, and then checked the water and added leaves from a small sack. He stoked the fire and turned the spit holding his dinner again. "In all my travels, there *are* no other Godstones."

Naturi's eyes widened in surprise because he had assumed everyone worshiped the god of Nor.

Trep smiled. He loved talking about religion. He found most people would vehemently defend the most outrageous beliefs. "Oh, I assure ya, other folks have their gods, but they're all different. No, I only pursue the legends that are somewhat the same everywhere. Those, I believe, are probably based on some truth. Like the ones that talk 'bout the location of ancient cities." He poured a fresh cup of wine for Naturi. "There's this legend about the Star of Genesis. I heard it when I's a boy. I jess cain't buy somethin' that has the power to turn the world into paradise. No, someone would have found it and used it by now." He waved his arm, gesturing to his surroundings. "Are we livin' in paradise? No. I think it's jess a made-up fable to give us hope."

Naturi almost choked on his wine, and it didn't go unnoticed by Trep. The traveler looked at the young man and wondered, *How odd! They've heard of the Genesis Star here. That's a legend I haven't heard much about north of Charltown. Seems that Narvin may have done some research on it. I'll have to ask him the next time I make it to Peireson Landin'.* Out loud he said, "As far as the Star is concerned, I jess wrote that one off."

Naturi asked cautiously, "If there really was a Star, and you found it, wouldn't you become a very powerful man?"

Trep smiled candidly. "Suppose I would." He looked at Naturi, and then brushed the question off as a boy's curiosity. The wine was obviously relaxing the young man. "If, and I stress *if*, there's any truth to the legend, then I guess I owe it to the world to put it to good use. World's been pretty good to me. But listen, do ya honestly believe there is a magic that can make people fly to the stars?"

Naturi said, "I never heard it could do that. Only that it would make the world healthy and happy."

Trep looked sideways at Naturi. "So, you've heard of the Star?"

Naturi panicked. He'd said more than he had intended. Conversation was too easy with this congenial man. The words tumbled out in a rush. "I have only heard stories about what the gods could do."

"The gods, huh?" he asked as he settled back in his chair. "Tell me about this Healin' family. How do they come by the learnin' of ancient writin'? Do you think I could talk to one of 'em sometime?"

Naturi cringed. It was obvious that Trep was not going to forget his blunder. Naturi was cornered and would have to come up with something. "Well, like I said before, I *think* they may know how to read the script. Maybe, I heard that once—when I was younger."

Trep sounded anxious now. "It'd please me to no end if y'all could find out. I've looked everywhere for someone who could read the ancient writin'. Cain't tell you how important this is to me. Bein' able to understand all the ancient writin' could change our world. They did some pretty fancy things in their time. If we figure out how they did things, well, that would be almost like findin' the Star itself, wouldn't it? Better even, I think."

Naturi sipped his wine and pushed another drawing toward Trep in an effort to change the subject.

Trep caught the gesture and inquired about a picture of an old man holding a torch to a pile of leaves. Naturi was grateful for the reprieve. "That's Hiram, the one who got in trouble with the bear." Naturi pointed to a long scar down the old man's arm. Outlining the torch and the leaves, Naturi continued. "When he was a young man, some people wanted to use some of the caves across the valley for more homes, but the Whitish lived in them. The only way to get rid of them was to build huge fires and fan the smoke into the caves. They say that the Whitish ran out of the caves and attacked the men." Naturi paused. "I drew this from what he told me as I was not yet born at the time." Feeling more at ease discussing the White Ones, Naturi refilled his cup and took another healthy drink.

Trep looked long at the picture. "Is that so? Do they attack often?"

"No, Sir, not usually, but four annums ago one bit Kairma."

"The pale looking girl who wears the scarf? Isn't she from the Healin' family?"

Naturi regarded Trep with mild surprise. Trep had an excellent memory. He scrubbed a hand over his face and his tongue felt thick and found it hard to focus. "Yes, but she was very strong and didn't die. Kairma's the *only* person to ever live through the White Fever. They say that most people die quickly. Not Kairma. Her hair turned white and she was sick for a long time." He set his elbow on the table and supported his chin with his palm. He worked his mouth to form the words, "The elders i'sisted she be taken to the Godstones, but Miral Isontra refused them." Naturi's forehead wrinkled, and he nodded thoughtfully. "She often refuses to listen to the elders." There was a hint of awe in his tone.

It was obvious that Naturi didn't drink often. Trep smiled and said, "I don't understand. Why would they take her to the Godstones?"

Naturi tried to clear his head. He started to take another sip from his cup and then pushed it away. "Well, when someone is ready to die, we believe that iss better to meet the gods while you still have 'nough strength to be 'ware. We take dying members to the temples and leave them with blankets, food, and water. The Healer takes more food and water each day until the gods receive them. One of the Healer's duties is attending to the gravely ill until it's time for them to be buried. When the time comes, everyone from the village attends the service."

Naturi's velvet voice took on a melancholy hue. "The Temples of the Godstones are for the dead. We go there to mourn or to visit with those who have left us. Sometimes I go up there to talk to my mother even though I know she didn't go with the gods. She wasn't even sick when she left us."

Trep said, "I'm sorry to hear 'bout your ma. The loss of my own mother was very painful." Trep studied Naturi for a moment. "Did I hear ya say Miral Isontra wouldn't let 'em take Kairma up to the gods and she lived through the fever?"

"We thought it was odd at the time, and some people are still upset about it. Diakus doesn't even consult the Healers anymore. But Diakus is wrong. Kairma lived."

"So Miral Isontra is a strong Healer? She's in charge of things around here, ain't she? She'd know how to read the writin' if anyone does, right?"

Naturi winced and tried to swallow the dryness in his mouth. "I'll try to find out. Have you ever seen a White One?" Again, Naturi attempted to change the subject.

"If I understand what y'all's White Ones are, cain't say that I have actually seen one." He dropped his voice to a conspiring whisper. "They must be pretty evil by the way y'all talk about 'em."

"You mean they don't have Whitish in the city?" Naturi asked pointedly.

"Not sure. I'd have to see one for myself. Seems to me there's a colony of Worms who live outside the city. They kinda sound like your Whitish here. Could be the same kinda folks. I think Worms have to stay out of the sun, but they never hurt anyone."

"Why do you call them Worms?"

"Like y'all's White Ones, they live in the dark, usually in large cellars. I guess since worms live underground, we jess started calling those folks Worms. Don't really mean nothin' by it."

"We believe the gods use the Whitish to punish us when we do something that displeases them. My father says this house is empty because Roak and his family refused to give tribute and the Whitish came for them."

Trep said, "I cain't help but notice that there are many empty homes. Are the other empty homes from families that have been taken by the Whitish? Thought ya said they didn't attack often."

"Most have fallen vacant because the families have come down with the coughing fever and died."

Trep nodded thoughtfully. "I think I'd feel a whole lot better if I knew a little somethin' about these White folks." Turning back to the drawing of the old man, Trep asked, "Ya think this old man might know more about 'em? Bet he'd be downright interestin' to talk to. Think he'd mind if we paid him a visit?"

"You might be able to talk to him at the Awakening Celebration tomorrow. I should warn you though. He is very skeptical of strangers."

Trep grinned. "Everyone here is skeptical of strangers!"

Trep thought about that for a moment. He had met many different people in his journeys, but none as secretive as these. He was determined to find out what they were hiding. He had been in this quiet little valley for almost four weeks now, and until yesterday Collin had been the only person to talk to him. Judging by the reactions of the other people in the village, he was thankful that it was Collin he'd met by the lake when he stumbled onto this reclusive society.

Trep walked back to the fire and took the crisp turkey from the spit and placed it on a wooden plate. *Naturi seems friendly enough, but I kind of get the impression we aren't having an easy conversation, but a calculated exchange of information. Course the wine helped a lot to loosen the young man's tongue. Kinda feel bad 'bout that.* Setting the meat on the table, he offered a leg to Naturi.

Naturi stood up. "I had best be going now. It is late and the hunters have brought home game to blood. I am needed at home. I have already spent much more time here than I had planned."

Trep stood up and grabbed Naturi's hand in his, shaking it vigorously, thanking him for coming. "The bird we shot is hot and ready to eat. Are ya sure ya gotta go right now?"

Naturi nodded and smiled. "I had a wonderful, and very enlightening, evening, but I really do have to go."

Yes, thought Trep. *It* has *been enlightening.*

After Naturi left, Trep ate his dinner. He was looking forward to tomorrow's Awakening Celebration. He hadn't had much of a chance to meet these strange people and he wanted to understand them. They weren't mean or rude to him; they merely acted as if he wasn't there. It was all very curious. The celebration would be a superb place to observe the community. Collin had told him there would be lots of food and drink. Trep loved the thought of a party.

🝔

As Naturi walked home he understood why Collin was fond of this man, but Naturi vowed not to be taken in by Trep's charm. He noticed Trep had a slight limp, and wondered how the man had gotten injured. He hoped it wasn't due to a violent clash with another person. Trep looked friendly enough, but some men had volatile tempers. Naturi felt the brisk wind working itself into a fury. He was thankful for the granite walls of the tight little canyon, knowing the storm would be much harsher outside. A chill ran down his back and he pulled his cloak tighter.

His mind wandered back to the weapon Trep had showed him. He realized the karrack could make hunting easier and defense stronger. *The karrack would make a marked difference in the conflicts with the White Ones, and might have even saved Kairma from the attack. If I can obtain these wonderful weapons, my place as Comad will be secured, even if Siede were to challenge me. I don't think Siede intends to do that, which leaves*

Efram or Collin. The elders respect neither of those boys. Jared is older. If he were to challenge me, it would be advantageous to have proven I can bring wealth to the community.

Naturi thought about that for a while. *This can be very good for the colony. Can it be time to change the old laws? Time to embrace new ideas? Can we learn to make things of alloy? Can the ancient writings teach us lost arts?*

He let out a long sigh as he pictured himself winning Kairma's hand at the Harvest Celebration. At the thought of Kairma, he remembered Trep's intense interest in the Healing family. *Is it this Star that led him here? Is it the Ancient Ones, or is it trying to find someone to read script? That would lead him directly to Kairma and the Crystal. I wish I had not said anything. Oh, why had the subject of script come up? I really let that wine go to my head. What if Trep finds out about the Crystal?*

Great Stones! Could Collin have blundered more than I?

Toric was tired from the hunting trip. He entered the home he shared with his son and placed his hunting pack on the floor by the door. He was a stocky man, once proud and tall, but now his eyes reflected the emptiness he felt from the loss of his wife. As he put his bow on the table and reached for a hot cup of terrid, he noticed Naturi's bow still hanging on the wooden spike where he left it. He cursed under his breath. He had taught Naturi how to hunt when he was only five. At fourteen, Naturi was the youngest boy to pass the Seridar. *Why did that foolish boy give up hunting? Is he so sure that he will mate with that white girl? That he'll never have to kill his own meat again?* The two long scars on the left side of his face turned red when he thought about all the annums he had spent training Naturi to be a Comad. *Kinter acts more like a leader than Kairma does. They should have given that girl to the gods when she was sick. Can't they see that there's something wrong with her?*

Toric began the daily ritual of cleaning and inspecting his bow, while cursing that awful annum of Naturi's last hunt.

It was near the end of a long and bitter winter, before the frost had left the ground, and the colony was badly in need of meat. A party of six men had decided to make the twenty-mile trip to the southern valley to see if they could find game. Naturi had been excited about going on the hunt that morning. He had hunted with the men before, but at sixteen Naturi was likely to have his first kill. They kissed Devon good-bye and promised to come home safely.

Toric had been right. Naturi killed a large buck—the largest of the hunt, but something happened that day that Toric didn't understand. Naturi became withdrawn and morose. He should have been proud of that buck, but his son didn't even join the men when they ate the heart.

They had been gone for a day and a half, and when they returned they were cold and tired. Leaving Naturi and the other men to dress the large buck, Toric went home. He pulled back the shaggy hide of the door and called to his loving wife, but no one answered. Devon was gone. He went crazy. He searched everywhere, but there was no sign of Devon, and no explanation for her absence.

A week later he had come to the conclusion that she had been kidnapped by the Whitish and wanted to search the caves. He asked the Healing family for support but Miral Isontra had refused, and even his close friend, Comad Tamron, wouldn't go against her wishes. Toric was furious with those who had let him down. One week later, a White One stole into the canyon and bit Kairma, but Isontra still refused to mount an attack on the White Ones.

❧

When Naturi came in, Toric was in no mood for conversation. He picked up his cup of terrid and headed toward the back room where he often spent hours thinking about his losses.

Naturi waited a long time before approaching his father with a plate of stew. Toric looked at his son with empty eyes and motioned for him to leave the plate and go. Naturi set the plate down and then sat at the table and looked at his father.

"Well, *what is it?*"

As if reading his father's thoughts, Naturi swallowed and quietly asked, "Do you think Kairma was cursed by the gods? I mean, do you think that is why she was bitten?"

"You're still planning on mating that mutant girl, and you know damn well what I think of that girl—and her family. When Hestra died we lost the Healing family." He scowled at Naturi. "Ever since Jettena was old enough to look like a woman, she has worked at destroying the Healing family line. Imagine, mating at fourteen annums, and to a stranger. Tamron isn't even Survinees! Miral Isontra did nothing. But then Isontra married an outsider too. Pooh! Grimly's right, the old woman isn't fit to lead!"

"But Tamron is of Efpec blood. And he was your friend once," Naturi reminded his father.

"Don't tell me who my friends are! That family is a nest of vultures. They make their living off other people's pain. They'll use you. Do you understand? Now, leave me to my supper." Toric waved his arm to dismiss him.

Naturi gathered his composure. "Trep says the ..."

Toric shot him an icy look, his shoulders hunched into a fighter's crouch. "You've been talking to the stranger? Have you got no brains at all? Hasn't the colony had enough bad luck? Haven't you learned anything?"

Toric was livid. He got up and paced around the room. "I guess not!" he shouted as he stormed out of the room. Naturi followed. He knew he was walking a fine line with his father. Although he never had in the past, Naturi feared at any moment Toric might strike him.

Naturi braced himself and spoke softly. "Father, Trep has shown me something that could make hunting much easier. I think it is worth considering. I would like you to see it."

"What would you know about hunting? You haven't even picked up your bow in four annums!" Toric shouted and stomped out the door.

Chapter 7

The canyon was alive with activity the following morning as people prepared for the first celebration of spring. Jettena and Kairma met with a small group of men who had just returned from the hunt. Once Kairma described the location of the wolf sighting, the men hurried away, hoping to return in time for the celebration. The Awakening was a religious celebration held each spring to thank the gods of Nor for seeing the Survinees through the winter. It was a joyous occasion filled with song and dance and lots of food.

The warm kitchen of the Chancery smelled of frying meat and baking breads. Jettena added wood to the stove and checked the biscuits once more. The center table was littered with baskets, stoneware bowls, and baking pots, leaving little room for Kinter to work as she stirred flour into the bowl of sticky dough.

Concern flickered across Kinter's pretty face. "Mother, are you sure this is sweet enough? Maybe we should put a few more berries in the next batch."

"Kinter, you've made these biscuits dozens of times and there are certainly enough berries in the batter. Now hurry up and fill those baking dishes. We don't want to be late for your first competition."

Jettena dumped luscious blackberry biscuits from hot clay dishes into a beautifully crafted basket and covered them with a hand towel. She placed the basket in a large box with several other provisions and called up the stairs. "Tames! Taren! Tadya! Are you boys ready to go? I need you down here right now, and get your sister while you're at it!"

Taking the heavy pans from Kinter, Jettena placed them in the stone oven. "You had better get changed now. We wouldn't want folks to see you all covered in flour. I laid out the yellow dress you like so much. Now hurry up! I'll watch the biscuits for you."

"Thank you, Mother. You're the best!" Kinter started up the stairs then turned back to her mother. "What is Kairma bringing to the Awakening? I haven't seen her all morning."

"She's entering the blackberry preserves she made last autumn."

Kinter groaned. "How could she? She knew I was going to make blackberry biscuits."

Jettena gave her daughter a sharp look. "Kinter, I am most certain no one will notice that you each made something with blackberries. Now go get dressed."

"I just hope they don't put *her* preserves on *my* biscuits," she spat, and then ran up the stairs.

Jettena shook her head and went back to cleaning up the kitchen.

At the top of the stairs Kinter saw Kairma coming down the hall toward her, towing three little boys behind her.

"I hope you're happy with yourself!" Kinter shouted. "You know, two can play this game!"

"What are you talking about? What game?"

"You know what you did!" Kinter shot back as she stomped into her sleeping room.

Kairma stared after her, wondering what she had done this time.

Rounding up the boys, who were more interested in playing than in getting downstairs, Kairma tried to think of a reason why Kinter would be so upset. When she walked into the kitchen, she saw Jettena wiping off the table.

"Mother, Kinter's mad at me again, and I haven't a clue as to why."

Jettena shook her head. "She thinks you planned to enter your blackberry preserves in today's contest because she was entering blackberry biscuits."

"Nothing could be further from the truth. I didn't even think about what she was going to enter."

"I know, dear, but you know how sensitive she is."

"Do I ever!" Kairma let out a long sigh and plopped down at the table. "What can I do now? It's too late to make anything else."

"Well, that is very sweet of you to think about entering something else. You do have some apple preserves you could enter."

"They aren't as good as the blackberry preserves, and everybody knows Theonia makes the best apple preserves in all of Survin. I might win with the blackberry preserves."

"I trust you to make the right choice, dear. I know how much this means to you and Kinter. It would be nice to have one of my girls bring home a prize." She smiled at Kairma. "We might be good at taking care of the sick, but the Healing family has never been known for their cooking. I'm going to go freshen up a bit. Will you watch the biscuits for a minute?"

"Yes, Mother."

Tears threatened as she watched her mother walk out of the room. *It's just not fair. Why did Kinter have to choose to make blackberry biscuits? She could have made something else. The right choice? The right choice? What is the right choice? Should I let Kinter get another one over on me and maybe give up a good chance of winning today? Should I do the nice thing? I'm really tired of always being the nice one.*

While arranging the dishes in one of the boxes, Kairma sipped on a steaming cup of terrid. She was trying hard not to be angry. When Kairma saw Kinter standing at the bottom of the stairs in her pretty yellow dress, she set down her cup and grabbed a box, calling to her mother as she led her brothers out the door, "I'm taking the boys to the festival now. I'm taking one of the boxes too. I'll see you there. "

The Awakening and Harvest feasts were always held at the base of the Gathering House. Like the hospital, the north opening of the Grand Hall was about twenty feet above the valley floor. Large stones had been brought from the temples to build the massive stairs to the entrance. The structure itself was made of two large, square tunnels through the huge cliff face. A gap of two to eight feet separated the two tunnels. Over the annums, the Survinees had walled in the space between the two tunnels, leaving the roof open. Here in its center, they built a massive fire to warm the room in winter, allowing the smoke to escape upward. The opening also helped to cool the room in summer. Around the edges of the Gathering House were tables and chairs and a small dais for entertainment. It was from this great hall that several young men were hauling furniture outside in preparation for the afternoon's celebration.

From the top of the stairs, Zedic called, "Here, help me with this table, Collin. I've only got three more to set out." Collin sprinted up the stairs, and the two young men struggled with the long wooden table.

Wiping the sweat from his forehead with the hem of his russet vest, Collin asked, "Do you think Naturi had a chance to talk to Trep last night?"

"I don't know. I haven't seen him this morning. I'm sure he'll be here before long. He always tries to get in some practice shots before the bow contest." They set the final table in place creating a large square around a raised platform.

Collin harrumphed. "Isn't Naturi getting a little old for the games?" He adjusted the table to the left and gave Zedic a wry look.

"Yeah, but until he takes a mate, he's still eligible to compete. Everyone knows he's waiting for Kairma to come of age."

"I'll bet that's got his father in an uproar." Even as he said it, Collin felt a surge of resentment for the ever-popular Naturi. Collin tried to be nonchalant, but it irritated him that Naturi and Siede were still waiting to take mates.

Haphazardly placing chairs in front of tables, Zedic said, "Toric used to want Naturi to mate with Kairma, but I guess that was before she was bitten by that White One."

"Still, it gets old seeing him win the bow contest every annum." Uneasy with the direction of the conversation, Collin motioned for Zedic to help him adjust the rest of the chairs. "Come on, if we don't leave a little more room in here the musicians will never be able to get to the stage tonight."

Once they had made sure there was enough room between the two tables on the south end to walk from the Gathering Place stairs to the dais, they started setting the torches in place. "Zedic, are you gonna play your flute tonight?"

"I guess that depends on how much I have to drink. A little bit of wine will give me courage; too much wine and I'll be more interested in other things!" The two boys laughed heartily.

Collin winked. "I know what you mean! I can't wait!"

Seeing Naturi come up the path carrying a load of targets for the games, Collin ran to give him a hand, asking, "Did you talk to him? What'd he say? Does he know anything about the things we found?"

"Slow down, Collin. Of course I did not show Trep the items you found. I need to learn more about him before we let him see those things." He handed a bundle of targets to Collin.

Collin frowned as he started setting targets out. "You said you'd ask him!"

"I will remind you," Naturi said, glaring at Collin, "that I said I would meet with him and assess the situation. I am in no hurry to share the secrets of our mountain with this stranger."

Naturi had flushed when he replied, and Collin thought it odd for a moment but said, "Come on, Naturi. What is there to *assess*? We don't even know if the Healers are gonna let him live."

"Yes, there is that possibility, but ..."

"You're gonna waste this chance to get some real answers, aren't you? I don't believe it! Well, you had your chance. I'm tired of always depending on the Ogs to tell us what we can and can't do." Collin set the target in place with a little too much force and it fell over.

"Collin! Watch what you say!"

"No, Naturi! I'm not gonna to let you ruin this, no matter what you and Zedic think. This is a real opportunity to learn something." Collin reset the target and stormed off.

Naturi looked around nervously to see if anyone had overheard the conversation. Luckily, the other young men were outlining the course for the races on the far side of the banquet square, and boasting loudly of past achievements and claiming future honors. Naturi was relieved.

Naturi looked at the nonjudgmental Zedic. "I do not know where he gets these outrageous notions. And really, someone should tell him he sounds ridiculous when he mimics Trep's accent."

Zedic shrugged and walked away with the remaining targets.

Each side of the banquet square was dedicated to one of the four gods of the mountain. Bowls of berries, apples, and assorted greens of every type filled the west tables. Cheeses, milk, and creamy sauces were laid out on the south side and mountains of breads and cakes were stacked on the east tables. The north tables were a little over three feet from the base of the Gathering Place steps. On them lay sliced meats, stuffed birds, and hearty stews.

On the stairs of the Gathering Place sat a small table dedicated to the god Nor. Here Kairma sat carefully tending the peyotel, a strong mint-flavored, alcohol-based drink that when ingested might cause mild hallucinations. Most of the adults would partake of the punch before the night was over and would dance and sing until nearly dawn.

Kairma watched the people filling the festival area. The women had put on their best dresses and the children were clean and trying desperately to find ways to change that. Every once in a while she would catch a child trying to steal a cake or roll. She would turn away, pretending not to see him or her approach, and then quickly spin around just before they could snag the prize. The children would scream and run away laughing, only to try again moments later.

Jettena came to relieve Kairma. Setting the blackberry biscuits on the table beside the other young women's entries, she kissed Kairma on the cheek. "Go watch the games," Jettena said. "I'll tend the peyotel. You'll have to be here most of this evening. Enjoy the games while you can."

"Thank you, Mother. I was hoping to see the sling contest. Do you think Zedic will win again this annum?"

"I wouldn't count on it. There seems to be a lot of competition today."

"I'll bet he does win. He's pretty good." Kairma waved good-bye to her mother and hurried off to watch the games.

A large semicircle of people had gathered around the competitors. Finding a place as close to the front as she could, she watched the men throw a knife at various targets. The competition was tough. People were taking bets on the winners and each time a contestant did better than expected the crowd roared. Zedic was out of the competition early and came over to stand beside Kairma. She nodded to him but kept her eyes on the next player. "Sorry to see you out of the match so soon. I hope you do better at the sling contest."

"Yeah, me too. I'm usually good with a knife. I don't think my heart was in it today."

They watched Dillon throw. The young boy fared well, but Naturi edged him out by two higher marking throws.

After a while, Kairma looked around. "Where's Collin? I thought for sure he was going to enter the match."

"I don't know. I saw him talking to Naturi earlier and then he took off toward Roak's house. I'm sure he went to find Trep."

"Do you think Naturi showed him the things we found?"

Zedic paused for a long while. "I don't think so. Naturi is very cautious. He probably just asked Trep a lot of questions and didn't tell him anything."

"You're probably right." She became quiet as she watched the rest of the knife contest.

Siede was the last to compete. He was accurate and extremely fast, taking first place easily. As Siede accepted the medal, Kairma saw Naturi watching him closely. Although the older man had never said anything that would lead one to believe he was interested in Kairma, the man had skills that would make him a tough competitor.

Collin hurried down the winding canyon. The snowmelt had come early this annum, and the creek that flowed through the center of the narrow canyon was almost overflowing. Here and there, little bridges had been built across the swift water leading to homes of varying sizes. The steep, stone canyon walls were slowly disappearing under the new leaves of spring. The air was fresh and the sounds of meadowlark and red thrush filled his ears, but Collin wasn't noticing anything except the old wood and stone home. He knocked on the doorframe.

A deep and strangely accented voice called to him. "Come on in! Door's open! Help yourself to some terrid."

Collin made his way to the hearth and filled a cup.

"Oh, it's you!" exclaimed Trep. "I thought Naturi would be here this mornin'. We had a great discussion last night." Trep came from the back room wearing only a pair of close-fitting pants and his socks. He was drying his thick dark hair with a towel and looking like he had just woken up. Collin noticed that there wasn't an ounce of fat on the older man. His chest was covered with thick, curly hair, and his hairy arms were thick and strong.

"Really? What all did you talk about?"

Grabbing a cup of terrid, Trep sat down on a long black bench. Reaching under the bench, he picked up a pair of sturdy boots and pulled them over his red woolen socks. Collin noticed, not for the first time, the close cut of the leather and the solidness of the sole. "Well, we talked about his drawin's and we talked about the city." He was struggling to pull on the well-worn leather boot. "We talked about the White Ones and about the Healin' Family."

"What? You talked about the Healing family?" Collin's eyes darkened. *That lying, no good...*

"Sure, that some kinda crime here?" Trep said, looking concerned.

"No. No, it's nothing. Just something Naturi said this morning, that's all."

"Well, did he tell ya about the karrack?"

"The what?"

"The karrack. It's used for huntin'—like y'all's bows, only much more efficient. I could show it to ya if ya'd like."

"Sure. I'd love to see—what'd you call it again?"

"A karrack. I'll give you a demonstration, but first I have to tend to my horse." He disappeared into the back room to get a shirt.

Collin sat quietly at the table, noticing for the first time the shear strangeness of everything Trep was—his clothes, his manners, and the way he spoke. Even the man's eating utensils were different. Collin tried to picture Trep's world and found himself hungry for more knowledge. He vowed to himself he would one day leave this mountain, law or no law.

Trep came into the room carrying a small satchel and an oddly shaped instrument of wood and metal. Trep set his wares down on the table and went over to check the fire. There were a few swallows of terrid left in the pot so he poured the remainder into his cup and downed it quickly. "This drink of y'all's is pretty good in the morning. Hope I can take some of it back to the city when I go."

The casual comment took Collin off guard. He always knew Trep would want to leave some day, but Collin had never explained just how difficult that might be.

Trep picked up the karrack, checked it over, and then put it into a leather holster on his belt. The satchel was stuffed into one of the many oversized pockets in his jacket. "Come on, boy. Got to check on Belle. Makes me kinda nervous leavin' her outside of town like that."

They walked out of the small home and headed north, toward the hospital.

"This is the first town I've ever been to where jess to get in, you had to scale a forty-foot cliff or walk through a buildin'. Don't that annoy the Healers to always have folks walkin' through their house?"

"Well, they don't really live in that part of the Chancery, at least not anymore. Besides, most folks don't ever leave the village. They have everything they need here except for hunting and fishing and they only do that a few times a moon."

"It still feels a little strange to have to leave my horse outside of town. Hope she's still there this mornin'."

"Sure she is. How'd you catch her anyway? I've seen wild horses around here and even tried to catch one. If I hadn't seen someone riding one when I was little, I'd have never thought of it. I don't think most folks believed me when I told them about it, at least not until you showed up riding a horse." His perfect white teeth gleamed as he smiled widely.

As the two comrades walked northward, they passed several people who were on their way to the Awakening meeting place. Uncomfortable with the presence of the stranger, the village people stepped to the other side of the path and tried to avoid catching Trep's eye. Trep had to stifle an overwhelming urge to shout "Boo!" at a particularly timid group of older women.

"I'm not gonna hurt 'em, you know," he said.

"Yeah, I know. It's our way, I guess. No one wants to change the order of things. Change is often the prelude to trouble."

"That's how folks grow, develop new ideas—become stronger. No offense, but y'all are kinda behind the times when it comes to modern conveniences, and y'all look like you coulda had the same father." He chuckled at the thought.

"You might say, we don't get a lot of new blood around here. Maybe you could mix it up!" Collin laughed now.

It was true. The Survinees people were extraordinarily tall and well-muscled. Their thick hair was very dark and their skin was a deep reddish bronze. They had little or no facial hair, and from what Trep had seen they had no chest hair either. Oddly, most Survinees had blue eyes. They reminded Trep of his mother's master, and that thought made him almost as uncomfortable as he made the Survinees.

When they reached the door of the hospital, Collin gave three short wraps on the doorframe and a brief high-pitched whistle before going in.

Whistles are an important part of y'all's language, ain't they?" Trep ducked through the doorway behind Collin.

"I guess they are. Never gave it much thought before. It's a good way to say something from a great distance."

"That's what I thought. Somethin' else to take back to the city."

Collin could feel the hairs on the back of his neck stand up. He looked cautiously around the large room, and hoped no one had overheard Trep mention leaving.

To one side, they passed by an assortment of cots and bedrolls and to the other side a huge table lined with chairs. In front of them the north doors stood open and a beautifully carved archway framed a majestic view of the Survinees' gods.

Collin stopped for a moment. "I love to stand here and look at this view. It can make you feel small but, somehow, taken care of."

"It's a priceless view. In fact, one of the pictures Naturi showed me last night was drawn from this very spot. Folks in the city would pay good money for that picture."

Collin's jaw tightened. "Naturi said you could trade his drawings to people in the city?" He was incensed.

"We talked about tradin' with folks in the city, yeah. Thought y'all would want to buy karracks. Whatever has got you so anxious today?"

Looking around, Collin grabbed Trep by the arm. "Let's get out of here. We can talk outside."

Walking over to the tiny creek that led to the lake, they found Trep's russet mare, Belle, munching on tufts of needle grass. As Trep pulled out a brush to groom his horse, Collin prepared himself to explain things to Trep. He was torn between being totally honest—running the risk of having Trep disappear in the middle of the night—or making up a grand story that would convince Trep not to mention leaving the mountain again. He opted for something in between. "You might say I'm a little upset about your conversation with Naturi last night. You have to understand, *no one* leaves the mountain with information that could compromise our location. This has been law for centuries, and no one knows this better than Naturi." Collin began to pace nervously. "I don't understand how he could even suggest we trade ideas with people from the city."

Trep stopped brushing Belle's mane and looked thoughtfully at Collin. *"He* didn't suggest it, I did. He was so thrilled 'bout the karrack—and I guess we had quite a bit of wine—he jess fell into the conversation. Cain't say he actually said he'd go with me, but it sounded like he might be thinkin' it."

It wasn't like Naturi to let his defenses down like that, wine or no wine. "Your karrack must be pretty impressive. The law forbids us to even talk about leaving the mountain." He stared off at nothing. *Maybe Naturi isn't happy. Now, wouldn't that beat all? The proper and pompous Naturi just as eager to leave the mountain as me.* After a moment he said, "Maybe I ought to see what gave Naturi such a change of heart."

"Sure, let's go over there, by that clearin'." Trep loaded the karrack while Collin watched intently. Trep explained how the small projectile would penetrate the skin of the target, much the same as an arrowhead, but from a greater distance. After searching for the proper target, a small rabbit, Trep took aim and fired. *Kaarraaaaccckk!* The thunderous noise echoed off the canyon walls, and the rabbit jerked a couple of times before lying still.

Collin stared at the rabbit and then looked at Trep. "Well, if the alloy slug doesn't kill you, the noise will probably scare you to death."

Trep laughed. "Guess I've gotten used to it."

"I remember hearing that noise last night. I knew it was too early in the annum for heat lightning, but I didn't know what else might have made that kind of noise."

Collin went over to examine the rabbit. "We should dress it out before we go to the Awakening." He took out his knife and slit the throat. Holding it up by its back feet, Collin let the blood run out onto the ground. As he did, he looked closely at the hole where the alloy ball had entered and the place where it had come out the other side of the rabbit's head. He shuddered at the thought of being the recipient of one of those deadly projectiles.

"I see why Naturi was impressed. Your karrack could be used for hunting and defense."

"It's y'all's for the askin'. All ya gotta do is come to the city with a few things to trade and y'all are on the way to the next level of progress." Trep wrapped the rabbit in a piece of leather to keep the blood from dripping on the floor as they prepared to walk back through the hospital.

"It's not that easy. I told you—no one leaves the mountain."

Trep stopped, deep furrows forming on his forehead in frustration as he almost shouted, "Why?"

"We can't let anyone know we're here."

"I know that, but *why*?"

"The Healers won't allow it. It's been the law for centuries. You can't expect them to simply forget everything they were taught. It's just our way."

"What if I showed this here karrack to the other folks in the village? If they saw how useful it could be, would that change some minds?"

"Yeah, right after they changed their leggings." Collin had said that with such seriousness that Trep burst out laughing.

Kinter had been scrutinizing all of the entries for the cooking contest. She felt pretty confident. Someone had entered a pastry of sorts. The crust looked tough. All of the bowls were exactly the same to ensure the judges wouldn't know who'd entered the dish. She saw the blackberry preserves, and Kinter felt her heart pound.

Gently stirring the peyotel at a table near the contest entries, Jettena said, "Looks like a good contest, doesn't it?"

Kinter nodded. "Yes, it does. We even have some new entries this annum. I think this must be a black bean soup." She uncovered a wooden bowl of what looked like it could be mud. "Yuck, that looks awful."

"Looks aren't everything. Squash doesn't look like much, but it's pretty good to eat."

Kinter disagreed—looks were very important.

As Kinter inspected the rest of the entries, Jettena said, "Could you watch this a moment? I need to relieve myself, and Kairma is watching the games."

"Sure, Mother. I'm not interested in the games. Take your time."

Kinter took her mother's place stirring the punch. The constant stirring kept the heavier fruit juices from settling to the bottom, but it was more tradition for a member of the Healing family to tend the peyotel than it was a necessity.

As she stood there, an idea crept into her mind. Finding the blackberry preserves, Kinter added a little ingredient of her own. She quickly stirred it in and recovered the dish. *That will teach her a lesson!*

There were only three contestants left for the final and most difficult round of the bow contest. A leather strap had been tied between two young aspens. A round ball, roughly a foot across and fashioned from dried branches, was placed in the middle of the strap. Pulling down on the strap, the supple aspens bent toward each other and when released they catapulted the ball into the air. Each contestant would try hitting the flying ball of twigs with an arrow. The man who could shoot an arrow into the moving ball the most times would be declared the winner.

Dillon took his stance and aimed his bow. There was a *whoosh* of air as the ball flew across the clearing. *Zzziipp!* Dillon's arrow as it found its mark. The ball fell, and the crowd roared.

Siede stepped into position and readied himself. There was a *whoosh* and a *zzziipp,* and Siede scored a good hit. With fists in the air, the crowd howled like wolves.

Now Naturi took his place. *Whoosh! Zzziipp!* Again the crowd howled.

It was a splendid contest. Dillon returned and brought down another lifeless ball, as did Siede, and Naturi once again. More betting had started with Naturi clearly the favorite.

Silently, Dillon stepped into place. *Whoosh! Zzziipp!* Another hit, and then more howling from the audience. Siede was three annums older than Naturi and had been the best bowman until Naturi passed his Seridar at the tender age of fourteen. He took his place. *Whoosh! Zzziipp!* A miss! The crowd groaned, and Siede bowed to the two remaining contestants. "A good match," he said. "May the best bowman win."

Naturi took aim. *Whoosh! Zzziipp!* A hit. More trinkets switched hands as the crowd applauded.

Dillon nervously wiped his hands on his vest and picked up his bow—another hit!

Naturi fired, hitting the ball. Dillon fired, and again the ball was pierced. Naturi. Dillon. The crowd had grown strangely quiet, intently watching. It was Naturi, and then Dillon, Naturi and then Dillon, and then a miss.

The crowd roared with excitement when, for the first time in six annums, Dillon, a boy of only fifteen, won the bow contest.

No one was more surprised than Naturi. He was used to achieving every goal he desired, and for a moment he felt angry for letting a child strip him of the honor he had carried for six annums. He thought about the match and decided his mind had been preoccupied with thoughts of the stranger. Walking over to where Dillon's friends and family were congratulating the new winner, Naturi smiled, graciously bowed, and placed the ribbon-clad medallion in Dillon's hand. "It was a good match and you beat me fairly."

"I can't believe I did it!" the excited youth shouted. "I practiced and practiced. I beat you! I can't believe it!"

Naturi couldn't help feeling cheered when seeing the joy on Dillon's face. He remembered the pride he'd felt when he won the match the first time. "Do not get too attached to that prize. I will take it back at the Harvest Seridar."

Dillon's face fell. Then he saw the twinkle in Naturi's eyes, and he laughed. "Okay, but you'd better start practicing!"

Trep and Collin returned in time to see Dillon win, and Collin whistled through his teeth. "I can't believe Naturi lost. He always wins at least two out of the four contests, and his knife skills aren't that good. He'd better hope Zedic decides not to press him in the sling challenge or the mighty Naturi will lose his place as our boy wonder."

The toughest competition of the day was the hand-to-hand combat. No weapons were allowed, and often the man with the most strength was the victor. The names of all unmated males over the age of fifteen were entered, and then drawn by twos to select combatants. Other men often competed for fun, but the contest was implemented as a rite of passage for young men. In order to be invited on the monthly hunts, a young man must win one of the four competitions. Since most men were mated by the time they reached the age of eighteen, the competition was usually evenhanded. In recent annums though, the available women had not selected any of the eligible men and now at least three of the men competing were over twenty.

Efram's and Zedic's names were drawn first and everyone gathered around the grassy meadow reserved for the contest. The two boys squared off, crouching as they circled, looking for the right moment to strike. Efram whispered, barely loud enough for Zedic to hear, "You know that if your sister weren't heir to the Crystal, Naturi wouldn't be interested in her at all."

Zedic ignored Efram's taunts and focused on the contest, keeping his anger in check as was his nature. He feinted to the right and Efram struck out, but Zedic was able to twist away and come up from behind the older boy. Annums of wrestling with Collin had taught Zedic how to use Efram's own momentum to pull him over. Zedic placed his knee between Efram's shoulder blades, and grabbing Efram's right wrist Zedic was able to lock his thumb over Efram's little finger, bending his hand backward, forcing Efram to stay down. The crowd cheered as Zedic whispered to Efram, "You've been able to mate for five annums now and I don't see a line of girls accepting your offers. Maybe if you were pale …" Zedic grinned as he got up.

Efram jumped to his feet and pushed Zedic backward, only causing Zedic's grin to widen into a full-blown smile.

The next two names drawn were Dillon and Siede. Murmured objections could be heard slithering through the crowd. Dillon, only fifteen annums old, was competing for his hunting rights for the first time, while Siede was almost twenty-five. Like Efram, Siede had placed his name in the ring to mate several times, but the three girls of mating age, Alyssum, Ember, and Rose, weren't accepting any offers. When Trep asked why everyone was grumbling, Collin explained. "Rumor has it all the girls are waiting to see what Naturi will do when Kairma comes of age. It's common knowledge that Naturi will be competing for Kairma. If he's taken, the other girls will likely accept offers from Siede, Efram, or Zedic. Since Jared lost his wife two annums ago, one of the girls will probably mate with him. The elders have allowed the girls to wait this long, but once Naturi is taken the girls will have to choose. The Harvest Seridar should be very interesting because Rossi and Dessa will come of age as well."

Trep studied Collin out of the corner of his eye. Collin's usual light tone held a hint of anger. Trep asked, "Are you gonna mate this fall?"

Absent-mindedly toying with a lock of hair as Dillon and Siede took the field, Collin said, "I'm not interested in taking a mate right now." He was suddenly uncomfortable talking to Trep about the Seridar. Luckily the contest between Siede and Dillon was over quickly and Naturi's and Collin's name were drawn before Trep could press him.

Collin made his way to the grassy circle and met Naturi's hard stare. Naturi was an inch taller and more muscular than Collin, but Collin was quick and cunning. Collin leaned forward in a crouch, making slow pawing motions toward his larger opponent. He launched the first strike, spinning Naturi off to the left, but Naturi recovered quickly and pulled Collin to the ground. Before Naturi could pin him, Collin rolled over and jumped back to his feet. Collin landed a blow just above Naturi's middle and was awarded the sound of a grunt as he quickly blocked Naturi's right hook. Naturi paced the younger boy and when Collin's eyes darted to the sidelines, Naturi attacked, but the momentary distraction was a ruse, and Collin capitalized on Naturi's self-assurance, locking his leg behind Naturi's knee, tripping him easily.

Before Collin could find the center of gravity and pin him, Naturi found the pressure point between the thumb and forefinger on Collin's hand. The look on Naturi's face was something close to hatred, and Collin was amazed by how much it hurt when Naturi pinched the nerve. The pain woke him up and he began to think of Naturi as a truly dangerous man. Through all the annums growing up together, he and Naturi wrestled often, but never hurt one another. He had a shot at Naturi's groin but didn't take it. If this were truly a fight to the death, he wouldn't have hesitated, but on the contest grounds, it was frowned on. He rolled off quickly, jumping up and pulling his hand away.

His fingers felt paralyzed, but he had no time to think about that because Naturi was on him again in seconds. Collin twisted away, spinning Naturi backward over a small shrub. With all his strength, he threw Naturi face down on the hard field. Naturi pulled Collin along as they fell and hit hard enough to knock the wind from Naturi's lungs. Collin scrabbled to his knees and pulled Naturi's right arm up behind his back.

For a moment, Collin thought he'd pinned him, but Naturi kicked with the force of a mule, throwing Collin off his back. The two men rolled in the dirt and the sweat on their copper skin turned the dust to dark umber mud.

Naturi's hands closed around Collin's neck, cutting off Collin's air. It was pure adrenalin laced fear that gave Collin the strength to break Naturi's grasp.

They were rolling once more across the grass, with spectators moving quickly as the two men approached the sidelines. As they neared a large juniper, Collin was able to break free and put the shrub between them. A wolfish smile crossed Naturi's face as Collin backed away. They were among the trees now at the edge of the field. Collin was repositioning to place a thick aspen tree in front of Naturi. Naturi ran at the tree, grabbed it with both hands and swung his legs out. Coming around the tree at chest height, his feet planted solidly into Collin's torso. The younger man went down hard and out of breath. Before he could catch his breath, Naturi had him pinned.

Cheers erupted and trinkets exchanged hands. Naturi got up gracefully and offered Collin a hand, all animosity forgotten.

Collin got up, rubbing his chest. "I'm going to have your footprints on my chest for weeks now. What made you think of using the tree like that?"

Naturi's voice was noncommittal. "It just came to me. Remember that." He smiled, but the warning in Naturi's eyes was clear. *You're no match for me, Collin.*

As the word spread that Naturi had won, Collin pulled Trep over to the bow field. Collin hadn't won any matches today, but there was something he could offer the village. Collin stepped up on a withered stump and called to the crowd gathered there. "I would like all of you to meet my friend, Trep. As you may have heard, he comes from the village of Peireson Landing. I'd like to show you the wonders of his world. He can teach us how to make many things we've never seen before." He motioned to Trep to stand next to him. "Hold up your foot, Trep." Trep's face crinkled in confusion, but he held up his foot. "See these. Look at the leather workmanship." Trep, now understanding what Collin was doing, began to model his boots. "Look at the tough soles. Imagine walking through snow with these." Collin pointed to Trep's coat and his pants. "These are but a few of the things Trep's world has to offer." He nodded his head for Trep to take it from there.

Trep offered the formal greeting of right hand to right eyebrow. A few Survinees returned the gesture, while others merely looked warily at the stranger. "Could I have y'all's attention, please? I've seen what y'all can do with a bow and arrow. Must admit, it's some fine marksmanship, but if y'all'd give me a minute, I'd like to show ya what we hunt with down on the plains." Trep smiled at Dillon. "That was some right fancy shootin' you did." He nodded to the crowd. Trep stood there some time waiting for a reply. Whispers could be heard as the Survinees wondered what this stranger was doing.

"I'd jess like to give y'all a little demonstration." Since no one told him he couldn't, Trep motioned to Collin for help. "Set this small log on top of that large gray boulder way over there. Thanks. Now step back."

The sound of the karrack startled the tightly knit group of Survinees who had gathered around him.

Collin picked up the log to show the crowd. A large hole through the center showed them that Trep had hit his mark. The crowd stared in wonder.

Trep reloaded the karrack and fired again. He missed. Twice more he reloaded and hit his mark fast and true.

Scowling, Toric approached. "I can't see that your noise maker is any better than our bows. A hole is a hole, and with that thing making that much noise, you would have certainly run off any other game around."

"True 'nough, my good man, but can ya do this?" Running to an oak tree, Trep grabbed a branch with one hand and pulled himself up off the ground. Firing the karrack an instant later, he hit the log just off center. "Ever been chased by a bear? Try to do that with bow!"

Toric chewed on his lower lip. "Animals are not always sitting still. It wouldn't be useful if you can't kill a moving animal."

Trep agreed. "True, but I could kill a deer on the run at a hundred feet. Think that would be about thirty meters by y'all's reckonin'. Birds are my favorite sport. Go ahead, throw somethin' in the air." He reloaded the karrack. "I'll show ya what I mean."

All eyes were on Toric as he looked around for something to throw. He picked up a stone and launched to into the air. Trep took aim and fired. He missed. Toric laughed. "So it seems your karrack isn't all that useful."

Trep reloaded again. "Well, I've never seen any game worth huntin' quite so small. Give me somethin' a bit larger and I'll show ya it does have possibilities."

Toric, feeling a little cocky, threw his hat up.

Karraack!

The hat fell to the ground with a hole large enough to put a thumb through. Trep smiled mischievously. "There ya go. That's one very dead hat!" He picked up the cap and handed it back to Toric. "I guess you'll be needin' a new one. When Naturi and I get back to the city, I'll get ya the finest cap available."

Toric glared at him. "You will not be taking my son or anyone else to the city. A fine cap will not replace a son!" Taking his hat, he briskly strode away.

Naturi gasped. *Trep thinks I will go with him to the city. I cannot leave. No one can leave. Collin should have made that clear to him. Maybe Collin plans to go to the city. Bringing back these weapons and new clothing would be beneficial to the colony. Those boots he wears are very fine. I should like a pair myself, but the elders would never allow anyone to leave.*

An agitated murmur swept the crowd as they watched Toric leave. Naturi followed close behind his father.

Watching Toric and Naturi leave the clearing, Collin felt his heart sink and whispered harshly to Trep, "Why did you mention going to the city? I was foolish. I should have been more adamant about our laws. We're as good as dead now."

Grimly hissed something about the Law of Fontas, loud enough for the small group of men who had gathered around him to hear. They solemnly watched for Comad Tamron's reaction. After a moment a woman shouted, "Take him prisoner! Don't let him leave the mountain! We must protect the colony!"

Diakus joined the commotion, protesting loudly. "Can't you see he's dangerous? He will only bring death and destruction! Institute the Law of Fontus now!"

Soon the crowd was pushing toward him and Trep became frightened. Collin stepped between the stranger and the treacherous crowd. The villagers huddled and the shouts returned to agitated whispers of fear and condemnation.

Comad Tamron held up his large hand to hush the crowd as he approached Trep. "I think it would be best if you do not show us anymore demonstrations. You have clearly upset my people." Taking both Trep and Collin by the arm, he pulled them to the side. "Things may be different where you come from, but here it is customary to ask permission before disrupting our tournaments. Collin should have explained our customs to you better."

Collin looked down at his feet for a moment, and then looked up, meeting Tamron's gaze. "I'm sorry, Sir. Trep really does have some very valuable things to offer us, but we should never have suggested going to the city to get them."

Trep cursed himself for being so brash. "Forgive me. I was hopin' to make a better impression than this. It's jess like me to stir up the bees when I'm tryin' to show someone where to find the honey."

Tamron nodded. "Yes, the bees are stirred up altogether too well.

Let us hope that no one gets stung." He looked down at the karrack in Trep's hand. "That's a unique tool. How do you come by it?"

"Down in the city, lots of folks have these. Cain't hardly get along without one. We have lots of other useful things too." Trep pulled the karrack up and aimed toward the tree. "I'd be right happy to show ya how to use it. Come on, we can go outside the village."

"No!" The venom in Tamron's voice startled Trep. "Put it away! Now! This is not the time or the place for another demonstration! We must discuss the matter first."

When Trep nodded and moved to follow, Comad Tamron clarified himself. "No, *we*, the Healing family, will discuss the demonstration and decide what is to be done. Do not leave the canyon!" He waved to three burly men standing to the side of the crowd. "Hamond, Loren, Joel, see to it that this man does not leave the gathering without an escort."

Tamron walked away, but then stopped and turned back to Trep. "Do I need to take your weapon?"

Trep assured him he meant no harm to anyone.

Tamron nodded curtly and joined Miral Isontra, who had been observing from a short distance away.

Chapter 8

O nce Tamron had joined Isontra, the crowd of observers followed Tamron's cue and began to melt away, leaving a bewildered Trep standing with Collin, Zedic, and his three sentries. Trep sat down on a large log and mumbled, "That went about as smooth as a square wheel." Hamond, Loren, and Joel turned to watch the musicians set up on the small stage, knowing they were close enough to tackle Trep if he tried to run.

Collin pulled Trep from his thoughts with a roguish grin. "I'm sorry. I should have warned you not to mention leaving. You probably scared the berries out of their biscuits. Give them some time. The Healers will talk."

"You did mention it. I jess wasn't listenin'." Trep shook his head slowly. He was mad at himself for not doing a better job of relating to these people. He watched the Survinees disappear into their little factions. "Doesn't anybody around here want to know what the rest of the world has to offer?"

"Hey, some of us do." Collin nudged the older man in the ribs and took a seat on the log next to him. "We have to do things our way, even if it's a little cumbersome." He grinned apologetically. "You said something earlier about setting up a trade for the things we might want from the city. What kind of things could we trade?"

Trep was thankful for Collin's friendship. The young man with the dark hair and green eyes had a way of making him feel welcome that was sorely lacking from the other members of this village. "Well, provided y'all's Comad doesn't decide to invoke the Law of Fontas—whatever that is—Naturi does some nice drawin's and I've seen some pretty fancy wood carvings. What do you do?"

Collin motioned for Zedic to sit down. "I don't do anything, nothing like that. I like to explore things, but I really don't have much to show for it." Zedic kicked him, warning him not to say too much. Collin understood. "The only thing I have is this yellow band I found in a cave." He pulled out the antique ring and showed it to Trep. "I think it's pretty, but since I don't know how it was made, I can't make any more."

Trep looked at the ring and gasped. "Where did ya say you found this? A cave? Somewhere around here?" He carefully studied the ring. "I'm sure it was made by the Ancient Ones. Look at these fine lines, and here, on the inside, writin'. Yes! Yes! This has to be from the Ancient Ones!"

Collin looked at Zedic, inviting him to pay attention, and then back to Trep. "The Ancient Ones? How did they make it?"

Trep turned the golden band over and over in his rough hands. "There's lotta things I don't know about the Ancient Ones. We can do lots with gold ourselves, but this craftsmanship is beyond us. This is a very fine piece. A valuable artifact, if ya can find the right collector." He held it up and watched the sun glisten off the delicate markings. "The gold is worth quite a bit by itself, but this workmanship is so much more precious."

Collin was getting excited now. He took back the ring and looked at the script on the inside. "I can't believe I didn't see it before. I've seen stone like this before, but it's much softer than this ring. The Healers like to use it because it is soft enough to make permanent marks in."

Zedic blanched and made sure Collin felt his foot that time.

Trep choked back surprise. "Really? You say y'all have more gold, and the Healers use it to make marks? What kind of marks? Like designs, pictures, what?"

Standing abruptly and straightening his buckskin vest, Zedic snapped, "The family has needs. It's private."

Trep smiled congenially at Zedic and said, "Now don't get y'all's saddle twisted. The use isn't as important as the possibility of findin' more. Folks down on the plains like gold, and if you have it, *y'all* are rich."

Before either of the boys could ask what the word *rich* meant, Collin's father, Diakus, walked up. Diakus was a large man, broad in the shoulders like Collin, and about the same height. His gray eyes flashed with anger. He had been drinking wine and was infuriated with Collin for some unknown reason. As annums of practice had taught him, Collin ducked the first blow. This only succeeded to make Diakus angrier. Grabbing Collin by the wrist, he gave a painful twist. "What kind of godless mischief are you up to, boy? What are you doing here with this outsider?" The venom in his voice sent a frigid chill down Trep's back. "Nor's piss! You bloody worthless excuse for a son! Your mother's been looking for you all morning! It's just like you to go running off when there's work to be done! She had to carry the pissin' stew up here herself!"

Collin got up to follow his father, who continued to shout obscenities at him. Every so often Diakus would turn and swing at the boy. Collin was prepared, but a few strikes hit their mark.

Appalled, Trep turned to Zedic. "Cornfeathers! Does that happen often?"

Sitting back down on the log, Zedic let out a painful sigh. "In the early annums, before Collin's sister and brother were killed, Diakus and Massie were good parents. Now, they spend most of their time drunk on wine." Trep noticed a disturbing look in Zedic's gray eyes. "When Collin was five, he saw some outsiders kill his sister, Ellen, and his brother, Cody. Collin was too small to do anything so he hid in the trees. I guess his parents blame him."

Trep watched Diakus take another swing at Collin and miss. "What happened? Why'd someone want to kill children? And how on earth could that man blame a five-year-old for bein' the only one to survive?"

Zedic shrugged and stared off toward the fire. "I don't know. I ask myself the same thing."

Trep sat quietly, waiting to see if Zedic was going to continue. He was about to bring up a new subject when Zedic spoke, "Collin doesn't talk about it often. They were all down at Stone Lake—Collin, his sister, and brother. I think they were fishing when two men riding horses, like yours, came up and started chasing Ellen around. She was about fifteen then. They caught her and started tossing her back and forth between them. She fell and tore her dress. Then one of the men started tearing off what was left of her clothes. Cody was only ten, but he tried to get the man to stop. The man pushed away Cody, who hit his head on a rock and never got up. The men did awful things to Ellen, and when they were finished they cut her throat. My father and eight men went in search of the killers, but never found them."

Trep could feel the bile rise in his throat, unable to say anything, as Zedic continued in a monotone voice. "When Collin told his father what happened, Diakus was so mad, he hit Collin and broke his leg. Collin came to live with us until he was better. Sometimes, I think, when Diakus sees Collin, it reminds him of how he lost his temper that day, and out of some kind of misplaced guilt, Diakus' anger only seems to get worse." Trep thought that was pretty insightful for such a young man, but he didn't interrupt Zedic's narrative. "His father beats him every time he gets drunk now." Zedic looked down at his feet. "It's been that way a long time."

After another long pause Zedic went on. "Collin's mother used to try to intervene, but Diakus started hitting her too. After a while, she gave up."

"That's too bad. Oh, that's really too bad. Collin's a good kid. Shouldn't have to put up with that. Why doesn't he leave? I'm sure he could take care of himself."

Zedic blew out a sigh. "Where could he go? He tries to stay away, but the canyon is only so big."

"Well, if he wants to go with me when I leave, I'd be glad to take him. He's pretty sharp, ya know. He'd make a fine partner on the road."

"The laws forbid anyone to leave the canyon, but, knowing Collin, he would go regardless. I worry that he'll try going to the city with you, looking for the men who killed Ellen and Cody."

"Well, he's certainly welcome. And if I could find those men, well, I'd … I'd … They jess better hope we don't find 'em, that's all!"

Zedic shook his head. "The elders won't let you or anyone else leave."

Trep swallowed. "Y'all are serious, ain't ya?"

Zedic stared off at nothing. "Absolutely."

Trep suddenly realized he hadn't been out of the canyon without Collin by his side since he'd arrived. It made him think twice about why Collin chose to sleep in his cabin.

Kairma came up to tell Zedic it was time to eat. She was careful to cover the small suede sack that held the crystal with her rabbit cloak. Just as she turned to head back to the fire, she heard Trep ask Zedic if anyone in the Healing family could read the ancient writing. She spun around and looked at Zedic, whose face was as white as her own. He stuttered something about having to go and jumped up to follow her. When they were out of earshot, Kairma turned to Zedic. "What are you telling him about us?"

"I never said anything. I don't know why he asked that. Collin showed him the ring we found. It has script inside the band, but Collin didn't say where we found it, or anything about reading script. Collin did mention that we use the gold rocks, but I stopped him before he could tell Trep what they were used for. I honestly don't know where that last question came from."

"I don't think we should trust him. He asks too many questions. And you had better keep close tabs on Collin too." They walked a bit farther and then Kairma added, "I think we both know he is planning to leave. I couldn't bear to see something happen to Collin because of some wild dream he has about finding the men who killed his brother and sister."

They walked the rest of the way to the fire in silence. Zedic didn't know if he could trust Trep, but he liked him just the same.

Trep found himself alone again. Now he could better understand the colony's reaction when he rode up that day on his horse, though he would have thought Collin would be more wary of him than the rest. Strange as it was, Collin was the first one to talk to him. Maybe Collin had his own reasons for wanting to go to the city. That didn't bother Trep as much as why he couldn't seem to learn anything about the Healing family. Every time he mentioned the community leaders, they acted as if he'd cursed their unborn children.

Trep filled his plate from the selection of foods and made his way back to the log at the edge of the banquet. He sat by himself, watching the social melee that was only beginning to get interesting. Children were chasing each other from tree to tree. Trep thought they were playing some kind of tag-and-run game. Most of the adults were occupied with eating, drinking, and storytelling. As the music became livelier, the younger people initiated a strange kind of snake dance that made Trep chuckle, while the elders moved into their various cliques.

Trep could hear people talking about the karrack and about him. They were asking each other questions that he would have gladly answered.

He saw Hiram sitting with some men and recalled the story Naturi had told him about the burning of the caves. When he overheard Hiram ask about the material used in the karrack, he felt this would be an opportunity to get to know him. Moving closer to the small group of men, he nodded to Hiram. "Couldn't help but overhear y'all ask about my karrack. I'd love to answer y'all's questions."

Hiram and the other men grimaced cautiously at Trep, looked over to the Healing family, and then got up and walked away. Trep went back to sitting on his stump, watching the village celebrate the coming of spring. Frustrated, he mumbled to himself, "Prairie dogs. They all act like a bunch of prairie dogs. Stand up, make a lot of noise, then run an' hide before ya can approach 'em."

Kinter was excited when the cooking contest began. This was her first competition and she had high hopes. All the girls who had entered dishes in the competition lined up to the west of the table and crossed their fingers in hopes of first prize. The judges consisted of the three oldest women in the colony.

The apple pastry was first. Addison tore off a small piece and tasted it. "Good flavor, sweet, but not too sweet. The crust is a little tough but definitely a very good entry."

Hannah and Martena each had a taste and concurred.

A green salad with a tart dressing was next. Martena had a second taste. "I think it must be a mint-based dressing. Very interesting. Is that mustard? Yes, this is very good"

The black bean soup was good, as well as the dried beef strips. Hannah clearly favored the apple preserves and the spice bars.

"Are these blackberry biscuits? I do like good biscuits." Martena had a nibble and smiled. "Yes, I believe these are about the best blackberry biscuits I've ever had." She passed a bite to Hannah. Kinter could hardly contain herself. If the three judges had turned around, they would have known without a doubt which girl had prepared the biscuits.

The potato soup was very well received and then came the blackberry preserves. Martena had the first taste. She didn't say anything for a few moments. She nodded to the others to taste. "Interesting. I can't quite make out that unusual aftertaste." Addison's nose crinkled. The judges tasted a few of the dishes a second time and then they were ready to announce the winners.

Starting with third place, the judges walked over to the table and picked up the winning dish. The unusual green salad with the mint dressing took third place, and a very happy Alyssum came up to recite the recipe.

Second place went to the apple preserves. Kinter turned white when Kairma took her place to recite the recipe. She was so upset that the blackberry preserves had been someone else's entry that she almost didn't hear the judges when they announced that her own biscuits had taken first place. In a daze, she recited the recipe, all the while wondering who would claim the spoiled preserves at the end of the day. Kinter felt that Kairma had tricked her again and thought bitterly that it was Kairma's fault. *It was always her fault.*

Trep walked away and found a seat on a rock outcropping where he could watch the crowd. He pulled out his hemp notebook and started to write. The language wasn't script, but a crude kind of picture book with symbols for common words. He tried to capture the essence of the celebration and the nature of the Survinees people.

The Healing family interested him most of all. He took note of Toric's adamant dislike of Kairma, who Naturi obviously liked very much. The royal family seemed to be well-respected in the eyes of the colony, but something was amiss. There was tension when Grimly walked past Jettena on his way to the banquet table, followed by some of the people who had been most vocal about his demonstration. Grimly's craggy face showed signs of unease as he gathered his supporters about him and Miral Isontra rarely took her eyes off him.

Comad Tamron and Vice Miral Jettena called everyone to the base of the stairs that led to the Gathering Place. Awards were given and announcements made. Dillon grinned broadly as he accepted a beautifully braided leather band that signified first place in the archery competition. He added it to the other bands that adorned the medallion Naturi had passed to him earlier in the day.

Kinter proudly handed out the awards when each winner stepped forward. Trep wasn't immune to the fact that Kinter was a very pretty girl. She was young, but with a few more years, Kinter would be a real prize. He mused over which of these young men would have the grit and conviction to take on that little ball of fire.

Once the winners accepted their honors, the adults moved over to the altar and took a cup of the peyotel. Collin had warned Trep not to drink the fruit and cactus punch, the effects of which included altered states of perception and feelings. Trep made notes of the ritual but stayed clear of the punch; he needed to keep his wits about him tonight.

Kairma monitored the peyotel. To the side of her, Tamron, Jettena, and Isontra talked silently at a long table on the stairs to the Gathering House. After a while, Isontra moved to take Kairma's place. "Why don't you go join the others in a dance."

Kairma shook her head. "I'm not much for dancing."

"Go on, you'll have fun." She nudged her gently.

Kairma shrugged and got up from the punch. She made her way across the square, looking for Zedic and Collin.

Jettena and Tamron watched the dancing for a while and joined in on a particularly moving number. Their movements were slow and graceful, touching each others palms at about shoulder height. Jettena's skirt swirled gracefully as they danced by.

She loved to see her parents dance. Her mother was beautiful and her father was the most handsome man she knew, with the possible exception of Naturi.

When she looked over to Naturi she saw, as usual, women surrounding the handsome man. Rose, Alyssum, Ember, Rossi, and Dessa all jockeyed for his attention. Each asked him to dance and Naturi was always accommodating. Kairma smiled and went to join Zedic and Collin, who were trying to see who could put the most food on his plate.

The dancing and music made Trep homesick for the market days in the city, where he was often in the company of many friends. He stared at the gentle Survinees, thinking about how they would fare in the big city. As the sun dropped behind the mountain, the crowd got livelier and quite a bit louder. The musicians were seated on a small stage in the center of the ring of buffet tables. There was plenty of room for dancing outside the ring and most of the young Survinees were dancing and singing along. Hoping it would relax him, Trep decided he would try just one cup of the punch.

Across the square, Trep could see a number of young women around Naturi. The handsome young man danced for a short time with each of the ladies and then retired to the side of Tamron. Jettena obviously enjoyed the young man's company as well.

Kinter walk up to the stage and, after a brief discussion, she joined the musicians. Pulling out a small pipe, she began to play. The tune made Trep's blood run cold with the beauty of it. He had never heard an instrument quite like it. Like the sound of a whippoorwill mixed with the loneliness of a mourning dove, it was hauntingly seductive. When she finished the song, everyone clapped and asked her to play another. She played a livelier tune this time and then began to sing. Her voice was as perfect as her pipe and Trep was lost in her music as he sipped on his punch. The next song she dedicated to someone she wouldn't name, but her eyes were on Naturi. The handsome young man didn't seem to notice because he was in deep conversation with Tamron.

Soon after the song began, Naturi excused himself from Tamron and walked over to Kairma. He greeted her formally and then asked her to dance.

Kairma felt her cheeks warm and shook her head. "I really don't dance well, Naturi. I'll just watch."

Naturi reached out and put a hand on her waist, pulling her gently into him. "Nonsense. You are a very graceful woman. You cannot do other than dance well." Kairma knew Naturi was lying. She was as clumsy as a goat, but his dreamy velvet voice had Kairma believing him, if only for a moment. She shyly acquiesced, and he led her away from her friends to the middle of the dance square. The evening was turning cool, but Kairma felt a fire building in her that had nothing to do with the weather.

As they moved around the square, Naturi's lips brushed past her ear and she felt her heart begin to race. She stumbled, but Naturi caught her and whispered, "I will always be here to catch you, Kairma."

Pulling back, he looked into her eyes, as round and as pale as the rising moon to the east. "You are a very beautiful girl, Kairma. I wish you could see yourself as other people do."

Kairma felt her cheeks turn hot and knew she was blushing again. She was sure she knew exactly how others saw her: the colorless girl who resembled a White One. Naturi laughed softly, and she melded to him and put her head in the hollow of his broad shoulder, forgetting for a moment who she was. While they danced, Kairma dreamed of a future where all her questions and fears were abolished.

Naturi laid his cheek against her head and murmured, "You know, I would be good for you, Kairma. You have been the center of my world for many annums now. From the time you were just a babe, I held you in my arms and knew you were meant for me. Everything you do now is of my concern. You need a companion who understands the weight you carry—someone who is strong and knowledgeable. I would be good for you."

Kairma knew this. She still didn't understand what Naturi saw in her, but she was sure he would be good for her.

By the stairs, Jettena commented on the young couple's apparent attraction to each other. "See how well they dance together. They make such a lovely pair."

Tamron smiled. "Yes, she does seem taken with him, doesn't she?" He reached over and took Jettena's hand. "She could do worse, you know."

Jettena leaned into him. "I really worry that she spends so much time with Zedic and Collin. She's always coming home covered in grime. It's all I can do to get her to wear a skirt."

Tamron kissed her lightly on the top of her head. "I know what you mean. The silly girl still wants to climb rocks and chase after her brother."

Stirring the punch as she listened to Tamron and Jettena, Isontra came to Kairma's defense. "She still enjoys the pleasures of being young, but she isn't foolish. She'll be prepared for her Seridar come autumn." She looked over at Collin and Zedic, who were eyeing the dancers. "Collin is her best friend. He's smart, and he has an ingenuity and strength we rarely see in our people."

Jettena frowned as she turned toward Isontra. "Don't tell me you think Collin has the skill to best Naturi at Kairma's Seridar?"

"Naturi is very well-bred, and Kairma does seem to like him, but I wouldn't count anyone out just yet. Let's see what the summer brings." Isontra pulled her beige shawl around her shoulders and returned to the gentle stirring. "I think everyone has had their fill of punch tonight, and we should head back to the conference room. We have a lot to discuss. That demonstration was interesting." Isontra got up, and Jettena and Tamron followed.

Kinter had been watching Naturi as he danced with Kairma. She cut the song short and walked off the stage while the musicians did their best to carry the remainder of the tune without her.

Stomping to the table where Ember and Rose sat, Kinter swore, "I hate him!"

Rose looked up at Kinter. "Who?"

"Naturi, that's who!"

"I thought you really liked him. Wasn't that the song you wrote for him?"

Ember jabbed Rose in the ribs. "Didn't you see? Naturi asked Kairma to dance to the song Kinter wrote for him."

Rose's eyes grew wide. "Oh! I see!"

Kinter glared at both young girls and walked to Naturi and Kairma. She grabbed his arm, pulling him away from her sister. "You're a real skunk! I'm never speaking to you again!" She whirled and left the square before he could see her tears.

❧

Naturi was struck dumb. Kairma sighed, "I'll talk to her. I'll figure out what you did wrong. I suspect it has something to do with me, anyway."

Naturi recovered. "She does have quite a temper. I do not believe I have ever seen her that mad."

"I have. *Several* times. I'm just surprised it isn't me she's mad at this time."

"Please, let me make it up to her. It is important to me that your entire family is comfortable with me." Naturi led her to the sidelines.

"I'm sure it will be okay," Kairma said. *Kinter's in love with you and you can't see it.* She waved to Zedic as they headed in his direction. "Give her some time. I think she's having growing pains."

❧

Naturi, Zedic, and Kairma were deep in conversation when a young man Trep hadn't noticed before began speaking angrily to Naturi. Trep never could contain his curiosity so he moved a little closer to the argument.

"How could you think about going to the city? You have to be crazy."

"I never said I was going anywhere. I only..."

"So are you going to take the White Witch with you?" He pulled on Kairma's scarf and it came lose.

Naturi stepped in front of Kairma. "Leave her alone, Efram! She has done nothing to you."

Tears sprang to Kairma's eyes as she ran off, and wanting to comfort her, Zedic followed.

Efram's words were venomous. "Holy Nor! What kind of little bastards will you have? Skinny white weaklings?"

"Kairma is perfectly healthy in every way," Naturi countered.

Collin walked up and stood behind Naturi, his arms crossed on his chest, feet slightly apart.

"Sure she is. You would know, huh? Been there already like her ma? Ugly little mutant girl probably can't even have children. If she could, you know, like her mother, we would be swimmi ..."

Crack! Collin's fist hit Efram's jaw.

Efram went down in a heap and didn't get up. Collin glared at Naturi coldly for a moment, and then turned and walked away.

As Trep watched, Naturi took a deep breath and picked up the pile that was Efram and haul him to the bonfire. Efram was returning to himself, but Naturi didn't stick around.

Collin had disappeared and Trep knew he would find him in the extra cot when he got home. Collin had shown up every night in the few weeks that Trep had been staying in the village, and now, after meeting Collin's parents and his conversation with Zedic, Trep understood why.

The fire had burned low and most of the people had gone home. The temperature was pretty cool on this early spring night. Trep watched as the full moon settled over the tops of the western forest. Not far away from him, sat Hamond, Loren, and Joel.

After a while, Trep wandered back to his temporary dwelling, contemplating the events of the day, with his guards following close behind. Once they reached Trep's cabin, the Survin men took turns standing watch outside his door.

Chapter 9

The four most powerful persons in the small village of Survin sat in the great room of the Chancery. The fire burned brightly in the hearth, sending tiny sparks flying into the room. A pot of terrid sat steaming on the rock trivet in the center of the long dining table. Kairma sat with her arms folded on the table in front of her, her head down and her eyes closed. She had seen her parents leave the celebration and joined them right after Efram had made his disgusting remarks. She didn't feel much like celebrating and knew her elders would be discussing the items Trep had shown them.

When Kairma arrived, her mother and father had been arguing about invoking the Law of Fontas. They were afraid of this man and what he represented. Jettena was adamant, but Isontra begged her to consider the need for new blood.

Jettena held her head in her hands and rubbed her temples while Isontra stared into the fire. Tamron paced as the minutes slid away.

At long last Jettena spoke. "I still see no reason to risk this. How much do you really think we would gain? What is the use of one man?"

Isontra sighed. "You know your father and your mate were both outsiders. We have much to gain. This would be a whole new bloodline, especially if he were to mate with Kairma or Kinter."

Kairma, appalled by the thought of mating with this stranger, and sensing her mother's acquiescence, said, "Trep won't mate with us. They do things differently in the city. Collin says he has a woman there. He would surely want her to come here if he were forced to stay with us. If he went to get her, he could bring us some of the things we saw today as well."

Jettena shook her head emphatically. "Absolutely not! It's one thing to allow him to join our colony, but we can't allow him to leave."

Tamron faced his daughter. "Your mother is right. We have no guarantee the man would bring back any of these wonders at all. He could just disappear or might even bring back others to take what they want from us."

Kairma's lips formed a thin white line. "That is why we need to send someone with him."

Jettena was shocked, but it was Isontra who replied. "You've been considering this for a while, have you? You think we should send our men to the city?"

Not looking up, Kairma said, "Collin wants to go."

"I know, dear, but that doesn't make it a wise decision," Isontra's said softly.

Jettena's voice grew slightly louder. "See! What have I always said about that boy? He's trouble."

Tamron sat down next to his wife and put an arm around her, pulling Jettena close. "He is a brave boy, and yes, maybe thoughtless at times, but he's got a good heart. I'm sure he only wants to go to the city because he's curious. You see the way he's always exploring the caves, even when we tell him how dangerous it is."

Jettena's pursed her lips. "And he's always dragging Zedic into danger with him."

Sitting up and facing her elders, Kairma said, "Zedic will go anywhere Collin goes, and Trep won't wait forever. You heard him today. He's willing to go back to the city and bring us new clothing and weapons. And we need more of his kind. He isn't full Efpec blood, but I believe he has enough to make a valuable member of our colony.

Maybe he knows others like himself." She could feel the intensity of her parents stare. They were outraged. It was one thing to send men to the far off city in hope of miracles. It was quite another to let one of those men be your own son.

Undaunted, Kairma held her ground. "Gramme and I have talked about our need for new blood before. We keep waiting for a miracle to save us. Well, maybe this is our miracle."

"No, Kairma. This is wrong." Jettena wrung her hands.

Tamron shook his head slowly. "There are so few young men left in the colony. We can't afford to lose any. This would be terribly dangerous and there is no way of knowing the final cost of a venture of this magnitude. We can't risk sending men away."

Isontra spoke quietly, but her tone always carried a sense of authority. "Kairma makes a good point. If we don't do something soon, there may not be anything to fight for. We have lost four family lines in the last ten annums alone." Isontra met Kairma's gaze and she sounded apologetic when she added, "But this is not a gamble I believe we need to take. We can add Trep's blood, and he will have to forget about the woman he left behind."

Kairma sat thinking of all the things to be explored in the great vault and all the things they could learn from Trep. She was certain the elders wouldn't kill Trep now, but she didn't believe he would stay willingly in Survin for the rest of his life. She also knew that condemning Trep would condemn Collin. She stood up and looked in the eyes of each member of the small committee. "We should let Trep go to the city and bring back his woman at the very least."

All three of the elders shook their heads. Isontra's voice was calm, but she wouldn't be swayed from her decision. "We will let the stranger live, but we can't risk allowing him or any of our people to leave."

Kairma was pleading now. "But think of what he could bring back. You saw the karrack. You saw what it could do. Collin says they make things like that. Think of what it could mean to us."

After the fire had burned to red coals, Kairma finally gave up her arguments. The next day they would discuss the Law of Fontas at the weekly service, but she knew they wouldn't be sending anyone to the city.

Collin woke early. He slipped out of the house, thankful that Trep was still asleep. He didn't feel like discussing what had happened the night before, and with any luck he would catch Zedic gathering wood. He headed down the winding path, past the fields where he saw Naturi tending one of the many herb gardens. Collin didn't wave as he went by. He was still angry that Naturi had done nothing when Efram said those hurtful things regarding Kairma.

Outside the canyon, he saw Zedic walking toward the east pass. Hurrying to catch up, he called, "Zedic, wait. I'll help you."

Zedic stopped and waited for Collin. "I was just going for wood. The way my mother cooks, she's going to use all the wood on the mountain, and that's just for this morning's meal."

Collin laughed. "Yes, but I'd gather wood all day for the pancakes she makes!"

Zedic glanced sideways at Collin. His mother had never been known for her cooking though she was improving daily. "Well then, you'll be happy to know she's making some this morning. Start picking up wood."

"Gladly. I'm sure gonna miss them."

Zedic stopped abruptly and turned toward Collin. "So, you're going to try to leave? I thought you might. You're going with Trep to the city, aren't you?"

Collin continued to stack small logs in a pile. "Of course. But I'm not gonna try. One way or another, I *am* going to leave."

"There are no few people who will stand in your way, not to mention what your father will do to you. You know the law. We could be put to death for even talking about leaving."

"Let them try to stop me."

"They'll kill both of you."

"I'm not afraid. I'm gonna get some of the yellow rock Trep calls gold and go to the city with him. I'll buy a horse and a saddle and see the world. I'll help Trep investigate the Ancient Ones. Who knows? Maybe someday I'll even come back here."

Zedic seriously doubted this. He went back to gathering wood and didn't say anything for a long time. Collin was his closest friend and he couldn't blame him for wanting to leave the mountain. He'd often wondered what the greater world held as well. "What will you do when you run out of gold?"

Collin thought for a while. "Don't know. I'll think of something, I guess. Trep does okay."

They each picked up a stack of wood and headed back to the Chancery. Collin paused for a moment and then turned to face Zedic. "You saw all the things they have there. You could convince Miral Isontra to let us go. She would understand how important this is, I'm sure."

Zedic shook his head. "Kairma pleaded with them all night and they refused. You know the laws."

Collin grimaced. "Yes, I do. I just wish they could see things differently."

"Our family has already done a lot of things that have caused the rest of the colony reason to question our ability to lead. You can't expect them to condone something of this magnitude. Just allowing Trep to live is in defiance of the laws."

Collin hoisted his load of wood to the other arm. "Well, if they're going to keep him, maybe I should show him the vault. I bet he can tell us about most of those things we found."

"We'll talk with him after the service. Just because the Miral and the Comad believe he should live doesn't mean the rest of the colony will agree."

Collin thought about sneaking Trep out of the village before the service but realized a trip of that scale would require a lot more planning than he had time for today.

When they arrived at the grand hall of Zedic's home, Isontra was busy going over last-minute instructions with Kairma. Today was the first time Kairma would perform the service at the Monument of Nor. Although she had attended the weekly meetings since she was a child, she looked very nervous about having to read the sacred script in front of the Survinees. She rehearsed it again and again until she almost knew the words by heart.

Collin couldn't remember her looking as pretty as she did that morning. She wore a beautifully crocheted lace scarf trimmed with delicate yellow flowers that brought out the cerulean in her pale blue eyes. The long white dress she was wearing was a bit too small for her. It had been passed down from her mother, who was an inch shorter and more slender than Kairma. It was made of velvet-soft suede, and she bulged in some very nice places. He found himself staring at her until his arms began to ache from the wood he was holding. Recovering his wits, he put the logs down by the fireplace and helped himself to a cup of terrid.

Collin enjoyed visiting the Healing family, and even Kinter's whining about not having anything to wear only made him smile. Zedic helped Jettena get the triplets dressed, and Collin joined him. By the time they had the boys ready to go, Kairma and Isontra had already left for the service.

Kairma mumbled her lines as they walked. She was painfully aware of the stares she received as they passed the other homes. She could see people scurrying about, trying to get things together to be on their way. The walk to the Nor monument was only a little more than a mile from the south end of the canyon, but it was all up hill.

When they reached the Gathering House, Naturi joined them. Holding his hand out to Kairma, he helped her up the steep stairway that led to the village social house. "You are looking quite lovely this morning, Miss Kairma."

Feeling her cheeks warm at the comment, Kairma's embarrassment doubled, which proceeded to make her mad. She hated that Naturi had this effect on her. Without meeting his eyes, she softly said, "Thank you."

As they continued to the monument, Naturi held her by the arm. Kairma could see her mother was pleased. Jettena told her that Naturi would be a fine mate because Naturi had a natural serenity about him. She was certain Naturi would be the stabilizing influence Kairma needed.

Kinter didn't feel the same. From a few steps behind, Kinter watched Naturi. She was still hurt by his actions the night before, but she couldn't help hoping he was waiting for her to come of age. Kinter was sure Naturi was more interested in the Crystal than in Kairma herself, and felt something had gone dreadfully wrong. Both Naturi and the healing powers should belong to her—she knew it in her soul.

Strolling casually behind the others with Zedic and the triplets, Collin tried to imagine some way to convince the elders to allow Trep to take him to the city. Keeping the triplets from running off, or finding something dirty to play with, often interrupted his thoughts. Collin would miss these little boys when he left, but he would miss Zedic most. The two of them had been close friends since he could remember. He didn't believe Zedic would be willing to leave Survin. Kairma, on the other hand, would jump at the chance if she weren't the heir to the Healing Crystal, but she was the heir and she would never hurt the colony. He could see her well ahead, walking beside Naturi. In six moons, she would be mated so there was no point in even thinking about asking her to go with him.

Chapter 10

The Nor monument was a spire of dark gray stone with arms of layered rock creating a circle around a squat stone altar. On the face of the spire was a brass plaque welcoming the Survinees to this mountain. From here, the Survinees could see heavily forested land to the horizon in all directions. Across the valley to the northwest, the magnificent faces of their four gods looked toward the hilltop where the colony gathered each week to give special thanks to Nor, the great savior who had given them this land. Rows of wooden benches fanned out in a graceful arc facing the monument. Today's meeting would last most of the day, as there was much to cover with the recent hunt and the revelation of the karrack.

As people filled the seats, Kinter sat in the first row next to her father and the triplets. She had a scowl on her pretty face as she held baby Sonty, partially because she wanted to be at the altar helping the Mirals, and partially because the three little boys were squirming in their seats and making rude noises. She grabbed the closest boy by the arm and whispered harshly, "Stop it, Tad! Sit still!"

She reached over to grab the second boy when Zedic and Collin, who had taken the seats directly behind her, came to her rescue. Zedic was very good with the little ones. He and Collin pulled the boys onto the seats beside them. Kinter put her fingers on her forehead as if her head was hurting and said, "Thank you."

Collin said, "You know I only tolerated these monsters out of respect for your family." But the laughter in his eyes told the truth. Collin often played with the boys, and they adored him. For the rest of the service, Tadya sat in Zedic's lap, Tames sat in Collin's lap, and Taren was secured in between.

Miral Isontra and Vice Miral Jettena took their places at the front of the gathering. Kairma came from behind the monument, carrying a basket of tributes for the service. She could feel her knees shaking as she lowered the basket to the small stone altar and began to unpack a basket of herbs to be handed out to the congregation. To honor them, the villagers rose to their feet, and in unison, they raised their right hands to their right eyebrows, palms outward. The religious leaders returned the formal greeting and took their places.

Jettena led the colony in a prayer of thanks for returning all the men safely home. She then asked Toric to report on the hunt.

He seemed removed from what was happening. There had been a time when Toric would have gone on at length, explaining every detail of the trip, but now he used only the briefest dialogue. After he took his place by the statue he said flatly, "It went well. Twenty-seven men killed two large bucks and three cattle. Owen was injured when he twisted his knee while chasing a heard of elk into Pine Canyon. He'll be fine." Toric looked at no one as he returned to his seat.

Jettena asked Kairma to hand everyone a piece of the dried venison as Pria came to the front to report on the goatherd. When the shepherdess finished, Kairma walked through the crowd as she handed out small pieces of cheese and filled small cups with goat's milk.

Once Kairma had returned to the altar, Jettena called upon Naturi to report on the fields. He proudly walked to the front of the gathering and thanked all the men and women who had helped him till the ground and plant the seeds. He sounded much like a happier Toric as he took great pleasure in telling the colony what had been planted. His mother Devon had taken great pride in the garden when he was a boy. She had specialized in flowers and herbs. Although some people thought it was a silly notion, after a few annums Devon's garden proved to be extremely valuable. Come harvest time, Devon had many of the medicines the Healing family regularly searched the forests to find. Finishing his report, Naturi asked for help in keeping the weeds and insects under control and he looked pleased when several women volunteered themselves and their children.

The fields were almost as long as the canyon and half as wide. Everyone benefited from the grains of the field. Cornbread and barley cakes were a standard at mealtime, but Naturi's green beans and hot peppers were prized vegetables. Jettena thanked him for his report and asked Kairma to hand out the small cakes wrapped in large green leaves.

Once everyone had received the tributes, Jettena motioned for her mother to make her report. Crossing to the front of the monument, Isontra lightly kissed her daughter on the cheek.

Isontra clasped her hands behind her back and, in a strong voice, said, "Over the past winter, I've worked hard to teach our future Vice Miral all that I know to be true and healing." There were whispers among the crowd and Kairma shifted in her seat nervously. She knew what some of the others were saying about her and how they felt. She actually understood their fear. She was afraid too. It seemed like far too much responsibility for someone so young and so different. She was glad Isontra and Jettena would be there to help her in the next few annums.

Trep woke with a terrible headache though he'd drunk only a few cups of wine. He momentarily wondered if someone had put peyotel in his food and realized he'd had at least ten cups of wine, not usually enough to make him stumble, but enough to feel it. Trep rubbed his head. *I always drink too much when I'm nervous. Hope I didn't do anything stupid.* He laughed at himself. *Well, anything more stupid than upsetting the entire village with my little show.*

He was thankful that he and Collin had cleaned up the rabbit and started a slow-cooking stew the day before. He would feel better after something to eat. Noting that Collin was gone, he fixed a cup of terrid and a bowl of stew and then sat down to look over his notes. It must have been the punch; most of his notes looked like gibberish.

After a few minutes, he remembered everyone would be at the Monument of Nor. Today was the colony's holy meeting day. Collin had told him specifically that he was not invited, but he couldn't resist the temptation to see what they did there. He had been to the monument two days before and was sure he could get close enough to observe what was happening without anyone seeing him.

He dressed quickly and headed for the door. That's when he remembered he had guards. He cursed to himself. *Of all the dang luck. I really wanted to know what their religion's all about. Odd that they would keep it a secret. Most folk cain't wait to regale ya with every notion of their belief system.*

Trep poured another cup of terrid and took it out to the man standing by his door. "So, Loren, isn't it?"

Loren nodded.

Trep handed him the cup and said, "Where is everyone? They leave ya here alone?"

Loren nodded, suspiciously this time. Trep smiled, and Loren relaxed a little. "Everyone is at the service," Loren said.

Trep offered, "Ya know, if y'all wanted to go ya might tie me up here or ya could take my karrack hostage. There's no way I'd leave this mountain without that."

Loren considered it for a moment. "No, I had better stay right here."

"Suit yerself. I had a long night so I think I'll jess go back to bed." Trep reached around the doorframe and grabbed a stool. "At least I can offer ya a chair."

Loren smiled a little wider and sat down.

Trep wandered around the cabin for a while, and then he noticed a small window in the back room. It was more like a vent than a window, but he was sure he could squeeze through it. The Survinees had little experience with prisoners and missed it.

He smiled as he wriggled his way out.

He walked behind empty houses most of the way through the canyon. When he reached the Gathering House, he paused. If someone was in the stone tunnel, he couldn't get through without being seen. He backed up as far as he could and tried to see inside the doors. He could only see in a few feet, but it looked quiet. Crossing his fingers, he took the chance and climbed the stone stairs to the room.

Luck was his friend today and he darted through the empty room and up the path to the monument. Once he was sure no one was following, he cut through the thick forest. Right before reaching the summit, he got down on his knees and crawled the last fifty feet, coming up right below the sitting area on the north side.

As he crawled a little closer he could hear Isontra telling Kairma to pass out herbs from her basket. While hiding behind a thick spruce, he saw Kairma take her place next to the stone monument. He could barely make out what she was saying so he moved up a little closer.

He distinctly heard the pale young girl say, "Nor, Life Preserve, Act of Con, Nor, Sta man, nor of so akot, builder, art lover, poet of nature, gentleman. His age of vision, which saw far ahead, far beyond. He felt the strong heart throb of his beloved people commanding to do greatly and be great."

The words sounded stilted and confused, but what astounded Trep was what he was seeing! Kairma looked like she was reading the plaque on the statue. *Why had Naturi lied about it? They should be proud to understand the ancient writings.*

Trep crept closer as Kairma went on reading, "In these mountains he found a wilderness for them and labored to preserve its beauty unspoiled for them and their children's children. He is still present in the towering love, and in the hearts of the multitudes who will enjoy."

Kairma turned to the congregation, the Godstones clearly visible from their vantage on the mountain, and said, "I give to you, my people, the four gods of life: Meat, Milk, Grain, and Herbs."

The congregation turned to face the Godstones, and for a moment Trep thought he would be seen. He slipped off to the side as Kairma raised her arms as if embracing the gods. Hiding behind a thick stand of aspens, he could hear their prayers drifting gently on the breeze.

"For the meat that sustains our strength, we give you thanks." The congregation slowly chewed the dried venison.

"For the milk that sustains our bones, we give you thanks." The congregation sipped from their cups.

"For the grains that sustain our blood, we give you thanks." They put the small cakes in their mouths.

"For the herbs that sustain our minds, we give you thanks." Then each one ate a small plant.

As the crowd turned back to face the young girl, Isontra handed her three thin sheets of gold. Kairma held her scarf-clad head high as she began to read. "The angel handed the Crystal to Amanda with the instructions to..."

Trep couldn't believe what he saw. *They use the gold to write on! How can a primitive village like this know how to read and write the ancient language? Maybe they use a different form of writin'. Certainly looked like Kairma was readin' that plaque and I know that's ancient writin'.*

Kairma continued, "And so the Crystal was passed to her daughter, and then to her daughter's daughter. We, the people of Nor, have been entrusted with the greatest power of the known world. With this power comes the obligation to heal the world, and the responsibility for its protection. We bring this power to you, our gods, here on the Mountain of Nor." She placed the small gold tablet on the stone altar beside her.

Then opening the soft cloth bag that hung from her neck, she brought out a multifaceted object, slightly smaller than her fist, which glistened with silver, and gold, and all the colors of the spectrum. Holding it high above her head, she turned and faced the Statue of Nor. "I am Kairma, Kairma of Jettena, Jettena of Isontra, Isontra of Hestra,

Hestra of Gwenvier, Gwenvier of Faithen, Faithen of Elsubeth, Elsubeth of Duray, Duray of Cammri, Cammri of Bettella, Bettella of Annise, Annise of Zeanna, Zeanna of Yeshesa, Yeshesa of Xennan, Xennan of Wentesa, Wentesa of Velain, Velain of Ulanna, Ulanna of Tressim, Tressim of Shamonda, Shamonda of Rozela, Rozela of Quensi, Quensi of Perridre, Perridre of Olainka, Olainka of Nikile, Nikile of Mishira, Mishira of Loisann, Loisann of Kitru, Kitru of Jazentel, Jazentel of Irrsa, Irrsa of Headra, Headra of Giannia, Giannia of Fontas, Fontas of Ellanda, Ellanda of Daebra, Daebra of Crysten, Crysten of Belendra, Belendra of Amanda, Amanda of the Angel who entrusted her and her heirs with the Healing Crystal until it could be returned to the Sacred Mountain of Nor."

Trep was actually shaking where he stood. *It cain't be. The legend of the star! It glistens like a star. Of all the places to find it. What was that she said about healing the world?*

Kairma knelt on one knee and held the Crystal to her breast. "I am Kairma, heir and guardian of the Healing Crystal. My lord of this mountain, I bring the Crystal to you, that you may heal us."

Sitting cross-legged before the statue, she placed the Crystal on the ground in front of her and look up at the colony. Her voice cracked with nervousness as she said, "I am your Healer. Bring to me your sick and weary that I may heal them."

Trep was astounded. *Can it really be the mythological Star of Genesis! I didn't believe it really existed! So that's what they're hiding! That explains why they don't want strangers askin' questions.* He thought for a moment about the names she had recited. *I don't even know my pa's pa's name and yet she must have listed at least thirty generations.'* He tried to remember everything else Kairma had said, but his mind kept going back to the Star. *How the hell did they come by it? Some "Amanda of the angel" gave it to someone else, to bring it* here, *the Mountain of Nor? It jess doesn't make any sense.*

He studied the simple villagers. *It cain't be as all-powerful as the legends claim. These folk don't even know how to work metal or raise cattle.*

Trep's mind was suddenly drawn back to the altar as Isontra stepped up and opened the discussion about *the stranger*. "I am opening the floor to discuss bringing the stranger, Trep, into our community."

A low angry murmur swept through the crowd.

"The bow and sling work well for us," Isontra continued, "but with his weapon we could improve our hunts and defense would be much stronger. More important than weapons is our need for new blood. We've lost many of our bloodlines over the past few generations and he appears to have at least a small amount of Efpec blood."

A few people nodded in agreement.

Grimly stood and bowed deeply. "Miral Isontra, am I to understand that you are in favor of allowing this stranger to live? I must protest this outrageous act of sacrilege. The Ogs are very clear in the matters of strangers and the renunciation of the colony." Grimly glared, menace in his eyes. "We have allowed strangers to join us in the past and it has *always* led to hardship."

Several members whom supported the orthodox vein of the church nodded and mumbled in agreement.

Trep felt the hairs on the back of neck rise, yet curiosity pulled him closer. He could clearly see the muscles of Isontra's face tighten.

The influential woman looked squarely at Grimly, hands clasped firmly behind her back. "Renunciation? I do not believe we have been considering anything of the sort. Vice Miral Jettena has merely proposed a small change in our traditions, not that we abandon our way of life."

Grimly shifted on his feet, his voice rising, "Experience is *knowing when you've made that mistake before.*"

Isontra put her hand up to silence him. "Experience is a lifelong process and is absolutely necessary for shaping future decisions, but, my dear Grimly, it is how you interpret the experience that decides your course of action." Then, addressing the assemblage, her voice softened. "Change is not always baneful. Witness the many changes as a child grows into an adult. Some of these changes are uncomfortable, yet all are necessary to acquire new abilities. Sometimes we stumble and fall, but I ask you now, where would we be if we had never learned to walk?"

Grimly sneered at the old woman. He said, "If we could see how this divergence from our most sacred laws would benefit us, we might be more willing to accept your ideas, but with the past as my witness, many foul things have come our way since Miral Hestra allowed the last outsiders to join us."

Isontra saw this as the personal attack it was, and she glanced into the faces of the congregation, searching out those who would support her. "Grimly, my good Sir, do you not see all the empty homes of our valley. Do you not witness the declining birth rate of our people? This man offers us a way to change this."

Grimly crossed his thick arms over his chest. "How do we know what we're supposed to do in any situation? We listen to you, and you say the Ogs tell us to kill strangers. Now you tell us to let them join us. Maybe if you let someone else read the sacred Ogs, we would know what to do."

Light danced in Isontra's gray eyes. "You complain to me that you don't like changes in our traditions, but what you're proposing now is unprecedented. The Mirals have been the only ones to learn how to read the sacred script, until now."

She paused for a moment, waiting for her words to sink in. "I'm willing to teach the script to anyone who is interested in learning. I have often felt the knowledge was too vulnerable, being held by so few. We have to make adjustments in a changing world and, as you know, both Kairma and Kinter are able to read and write the sacred language of our ancestors."

Grimly cursed under his breath but returned to his seat.

Martena stood. "I realize we have let strangers live in the past. But this stranger told us yesterday that he intends to return to the city."

Voices rose and Isontra sighed heavily. "Although I would like Survin to have some of the items to which the stranger has access, you are right. We won't let him leave the mountain with knowledge of us."

The murmurs of the populace grew louder and Isontra had to almost shout. "We spent many hours discussing our options last night. Yes, there is a danger involved whenever we do something different, but this stranger may truly help us." The crowd settled a little.

Isontra paused until she was sure she had the full attention of everyone present. "I had a dream in which all we know is changed. The signs are clear that we are the chosen people." She motioned to the statue behind and the great stone carvings before her. "We are the guardians of the Crystal. It is our people who will protect and keep safe the healing power."

She raised her arms in appeal. "Now the time has come. We cannot sit idle and hope for a miracle. We must test our faith and our honor. I cannot say what is to be the future of our people; only that winter turns to summer and in each end there is a new beginning. May the changes we adopt today provide us with the fruits of a blessed summer."

The community was at odds with each other and Trep wasn't sure it wouldn't get worse before it got better. Suddenly all of Collin's warnings had depth. He hadn't realized how precarious his position had been until now. He knew he was in danger, but after seeing the star he couldn't walk away.

As the service came to a close, Kairma passed out the animal gut string used for the prayer of the Thirty Blessings. Everyone took their string, stretching it between their fingers as Kairma began the litany. "Lord of Nor, we thank you for the Thirty Blessings that guide us and keep us safe." Placing the string between two teeth she said, "Life." The others imitated her movements and invocation. Moving the string to another tooth, she said, "Love." Another tooth was cleaned, and another miracle was enunciated. She repeated the ritual with *loyalty, honor,* and *respect.*

After these five miracles, each person rinsed his or her mouth and continued through the next five miracles: *sight, touch, scent, hearing, and taste.* After another rinse came *courage, compassion, tolerance, faith,* and *friendship,* followed by *joy, music, art, literature, language, then hope, knowledge, inspiration, intelligence, resilience,* and finally *health, harmony, medicine, community, understanding.*

Once the meeting was concluded, the people stirred to their feet not a little unsettled. It was an acute sense of fear mixed with confusion that arose from the top of the mountain that day. There several small arguments, but no other decisions were made. Slowly people began to break up and head back down the mountain.

Chapter 11

Trep scarcely had time to slip into the house before he heard the light rap of Isontra's walking stick at the door. He quickly tossed some of Naturi's drawings on the table, composed himself, and went to let her in.

With her silver head held high, Isontra walked purposefully to the center of the room, with Kairma at her heels. "We would like to discuss a matter of great importance with you." Her eyes briefly assessed the room and she noted that the fire had burned down low and it was quite chilly. As she walked to the table, Trep greeted her formally, then bowed slightly and motioned for the community leaders to have a seat.

"I'm sorry, wasn't expectin' company. Here let me clear this off. I was jess lookin' over some of Nate's stuff."

Isontra eyed him cautiously. "Really? You must have very thick skin. It feels as if you have neglected your fire. Would you mind? These old bones chill rather easily." She gestured toward the cold hearth.

Trep stoked the fire and put on a pot of water for terrid. "I must admit, dear ladies, I am quite honored that y'all have paid me a visit. Seems most folk don't want to have much to do with me."

To Trep's great relief, Isontra smiled and said, "We are a rather private people and do not warm well to outsiders." She looked at him thoughtfully for a long time. He was beginning to feel uncomfortable when she said, "One never knows whom one can trust. Could it be that you were not sitting here studying those drawings as you claim, but in truth you had only arrived here moments before us?"

Trep felt awkward as he took a seat at the table. "Please forgive me. Of course, y'all are right. I did jess get in. I really mean ya no harm, though. Honestly, I'm jess curious 'bout so many things, and I find y'all so interestin'. I love meetin' new people, and learnin' 'bout how they live." He shifted slightly under Isontra's icy stare. "Sometimes, I get a bit carried away. I treasure y'all's little society here." He paused briefly. "Well, I guess y'all are not that friendly to me, but y'all are real interestin' and seem to be downright honest folk."

Isontra nodded. "Shall we begin again?"

Admonished, he replied, "Yes, please."

"Let us start by having you tell us what you know about us. We will decide from there what is to be done about you."

Trep swallowed the hard lump in his throat. Then he got up quickly from the table, chiding himself for trying to fool the proud Miral. He had hoped to be in better control on his first introduction to Isontra; she could be a very intimidating woman, without so much as raising an eyebrow. Mentally, he vowed to be honest with her in the future—at least to never be caught in a total untruth.

He pulled three pottery cups from the finely carved wood shelf above the hearth. "I know y'all don't like outsiders. Cain't blame ya after what happened to Cole's kin." He filled the cups with steaming terrid and set them on the table. "I know a little bit 'bout y'all's gods from what Cole and Nate have told me." Kairma looked up from her cup, a little puzzled. Her stunning pale blue eyes unsettled Trep; he quickly looked back to Isontra. "Sorry, I mean Collin and Naturi. As y'all know, Collin asked ya the first day I came here if I could use this home, and he's been teachin' me y'all's way of talkin'. He's a real bright boy. Makes me think I'd like to have a son someday. And Nate, yeah, he's real smart too. He's told me a bit 'bout y'all's trouble with the White Ones. He tells me ya never let anyone leave the mountain. Must admit, made me more than a touch uneasy. Thought y'all were gonna do me in." He chuckled nervously. "I'm real sorry 'bout the way I barged into y'all's games uninvited. Jess thought I had somethin' important to show ya."

Isontra took a sip of her terrid and closed her eyes. "I believe Collin invited you to show us your weapon."

"He did, at that, and I don't think he meant any harm."

"Trep, can you tell us from where you have recently returned?"

He looked into his cup, feeling like a child who had been severely scolded. "I was told the meetin' at the Monument of Nor was private, but ..." Trep smoothed his unkempt hair. "My curiosity got the best of me, and as much as I hate to admit it, I did overhear some of y'all's discussion this mornin'."

"I thought as much." Isontra was calm, but Kairma blanched visually as she chewed on her lower lip. "Though I didn't realize this until we arrived here. How much of the meeting did you overhear?"

Trep squirmed in his seat. "I heard y'all argue 'bout killin' me."

"Then you must have learned that we have decided to let you live." Her tone was serious, but Trep thought he detected humor in her steel gray eyes.

"Yes ma'am, and I thank you. Seems not everyone felt the same."

"This is true. You do present us with a problem, and an opportunity."

"I understand that y'all are interested in my blood. I'm guessin' ya want me to mate with one of y'all's women."

"Yes, we are most interested in that."

"I have a lady in the city. She's real special to me. If I could go get her ..."

"You will not. I'm sorry, but that part of your life is over. I know we seem harsh to you, but our precautions are necessary."

Trep would have argued the point, but he understood why they would want to keep the star secret, if it was indeed the Star of Genesis.

❧

Kairma was surprised at how drained she felt. Something told her Trep wasn't being totally honest with them, not that he seemed harmful but that he was hiding something. Glancing at her grandmother, she realized that Isontra was very tired as well.

The two women walked to the door, and then Isontra suddenly turned back to Trep. Her voice was as brittle as ice. "If you fail to prove true, make no mistake, you will be put to death. Trust Zedic and Collin to tell you what you must know, yet ask no more questions."

They bid Trep farewell and slipped out into the midday sun. Isontra leaned on Kairma's arm as they walked home in silence.

Walking down the canyon, the sun bright overhead and the sound of spring birds singing in the trees, they saw a few small cliques of people discussing the resolution made at the morning service. Kairma could feel the eyes of distressed people follow as they walked by. It wasn't a popular decision, but popularity was never one of Isontra's goals. Kairma wondered if she, herself, would ever have the confidence to stand behind an unpleasant choice because she felt it was best. She admired her grandmother's fortitude. Isontra held her silvered head high and smiled as she passed. Few people had the courage to go against the Miral's wishes. As they walked on, Kairma felt the slow warmth of determination swell in her own chest.

The next afternoon Zedic found his father examining the gash in the log Trep had used in his demonstration. Although Tamron thought the karrack was interesting, he was appalled at Kairma's suggestion of letting anyone go to the city. He was anguished by her proposition that Zedic go along with Collin to trade for these weapons. He knew his daughter well, and from her tone knew that the young people had discussed the matter at length.

Seeing his tall son watching him, Tamron asked, "So, you think this karrack is worth risking your life for, and maybe our lives as well?"

Zedic examined the hole in the log. He was holding his hands under his arms so the twitching in his fingers wouldn't betray him, but his voice gave him away. "It isn't that much of a risk. Trep has traveled safely across the land. And the other night Kairma and I were surrounded by Whitish, and even though they outnumbered us they didn't attack."

Tamron turned to his son. "You were protected by the gods. It was a Tribute Moon. Have you already forgotten the pain your sister suffered from the attack only four annums ago?"

"No, Father. Kairma still suffers because she looks more like a White One than one of us. But that night we saw the Whitish going down to take the tribute food. Trep believes those are statues of the Ancient Ones, not gods at all."

Tamron's temper flared and he backhanded his son. "How dare you speak such blasphemy? The gods will surely strike you dead for this nonsense!"

Although Zedic stood half a head taller than his father, the blow caught him off guard and knocked him to the ground. Getting up slowly, he did his best to steady his voice. "I'm sorry, Father. I didn't mean to upset you." He brushed his hair from his eyes and in a tight voice said, "I think there are many things we don't understand about ourselves and our beliefs. We may find answers that have eluded us for generations. Yes, Collin and I would like to go to the city with Trep."

Tamron was shaking with anger. "You have responsibilities. You have only now passed your Seridar. You need to think about your family. Your brothers won't be hunters for at least nine or ten more annums." He had never before struck one of his children. He knew his anger was caused by the fear of losing his son and not because of anything the boy had said. Tamron started to walk away but turned slowly back to Zedic. The life had been hammered out of his voice as he said, "It makes no difference. The elders have decided to keep the stranger, and there is no circumstance that will convince them to let anyone leave. You will stay here."

He left his son standing on the archery field.

Collin found him there, weaving long blades of grass into a net. "You planning to go fishing?"

Zedic looked up, and Collin saw the bright red mark on the side of Zedic's face. "What happened? You run into Efram?"

Zedic's lip curled wryly. "No. I asked my father if I could go to the city."

"You didn't!"

"I did."

"I can see he was all for it." Collin tried to sound flippant, but only succeeded in sounding angry.

"I think I surprised him."

"I *bet* you did!"

"The elders are never going to allow anyone to leave here."

"I can't believe you asked him to go. I know I said I was leaving, but I never dreamed you'd ask Tamron before at least trying to convince Isontra."

"He was looking at the hole Trep's karrack made in the log over there. I thought he looked interested in having a karrack, and it just kind of fell out of my mouth."

Collin looked incredulous. "Zedic, nothing ever just falls out of your mouth. I have to drag it out kicking and screaming."

Zedic gave him a lopsided grin. "Most times."

Collin sat on the log next to Zedic. "So where does that leave us now?"

"We need to get back to the vault. I think there's enough information up there that if we could understand it, we might be able to convince the elders to let us go."

"I can't go for a few more days. I have tanning duty, and Isontra won't let any of us outside until they find that wolf."

Zedic wrinkled his nose. Tanning was a very smelly job. "I drew roof repair this week. I'd offer to trade, but …"

"Sure you would." Collin smiled, and Zedic began to relax.

Collin began working long grasses into a braid to augment the net Zedic had started weaving. "We should make plans anyway. See if we can take Trep to see the temples. Maybe he can kill that wolf with his karrack. Now that'd be something to show the elders! The only time he's been allowed outside of the canyon is to care for his horse. Now that he has his regular guards, I'm not even sure they'll let him do that. I should have realized how the rest of the colony would react to his karrack. I tried to tell him we aren't accepting of strangers."

Zedic stood and stretched his back. "Kairma tells me she and Isontra had *the talk* with him yesterday, after the Nor Day service. If he didn't know it before, he knows it now."

Three days later, Collin, Zedic, and Kairma met on the north side of the west cleansing station. The buildings housed separate cubicles where village members could relieve themselves. The waste ran down into a wide ditch where water from the shower helped wash it away.

In the center of the building was a room where members could shower. A large earthenware barrel held water. By pulling on a rope, the barrel rotated on a stone axel, tipping toward the user. Small holes were drilled into the lip of the barrel causing a sprinkling effect when the water reached the top. In the summer, the sun kept the water a comfortable temperature, and in the winter, a fire under the barrel helped keep the water, if not comfortable, at least not frozen.

"Whew, the scent is potent today. Let's go over to the grain shelter and talk." Collin held his nose and motioned for the others to follow.

Zedic jabbed Collin in the ribs. "See if we ever let you pick the meeting place again."

They checked to see if they had been seen, and then scurried to the top of the old stone building. Pulling Kairma up to the roof, Collin said, "Well, I knew there wouldn't be anyone hanging around to listen to us there. I didn't want to take the chance of being overheard."

Kairma found a comfortable seat, her legs dangling off the side of the low roof. "I don't have much time. I have a lesson soon, and Gramme's not been in good spirits lately. I think she's worried about bringing Trep into the colony. The rest of the elders aren't fully committed to the idea."

Collin's arm brushed hers as he sat next to her and she playfully shoved him with her shoulder. He shoved back until he saw Zedic roll his eyes at him. Kairma giggled and snuck in one more little push. Her husky voice suddenly turned serious. "I think we're safe enough here. So what is this all about?"

Collin glanced at Kairma. She had been so busy over the last few days he hadn't had much time to talk to her. Somehow she seemed older now. He decided it was the responsibility of her position, and he was unexpectedly saddened, knowing their days of skimming stones down at the lake and climbing cliffs were over.

"I'm going to the city with Trep," he said, "but I think we should show the vault to him before I go. Find out what he thinks of those things. Maybe they would make good trade items."

Zedic frowned. "Don't you think he'll start asking questions? What if someone else finds out? Before you know it, we'll either be punished for digging around the Godstones or we'll have the whole village rummaging through our find."

"We don't have to tell anyone else, and Trep couldn't care less about our religious laws. What's the problem?"

Zedic looked at Collin and considered at length. "Trep may not care that we broke a religious law to get these artifacts, but he cares very much about where we found them. I think he would be *most* interested in our find. Maybe even enough to decide he wants to stay here, forever."

Collin blanched. "Zedic, you could be right. I can't let him know about the vault until after we're in the city."

Kairma looked uncomfortable. "Collin, the elders will never let you go to the city. I did my best to convince them the night after the service, but they said no."

Zedic said, "I think you should stay here with me and Kairma. We should try to make sense of what we found. This has got to be the biggest discovery of the last five hundred annums."

Collin got up and started to pace back and forth. The roof span of the stone building was so short he appeared to be walking in circles. "I know it's important. I really do want to study those things, but if I'm going to the city I have to leave soon or I won't get back before the harvest. Trep said it was impossible to cross the plains in the winter. It's now or never."

Shaking his head as he paced, Collin said, "Look, the temples have been there for centuries and have survived just fine. It can't possibly hurt to wait another annum. It has to be kept secret until we get back. I have to get Trep out of here."

Zedic stood up slowly. "Collin, stop pacing, you're making me dizzy." Collin stood still, and Zedic continued, "The only way you'll get to the city is to defy the elders and if they find you, they'll kill you."

Kairma eyes were wide with fright. "Collin, Zedic's right! They'll kill both of you. You can't leave without the elders' permission. I'll do my best to talk them into letting you go, but promise me you won't do anything stupid." She sounded close to tears. "Please, Collin. Give me a couple of weeks to change their minds. If it can be done, I'll do it. You know I will."

Collin pulled Kairma up and threw his arms around her. "I could just kiss you, Kairma! You're the best! Having the elders' permission would mean Zedic could go too." He held her a moment longer than he should have, and then immediately felt awkward. He quickly disengaged and jumped off the low roof. Cheerfully, he said, "Let's go up to the vault tomorrow. I should be finished tanning hides by mid-morning."

Kairma jumped down behind him, almost knocking him over. "Gramme won't let us out of the canyon until she knows there isn't a hungry pack of wolves waiting for us."

Ever graceful, Zedic jumped lightly down from the roof. "She's right, Collin. I think my father might be planning to hunt it down, but I haven't heard any solid plans yet. I'm sure they'll talk about it at the next Nor Day service."

The three comrades headed toward the hospital where Kairma would meet Kinter and Isontra for her afternoon lessons.

Chapter 12

They didn't make it to the vault the next day, or the day after. The tanning took two more days—some jobs couldn't be rushed—and the Nor Day service ate up the next day. Tamron had suggested looking for the wolf, but he didn't appear to be in a hurry. Collin felt he would have to get rid of the wolf himself, or Isontra would never allow his friends to hike up the mountain.

Siede was a few annums older than Collin and one of the few people Collin trusted. Luck had it that they had both drawn cordwood duty at the Nor Day service. This would require them to range pretty far from the canyon, all the wood close by having been used up during the winter months.

When Collin reached Siede's home, the older man was just finishing breakfast. Collin let himself in and sat at the rough-hewn table while Siede gathered his things.

Collin watched Siede tie his long hair in a leather thong. As Siede tied his moccasins, Collin said, "I think you should bring your bow."

Siede paused and looked up at Collin, who wore a bow on his back. Puzzled, Siede said, "We're gathering wood, not hunting."

Collin smiled mischievously. "Well, maybe we should do a little of both. You know that wolf that's been hanging around has made it hard to go fishing and I thought we might see if we could find it."

"Wolves aren't easy to hunt."

"I know. But they like meat. I thought if I took some meat with us, tied it up in a tree, the wolf might come to investigate."

"I think they like to kill their own."

Collin blew out a sigh. "Let's just try it. Neither one of us did very well at the games this annum. Maybe bringing home a trophy like that will help them forget."

"Thanks so much for reminding me. I was trying to forget." He sounded harsh, but the twinkle in his blue-gray eyes admitted the idea had merit. "I'll get my bow, but I think we might be wasting our time."

Once they were outside the northern doors, Collin showed Siede the dead rabbit he had in his pack. "We were about a mile from the Grand Hall when Kairma saw the wolf. I'm guessing it's got a den nearby."

They walked through the trees about a mile from the north end of the hospital. Collin pointed to a low ancient wall. "Kairma said she saw it over there. First thing we need to do is see if it's still around. I've been practicing my howling since I was ten. Let's hope it pays off." He climbed up the hill behind the stone barricade. "Watch my back. She might not be far away."

Siede felt his skin crawl when Collin began to howl. It was an almost perfect imitation, and to have it come from ten feet away sent chills down his back.

After about five minutes Collins throat was beginning to hurt. He was about to suggest they move deeper into the forest when the answer came—and it was close.

Collin burst out laughing. "It worked!"

He jogged back to Siede. "Now we bait the trap." Colin pointed to a tree fifty feet away. "You can get in that tree over there. I'm going to get up that tree on the other side of the trap. I'll call her again. If she's close, trying to challenge me, I'll switch to squeaking like a wounded rabbit. I'll leave the rabbit here tied to a string. If she comes into the clearing, I can pull on the rabbit. That should take her mind off looking for me."

Siede began to move off toward his tree. "Let's hope she's alone. We won't get more than one shot."

They found their places among the trees and Collin howled once more. After a minute he was answered with yipping and barking. It still sounded like only one animal. Collin tried to squeak, but his voice was too raw. Siede took over and did a fair dying rabbit.

The wolf took the bait and cautiously moved into the clearing. Collin pulled on the string and the wolf jumped at the moving bait. Collin's arrow caught the predator in the flank, but Siede's arrow went deep into the chest.

She didn't die quickly so Siede used his knife to finish the job lest she suffer needlessly. "She's an old one. Tell Kairma not to worry about pups."

Collin came to his side and they began the arduous tasks of skinning the animal. If meat was scarce they would have eaten it, but carnivores aren't the best tasting. The hawks and vultures would finish off what the men didn't take.

The hide was a little mangy, but it would still make a warm winter cloak. Even though he had made the kill, Siede offered the skin to Collin. "I never would have had a shot at her if you hadn't sounded like a love-starved alpha."

Collin gladly took the hide. He was rooster proud.

When the young men showed the hide to the rest of the colony at the Gathering House, Siede made a point of telling everyone how Collin had lured the she-wolf to her knees. "I thought she was going to mate with him right there in the clearing."

Collin demonstrated his eerie wolf call until he had no voice at all. Fortunately, lots of wine helped sooth his raw throat.

Chapter 13

Over the next few days, Collin and Zedic tried to get up to the vault as often as their chores would allow. Kairma's lessons usually kept her securely locked inside the canyon walls, but on occasion, she convinced her grandmother to allow her to search for herbs near the temples and managed to get away for the afternoon.

Collin wanted to take a few silver cylinders to trade in the city, but Kairma convinced him to leave them in the vault. "You won't want someone to see these and start asking where you got them, besides, if you take them to the city I won't be able to figure out what was written on them." After several trips to the vault, Collin had only a few odd-shaped pieces of metal, some wood writing utensils, and a colorful mug made of a hard but lightweight material.

Zedic's father had taken an interest in Zedic's free time and Kairma's lessons were daily, so the time Collin spent alone was considerable. He spent much of his time near the lake where he'd found a cache of pretty, colored stones annums ago. Many of the stones were cut into fascinating shapes, like miniature crystals. When he showed Trep his favorite stones, the traveler said that they were valuable and the people of Peireson Landing would be willing to trade wonderful things for them. Knowing the stones were actually worth something to someone else made Collin feel a lot better about all the time he'd spent digging and diving for them over the annums.

Coming back from one of his forays near the caves, Collin, lugging a substantial leather bag of his precious rocks on his back, saw Naturi clearing weeds from the water canals that separated the fields. He set his burden down under a tall blue spruce and waved. When Naturi acknowledged him, Collin said, "Naturi, come take a break. You work too hard. Makes the rest of us look lazy."

Naturi could see Collin was in a good mood and was curious why he'd come to speak to him, especially after the way he'd trounced Collin at the Awakening contest. *He was really mad, but how could he have thought it would be different? I have not lost a hand-to-hand contest in four annums.* He wiped his hands on a soft piece of leather and dabbed the sweat from his forehead. He could use a break. He had been working all morning and, by the looks of things, he would still be clearing weeds for the next few days.

Grabbing his lunch pack from under the edge of a nearby rock where he'd put it to keep it out of the sun, he went to join Collin. Naturi tried, but failed, to keep the accusation out of his tone when he asked, "What have you been doing the past few days? We sure could have used some help. The last snow washed about a thousand kilos of debris into the canals."

Collin's eyes narrowed for a moment, and then his smile returned. "I drew cleansing stations duty yesterday. He handed Naturi a waterskin fashioned from the stomach of a longhorn bull and motioned for him to have a seat in the shade. "It was tanning the week before that. It seems like you're the only one who always draws field duty."

Naturi lowered himself onto the log. He took a deep drank from the waterskin. "I often draw other duty, but there is always someone willing to trade." After carefully tying the top closed, he handed the skin back to Collin.

Collin nodded in understanding. There were certain duties everyone tried to trade out whenever possible. He motioned to the sack on the ground at his feet. "Today I've been busy collecting the rocks Trep told us about. The ones he said were valuable. I've got a whole sack here. Trep says we can buy a karrack with just one or two of the smallest ones and I've got dozens here." Collin leaned back against the tree and smiled.

Naturi stretched out his long muscular legs and rubbed the back of his neck, his eye twitching again. "Why do you say such silly things? You know the elders will never let you or Trep leave!"

"I'm just making sure I'm ready if I ever get the chance."

Naturi knotted his fists as he turned toward Collin. "The teachings are very clear in regards to leaving the colony!" He took a deep breath, and said in a gentler tone, "I know we have not been the best of friends recently, but just talking like this can be reason enough to have you put to death."

"But if they said you could go, wouldn't you want to get some of the things Trep has? I know Zedic wants to go."

"Vice Miral Jettena would never let her son leave."

Collin's eyes twinkled, and his cheeks dimpled slightly. "We all know who wields the power in that family."

Naturi shook his head. "I find it difficult to believe Miral Isontra will ever be in favor of allowing anyone to leave."

"Times change," Collin said as he sorted through his collection of rocks. "I haven't talked with Isontra for a while, but ..." He examined a deep green cut stone in the sunlight. "From what Kairma tells me, Gramme's very interested in Trep's knowledge." Seeming satisfied, he returned the stone and tied the sack closed again.

Naturi grimaced at the blatant use of the familiar. "*Miral* Isontra has encouraged a number of changes in her time, but I will not go against the teachings of the Word."

Collin stood up. "I's just wonderin'. It's really not important at all, 'specially since no one can leave. Right?" Collin took his leather sack of stones and headed toward Trep's cabin.

Naturi watched Collin saunter away while whistling a familiar tune. It irritated him that Collin never used proper titles, and he found

Collin's attempt to imitate Trep's speech patterns especially annoying. He vowed that when he was made Comad, Collin *would* call him *Sir,* or *Comad Naturi.*

Naturi went back to cleaning weeds from the canal, but the more he thought about what Collin had proposed, the more uncomfortable he became. However, it wasn't the thought of leaving the canyon that was giving him second thoughts. Possession of the new weapons would be a major boon to the colony, and Collin's name had been on every tongue since he'd come home with that wolf skin a week ago. Naturi found himself torn between wanting to stop Collin from leaving and wanting to bring back those gifts himself. Just the right word in the right ear, and the annoying Collin would never be a threat to him again. But if he did so, he would also lose the chance to gain the karracks. Collin was also Kairma's friend, and if she discovered he had anything to do with Collin's demise, she would never forgive him.

Coming home from the Nor Day service, Collin walked with Kairma and Zedic. They had been to the vault three more times during the past week and noticed the inside of the vault had similar features to the two temples above the amphitheater. Collin suggested they take Trep up to the temples. "He could tell us a lot about those buildings. He's been studying ancient ruins for a long time."

Zedic shook his head. "Maybe it should wait until we know more about Trep. We should keep it to ourselves."

It was Collin's turn to frown. "I'm not suggesting we show him the vault, yet. I don't want him too interested to leave if we get the chance. I want to show him the temples. Maybe he can tell us how they were made, and we'll learn more about our vault."

Kairma touched Collin's arm lightly. "I agree. We should show him the temples, but I want to go with you. I want to see for myself what he's like."

Zedic shook his head again. "No, the Crystal has to stay here. Collin and I will take him."

"No," she said flatly, "I'm going with you. I'll hide the Crystal someplace safe."

Collin grinned mischievously, winking at her. "Boo, you little law breaker, are my rogue ways rubbing off on you? Seriously, though, you can't hide the Crystal. What if something were to happen to you? The Crystal could be lost forever."

"I can tell Naturi where I've hidden it. He plans to be the next Comad. He should know where it is."

The casualness of her words cut him like a new blade. Without meeting her eyes, he said, "Right, and he'll tell Tamron before you make it out the north door."

"The only other choice is Kinter."

"Kinter is as likely to tell on you as Naturi—she just has different motives."

Kairma crossed her arms. "I'll make sure she won't tell anyone."

"What are you going to promise her this time? She's already attending your lessons. What more can you offer her?"

"I'll think of something."

There was a long silence before Collin asked, "Well, what are you going to tell her?"

"I'm thinking. Give me a moment." She chewed on her lower lip.

Zedic nodded thoughtfully. "You know how much she hates to make soap."

"Ugh! There's a reason she hates to make soap! *I* hate to make soap!"

"It's either soap or stay home."

Kairma grumbled as she went to find Kinter. Her sister took the bribe easily and for a moment Kairma thought she was going to betray her the moment she left for the temples. But Kairma's anxiousness was put to rest when Kinter said, "You keep following Collin into danger and leaving the Crystal with me. One day you won't come back. All I need do is wait."

Kairma shrugged off the words, but part of her feared she might be right.

As a member of the Healing family, Zedic wasn't required to place his name in the weekly duty lottery, but like his father he felt better joining the community in regular chores. Zedic had drawn tanning duty yesterday, so Collin went to the tanning house to help him as he usually did when his own chores were light. Since the majority of the hides had been cleaned and tanned the first week, Zedic's job was repairing equipment.

Picking up a spool of hemp string, Zedic asked, "Are you finished already?"

Collin held the corner of a frame together as Zedic secured it with new string. Collin said, "I had the pleasure of fixing the leather hinges on the Gathering House door this morning. I think they should leave the doors off when the weather gets warm, then we wouldn't have to replace them as often."

"I had to replace the ones on the hospital a few weeks ago. We either need a better system or buffalo with tougher hides."

"I was hoping to see if we could take Trep up to the temples tomorrow."

Tying off the end of the string, Zedic shook his head. "Kairma said she wanted to go with us. We'd better see if she can get away before we make any plans."

"She can go the next time."

"Collin, I have to live with her. You don't." He put the frame in the storage area. "She should be ready for lunch soon. We'll go press Gramme for her freedom."

They found Kairma eating a light snack in the dining room of the Chancery. It wasn't Isontra they had to convince to let Kairma go, it was Kinter. Kinter was bored and wanted to tag along, but after an elaborate story about visiting with Trep and learning how to use the karrack, Kinter decided she didn't want to go with them after all.

The trio arrived at Trep's cabin where Kairma stood in the doorway like a rabbit ready to bolt at the first sign of danger. She was nervous because Trep studied her from the corner of his eye.

The strange man said, "Come on in. Have somethin' to eat. I was just making some flat bread." Loren, one of Trep's regular guards, rolled out dough at the table.

Helping himself to some warm bread, Collin said, "We thought you might like to go see the temples tomorrow." Collin nodded to the guard and added reassuringly, "Zedic and Kairma will be with him. You can come if you'd like."

Loren shook his head. "Graveyards are for the dead."

Trep couldn't hide his excitement. "Thought y'all'd never ask!"

Collin said, "I have chores to finish, but I'll come for you when I can." He grabbed Kairma by the hand and led her from the cabin.

Kairma turned in time to see a bemused Zedic follow them out the door.

Once they were out of hearing range, Collin turned to Kairma. "See. I told you we could trust him."

Kairma shoved Collin playfully. "We weren't there two moments. You can't judge someone's character in two moments' time."

"Yeah," Zedic said, "I thought you were finished with your chores. What gives?"

"I am, but I forgot he'd have a guard and I didn't want to say much in front of Loren. Trep will need to pack some things, but it didn't sound like we'd have trouble getting him away from his guards."

Zedic picked up a rock and threw it as far as he could. "Collin, we're taking him to the temples and back."

Kairma's lower lip puckered. "You promised you would give me a couple weeks to convince Isontra to let you go. Don't you dare take off with Trep!"

Collin wrapped a muscular arm around Kairma's shoulder and leaned near her ear. "You have one more week, then I have to go."

Two days later, Kairma was no closer to convincing the elders to let Trep return to the city, and Isontra had warned her not to bring it up again. She wanted to know what Trep thought of the temples, but she also hoped he would be so intrigued he wouldn't want to leave. It seemed the only way to keep Collin safe. Collin hadn't arranged for the trip up the mountain and time was running out.

It was late in the afternoon when Trep usually went to care for his horse. Kairma was sitting on the front porch of the Chancery when Trep walked by. Loren was at his side as usual. Kairma motioned for the two men to have a seat.

Loren shook his head. "I need to get home now. Joel should be here soon to take over the watch. Will he be okay here with you until then?"

Kairma nodded. "He'll be fine. We haven't had much time to talk." Over the weeks, Collin had told her so much about the man that he felt less like a stranger come to visit. She still didn't fully trust him but did her best not to show it.

Trep lowered himself onto one of the wooden chairs. "I'm mighty glad to see ya here 'cause I was hopin' to find out if we were ever gonna visit the temples. Y'all come by two days ago. What happened?"

Kairma waved good-bye to Loren as he left. Turning to face Trep, she said, "My lessons keep me pretty busy, and I told the boys I would be going with you."

"That's good news. I'd like to get to know y'all a little better." He blew out a sigh. "Yeah, I'd very much like that. Ya know, I saw those carvin's from a distance when I first got here, but never got a chance to see 'em up close. After Collin introduced me to the village, I ain't been allowed outside for any more than takin' care of Belle."

"I know. I'm sorry it has to be that way. I hope you'll understand someday. I'd love to take you today, but now we'll have to wait until Zedic or Collin can get away from their duties long enough to join us." She rolled her eyes playfully. "Rules, you know. I can't leave the canyon by myself any more than you can."

"'Cause you're one of the Healers?"

"Yes. They don't trust me not to get into trouble. I'll talk to Zedic tonight. Maybe we can go up there in the morning. The moon will be full next Nor Day so the men are preparing for an extended hunt. I'll be required to take the tribute to the temples tomorrow, and I think I can convince Zedic and Collin to bring you along." She knew Kinter would be glad to stay home and mind the Crystal for her.

Trep saw Joel walking toward the Chancery and got up to meet his new guard. "Ya know, someday y'all are gonna get tired of babysittin' me."

Joel greeted Kairma and Trep. "I'm already tired of it. Shall we go? It's your turn to cook supper."

Trep winked at Kairma. "Don't let him fool ya. He loves my cookin'. Tonight we're gonna have pheasant rolled in cornmeal and mulberry wine." Turning to Joel, he asked, "Is the little missus comin' over tonight?"

Joel nodded.

Kairma watched them walk away. *All in all, things could be worse for Trep.*

❦

Kairma spent the next morning in the clearing south of the Grand Hall accepting the tributes from the members of the colony, while thinking how to keep Collin from running away with Trep. She and Zedic would be no match for him if he were set on leaving. She'd been able to convince Zedic to come with her today, and bring Trep along. She wasn't sure if her plan to entice Trep would work. Zedic told her that Collin would wait the full week, but she paced uneasily as she placed a loaf of bread in the old wooden cart and thanked the young boy who'd brought it.

Other tributes were brought and soon the cart was filled. She waited to see if Zedic would be able to get Trep away from his guard for the day, but when the sun began to beat down through the spring leaves she decided to use the cleansing room before the long hike up the mountain.

Collin and Zedic found Trep in his cabin, playing some kind of dice game with Hamond. Trep was excited when the boys told him they were finally taking him to see the temples.

Trep had been making his way toward the mountain when he met Collin. Little did he know that by accepting Collin's offer of food, he would be taken prisoner in a small village. Escaping wouldn't have been difficult, but Trep learned early on that a man gets more information when people liked him. Somewhere in the back of his mind he knew he would have to find a way to escape one day, but, for now, he was happy to study these bizarre people.

Chapter 14

At first, Hamond had been unsure about letting the boys take his prisoner, but Zedic handed Trep's weapon to the guard, and that seemed to satisfy him. Collin's plan to take off with Trep and Zedic had been abruptly halted when Zedic insisted on accompanying Kairma to the temples today. He hadn't had time to prepare Trep for their departure, and he couldn't leave Kairma alone at the temples.

As they walked toward the Chancery, Trep said, "I'm not real comfortable leavin' my karrack behind. Ya never know when ya might need to defend yourself."

Collin spit out a blade of grass he'd been chewing. "We'll watch your back. We make this trip often. There's nothing to fear."

Zedic nodded. "Even Kairma and Kinter go to the Godstones by themselves."

In the distance, Collin could see the full tribute cart and looking up at the mid-morning sun he asked, "Speaking of Kairma, where is she?"

Zedic pointed back up the canyon where a slightly clumsy white-haired girl was running to catch up with them. She tripped over something in the road and fell. Scrambling to her feet and lifting her skirt high above her knees, she began running in earnest.

When she reached them, she was panting hard and unaware of the blood dripping from a skinned knee. "I have the tributes ready to go. Kinter said she would be happy not to go with me this time. We have to make soap day after tomorrow and…" She glared and her point was well established with the two boys. "I hate making soap."

Collin and Zedic just grinned.

A moment later, Collin looked down at her knee and began searching his pack for something to clean the cut. Following his gaze, Kairma looked down, embarrassed that they had seen her trip. She dropped her skirt. "It's okay. It's only a scrape." She used her skirt to wipe away the blood. "There. It's better now."

Zedic rolled his eyes, and Collin laughed. Kairma blushed and tried to act as if she didn't care. She purposefully strode ahead and tripped on a root sticking up in the path. Collin grabbed her before she could fall, and as she pressed into him, his body reacted suddenly to her warm soft skin touching his bare arms. It angered him that his body would betray him at the most inopportune times, and over the most absurd things. Feeling the heat rise to his face, and hoping the others hadn't noticed, he let go of her and walked quickly ahead until he had his emotions under control once more.

Kairma had barely regained her balance and called to him, "What's the hurry Collin? Wait for us!"

Collin didn't slow down. "It's past noon and if we want to do any real exploring we need to hurry."

The rest of the group trotted quickly to catch up with Collin.

When they reached the Grand Hall, Kairma grabbed the handle of the wooden cart of food. Before she'd gone ten paces, Trep had taken her burden from her. Inside, Jettena was airing out the room and dusting various oddities that lined the shelves and sat on the table.

Trep pulled up short, dumfounded. The previous times he'd passed through the hospital, the shelves had been covered with draperies. Now, piled in the middle of the long conference table, he saw what had been stored in the darkness along with medicines. It was the largest collection of ancient artifacts he'd ever seen outside of a museum. There were several ceramic mugs with colorful pictures of the Godstones, and on each one, in beautiful gold script, was the ancient writing. There were matching plates, metal spoons, and an array of odd statues in rose quartzite and tourmaline. Trep would have given anything to have a few minutes to examine the artifacts. He sighed. *Never fear. I* will *be back.*

Jettena saw him staring in wonder at the collection. "The gods are good to their children. These items have been passed from generation to generation for several hundred annums now." She held up the plate Trep was gawking at, cautious not to stand too close to him. "Most of these were found in the temples. There was a storehouse of goods left for us. Nor knew his children would come and He provided for us." She let him hold the delicate plate.

"Will we find more of these things at the temples we're gonna visit?"

"No. I think over the annums we have brought them all here. It's not safe to leave things to the weather and dust. Who knows how many things have been lost already." It wasn't a question.

Trep couldn't agree more. He smiled and thanked her for letting him examine the precious artifact.

"Please be careful with my children. They're worth much more to me than all of this." She waved her hand across the table. Zedic's cheeks flushed and Kairma loosed an exaggerated sigh.

"I'll do my best ma'am. I'm pretty partial to them myself." He set the plate down gently with a slight bow to Jettena. When they reached the last door of the hospital, each of them looked up to the massive Godstones framed there like a living picture.

Trep said, "I noticed y'all use the artifacts from the temples in your daily lives, ya know, plates and cups. Do y'all have so many that ya don't care to keep 'em safe?"

Zedic shrugged. "We use them when they lose their markings, or when time begins to crack them. At one time, there were hundreds of them."

Trep stopped short. "Hundreds?"

"Yes. Many of them have been damaged, but Mother still protects the ones in good condition as best she can."

Trep's thoughts strayed to the artifact collector he knew in the city. That man would give his right arm to have such a collection.

Zedic helped Trep carry the cart down the stairs to the ground level. "As they turned away from the lake, Trep asked, "Shouldn't I get Belle?"

Collin replied, "Not this time."

Kairma looked up sharply at Collin, but didn't say whatever was on her mind.

After about a mile and a half, the trail widened enough for the four of them to walk abreast. Collin and Zedic were seeing who could kick a rock farther when Trep turned to Kairma and said, "Seems strange that I'm y'all's only prisoner."

Kairma sounded embarrassed. "Sorry, I guess it would be better if we had a way to warn people away from here. It really is rare that we have to take someone prisoner."

"I seem to be the only one who's come along in more than ten years."

"My father came here as a stranger."

"Really? He looks jess like the rest of y'all. I thought he was part of y'all's tribe."

"He's of Efpec blood."

Trep tilted his head as he considered her words. "Efpec blood?"

"Yes, we are all of the same blood."

Trep thought about it for a long time as they continued to walk.

As they strolled up the broad path to the west, Zedic explained the finer points of the temples. The ancient buildings were made from quarried granite of gray and rose. Although the roofs had been lost hundreds of annums ago, most of the walls were intact with the exception of the large stones the Survinees had used to augment their homes. In the most recent times, taking anything from the temple grounds was forbidden, but Collin, never one to follow the rules, had found a cache of gemstones by digging out some of the temple floor.

After a couple of more miles of hiking, they reached the granite ridge where they could once again see the faces carved in the mountaintop. Trep pulled up short. "Well, dance on my grandmother's grave! I never even suspected they were this big! I'm only a pimple on their noses!"

Collin grinned. "And a little pimple at that!"

In awe, Trep said, "Each face must be 'least fifty to sixty feet tall."

Kairma came to stand beside him. "It makes you feel insignificant, doesn't it?"

Trep sobered. "That it does. *That* it does. This is amaaazin'."

"Come on," Collin called to them. "Wait till you see inside the temples!"

Once they reached the ruins, they climbed over fallen stone and entered the building on the right. Trep took measurements, drawing the layout of the buildings on his hemp pad.

Zedic and Kairma took the tributes to the terrace and set it out on the granite parapet that served as the upper altar. Below, the ancient stone seats spilled out, meeting hundreds of graves at the base of the carved mountain. Kairma said the blessing over the tributes and returned to find Collin digging in another corner of the temple, looking for buried treasure.

The sound of karracks firing and men shouting interrupted the peaceful afternoon and everyone scrambled to find a place to hide inside of one of the two temples. From the top of the thick granite wall, they could see the trail below. Four men on horseback were riding hard, westward, firing their weapons over their shoulders. Behind them, ten or more White Ones gave chase on foot, bows drawn and arrows flying. An arrow brought down a buckskin horse. The leading White Ones quickly overcame the small rider.

As the men drew even with the stairs of the temples, one of the arrows pierced the leg of the lead rider. He stayed upright in his saddle as deadly arrows brought down a second man. In less than a heartbeat, the first two were around the bend and out of sight.

Kairma turned to the men with her. "Who are they? Why are they here?" Having never seen a man killed, she was in shock. "They killed that man." Her body shook as a cold tremor swept through her.

Trep whispered, afraid there might be other men nearby. "They come from the city."

Anger flared in Kairma's pale eyes. "You know these men? Did you bring them here?"

"No. I jess recognize the saddles. They look like the ones they make in Peireson Landin' and I think I've seen the red-haired man before."

"What do they want? Why are they here?"

"I'm sure they wanted to see the temples here, same as me. Y'all have no idea what an incredible find this is. There's a man in the city who would pay top dollar for information 'bout this."

As they watched, several White Ones collected the two dead men and began to carry them. They also carried one of their own who had been killed. Kairma's mouth began to sweat, and her stomach gurgled, dangerously close to rejecting her light lunch. Her voice was barely audible. "What are they going to do with those men? Do you think they're going to eat them?"

Collin shook his head. "I don't think so, but it's odd. You don't usually see the Whitish in the light. It looks like they're bringing them up here to the temples."

The travelers held their breath and crouched down on the top of the wall as the White Ones filed past, carrying the dead men.

Zedic softly whispered, "They're taking them down to the lower altar."

The creatures continued past the upper altar, climbing down the seats and stopping at the stage below where they placed the dead men on the lower altar. Deep afternoon shadows hid the fullness of the stage from view, but the intent was obvious. Once there, the White Ones laid the men out on one of the seats and began to cover the dead men with the loose stones left over from carving the mountain.

Kairma's heart pounded in her chest. "They're burying them. They must have seen us bury our dead, and they're copying us." She was, at once, appalled and amazed.

Collin nudged Zedic. "They only buried two men. The other two must have gotten away."

Trep rolled to his side, facing Collin. "Those men'll be back, and they'll bring help next time. Most likely they hadn't figured on runnin' into opposition here."

It took a long time, but once finished with their task, the White Ones filed past the ancient granite wall where the Survinees lay hidden and disappeared into the long, early evening shadows of the forest.

Trep sat up and said, "If y'all don't want a hundred or so strangers comin' to investigate this site, y'all better stop those men before they get to the city."

Collin said, "They're headed west, and there's only one way off this mountain in that direction. We can get Toric and some of the other men to track them down."

Zedic cringed. "Most of the men left on the hunt this morning."

Pulling the cart from the altar, Kairma said, "I didn't see Toric go with them. He stopped by yesterday complaining of a trick knee. Isontra has him resting it."

Taking the cart from Kairma, Zedic asked Trep, "Those men were heading west, but the city's to the east of us, isn't it?"

Trep nodded. "Yeah, but most likely they'll circle 'round the back side of this here peak and head back east. Y'all will never catch 'em without horses."

"Toric's a good tracker."

"I'm shore he is, but I know where they're headed. I can show you where to cut 'em off. The city's a long way from here, and y'all would never make it there without my help."

Collin climbed down off the wall. "I'm going with you."

Kairma tried to jump down the last couple feet and stumbled into Collin, knocking them both over. "Sorry. I misjudged that last drop." Collin helped her up, and she dusted herself off, saying, "The elders will never allow it. For the entire past moon, I've been trying to convince them to let you go to the city with Trep to get weapons like the one he carries. They're going to think this is only a ruse."

Trep went to pick up the hemp pad he'd dropped. "We could dig up one of those boys there. That should be proof enough."

Kairma grimaced. "I was thinking of something a little easier to transport."

Collin picked up his pack and joined Trep at the base of the wall. The dead buckskin horse was about sixty feet away. "How about we take the saddle off that horse the Whitish killed?"

Kairma nodded. That should do for proof enough. "It's going to be dark soon. Even Toric can't track well in the dark."

Trep unsaddled the horse with difficulty. The animal was heavy and the stirrup was caught under its dead weight. Trep cursed. "It upsets me to see such a fine animal killed." With the help of Collin and Zedic the saddle finally came free. "This here belonged to a professional rider. See how much smaller and lighter it is than mine." No one there had studied Trep's gear enough to see the difference, but Trep seemed impressed. Hoisting the saddle over his shoulder, he said, "This cost that man a chunk of money." The Survinees didn't really understand what he was talking about as he joined them on the eastward trail.

Kairma knew the White Ones were still nearby. There was that similar sense of apprehension, like a dull ache in her chest and a tightening in her shoulders. She moved as quickly as she could in the lowering light. Before they turned at the bend in the trail, Kairma looked back and saw a dozen White Ones, blood on their pale hands and bare feet as they cut the dead horse into pieces.

Chapter 15

When they reached the Grand Hall, Jettena could tell something had gone wrong. Before she could ask, Zedic and Kairma took off to find the elders.

Setting the saddle on the floor by the long conference table where Jettena was finishing her dusting, Trep said, "I think I should let the others explain."

Jettena turned to Collin, who shook his head. "I'll let Zedic tell you." He went to the hearth to add a few small logs to the bed of coals. Not really addressing anyone, Collin said, "This will likely be a long meeting. Might as well get comfortable."

Jettena paced. Several minutes later eight people filed into the Grand Hall and took seats at the oak table.

When Zedic explained what had happened while taking the tributes to the temple, worried looks plagued every face in the room. He urged, "We have to stop them from reaching the city. Trep says they will bring back a lot more men to study the temples. It will only be a matter of time before they find us here."

All eyes searched out the stranger. Trep cleared his throat and explained why he was sure the men would return. "That mountain can be seen for miles and I'm not the first one to see it. I heard about it from another traveler. Most folks thought he was touched in the head, but I had to make shore. Never dreamed it would be this big a find. Those men will go back and tell others, and they will be believed this time. If y'all want to keep this place a secret, ya best stop those men from ever tellin' another soul about this place."

The Law of Fontas was often referred to in their daily lives, although it had not been invoked for several generations. The need to stop the men was not the issue. It was the genuine fear of chasing these hostile men across unknown lands that concerned the Survinees.

Collin stepped away from the wall, adjusted his clothing, and formally addressed the Healing family. "This is a risk we have to take. Trep has offered to lead us. He says that he knows where we can find these men because he knows where they're headed. It may be a journey of several days, but Trep's been able to cross the plains without harm. You only need to decide who will accompany him, someone you can trust to ensure Survin is not compromised—and someone who will ensure Trep's return. I'm willing to go and bring back these men, dead or alive, as you wish."

Jettena was caught off guard when her oldest son, Zedic, stood and addressed her directly. "Trep tells us Naturi's drawings could be traded for goods. If we go as far as the plains, we should consider bringing back more than dead men. There are karracks and fine cloth in the city too. I know you don't want us to go there, but think of what we can bring back for Survin." Zedic nodded to Collin and sat down on a chair by the wall.

Jettena was appalled. "No! You will *not* go to the city. We have everything we need right here."

Kairma took a deep breath and let it out slowly. "Zedic makes a valid argument. If the men have to go that far to capture the Madics, why not let them bring back the new weapons as well?"

Jettena tersely addressed Kairma. "Your point has been made…" She now scowled at Collin. "Numerous times!"

An old man stood, taking a few moments to compose his words before speaking. At ninety-eight-annums-old, Noah needed to hold on to the large table to steady himself. "I understand wanting to stop these men, but it would be suicide to travel that far. We have the White Ones to consider. You know how nasty a Whitey can be? How can we risk such an uncertain trip if we don't even know if we'll gain anything from it? I say, let those men go and good riddance."

Collin motioned to the stranger standing beside him against the cold gray wall of stone. "Trep tells us the men will return and bring others with them. One of the riders was wounded. That may slow them down a little, and if they have to go around the peak to the north that will give us a good opportunity to cut them off."

Naturi stood, giving the elders a formal greeting. "Miral Isontra, Vice Miral Jettena, I believe you should consider me for this venture. I am excellent with a bow and a knife, and my hand-to-hand skills are above reproach. I could bring back these things you desire."

The murmuring of the crowd grew louder when Toric walked to the front. "These men already have several hours lead on us. Naturi is his own man. If he wishes to throw his life away on a foolhardy adventure, I can't stop him, but ..." He glared at Trep. "A fine cap cannot replace a son!" With that, he put on the cap with the large hole in it and turned to leave the meeting.

An errant thought crossed Jettena's mind. *If Collin is gone when Kairma's Seridar comes, I won't have to worry about the two of them doing something foolish. Naturi will surely best any other contestant, and Kairma hasn't shown an interest in anyone else.* Placing a hand on Toric's arm, she stopped him from leaving. "Naturi cannot leave. He has made it known he wishes to contend for Kairma this Harvest Moon. I'll not agree to risk him on a venture like this." She turned to Naturi. "I know you see this as a duty, a way to protect us, but your first duty is to become a father and our future Comad."

Trep stepped gingerly to the table. He wasn't one of the decision makers, but he had a lot to say that might change their minds. "If y'all chose to let me lead you, I know we can catch the men. They have horses, so it won't be quick, but I do know where they're goin' and I can move pretty fast. They're gonna have to follow the river east and

I know that river pretty good. If I only take a couple men with me, we can catch them." He paused for a moment, his hat in his hand as he looked to Isontra. "I only ask one thing of y'all. I left a woman in Peireson Landin' and I really, really want to bring her back with me. If we get close to the city, would y'all let me get her? Please?"

Isontra's steel gray eyes burned into his. "It is your intention to return to us then?"

Trep was quick to smile. "Yeah, I would like to come back here. Y'all are fine folk with good morals. Hell, I'd stay on a good long time if y'all'd have me. There's so much to study here. It's jess that my girl is expectin' me to come back to her. And I really do miss her. I've been gone two years now."

Isontra studied the rugged face of the traveler, debating how much she wanted him to know about their situation. "I don't like this. I feel as if I've been backed into a corner. I know the Madics have to be stopped. It is also true that our people have been here for many generations, with very little diversity. Our homes are not filled with many children so the introduction of a new family line would be most welcome, but I hesitate to send out young men so far from home."

Collin insisted. "Zedic and I are fully aware of the danger and we will take every precaution necessary to return Trep and his woman safely to Survin. While we are in the city, we can also dispel any tales about the Godstones." He looked intently at Jettena. "But if we don't do something about those men, by this time next annum we may have hundreds of Madics swarming our home."

Isontra glanced at Collin, and then at Zedic, and then she addressed Trep. "It is because of this that I will allow you to take Collin and Zedic. Keeping them here on the mountain will only prolong the inevitable a few more generations. During this trip, you will be given the chance to prove your heart." She folded her hands on the table in front of her. She paused for a moment, feeling anxious about what she was proposing. "If you should find yourself very near the city, you may trade for some of these weapons you showed us. Once done, you and your lady friend may return to us as Survinees."

Kairma's tone was somber. "Thank you, Miral Isontra. The men should go now, before those Madics get too far away." Turning to Trep she asked, "What should we give you to trade for those weapons?"

Trep visibly relaxed now. "Cole showed me a few nuggets of a gold rock he claims is rather common 'round here. I've also seen some other gems he has. I think the charm he wears, the green stone in the wooden eagle claw, now, that might fetch a good price too. In the city they use these stones in jewelry. And there's that little ring that appears to have been made by the Ancient Ones. That would be worth a great deal. Y'all could use these things to buy karracks and metal pans too."

Isontra implored, "Trep, you're our best chance of success. Let us please have our sons back before the Harvest Moon."

Jettena relented, but there was real bitterness in her tone. "If you think this is best, I won't stand in your way. But you had best see to it that nothing happens to my son!"

Pushing a long dark lock of hair away from Jettena's blue gray eyes, Tamron said, "Indeed! The time has come for Zedic to make his own choices, in life as in death, and time changes many generations. We did our best to raise our children to have good sense. All we can do now is hope we taught them well."

Tears threatened to break through Jettena's austere demeanor. "Why did this traveler have to come here and fill our children's heads with strange ideas?"

Tamron sighed heavily, touching two fingers to his head, then to four corners on the table, then his lips. In silent prayer, the others did the same.

With the decision made, the elders left the room to let Trep, Collin, Zedic, and Kairma discuss the logistics of the journey.

Kairma rubbed her temples as she watched the elders file out of the Grand Hall. Although she had sought this decision for weeks, once made, she wanted to undo it. It took a moment for her to realize that she was jealous of her brother. Zedic and Collin would be seeing strange places while she spent the summer alone. She looked up when Trep suggested a few of the ceramic mugs that lined the shelves would be good for trading.

Zedic frowned. "Those are religious objects. Mother would never let me take them, but I do have some that Grimly made last annum."

Trep shook his head. It's the ancient writing on 'em that makes 'em so valuable. Y'all have so many, couldn't we take one or two?"

Zedic closed the curtain over the mugs and plates. "If we end up near the city, and are in the position to convince the people that the great carved mountain is a myth, we best not take anything that would lead them to believe otherwise."

Trep sighed. "Y'all are right. I wasn't thinkin'. I'd love to have those beautiful mugs appraised by a genuine collector, but y'all are right—that would only lead to more questions." He walked to the door. "Make sure y'all have enough food and water for several days, and Collin, bring those gemstones ya showed me."

Once Trep went back to his cabin where they were to meet in a few hours, Kairma turned to her two dearest friends. "With the two of you gone, how will I figure out what all those things are in the vault? I can read some of the writing, but I can't go there alone. I really need someone here to help me."

Collin went to the table where Kairma sat and grabbed her hands. He looked pleadingly into her eyes. "You have to promise not to let anyone else know about the vault. Promise me, Kairma! No one can know about it until I get back!"

"*Okay, okay.* I won't tell anyone!" She started to pull her hands away, but Collin gave them a slight squeeze and leaned his face close to hers.

"I'll be coming back with the answers you're looking for. Promise to wait for me, Kairma."

Staring at his lips only inches away, Kairma wondered what it would be like to kiss him.

Collin looked over at Zedic. "I've already gathered some of the small gemstones and gold rock. I'll get my bow when I pack extra clothing. Kairma can make sure no one finds the temple while we're gone."

He looked pointedly at her again, and Kairma sighed. "Don't worry. I'll keep quiet until the Harvest Moon, but you had better be back by then." Dejected, she said, "Gramme will keep me busy all summer and with Kinter as my shadow I can't do much research anyway. Your secret's safe with me."

Getting up from the conference table, Kairma went to the kitchen in the Chancery to get flat bread and venison stew for the travelers to dine on before they left on the lengthy journey. Kairma felt numb. It was going to be a long and lonely summer.

Before Collin could leave the Grand Hall to pack his things, Isontra asked him to come to her suite of rooms. He helped Kairma take the empty terrid cups, bowls, and bread plates back to the kitchen, and then made his way down the long hallway to the western rooms.

He found Isontra standing by the fire when he entered the room. She was older than her appearance. Her silver hair, coiled in soft braids, framed a delicate face, but Isontra wasn't a delicate woman. As the leader of Survin, she had heavy responsibilities. Raising his right hand to his brow, he gave her a formal greeting.

She returned his greeting. "There you are. I was hoping to have a private word with you before you left for the plains." Taking a seat on a well-worn rocking chair by the hearth, she smiled graciously at Collin, motioning him to sit as well.

Collin straightened his vest. *I wonder if this has to do with what might have happened to Kairma at the temples today. It was more dangerous than I'd thought. I never thought the White Ones would attack like that. We should have had Trep's weapon with us.*

Taking the chair across from her, he asked, "Miral Isontra, what can I do for you?"

Isontra held his gaze for a few moments before speaking. "You know why I'm allowing the stranger, Trep, to take you to the city?"

Relieved, Collin nodded. It was the conversation he was hoping to have with her, a safer topic to be sure.

She squared her shoulders and asked again, "Do you understand why I made this decision?"

Collin looked out the open window to the south. "Not really. I mean, I know we have to catch those Madics before they can tell anyone about the temples. I've always been taught to respect the teaching of the Word, and leaving the mountain is expressly forbidden. I was surprised when you suggested we go into the city if we found ourselves nearby."

"Yes, this does seem impetuous, doesn't it?" The corners of her mouth twitched in a half smile. "You can thank Kairma for that. She was very persuasive, not to mention she never once gave up on the idea that we needed these modern weapons."

Isontra stared into the fire. "We came to this mountain more than five hundred annums ago and there are still less than two hundred people in this valley. The most we have ever recorded living here was three hundred and sixty four. Disease has taken its toll. Since we have lost many families the past few annums, what we need more than anything now is new blood."

She reached over and took Collin's hand in hers. "I need you to understand the necessity of adding new members to our colony."

Collin was thoughtful. Understanding slowly dawned on him. "You want me to find people to bring back here?"

"Yes, son, I want you to go all the way to the city, regardless of where you encounter the men you seek. If there are people of Efpec blood in the city, see if you can speak with them without compromising Survin. See if any would be willing to come back with you."

Collin considered this a moment. "You're asking me to return with new members, more than just Trep's woman, but I am not to tell them where they are going until they get here?"

Isontra chuckled quietly. "Something like that." When Collin didn't answer, Isontra continued. "Zedic is a good boy, but you're smarter than most people give you credit for. I know you will find a way to do what's right. I'm also very grateful to have you watching over my grandson. I expect you to bring him back to us."

"I understand. I'm honored that you believe in me. I will do my best to fulfill your request."

Chapter 16

Several houses away, Naturi was slicing strips of venison for the evening's meal while Toric sat at the table, staring out a small window at the drizzling rain that had begun to fall. Without looking at Naturi, he quietly said, "What*ever* were you thinking when you told Isontra you wanted to help capture those Madics?" Toric's gruff voice held dark emotion. "You plan to leave your old Pa here to die alone, don't you? It's just like you to do that. Same as your Ma did. Don't think about anyone but yourself."

Naturi was taken aback. He didn't think his intentions were so obvious.

Naturi's throat tightened. "I thought the colony could use the karracks. They would help us to hunt better and …"

Toric cut him off. His words were heated now. "What would you do with a karrack? You spend all day doing woman's work in a field." He turned toward Naturi and glared. "You haven't been hunting in four annums. The only reason the rest of the community doesn't say anything is because they all know how you feel about that little mutant Healer." Under his breath he muttered, "It's not like anyone else would mate with a White One." Turning back to the window, he watched the rain gather on the stone steps of the house across the way. "After all, someone will have to mate with her. I guess it may as well be old Toric's boy. They should have given that child to the gods annums ago."

Naturi could see that his father's eyes were red, though he wasn't sure if it was from unspent tears or the smoke from the fire. He gently pleaded. "Please, Father, do not be angry with me. I merely wanted more for our colony than …"

Toric slammed his fist on the table. "More than what? You're willing to go half way across the world to get these karracks. Something you won't even have the courage to use. You think that's what being a Comad is all about? New fancy ideas?" Toric got up from the table and stomped out of the room, and it wrenched Naturi's heart to see his father so angry.

Naturi finished preparing their supper and called to his father. They ate in silence.

Toric sat staring into space while Naturi cleaned up the dishes. He was used to his father's long silences, but his suggestion of leaving the mountain had caused a violent and unexpected reaction. How long ago had his mother disappeared? Why? That was the real question that burned in his heart. He heard the talk among the colonists. Rumors of how Toric drove her away. They didn't remember what he was like before. They only saw the shell of the man he once was.

Evening fell over the mountain and the rain began to increase, blocking out the light of the rising moon. Naturi sat on the threshold of their doorway and watched as people darted to and from the cleansing room across the road. Sometimes they would see him and shout, "Hello!" He would smile and wave back to them—*his* people. He couldn't remember when he began to think of them as *his* people. How could he leave them like this? On the other hand, how could he let Collin come back a hero, while he sat waiting for his life to begin?

When darkness filled the canyon, Naturi went back inside, and sitting in the russet, bearskin-covered chair, he finished a drawing he had started a few days before. As he sketched, he mulled over the idea of going with Trep. Jettena had forbidden him to go and the uneasy feeling that he was about to commit a grievous sin clung to the back of his neck. It wouldn't be easy to put twenty annums of ideals behind him and risk the unknown. Toric sat in the other chair, staring into the fire. The only break in the silence was distant thunder.

The rain had slowed to a steady drizzle so Naturi put away his drawing. He had made his decision. Throwing a wrap over his shoulder, he walked out. Toric didn't look up.

Naturi stopped at the home of Morgaina to seek help in managing the fields. The older woman hadn't been at the meeting earlier in the evening. Naturi hoped she hadn't heard all the details. She was a strong and confident woman. Having two nearly grown daughters, Naturi knew she would have plenty of regular help. The fields didn't take a long time, but they had to be tended daily to keep the weeds and insects from taking over. Morgaina was well-liked in the small community and wouldn't have any trouble soliciting additional help when needed.

The fields had become Naturi's passion after his mother left. He could get lost in the mud and feel he was contributing a great deal to the colony at the same time. In the past five annums the colony had managed to grow enough produce to sustain them with less and less red meat. He also realized that this fact further alienated him from his father whose skills at hunting were legendary. Still, Naturi was gaining a strong reputation on his own merits and that was extremely important if he was going to become the next Comad. Without actually telling her what he planned to do, he enlisted her help for the summer.

Morgaina said she would be happy to help him with the field, although she grumbled about the gossip circulating the small village. "How could such a good boy as Zedic go against the teachings? For generation on generation, no one has left the community, and *never* have we allowed strangers to come and go." She shook her head slowly. "I know something bad will come of this, and to lose one of our brightest children. My, my, my, what has the world come to? Someone should talk to Miral Isontra. Jettena must be beside herself."

Naturi thanked her for her help, and as he walked down the small stone steps that led from Morgaina's door hoping that what he was about to do wasn't some silly adventure that would get them all killed.

Toric was asleep when Naturi returned home. He quietly began packing his travel sack and tried to think of what more he could say to his father. Traveling for several weeks was much different from an overnight hunting trip. He wasn't even sure what he would need. He would definitely take his cookware. Naturi didn't think any of the other travelers were experienced at cooking, unless Trep was. He had seen some metal pans that were unfamiliar when he had visited with Trep. Somehow the man had made it all the way to Survin from the city and he didn't look like he was particularly starving.

Midnight was cold and wet, with rain dripping from the trees and puddles soaking his leather moccasins. Collin was the first to arrive at Trep's door. "Well, I'm ready to go, are you?" He asked, setting his meager pack on the floor by the hearth. "It's getting late. I was hoping we would be on the plains by midday."

Trep looked up from the hide he was studying, and leaned back in his chair. "Whoa. Slow down a bit. Why don't y'all have a cup of terrid and warm your bones a minute. Even if we left yesterday, don't think we could make it to the plains by nightfall. It's farther than ya think." He poured the hot liquid into a cup and handed it to Collin. "I know we need to hurry, but we can spare a few more minutes. Good plannin' saves a lotta wasted time." He moved to the table and began throwing things into a leather satchel. "We should have 'bout half a day or more to spare. The man with the arrow wound won't move fast, and with any luck it will be a long way around that mountain to the north."

Collin took the cup from Trep and sat on the wooden bench by the fire. "I guess I just want to catch those Madics before they get too far." He hadn't told his parents that he was leaving, and he knew they would be looking for him at first light. Hiram and Grimly would be angry about the elder's decision when they returned from the hunt, and when his father learned about it Collin wanted to be as far away as possible. "It sure is cold tonight. I wore my warmest leathers, but it still chills me to the bone."

Trep wrapped up a small drawing and stuffed it in his pack. "Ya heard from Zedic yet?"

Collin took a long sip, "He should be here soon." Moving closer to the fire, he asked, "What's all that stuff you're packing?"

Trep looked over at Collin's meager bag. "Well, I need something to sleep on and some food, water, cooking utensils, clothes, my karrack, some rope …"

As Trep went on to name the things in his pack, Collin's eyes widened. "I didn't think about all that. I guess I should get a few more things before we go, huh?" Collin finished his terrid and slipped out the door, unsure of how he would get everything he needed without waking his parents.

Trep was sitting at the wooden table, making mental notes of things they would need for the long journey, when Zedic came in and set his bundles down. The young man walked to the hearth and poured a cup of terrid, commenting that it tasted wonderful on this cold and rainy night. A little stiffly he added, "Mother is still very concerned. I told her I'd be careful." He warmed his back by the fire. "It's not that dangerous, is it?"

Trep looked over at Zedic's bulging pack and noted that he seemed to have at least two of everything he would need. "I wouldn't say it was a really *dangerous* trip. The hardest part will be confrontin' those men. I hope y'all are ready to do what's necessary." He paused, studying the severity in Zedic's face. "You're a bright boy. I think you'll do jess fine on the road. For the most part, I'm sure you'll jess get real tired of walkin'."

Zedic made himself comfortable in an overstuffed chair and began rearranging his bag. "Where's Collin? I thought he'd be here by now."

"He went back to get a few things."

Trep watched Zedic as he refolded his bedroll and counted his waterskins. He had eight skins of water and five of wine. Trep laughed. "At least ya won't die of thirst on this trip." He walked over to where Zedic sat by the fire. "I think y'all can leave a couple of these behind." He set three of the water bags aside. "This will last till we pick up the river. We'll be followin' it most of the way." He picked out a couple of clay bowls and set them aside. "Ya need to carry all the necessities, but not too much. I think this'll do." He set aside an extra tunic and an extra pair of leggers. "We won't need to change our clothes that often. Y'all will be okay so long as ya got somethin' warm, somethin' cool, and somethin' to change into if ya get wet. There. Ain't that a little lighter?" He set the pack on Zedic's shoulders.

Zedic grinned sheepishly. "I didn't want to run out of anything."

"Better too much than too little."

Trep invited Zedic to have a seat at the table. "I was jess goin' over the trip." Trep motioned to the large deer hide on the table. "See this mark here," he said, pointing to a large circle on the hide. "This is Peireson Landin'— the city those men are headed for."

Zedic was impressed. The hide had a long squiggled line running up from the lower right-hand corner to the center of the hide and then it turned to the left and crossed the hide. On the far right-hand side was a large sun and on the far left was a crescent moon.

"What are these for?" Zedic said as he pointed to the sun and moon.

"That's where the sun goes at night, and this is where it comes up in the mornin'. That's how I know which direction I'm goin'."

Zedic noticed two little circles sketched in a line toward the lower right corner of the drawing. "What are these?"

"This one is Charltown, the city I come from, and this is the great river." He put his finger on a drawing of fish. "This is a lake." And then he pointed to a few small pictures of deer. "And these are good huntin' lands." Indicating a number of small triangles, he said, "These are y'all's mountains. See here, at the end of this river. This is where I turned off and ended up here."

Zedic pointed at a few odd-shaped symbols. "What are these?"

Trep let out a rugged laugh. "Those are landmarks. Rock formations and trees."

Zedic looked sideways at him. "Trees?"

"Okay! An artist, I'm not. I was hopin' Naturi would be comin' with us and at least redo this part of my map. Not sure anyone could recognize my landmarks this way."

Zedic looked toward the door. "Naturi won't be coming. Isontra forbade it and he takes his responsibilities very seriously. He plans to be our next Comad, even though his father is against it."

"Could his pa stop him from becoming the Comad? I thought it was decided by the elders and a matin' with the Vice Miral."

"That's true, but Toric could make things pretty rough on him."

"I thought the healin' family were the leaders. What's Toric's position?"

"He used to lead the hunts. He's a very good hunter—the best, in fact. That doesn't exactly make him a leader, but with all the trouble within our family, a lot of people look up to him. I think he could sway people not to listen to Naturi if he wanted to."

The long buffalo hide that covered the door was pulled aside and Naturi proudly strolled in. "I will be going with you!"

Zedic's jaw dropped. "Well, I'll be Nor's bastard!" He blinked several times before stammering, "Jettena and Isontra forbade you to go!"

Naturi admonished, "Zedic! Watch your language!"

Recovering, Trep jumped up from the table. "Come in! Come in! Here, have somethin' warm to drink. I'm glad ya decided to come with us."

Ignoring Zedic's accusation, Naturi walked over to the table and looked at the deer hide. "What is this?"

Trep smiled meekly. "That's our map, to tell us where to go. I was hopin' I could talk ya into makin' a better copy for me."

Naturi studied the map as Trep explained all the markings. He laughed out loud, and then quickly apologized when Trep pointed out his interpretation of the Godstones.

"That's okay. I know I don't draw good. But it does help to have somethin' to go by. I mostly try to follow a river or major stream. Best chance of finding people and supplies."

Turning to the two younger men, he told them to roll up the map and get ready to leave. "We should get movin'." He took one more look around the dwelling, making sure he had everything he needed. "Where's Collin? He went to get some more gear, but I thought he'd be back by now."

Zedic scooped up his things and headed for the door. "Don't worry, he'll be here, even if he has to sneak out of his house. And if I know his father, he will." Zedic looked incredulously at Naturi. "I'm guessing you had to sneak away too. I still can't believe you're going to disobey the elders."

Naturi's mouth pinched tautly as he helped Trep put out the fire. "Sometimes, you just have to do what you think is right."

Chapter 17

The rain had let up a little and was not much more than a cold black drizzle. It wasn't the best traveling weather, but at least it wasn't pouring anymore. They decided to wait for Collin at the north edge of Survin where Trep kept Belle tied.

Heading through the canyon, the weight of what they were about to do began to settle over Naturi and Zedic. Their grim faces peered through the rain at the homes they were leaving behind, but in their hearts was the hope they would make their friends and families proud.

They passed through the Grand Hall where heavy wooden doors set on each end of the long tunnel kept out the cold in winter and, if necessary, hostiles. At the moment the great doors were closed on either end. Slipping quietly through the hall, they silently bid good-bye to Survin.

It was a short walk down the narrow trail that led to the lake where Trep's sorrel horse was tethered. Trep saddled Belle, and put his pack on the mare's back, arranging the remaining bundles so no one had to carry more than a small backpack. Trep nodded solemnly toward Belle. "These wonderful animals can be y'all's best friend or worst enemy. They deserve genuine respect and love." Both young men heeded the warning and were cautious, standing well clear of the large animal.

They each checked their gear again and waited. After a short while the rain began falling heavily again. Zedic pulled his cloak up around his neck to help ward off the downpour and mumbled to no one in particular, "I think we might be crazy."

A moment later, Kairma came running up to them from the west, holding a small covered basket.

Trep instinctively looked for the suede sack that held the Crystal, but Kairma's fur wrap was tied tightly at her neck. *Wish we hadn't needed to take this trip so soon. I'd of liked to have more time to find out 'bout that Crystal. It fits the description of the star, and there's no doubt the Survinees believe it has some kinda power, but to have ended up here of all places...*

Kairma was winded, having run quite a distance. Breathlessly, she said, "I would have been here sooner, but I wanted to pack some plums for your trip." She handed the basket of yellow underwood plums to Zedic. They were small, and probably could have used a few more weeks to ripen fully, but they would add diversity to the travelers' diet.

"I saw Collin," she said. "I think his father may have beaten him again. He lost his pack, but he said that he has the gemstones in the alloy cart. You're to meet him there."

Zedic said, "I guess I'll be needing those extra things after all. I'll be right back." He took off for Trep's cabin to grab the extra waterskins and clothes he had left behind.

Kairma paced nervously as they waited, her eyes darting to Naturi several times. Finally she couldn't control her curiosity any longer. When she approached him, Naturi pulled her out of hearing range.

She asked, "Does Toric know you're here?"

"No, and he will be very upset with me, but I think you were right when you first suggested we send a team to capture these men."

Kairma nodded. "I'm just really surprised. I can't believe you'd defy the elders, but I'm glad you'll be there to help keep an eye on Trep. I want to believe in him, but if he isn't the man we hope he is ...Well, I'll feel better knowing there are three of you." She fretted about sending Naturi. Not only had the elders forbade his going, but if something happened to him she would be forced to mate with Siede or Efram. Siede was nice enough, but Efram made her skin crawl. When Efram deemed to acknowledge her at all, he made the most horrid remarks, usually referring to her as the white witch.

"Thank you," Naturi said. "I do hate to defy Isontra and Jettena, but their argument makes no sense. I can still be back in time to fulfill my duty to you."

As Kairma began to turn away, she replayed his words in her head: *"I can still be back in time to fulfill my duty." Is that how he feels? That I'm a duty to be fulfilled?* She was about to tell him it wasn't necessary, when he pulled her into his arms and held her for a moment. His breath was hot on her neck and she began to panic, not sure how she should respond. His strong arms around her felt wonderful and warmed her in an odd way.

He whispered, "I will make you proud." And then he let her go.

She almost staggered back to the others, fighting down the conflicting emotions that raged through her.

When Zedic returned, they put the additional gear on Belle and headed away from the small grazing area. They were walking around the north side of the lake when Naturi stopped them. "Kairma, you must return home. It is very late, and I do not wish to endanger you further."

She frowned at him. "I want to say good-bye to Collin."

"No, there are White Caves that way. Return to the Chancery." To Trep Naturi said, "We should take the south side of the lake. It would be safer."

Zedic looked at Naturi. There would be no changing his mind, so Zedic said, "I know where Collin is. The cave he's waiting by is north of the lake. I'll go get him and meet you east of here, where the creek runs. It won't take long."

Trep agreed. "That's a good place to meet. That's the way I came in."

Naturi grimaced. There were caves all around to the north and east. "We are too close to the caves now. Are you trying to get us killed before we even get out of the mountains?" He gestured off to the southeast. "We will meet in Graystone Valley. If you and Collin can get away from the Whitish, meet us there."

Trep asked Naturi, "Where's this Graystone Valley?"

Zedic said, "It's straight southeast of the lake, about eight kilometers from here. The hunters camp there often. There are two large walls of gray boulders on the east and south sides. The cliffs are taller than three pine trees put one atop another."

Trep nodded. "Oh, I know the place. Not an easy place to forget, once ya been there."

Zedic was already on his way. "Yeah, I know, we'll meet you there."

"Wait for me!" Kairma took off after Zedic before Naturi could stop her.

Zedic and Kairma found Collin sitting with his eyes closed, just inside the square opening of a cave and out of the rain. His left eye was turning a deep blackish-purple and his lower lip was swollen and bleeding.

Zedic cleared his throat as he walked up. "Looks like he was pretty tough on you. I take it he knows where you're going."

Collin winced as he smiled sardonically. "He sure does, and he doesn't like it a bit. I should say, he didn't like it at first, but now he's insisting I go. That is, as long as I never come back!"

Zedic whistled softly, "You *are* planning to come back with us, aren't you?"

"Sure. But I guarantee he'll never hit me or my mother again, not if I have a karrack." Zedic winced, but Collin continued. "You know, I probably should have killed him annums ago." He stood up uneasily and limped out of the cave. "Lo, Boo. Are you coming with us?"

She smiled shyly. "I only wish."

Zedic offered him a shoulder to lean on and said, "I've got another surprise for you. Naturi's with Trep right now."

Collin stopped short and looked at Zedic. "Great Stones! Naturi's defied the elders?"

Kairma tried to help him on the right side, but Collin insisted he was okay.

Zedic searched the dark cave opening. "What did you do with the rocks?"

Collin pointed to a dark leather sack next to a rusted cart. "I wish you'd stop calling them rocks. Trep calls them gold and jewels. When you say rocks, it sounds like they're worthless."

"I know, but it's pretty hard to imagine someone would be willing to give us karracks for them." Picking up the heavy sack, he went back to help Collin.

Kairma's voice was filled with concern. "Are you going to be all right? You have more than eight kilometers to go to catch up with Trep. They're waiting for you in Graystone Valley."

"I'm a little stiff, but I'll be fine."

Kairma dug through the little satchel she usually carried and found something for pain. "I know this is bitter, but it works. Zedic knows what kind of trees to look for if you need more."

Collin ate the medicine. "You're a handy little thing. I'm gonna miss you."

Kairma' heart ached. She would miss them too. Sadly, she would have to leave them soon and return home; she was already as far from the village as she had ever been at night before. It felt strangely invigorating. Wrapping her arms around Zedic, she said, "You take care of yourself. It's going to be a long summer without you." She looked at Collin. "Both of you, be careful and come home soon." She wiped away tears with the sleeve of her light beige blouse.

Zedic hugged his little sister until she thought she would break, his dark gray eyes glistening with the threat of tears.

She walked to Collin and kissed him lightly on the cheek. He tried to turn away, but before he could go anywhere she held his face in her hands and checked his eye once more. Sternly, she said, "You take care of that leg. It's not good for you to be chasing dangerous men when you're hurt, but I know it would be a waste of time to insist you return home with me."

Collin's eyes twinkled, denying the pain he was surely feeling. He put his hands on her hips and said, teasingly, "Your offer is tempting."

She grinned. Giving each another hug, Kairma bid them good journey as they turned to leave.

The rain soured her mood even more as she stood watching her brother and best friend make their way down the slick, muddy hill. The light bands of colors around her friends grew brighter as she relaxed. Once they had disappeared into the dark of night, Kairma turned and headed back to the comfort of her home. Wrapping her wet cloak tightly about her, she began to run. The sun was still more than an hour from rising, and the dark forest was suddenly filled with the sounds and smells of danger. She didn't have to look into the shadows to know the White Ones were near. Tripping over a small branch, she tore her skirt again. Her mother wouldn't be happy with her, and Isontra would surely scold her for going out alone in the dark. She had wanted to see the guys off, wanted to say good-bye one last time, but if the White Ones caught her now, Isontra and Jettena would be the least of her worries. She began to run faster. From the edge of the trail, she could see two of the White Ones watching her: a small boy of about twelve and an older, wrinkled man. Kairma thought he looked like he was a hundred and fifty annums old or more.

As they limped along, Collin found a tree limb about six feet long with a fork in the top. "Zedic, what do you have in your pack? Got an extra tunic?"

"Sure. Kairma said you had to leave your pack behind. I just so happened to have packed a few extra. Are you cold?" He handed the shirt to Collin.

"No, I'm gonna relieve you of having to carry me all the way to the city." Collin grimaced a little and took the clothing from Zedic. He wrapped the shirt over the fork of the branch then measured it under his arm. It was a little too long so he cut off the straight end and had an adequate crutch.

Zedic smiled. "You're pretty smart. I never would have thought of that." Collin adjusted his crutch a little more. "You remember when my dad broke my leg when I was five? Isontra gave me a crutch a lot like this; only it had a nice little handle to help with the weight. My armpit's gonna be in bad shape soon if I can't find a better branch." Collin thought it would have been so much easier if his father had gone hunting with the other men instead of spending most of the night at the Gathering House cursing his lot in life. The rain continued to fall, making it difficult to move quickly, but they walked. Zedic talked about the adventures they would have and it raised Collin's spirits once more.

The sun was low in the eastern sky before they reached Graystone Valley. They could see the campfire as they came over the small ridge, and both thought about how good it would be to get into something dry and have something to eat.

After a quick meal and a brief rest, Trep began loading their lunch items onto Belle. "We best get movin'. That wound won't slow 'em down that much." He tied the bundle to the saddle horn. "Most likely, they went around the peak and will be catching the river northeast of here. I came from the southeast, along the creek, but we cut 'em off sooner if we head north once we clear the hills."

The sky was a dingy gray and the steady rain had soaked everyone's clothing. Trep let Collin ride Belle to rest his sore leg. The injury was a mild sprain in the knee, but walking on it made his leg swell, and even the birch bark medicine did little to ease the pain. Having not slept the night before, the travelers were exhausted by nightfall and made camp under a large overhanging rock just after sunset. The space was small, but it got them out of the rain for a while, and the bits of dry wood they could find made a meager, though sufficient fire. The steady rain had chilled them to the bone.

Trep began to strip off his shirt. "I'd suggest y'all get out of those wet clothes so they'll dry faster." Collin and Zedic were no strangers to being away from home and wet. As boys, they had been caught in violent summer storms many times during their explorations of the mountain.

Naturi, being a more private person, felt uncomfortable taking off his clothes, but with a little prodding he succumbed and the fire did indeed feel much warmer against his bare skin. Once they had changed into dry clothes they each rummaged through their packs for something to eat.

Naturi had a small sack of crushed wheat and a few herbs, so when he offered to cook dinner, no one objected. He dug a small hole and filled it with stones as the others watched, and then took a large cut of elk that Zedic had brought, rolled it in the wheat, and added herbs from another small bag. Wrapping it all in some green leaves, he placed the supper in the hole and covered it with red-hot coals. "This will take some time. We should probably get comfortable. This morning, as we walked, I picked collard greens too."

Collin made a spit out of rocks and a green tree limb, while Zedic took a large pottery dish to the creek and filled it halfway full of water. Naturi added a few herbs to the greens he'd picked and hung the pot over the fire. They rolled out their bedding and waited for the meat to cook.

Unpacking a small jug, Zedic beamed at the others. "I thought this wine would bolster us. This seems like as good a time to open it as any."

Collin smiled. "I'll say. That's exactly what I need to deaden the pain in my leg."

They passed the jug around the fire and Trep told the others what they could expect to find once they reached the plains. "There's a lot of grass between here and the big river. I expect we'll see signs of those men in three, maybe four days, six at the most. They have to sleep too." Trep accepted the skin of wine from Naturi. "While we're on the plains, y'all best beware of wild dogs. They aren't afraid of men like most animals. Oh, and if y'all hear a rolling thunder, *run like hell!* Buffalo stampede ain't no place for the likes of us."

As they talked, Collin got out the sack of stones and suggested they review the contents of the bag. Naturi stared in disbelief when Collin pulled out the stones. "They really trade for that? I find it hard to believe."

Collin gave the stones to Trep. "If you hadn't told us about these, I'd be packing deer skins."

Passing the skin of wine to Zedic, Trep said, "Hey, it's all in a good day's work. I have to caution ya, though, not everyone in the city is honorable. Some swindlers might try to take this away from us. Best not let folk know how much we have." Collin continued to sort the last of the stones. When he finished, they counted five gold pieces, fifteen fair-sized colored stones—one, half the size of his fist—and two-dozen smaller gems.

Trep whistled. "Y'all have enough wealth here to buy anything ya want. I've never seen so many precious stones in one place."

The evening passed quickly as they discussed what they should do about the Madics when they found them. Trep was the only one with real-world experience, but he admitted to the boys that he'd never killed a man. Collin and Zedic didn't seem concerned about how they would do it, only when and where. Naturi sat silently watching the others.

When the meal was ready to eat, Trep watched each of the men place their food in precisely the same place on their plate. Each man pressed two fingers to their forehead, and then touched four places on their plate, followed by touching their lips. Although they didn't say the words out loud, Trep had recognized the prayer. He had learned through his travels that most people appreciated the gesture when he adopted their greetings and other customs. So placing his food as he had seen the others do, he made the small hand gestures that invoked the prayer.

The supper was delicious. As they finished, Trep suggested that Naturi should be the designated cook for the rest of the trip. Naturi smiled proudly and accepted the honor.

Collin plucked a long blade of grass and began to chew on it. He often mimicked Trep's language and mannerism. Leaning back against the hard stone, Collin drawled slowly, "The way I figure it, if we catch those men before long, we can go all the way to the city and we'll only be gone for about two moons." He looked over to where Naturi was fidgeting with his pack, and noticed how tense he was. A small amount of sympathy stole into Collin's thoughts. Naturi was a good person, never one to break the rules. Collin understood how defying his father, and the elders, was chipping away at Naturi's composure. Trying to hide his concern, Collin's tone was lighthearted. He'd hope Naturi would hear comfort in his words, not pity. Naturi was proud and would only be angered by pity. Collin said, "You know, if you'd asked him, your father would've let you go. You heard him at the meeting. He said you were your own man. Hell, he could have come too. He's a great tracker, and he knows hunting well enough." Collin took a drink before he went on. "I know you're worried he's going to be upset when he finds out you came with us, but he might actually think it was a brave thing to do. I certainly didn't think you had the stones for it."

Zedic asked Collin, "What is this word, *hell*?

Trep barked a laugh. "Hell is a very bad place to be. I sometimes use it to express my awe or displeasure. Kinda like y'all say *Stones*."

Zedic shook his head. Turning back to Naturi, he asked, "What do you think will happen when we get back?"

Naturi gazed across the small glen filled with thick grasses. "I do not know. Two moons is a long time to be away from the mountain. We will barely get home in time to harvest the fields. My father may have allowed me to leave, if the elders had not forbidden it. Now, only time will tell us."

Darkness enveloped them and the small group had become quiet. Beyond the edge of the firelight was total blackness, the stars and moon hidden by thick clouds. After a while, Trep broke the silence. "I'll take the first watch. Who wants to take second?"

Naturi unrolled his blankets and noticed the rain had seeped into his pack and dampened everything. "I guess I'll take second. It will take most of the night for these to dry out anyway."

"Since I won't be using my blankets for a while, y'all can warm 'em up for me till I wake ya."

Naturi nodded. "Thank you, Trep. That is very kind of you."

Zedic wrapped his cloak about his shoulders. "I'll watch with you."

"No need for that. One man can handle it."

"I'll watch." The certainty with which the words were said informed Trep their trust would only go so far—he would always have company on watch duty. "Very well, then. Y'all take that direction," Trep said, pointing to the west.

Exhausted, Collin and Naturi quickly fell into a deep sleep.

Chapter 18

The darkness of night was gradually replaced by a dull gray as Kairma slipped back into the Chancery. Everyone in the household was still sleeping, so she stripped out of her wet clothes and hung them on a rod by the fire. A blanket of harsh goat hair lying on the large chair near the door served as a warm and dry wrap for the frightened girl. *I don't understand why the White Ones let me pass this morning. Surely they could see I only had a small sling, and I'm not really very good with it.* She added more wood to the fire and set a kettle to heat water. *I wonder why they've been so active lately. For annums, we never saw them at all.* But she drifted off before the water boiled, thinking about the mysteries surrounding the White Ones.

Isontra roused her and told her to go get dressed. "I hadn't realized you stayed up to see the men off. I should have known. You must have stood in the rain awhile to do it."

Kairma gathered up her still damp clothes and headed to her room. "It didn't take long. It was raining pretty hard when they left." She hoped her grandmother wouldn't ask her too much about the men's departure. It was only a matter of time before they would discover Naturi had gone as well. Kairma hoped it would be too late for them

209

to call off the quest, and that she wouldn't have to admit she knew he'd gone. With any luck, no one would ever know the whole truth.

A few minutes later, she'd dressed and returned to the great room with Kinter in tow. The morning was overcast and wet. The frequent spring rains kept the villagers inside and the kitchen of the royal family was warm and inviting. Breakfast consisted of hot oatmeal and dried berries—Kairma's favorite. The regular Nor Day service would be held when the weather cleared, so while they ate, Isontra laid out the lesson for the day. Today would be a good day for preparing medicine.

The morning passed, and as a fire blazed in the oversized hearth, Kairma, Kinter, and Isontra went about their duties.

"Kairma, stir more slowly. We don't want to get air bubbles in it." Isontra looked over her shoulder and nodded. "That is better. Analgesic has to be made carefully if it is to work."

Kinter looked up from the rose hips she was chopping. "Gramme, how come you let Zedic go with Trep? I thought there were very strict laws about leaving the mountain? Weren't we supposed to kill Trep?" The ease in which Kinter said *kill* gave Kairma a chill, but she didn't say anything.

Isontra put a few more pieces into the white bark potion Kairma was stirring and then turned to Kinter. "It is true that the laws are quite clear. The law says all strangers should be executed immediately. I've thought about this since the first day Collin brought Trep to us. I even discussed the possibility of imposing the Law of Fontas with Kairma, your mother, and your father. Of course, if we had always done that, I would not have married Petar and your father would not be here today." A teasing grin crossed her face briefly. "I might have had to mate with Grimly, and then he would have been your grampe."

Both girls looked up in horror. The girls had often said they thought Grimly was a wicked old man. Isontra smiled as she continued her teaching. "Laws are meant to guide us to the right decisions, not make them for us. We wouldn't have sent them out there if those Madics hadn't found the temples. We had to weigh the danger of being discovered against the dangers of sending someone after them."

Kairma stretched her shoulders and neck. She had been sitting there for almost an hour. She had questions for her grandmother too, but they were different from Kinter's questions. "Gramme, can you tell me about my Seridar? I know the boys who wish to take me for a mate have to pass some kind of test, and I'm supposed to mate with the winner, but what if no one contends me?" Her face flushed a soft pink.

Isontra patted her hand and said, "Don't you worry, my dear, I know at least one young man who has had his eye on you for several annums now, and I wouldn't be surprised if a few other men weren't considering their chances as well."

Kinter frowned. Everyone knew Naturi saw himself as the next Comad. She started chopping her rose hips with greater conviction.

Isontra noticed the change in Kinter's bearing. Placing a gentle hand over Kinter's hand to slow her vigorous chopping, Isontra said, "This Harvest Moon, there will only be five men for Kairma to choose from, and unfortunately only one other boy will come of age by the time you're old enough to mate. It would be nice if we had lots of young people in Survin, but we are quite limited. We'll have to see what happens." Isontra got up from the table and took the heavy black pot from the stove and set it on a cooling rack.

Kinter said quietly, "I'm going to be Naturi's mate."

Isontra looked up at Kairma, but Kairma just shrugged. Every female over the age of ten wanted to mate with the charming and handsome Naturi.

"Kairma, will you please get the wooden box from beneath my bed?"

"Yes, Gramme." Kairma hurried down the hall to her grandmother's suite of rooms.

Kairma loved the smell of these rooms. A combination of herbs and musk permeated the richly paneled walls. A cool spring breeze blew in the scent of daffodils mixed with apple blossoms.

The finely carved box was easy to find. She carefully pulled it out from under the white crocheted coverlet. Another small box that had been sitting on top fell to the floor, spilling the contents in front of her.

There in front of her, she saw a picture much like the one Zedic had found behind the Godstones. This one was of the Godstones themselves. The great temples at the base of the mountain were clean, all the vines stripped away. After close scrutiny, Kairma realized, this was a picture of the Godstones before vegetation had taken over. A shiver ran down her spine. It was faded and very old. She could make out the images of dozens of people going in and out of the temples. They were dressed in strange and colorful clothes, like the boy and girl in Zedic's picture.

Kinter's voice sounded irritated. "Kairma, come on. What's taking so long?"

Kairma stashed the picture back in the box just as her sister came around the corner. "I'm coming. I knocked something over and had to clean it up." She picked up the box her grandmother had sent her for and hurried out the door. With Kinter on her heels, she dashed down the hall to the kitchen, where Isontra waited patiently. "Sorry, Gramme." Kairma set the box on the table and began to take out the ancient bottles they used for storing medicines.

Isontra began to ladle the contents of the black pot into one of the bottles. "Where was I, now? Oh yes, we were talking about allowing strangers into the colony. Once in a while, we should question our actions and our beliefs. We've been secluded on this mountain for centuries and little has changed in the way we do things. All the while, the rest of the world has evolved into something quite different." She handed the filled bottle to Kairma, who sealed the top with soft leather dipped in hot bees wax. "I still believe the protection of the Crystal is our primary reason for being, but that doesn't mean we don't need to protect ourselves from other dangers a well."

Kinter looked up sharply. "Do you mean like the White Ones? Can Trep help us get rid of the White Ones? They're really ugly. I hate them."

Isontra handed Kairma another bottle. "At the end of their journey, we'll know if he can give us what we need. Kinter, chop those rose hips a little finer. I have given the young men very explicit instructions. They know what to do."

Toric stumbled out of bed. His knee was bothering him again. The dampness seemed to aggravate the old injury so he poured a little analgesic into his terrid and sat near the fire. It wasn't unusual for Naturi to be out in the fields at dawn, but the steady rain would make fieldwork difficult at best and Toric was surprised his son didn't have breakfast waiting. *Naturi must be at the Gathering House. That's where most men go when the weather keeps us from our work.* He refilled his cup and fried up some flat bread. It was always nice when Naturi cooked for him, but Toric was no slouch in the kitchen. He slathered apple preserves on the hot bread, and through the crack in the shutters he watched the rain falling in heavy sheets, turning the tiny creek that ran through the canyon into an impressive little river.

After breakfast he cleaned his hunting knives and mended a broken bow. He was feeling bad for the way he'd spoken to Naturi the night before and vowed to apologize as soon as his son came home, but morning turned to afternoon, and afternoon turned to early evening, and Naturi still hadn't come home. *He must be pretty angry with me. He never stays away through dinner.*

The sun dropped down behind the mountain, drenching the wet canyon in darkness, and the rain eased up to a fine drizzle. It would be difficult to keep a torch lit in this rain, so Toric opted to let Naturi have his retaliation. He would see Naturi in the morning and with a little coaxing, Naturi would forgive him.

But morning came and Naturi's bed was cold. The rain had eased a little, but it was still too wet to work in the fields. Toric grumbled. *This is really going too far. I might have been rough on him, but he can't stay away forever. Naturi must have stayed at the Gathering House all night. I suppose with the rain, there were plenty of people to keep him company.*

By afternoon Toric was starting to worry. He pulled down a thick deerskin cloak and wrapped it over his head. The Gathering House was about a half mile to the south of Toric's home. The path was muddy from two days of rain and his moccasins were sticky and cold in minutes. He reflected on the boots the stranger wore, and for just a moment envied the man. Toric's cap was sitting on the table in the dining room, its fresh hole making it useless in the rain. Nothing moved in the gray morning light as he approached the large stairway leading to the door of the colony's entertainment lodge.

Smoke wafted past him as he opened the door. It was dark in the room, but the fire was well tended, making the room warm and inviting. Rain always brought the men together to play games and tell stories. The hunters who had recently returned were discussing the Healer's decision to send men after the Madics. Toric looked around but didn't see his son. He walked up to the long oak table that served as a bar and spoke with Efram. "Have you seen Naturi? He didn't come home last night. I was sure I'd find him here."

Efram shook his head. "Hasn't been in this afternoon, but we only returned from hunting a little while ago. You want something to drink? We have some hard biscuits too."

"No, not right now. Who was here last night?"

"Most everybody was hunting, but Diakus was here until after dark," Efram said, pouring a cup of hard cider for Jared, who was standing at the edge of the bar. "Hey, Diakus, you see Naturi last night?"

The bitter man sat hunched over in a chair by the hearth. "No. I haven't seen him for about two days. Last time I ran into him he was working in the garden."

Morgaina was weaving a blanket in the far corner of the lodge. "I saw him night before last. He came by to see if I'd help him with the gardens this summer."

Toric crossed the room to speak with her. "When did he come by?"

"It was late, after dark. He had a torch with him. We talked for a few minutes about the garden and that ridiculous decision to let the stranger take Zedic and Collin on a hunt for those Madics."

Toric spun around, addressing everyone in the smoky room. "Has anyone seen my boy since yesterday? Anyone at all?"

As the people in the room shook their heads and murmured to each other, realization dawned on him and Toric's face paled, his mouth dropping open. *My boy, my perfect boy, has gone with that stranger. I would expect something like this from that rogue boy, Collin, and maybe even Zedic, since the two are rarely apart, but not Naturi. Naturi would never defy me like this.* Toric crumpled into a chair and stared at the walls, seeing nothing but the face of his lost child. An all too familiar pain tightened his chest, making it hard to breathe.

Grimly managed to piece together what had happened. "He went with them, didn't he? Great Godstones, man! Why would he do that?"

Toric nodded, but couldn't answer. Naturi's leaving ripped open the festering wound left by Devon four annums earlier. His guts twisted in a tight knot and his eyes burned. His hands were cold and seemed to belong to someone else as he stared down at them.

Grimly shook him by the shoulder. "We have to go get him. The Miral made it clear that he wasn't to go on this hunt."

Efram came out from behind the bar. "I'll go with you, Grampe. We can leave as soon as I grab my hunting pack."

Dillon volunteered as well, but Siede and Jared told him to stay behind. He would have other chances to prove himself. This would be a hard, fast run and Dillon was untested.

As the day wore on, Toric's despair hardened to anger. In the Grand Hall he addressed Isontra with bare civility. "It's your fault those boys are out there. If you had invoked the Law of Fontas in the beginning, I wouldn't be on my way across hostile land tracking down my son."

"None of us would have believed him capable of doing this. We had no idea he wanted to be a part of the hunt that badly."

Isontra pleaded for Toric to understand, but Toric's words hit her like hard stones. He said, "I'm taking Efram, Jared, and Siede with me. You best pray we find him safe."

Kairma stood in the doorway, fidgeting nervously and looking torn. In a subtle voice, she said, "Zedic said they were going to follow the stream that runs east from the lake. Trep said that it joins a big river that leads to the city."

Toric studied her for a moment. She looked so much like a White One that her paleness made his skin crawl. This was the future of the colony, and the girl his son desired. She was meek and clumsy and Toric didn't know how to accept this future. Turning back to Isontra and Jettena, he realized the entire Healing family was less than he desired in his leaders. The family had made so many foolish decisions that his respect had been slowly crushed, annum after annum.

Kairma stepped quickly aside as Jared and Siede came in bearing heavy packs. She hadn't moved far enough away, and Efram pushed her into the wall as he came through. "Don't worry your little white head, witch. We'll bring back your man. Can't say that I blame him for running, though." He sneered at her and she dropped her eyes to the floor, making him laugh raucously.

The men headed east as fast as they could travel, and although the rain had let up, it washed away all signs of previous passing so the going was much slower than they had hoped.

Coming to the east side of the lake, the trail narrowed and they moved in single file. Once they found the first campsite, Grimly suggested they stop and rest for a few minutes. Jared pulled out some food and offered dried meat and bread to the other men. It would be dark soon. Toric paced nervously and then took off down the trail.

Jared jammed his lunch into his pack as he watched Toric disappear around the bend. "We best catch up with him. I'd feel a lot better if we all stuck together."

Grimly rested on an old fallen log. He was in good shape for a man in his mid-sixties, but the jog had winded him. "Just need a few minutes. He won't get far."

Before the four men could move, several black arrows struck the dirt at their feet. Jumping back, they looked around to find themselves surrounded by White Ones. Siede raised his bow, but Jared forced it down, saying, "There're more than a dozen of them. If you fire, they will certainly kill us. They could have killed us with those first shots. I think they meant those as a warning. We must be in their territory."

Grimly spat gruffly. "I should have known we'd never get far. The White Ones don't usually come out during the day, but with all this coming and going they must be making exceptions."

The White Ones parted to the west, leaving clear passage for the men to go back the way they had come.

Siede looked wistfully toward the trail Toric had disappeared down only a few minutes earlier. "What about Toric? He's out there alone. We can't just leave him."

Jared dragged Grimly by the arm. "I don't know what's become of him, but if we value our lives, we had better go back the way we came."

Siede pulled up close to the other men. "Why don't they kill us? Clearly, they have the advantage."

Efram began to jog ahead. "I don't know, but let's not give them any reason to change their minds."

Chapter 19

When the men safely reached the canyon once more, Isontra was distraught. When she'd allowed Trep to take the young men, she hadn't expected the White Ones to interfere. Since Grimly and his team had been forced to return, but left unharmed, Isontra hoped Trep and the young men had slipped safely passed.

While Grimly was in the Gathering House, railing against Isontra and the White Ones, Kairma slipped into Isontra's room with a kettle of terrid. "Gramme, I don't think you should worry about Trep or even Toric."

Isontra stopped pacing long enough to fix a stare at Kairma. "And why is that, child?"

Kairma poured two cups of a spicy, hot drink. It was a new recipe she wanted to try. "I walked with them as far as the north shore of the lake. The White Ones were there, but they didn't try to stop the men from leaving."

Isontra sipped the drink Kairma offered her and made a face. The taste was different, but not unpleasant. The face was a reaction to learning Kairma had been so far from the village late at night and all alone. Her tone was measured but dripped with exasperation. "You were there? You saw Naturi was with them? And you said nothing to anyone about his leaving."

Kairma looked down, embarrassed by her lie of omission. "Yes. He really wanted to go, and I thought it would be better to have three men to watch Trep, in case something happened to Collin or Zedic. It's possible Trep could hurt one of them while the other one slept."

Isontra blew out a frustrated sigh. "You do realize that you allowed two of your slim choice of five mates to leave the village, with no guarantee that either of them will return safely. Not to mention, you were out there in the middle of the night by yourself."

Kairma studied an imaginary spot on the table in front of her. "Yes. I know, but I left the Crystal here on my bed."

"Child, I don't know what I'm going to do with you. You seem determined to hurt yourself." She studied her granddaughter over the tips of her fingers. "Why do you think Toric is safe?"

"I think the White Ones would have turned him back if they could, but I don't think they want to kill any of us."

"They had no qualms about killing those Madics at the temples."

"The Madics were shooting their karracks. We saw them kill at least one of the White Ones."

Isontra thought about this for a long time. The spicy taste of the terrid grew on her as she sipped it. "That was a very big risk. You should never have been that far from the canyon by yourself. I can't seem to instill a true sense of your responsibilities in you. Maybe I shouldn't have let you run with Collin all these annums. He was always a risk taker, and now I think his ways may have influenced you beyond repair." Isontra searched her granddaughter's eyes. Kairma was right to send an additional man, she only wished she'd thought of it herself. Toric would have been the logical choice. As she set out the Ogs for today's lessons, she realized, planned or not, Toric was probably with them now anyway.

The next day was warmer, but the rain continued. After a while they came to a wide area with few trees. Trep told them it was the remains of a road built hundreds of years ago. The road, similar to the last two miles to the Godstones, was fairly smooth and gently sloped down toward the plains. In some places they could see how it switched back and forth on the steeper part of the mountainside. When they could see the road below, where it switched back, they would climb down to the lower road and continue on. As the sun lowered in the west, Trep led them confidently, while the rest of the party was hopelessly lost.

From the forest behind them they could hear the sounds of something following them. The trees were too thick to make out what kind of animal might be on their trail, so the men began to move faster. A clearing opened up and Trep suggested they keep to the trees, and wait to see what was behind them. "Whatever is followin' us is big and noisy. Most animals that loud aren't afraid of the likes of us. If it is a predator, it will surely catch us out there. Keep y'all's weapons ready and watch for it to reach the clearing."

Sitting patiently, weapons at the ready, the four men waited for the animal to appear in the clearing. A branch moved to the side and they could see the deerskin plainly in the lowering sun, but the animal walked upright, on two feet—not four. He was moving slow, panting hard, tired from running. Tears leapt to Naturi's eyes as he recognized his father, but anger was blazing in Toric's eyes as the four men came to meet him in the clearing.

Toric raised his bow, notched a long arrow, and pulled the string tight, aiming it at Trep. "Why have you taken my son? I should kill you where you stand!"

Collin pulled Trep to the ground and the arrow flew past at a deadly speed, missing Trep's head by less than two inches.

By the time Toric had notched another arrow, Naturi was at his side. "Father, don't do this! This isn't his doing! It was my choice! I chose to come. I wanted to be here."

Toric shook with anger as Naturi wrapped his strong arms around his father, holding his bow down. "Please, this was my decision. I was the one who showed up uninvited."

"Why did you leave me? Do you hate me so much? Did I drive you away like I drove away your mother?"

"No, Father. I chose to come because …" He wasn't sure he wanted his father to know the real reason he'd come. He wasn't sure he wanted to admit to anyone that this had more to do with Collin than anything else. It was also possible that if Naturi hadn't come, Collin could return before the Seridar bearing gifts and weapons of untold value. "Because two men are not enough to watch over a prisoner, and until we know Trep is honorable, he will be our prisoner."

"You could have told me. I would have volunteered to be the third man. Or Jared or Siede. Why was it so important that you do this yourself?"

Toric had calmed down some, so Naturi led him to a place in the shade to sit. "I needed to know I could do it."

When Naturi didn't say anything more, Toric asked, "You needed to know you could do what?"

Naturi sat beside his father for a long time without speaking. He needed to know he was better than Collin at everything, but he really didn't understand why. The elders had always held him in high regard, and often spoke disparagingly about Collin, but it was the look in Kairma's eyes he sought to change. There was laughter in her eyes when she smiled at Collin, and Naturi longed to see that kind of happiness in her eyes when she smiled at him. He'd won over the hearts of the village, but it was Kairma's heart that mattered most. He couldn't tell his father this. Toric cringed whenever Naturi spoke her name. "I won't go back now. You can join us or return alone."

Toric stared up at his son, now fully three inches taller than him. "There'll be no changing your mind?"

"No, Father. When I chose to defy the Miral, I chose to complete this hunt. I will not go back with my tail between my legs."

Naturi thought he saw a flicker of pride cross his father's face. It surprised him, making his heart skip. Maybe Collin had been right when he'd said Toric might respect his decision to come.

Toric sounded gruff, but less angry. "I may as well go with you. I can help with the tracking, and maybe we can get you home quickly."

"You are the best tracker we have. We should have insisted you go from the beginning."

"I think I made my opinion of this hunt pretty clear the day of the meeting. I still don't like the idea, but since we're already two days away from Survin, we may as well finish it."

Trep told them to look for a campsite, and although it seemed to take hours Naturi finally spotted a large rock ledge jutting out from the mountainside. "That looks like a pretty good place. At least it will be dry under there."

All evening, things were very tense between Toric and Trep, but Toric hadn't threatened to kill the traveler in several hours, and everyone was slowly beginning to relax. Naturi blessed them with another wonderful meal as they huddled under the shallow ledge.

Trep and Naturi offered to take the first watch and Zedic took the second. When Zedic woke Collin for his watch, the rain was pattering on the rock above them, dripping annoyingly down the side of the small cavern. The fire was sputtering and hissing as rain found its way onto the hot coals.

Collin found it difficult to stay awake as he sat staring into the blackness around them. As the sky lightened to a deep gray, he nodded off.

He snapped awake to the sounds of a deep growling. At first he looked to see if it was coming from one of his friends, snoring or having illicit dreams; it wasn't. Searching the forest in the fragile gray light, he could make out the largest, unblinking eyes he'd ever seen. They were bright orange, like firelight. It took him awhile to realize the eyes were, indeed, reflecting the light of his small fire. The huge eyes belonged to a cat, a very big cat, in fact—the largest cat he'd ever seen. Sweat drenched his back and made his hands slick. He wiped them slowly on his vest, and from the corner of his eye he searched for the karrack he'd dropped when he'd nodded off.

A sleepy Trep picked up the karrack Collin had dropped and pointed it at the huge feline. The growl deepened, waking Naturi and Zedic. The young men held as still as stone while Trep seemed to study the cat.

Toric, awake now, tugged gently on Trep's arm "Well, are you going to kill it, or are you going to let it eat us?"

"I know this cat. Don't think he intends to hurt us." Trep motioned for Collin to get behind him, and Collin didn't need to be told twice.

Soon a very tall man stood next to the cat. At seven and a half feet tall, the man was at least four inches taller than the tallest Survinees. The man was broad as well, looking like he could take on the whole lot of them, with or without the help of the cat. Zedic moved back against the wall of the meager shelter, as did the other Survinees. "Great Stones! He's half again as big as Trep!"

A broad grin, showing strong white teeth, swelled on the giant's face. "Well, well, well, if it isn't my old friend, Trep! I thought you always traveled alone." He placed a hand on the big cat's head and began to scratch it behind the ears. The cat purred even louder than it had growled. He stroked his large hand down the back of the animal, and immediately, the cat sat down and proceeded to clean its fur. "So, what brings you to my mountain this time, and who are all your companions?"

Trep was visibly relieved. He placed the karrack beside the fire and invited the giant man to come in from the rain. "It's good to see ya again. We're looking for some men headed toward the city. Has anyone else come through here?" Naturi offered the man something to eat, but the man declined, saying he'd already eaten.

"No one's come this way since you were here last."

To the others, Trep introduced his friend. "This is Zacar, and that ball of fluff out there is Purder. Last summer while wandering around, looking for your Godstones, I fell and broke my leg. There I was, hardly able to move and half starved when this big tawny cat comes up to me and starts yowling." Trep's grin widened. "I thought I was his dinner for shore, but that cat kept making this god-awful noise. That's when Zacar found me. Took me back to his cabin and nursed me back to health like a babe."

Zacar smiled gently and motioned to the others. "You men look wet and cold. Why don't you come up to my cabin?"

After putting out the coals of their fire, they followed Zacar down the mountainside to a large stone and pine log cabin. Wood smoke drifted lazily from a large stone chimney. A wide porch ran across the front of the cabin with an oversized rocking chair by the door. Pinewood rails outlined a small patch of grass in front of the home. A big black dog trotted up to them as they approached. Zacar said, "This here's Jesse. She won't bite neither."

Although they were in a hurry, they accepted Zacar's invitation to get out of the rain for a while.

The wet and worn travelers were treated to a fine breakfast and a wonderful story about how he had found Purder as a kitten. "His mother had been killed. I think it must have been a bear. Not too many things here take out a big cat, you know. Took me a week to get him down out of that tree. Jesse there," he said, pointing to his dog. "She'd just had pups. It was quite a sight watching her nurse that big cat with those two little pups." His laughter filled the room.

Trep chuckled. "Still remember the first time I saw one of those cats fully grow'd. Damn, they're fast. I barely got my karrack up before it was on top of me. Still got a scar halfway down my back." He pulled up the back of his shirt, showing the others three long red marks that ran from just under his shoulder blade and disappeared into the waist of his pants. Zacar started showing off several of his hard won scars and soon everyone had a scar and a story to tell.

To repay him for the hot breakfast, the early part of the morning was spent helping Zacar with a few chores. Although he'd invited them to stay overnight, they needed to hurry, so, after wishing Zacar well, they headed east again, feeling warmer and refreshed.

The sky was still overcast and spitting just enough to make the walk miserable. A break in the clouds came at the same moment as a break in the thick forest. There was a great deal of excitement as they got their first glimpse of the vast plains. Collin was in a hurry to reach the plains, but Trep assured him it would be at least mid-morning the following day before they would actually set foot on the plains. When the sun began to drop they talked of stopping for the night, but finding a dry camp was difficult, as the rocky landscape had given way to rolling hills and sparse forest. They continued for another two miles before finding a place to camp for the night. They made a small lean-to and shared the cramped quarters without much talk.

Chapter 20

The next morning, a bright yellow sun rose in a clear sapphire sky, a wondrous relief from the cold rain. Setting out early, everyone was in better spirits as they started to follow a broad pathway that was carved into the side of the mountain. It followed the creek, winding to the north and to the east.

Trep had seen many of these roadways, and was about to speculate on the possibility of the Ancient Ones being the engineers, when they reached the edge of the mountain pass. There, in the bright sun, they could see the vast plains stretching out like an ocean of tall grass before them. For mile upon mile to the north, east and south, all they could see was the soft waves of a green on a treeless land. As they looked back the way they had come, the mountains seemed small and somehow insignificant when compared to the sweeping plains. What was once their whole world, now felt intensely fragile. The small band of friends stood in silence for several minutes, staring at the ocean of grass. Now they fully understood how far their duty lay.

Trep understood the anxiety the Survinees experienced when seeing the plains for the first time; he well remembered the sense of disorientation the first time he found himself in the mountains. On the plains, he was able to see for several miles in any direction, but in the mountains, rocks and forest blocked every view and turned a person around. It was a long time before he could distinguish one tree or rock from another.

Collin was the first to shake off the awe. "It would be a lot easier to cross that if we all had horses to ride. I feel bad that you have to walk while I ride."

Trep smiled in agreement. "When we get done with this job and go to Peireson Landin', we can buy some horses. It will definitely make the trip back easier."

Zedic, who was leading Belle at the time, sighed. "I can't wait. I saw a beautiful white horse down by the lake several annums ago. I want one exactly like that!"

Toric pulled up short. "What's this? I thought we were tracking outsiders."

Naturi said, "We plan to go all the way to the city. Isontra has given Trep permission to bring back his woman."

Toric spit out a few profane words. "That's craziness. She said, 'If you find yourself close to the city.' There's no reason for you to risk your life by going into a wolverine's den if you don't have to."

Naturi was firm. "I want to go all the way. I need to know what the rest of the world is like. We can gain much by trading with the city."

Toric spit. "And you can lose everything!" Knowing he would never change his son's mind, he joined the other men walking toward an endless vista of grass.

Hurrying the men along, Trep said, "We'll head northeast from here. That tiny line of trees down there is the river. We should have 'least one more day of water before we need to refill the skins, so we'll save 'least half a day or more by cuttin' across that valley. I'm guessin' we'll catch up to those men by maybe day after tomorrow, if that wounded man can still ride. Couldn't really see how bad he might of got hurt. Let's hope it was fatal, save us havin' to do the deed."

The rest of the group just stared at Trep. Although, they understood the necessity of stopping the Madics, even if that meant killing them, it was a bitter medicine.

They made their way down the rolling hills and into the wide valley. The air was thick with the smell of honey from huge swaths of clover as the Survinees fought their way through thick prairie sandreed nearly four feet high. The mountain meadows rarely had grasses over two feet high, and the pine trees limited most other ground cover to bare inches. Yellow patches of cleft gromwell and western wallflower greeted them on the lower hills, while bright clumps of lanceleaf blue bells broke up the ocean of green and yellow fur covering the hillsides.

Trep raised a hand to cover his eyes from the bright sun. "Looks like a buffalo trail 'head of us. They must of come through here a few days ago. It'll make walkin' a lot easier, not havin' to fight waist-high grasses. We'll make good time now."

Behind them, the jagged peaks of the mountain turned from soft azure to pale indigo as they came upon a strange metal structure. There were three metal shafts three feet by six feet wide that rose in a gentle arc to meet in the center some ten or more feet above their heads.

Zedic asked Trep what it could be. "I'm not sure, Zed. I saw it on my way here and studied it at length. I'm sure it was left by the Ancient Ones, I think it could be some type of religious temple, or what's left of it."

"Do you think it had walls before?"

Trep examined the shafts as they passed. "I would think it must have, though I cain't see a sign of anythin' ever havin' been attached to it."

Naturi replied, "Maybe it was a message post, or a kind of gate separating the mountains from the plains."

"That's a thought. Seems kinda like a waste of good metal. I don't understand much about the Ancient Ones. I guess it could be anythin', but I think it was important."

Collin looked it over and laughed. "Maybe they made it just to look at. Like Naturi makes his drawings."

Trep turned. "I'm sure it had a purpose. Everythin' the Ancient Ones did had a purpose. They were far too advanced to waste their skills. No, this must have had religious meanin', probably a temple or a place of worship."

Zedic cocked his head to one side. "Who or what did they worship?"

"Cain't say as I know. Maybe while we worship the Ancient Ones as gods, they worshiped even older folks." Trep chuckled at the thought.

Toric brushed past the others. "We don't worship your Ancient Ones, and I think it's foolish to believe the gods have anything in common with us." He stood with his hands on his hips. "How far before we find those men? Seems like we're taking our sweet time. Wasted a lot of time at your friend's house."

Trep sobered. "This is a good place to rest and we're makin' good time following that buffalo swath. It won't hurt to take an extra hour tonight."

Toric mumbled something about chasing ghosts and turned away from the others. After setting up their camp at the base of the strange monument, they spent the dinner hour discussing the possible reasons for its existence.

On the fifth day from Survin they reached the river once more. Off to the east they could see desolate hills. Where they walked, the grass grew lush and high, but less than a stone's throw from the river the land was dead. Windblown, desolate pinnacles of delta clay and sandstone rolled on for miles, cut by deep chasms and narrow ravines. Occasional patches of sage and rabbit bush dotted the hills like a scattering of stars on a cloudy night. Pointing out the barren landscape, Trep whispered, "I'd never think of crossin' land like that. Scares me just to look at it. I've seen a few holes in the ground where nothin' grew, but not like this. Y'all can see this goes on forever."

They stopped to take a break from walking. The men were tough, but five days of walking was hard on them, even considering the last day was crossing flat grassland.

Collin's leg had healed enough that he no longer needed his crutch when he wasn't riding on Belle. Laying it aside, he rubbed his sore armpit. "Don't know what hurts more, the leg or the arm."

Zedic gave him a waterskin. "I'm glad you weren't hurt worse. I'd hate to listen to you whine for another week."

Collin threw a small rock, and dodging the missile Zedic laughed.

Toric grumbled something under his breath about being juvenile, making the boys laugh even louder.

Naturi took off his moccasin and rubbed his foot. He noticed Trep was the only one who didn't seem to have sore feet. "I would like to have a pair of boots like yours. They appear to be good for walking."

Trep looked down at his leather boots. "They do help, but ya gotta remember I'm used to walkin' long distances. Don't usually stop anywhere for more than a few months. There's always somethin' new to discover."

Toric said, "It would be nice if you could discover the men we chase. Tell me, Trep. Are you certain about their destination?"

Taking off the other moccasin and putting his feet in the cold water, Naturi asked. "Do you think those men came through here? We have yet to see any signs."

"If they came around the north side of that peak, we should catch them before the river turns east again. They gotta follow the river to get back to the city."

Collin followed Naturi's lead and soaked his sore feet. "How far is the city?"

"Hate to tell ya this, but it's a lot farther away than we've come. My best guess is we've come about a third of the way."

There was a collective groan from the Survinees.

"The part we jess came through is the hardest. Had to stay on the river the whole time 'cause the hills are too steep through the mountains. Now we can stay more to the flat lands. Jess gotta stay close enough that we don't lose sight of the river. You can see the line of trees from a mile or better, I mean, *kilometer* or two. Course, the hard part will be findin' where those men chose to walk. If we stick close to the river here, we should be able to see where they cross over. Find that, and we find the men."

The men put their moccasins back on and began walking through the coarse grass once more.

Chapter 21

The morning sun was shining through the east window, warming Kairma's back as she helped Isontra sew lace to the bottom of several white veils. The veils were for Kairma's rite of passage—her Seridar. She felt nervous about asking her grandmother the questions she had been thinking about, so she started with what she thought was a safer subject. "Why does Grimly hate you?"

"I don't believe he actually hates me." Isontra smiled at Kairma. "I believe he's afraid of new ideas and he doesn't like the direction I'm leading the community. You see, I'm convinced you can change a society's attitude by *not* teaching old ideas as well as by teaching new ideas. New ideas carry a strong possibility of being rejected if they appear too radical. Most people are slow to accept change. Grimly is no exception."

Kairma handed her grandmother a finished piece and began making tiny stitches on a smaller veil. "What will you do? He's been very disruptive and outspoken about the decision to hunt down the Madics."

Isontra held up the white blouse she was hemming and checked to see if the stitches were showing through. Laying it across her lap, she looked over at Kairma thoughtfully. "I may not be able to do anything about Grimly. I hope to introduce some new ideas that will eventually be accepted by asking questions and letting others discover their own answers. I believe it's natural to question things that have not been sufficiently explained, and it's a more subtle way of changing the direction of a group. By guiding the questions and helping people to find their own answers, new beliefs take on a life of their own."

"What are the changes you're trying to bring about? I know you want us to have weapons like Trep's, but what other things are you trying to change?"

"Well, by not teaching, or I should say, not dwelling on the old ways of killing outsiders and the White Ones, I hope to have opened people's minds. Now, as new questions are raised, I can reply without many of the old prejudices and fears shading the answers."

Kairma considered that for a moment. "Don't all the strangers who come here want to steal the Crystal? I thought that's why we had to stay hidden all these annums."

"What was once good policy for protecting our relic may have grown into an unrealistic fear of strangers. As time passes, the original reasons for many of the things we do become more and more of a mystery." Isontra paused briefly as if remembering something important. "I think the loss of my Gramme at a young age led my mother to find her own answers to some of these questions. She in turn led me to do the same."

"Well, maybe not all strangers are bad, but we have always fought with the White Ones. Aren't they evil? I know Collin thinks they aren't bad, only really hungry. He thinks they take the tributes we leave at the Godstones every full moon."

"You've stumbled onto a curious question. Are the White Ones really people like us or are they some kind of wild animal? After many annums of studying the past writings in the Ogs, I believe what once was a simple form of defense may have become an unjustifiable hatred. If you don't want a child to get too close to someone or something, isn't it easier to make the child fear the person rather than try to explain why they should stay away?"

"So, you do think they're people. If that's true, why can't you tell everyone what you think?" Kairma found this confusing. She never thought of her grandmother having to do, or not do, anything she wanted. She always seemed so powerful, almost omnipotent.

Isontra sighed and handed Kairma the blouse to try on. "It's a very slow process to change a belief system. Taking something on faith often has little to do with common sense; by its very nature, it refutes logic."

"Then how do we change what people believe if we can't use logic?" Kairma asked with conviction.

"Older people will not usually change their minds, and when asked, they will usually give a child enough reasons to hate what they hate. But if that hatred is not reinforced, the child may begin to question it. And there will always be a few children who will not follow with blind faith, and those are the children who will shape the new world."

Slipping the blouse over her head and straightening the sleeves, Kairma asked, "Do you think we can do this? I mean, can we change the world?"

"I don't believe our people are ready to accept the White Ones yet, although you may very well be the bridge that takes our people to the next level. Since your illness, you don't appear to belong to us or to the White Ones."

Kairma cringed at that thought. "How can I be expected to lead the community when most of its members believe I'm one of our most-hated adversaries?

Tugging the blouse in place, Isontra said, "I know this is difficult for you. The old hate is strong and it will be tough to break down these walls. I doubt if you or I will see a major change in our lives. We do this for the future of our world, not for the benefit of our own existence." Isontra held Kairma by the shoulders, and then slowly turned her around so she could check the back. "Is this too tight across your breasts? The waist looks like it fits well."

"It's beautiful, Gramme!" Kairma went to the wall where a large horizontal plate of alloy served as a mirror. Turning back and forth, she checked her reflection and sighed. "Oh, Gramme, white on white on white. I'll have to wear some really colorful flowers in my hair."

"You will be beautiful."

Coming back to the table, Kairma said, "I want things to be different now. You're so unselfish. I hope I can be like you, someday. Sometimes, I wonder if I'll ever grow up, and other times I'm terrified that I will."

Isontra laughed. "One could argue that you are grown up. You can feed yourself, find shelter, and bear offspring. I would say that makes you an adult." Kairma shuddered and Isontra smiled at her. "Growing up is a lifelong process, not a goal. The day you stop growing up is the day you stop living. Look closely at the people around you. How many of them are still aging, but have stopped living?"

Kairma carefully took the blouse off and went back to stitching hemp lace to a veil. "I don't feel like an adult. I'm so unsure of myself. Why is the Crystal given to someone who is so young? You are so much wiser. I would think it would be better if you kept it until I was ready."

Isontra folded up the blouse and began to work on the long white skirt. "The Crystal is the symbol of who you will become. It instills a sense of responsibility in a person not otherwise achieved. It is a constant reminder that you belong to the people of Survin." Isontra picked up a new piece of sun-bleached suede. "Your youth is important. You're young enough to have, and to accept, new ideas. You're also more flexible than me. You're willing to take risks because you haven't formed so many biases. You have energy, and you have hope." Isontra chuckled quietly. "Most young people think they're fireproof, they're fearless. For all these reasons, these people need you whether they know it or not. I need your zest for life as well, Kairma. You keep me on my toes."

Kairma didn't feel fearless. She was terrified, sure she would end up doing the wrong thing. "How will I know when I'm ready to be a Miral—ready to be responsible for Survin? When will I *feel* grown up?"

Isontra's eyes twinkled. "You'll just know when you know. For everyone, it's different."

Kairma was in a sour mood. Although it had been a relatively short time since the men left on their mission, she was already missing her best friends. A whole summer seemed like a lifetime to be away, and Kairma was dying to investigate the vault again. With Kinter as her perpetual companion, Kairma couldn't get away. Kinter's constant remarks about her having a better memory for facts than Kairma was one more thing Kairma found irritating. Looking over at her little sister, Kairma was sure Kinter knew just how expensive the bargain for her silence had been.

Kinter seemed to feel Kairma's eyes on her. "Where do you think they are now? Bet they killed those men and are already in the city."

Kairma shook her head. "Trep said it would take almost a full moon to reach the city, and that's if they were able to take care of those Madics without any trouble."

Kinter's cobalt eyes widened. "A whole moon? I get tired just walking to the Godstones and back. I'd never want to walk for a whole moon."

"I guess if you really want something bad enough, you'd be willing to do almost anything."

Kairma thought about what it would be like to chase someone down and capture or kill him. In the abstract, it didn't seem difficult, but when she visualized herself taking part in the action, she didn't think it was something she could follow through with. She wondered if the men who had been assigned to the duty had similar feelings. She knew she would have walked the distance if given the opportunity—she couldn't imagine how interesting the city would be—but she was thankful it wouldn't have to be her hand that took the lives of those men.

Most of the girls' days were filled with helping Isontra treat various injuries and maladies. Today, Jacom brought in his youngest son who had discovered a patch of poison ivy. Isontra said it was a good chance to test the girls on their Healing skills. Kinter was the fastest to procure the juice of jewelweed to dry up blisters and rose hips to use as an antihistamine. Kairma remembered that a rub made of crushed plantain broadleaf would stop the itching but didn't know where to find it.

Morgaina stopped by, complaining of elbow pain. Isontra said it sounded like bursitis. Kairma was quick to put together a poultice of comfrey wrapped in suede. "Drink this herbal tea consisting of two parts chamomile, one part powdered skullcap, and one part roughly ground root of Lady's Slipper. At bedtime, add hops."

Collin's mother, Massie, came to see them the same morning. She waited until Morgaina had gone before taking a seat on one of the cots that lined the hospital. "I can't sleep at night and I feel so tired."

Isontra felt her pulse and looked at her eyes. "How is your general mood lately?"

"To be honest, since Collin left, I just don't feel alive anymore."

"Are you still spending a lot of time at the Gathering House?"

"Not really. I go there sometimes with Diakus, but mostly I stay in bed, trying to sleep."

The village was small and there were no secrets. It was true that Massie stayed home most of the time, but while there she consumed a fair amount of wine.

Isontra went to the shelves along the west wall and pulled out a few jars. "I'm going to ask you to drink this terrid made from soy, evening primrose, and St John's wort. Don't mix this with wine." She handed Massie a small bag of herbs. She reached for another and began mixing a few ingredients together. "Every night place this lavender poultice over your eyes. This should help you sleep."

Massie thanked her as she left.

Kairma placed the jars back on the shelves. "She sounds so sad."

Isontra nodded. "I'm afraid she's quite depressed. I've tried to convince her to give up the wine, but she's a stubborn woman."

"Do you think it's because she misses Collin?"

"It's hard to say. The wine has a lot to do with it. Losing your two oldest children would be hard on anyone. I think that, mixed with Diakus' reaction, has done her more harm than anything."

"Diakus is always so angry—even more angry than Toric."

Isontra deliberated a moment. "They both lost someone dear to them. It's hard to understand why bad things happen to us and sometimes it makes us angry."

Kairma thought about this. Bad things had happened to her, but nothing to compare to the losses dealt to the two men in question. "When Grampe died, did you get angry?"

"Yes, for a while I was very angry. He was killed in an accident at a very young age. With time, I became sad, and eventually I got over the pain."

"Why haven't Diakus or Toric gotten over the anger?"

"I knew when Petar died it was an accident. I didn't like it, but in most ways I understood. I think for Toric the question of why Devon left is what keeps the wound open."

"And Diakus?"

Isontra tapped her fingers to her lips, thinking. "I think the sheer tragedy of the act caused him to seek solace in wine, and the wine now keeps the wound fresh."

"I wish I could help them."

"So do I, dear. So do I."

The daily lessons continued and the two girls silently competed to see who would win Isontra's favor each day. The weather had turned cool again, but the budding aspens told them it was time to plant in earnest. So, Kairma and Kinter sat at the large table in Isontra's room, sorting seeds. Empty, small leather pouches lay on the wooden chair next to them. The girls looked closely at the seeds, determining if they looked healthy enough to plant. Kairma looked up at Kinter. "Would you put more wood on the fire? It's getting a little cool in here."

"Is your arm broken? If you're cold, you know where the wood is."

Kairma blew out a sigh and got up to stoke the fire. "You're sitting right next to the wood pile. Would it have killed you to reach over and toss a log in the hearth?" She turned a few pieces of burning coals and added a pine log. Kinter never looked away from her sorting.

The girls continued to sort in silence until Isontra came into the room. Both girls greeted her with right hands to their foreheads. Isontra returned the greeting and looked over the piles of seeds. "You girls have done a fine job. I think we'll have a nice garden this annum." She looked through Kinter's selection of seeds. "Very good. These will surely sprout." Turning to Kairma's somewhat smaller piles, she said, "These look good too. Oh, here's one I think is bad." She looked closely at the broken seed. "Don't be in too much of a rush to finish, dear."

Kinter beamed, and Kairma blushed. It wasn't a reprimand, but Kairma had rushed through the job, and had been caught making mistakes. She had seen Kinter's piles of good seeds growing faster than hers, and not wanting to appear incompetent, she hurried. *Stones. Kinter knows her seeds. At least I can still read better than she can.* She rechecked her seeds as Isontra and Kinter filled the small bags.

Kairma began splitting pieces of pine that would label the rows of plants in the garden. She was also better at writing script so the task of making labels fell to her. She took several pieces of wood about as big around as her wrist and with a small knife she split them in half. Before she could write the letters, she needed to make the wood as smooth as possible. Using a rough piece of granite she sanded the face of the wood. Once she was satisfied with the surface, she carved letters on the flat side of the split limb using the small stone knife.

❧

The sign-making would take most of the day, so while Kairma carved Kinter and Isontra planted the seeds in the garden. Kinter actually liked planting the garden every annum, and she showed off her knowledge to her grandmother with aplomb.

"The lavender is used for insomnia, headaches, or depression. The

St John's wort is used for depression too." She carefully covered a row of seeds. "Valerian, catnip, and hops can treat nervousness or be used to aid sleep."

Isontra handed her another small bag of seeds to plant. "What do we use to treat a sore throat?"

Without a pause, Kinter said, "Cloves, honey, golden seal, licorice, and raspberry leaves."

"What would you do for someone with a fever?"

Kinter placed the small seeds in the shallow trench she carved in the black dirt. "The easiest treatment is a terrid made from catnip, dandelion, and lobelia. If the patient gets an upset stomach, cut back on the lobelia." She covered the seeds and moved to the next row. "You can use feverfew if the patient isn't pregnant. Black thorn, white bark, and poke root might be helpful." She sat back on her heels and looked up at her grandmother. "The patient needs lots of rest, lots of water, and little food. If the fever gets really high, a cool bath will help, but always look for a wound that may be red and inflamed. If you find one, treat the wound first."

Isontra looked pleased. "What would you recommend for an infected wound?"

Kinter had an excellent understanding of medicine. She smiled as she took another sack of seeds. "Clean the wound with clear antiseptic. Coating the wound with honey will help draw out the infection and a poultice made with lobelia and slippery elm bark will be soothing and help fight further infection."

As they finished the last row of seeds, Kairma waved to them. Kinter stood up and brushed the dirt off her hands, feeling a sudden sadness. Every annum until now, Naturi had helped her plant the annual herbs. She took the signs from Kairma, and placed them in the appropriate locations while wondering what Naturi was doing at that moment. *Does he miss the spring planting? Does he miss his home? Does he ever think of me?*

Chapter 22

Toric had made rude remarks about Trep's tracking abilities from the first day he'd joined the hunt, but as of yesterday Toric's remarks were more pointed. After two days of following the river, they still hadn't seen any signs of the Madics, and Toric began to suspect Trep had lied to them. "Why are you so sure those men will come this way? Could be you're leading us on a fake ferret hunt."

Trep explained once more why he thought the men would return to the city. "The saddles they have are from Peireson Landin'. I've only been to two other towns big enough to have a livery, and each place makes saddles a little differently. Saddles from Peireson Landin' have a sturdy horn used for ropin' and a wider seat. Men around here spend a lot of time on their horses. Down south, most horses are used for pullin' carts or as pack animals. Oh, they do a bit of fancy ridin' but mostly they travel by means of the pedal-cart."

Everyone stopped and looked at Trep. Naturi was the first to ask. "Lacking your worldliness, we have never heard of this thing you call a pedal-cart. Is it an animal similar to the horse?"

"Gods no, boy. It's a cart you sit in and pedal."

"What does this mean, pedal?"

Trep made pedaling motions with his hands, but the Survinees were still confused. "The city in the south, Charlton, it's mostly flat, except by the river, so folks have these little four-wheeled carts that they pedal around in."

Toric was getting irritated. "I want to know why you think these men will go back to your city? Enough with talk of strange places we'll never see."

Trep sobered. "When I got to Peireson Landin' about four years ago, I was lookin' for artifacts, things left by the Ancient Ones. See, it's kinda a hobby of mine. I do a little tradin' with the items once I've learned all I can 'bout where they come from and what they was used for." He stopped and took a long pull on his waterskin. "When I got to town, I had a few things to unload and I needed supplies. I was introduced to a man called Narvin. Seems he has an affinity for old things too. One thing led to another, and I ended up sellin' my whole collection to the man." He stopped and knelt by the river. After looking through the tall grasses he went back to his narrative. "Now, Narvin had a fair collection of his own before he met me. He tells me his grandfather was a nobleman who watched the treasury of a little fiefdom near the ocean. That treasury supposedly contained hundreds of these ancient objects, some that could still be used, until somethin' happened and Narvin's cousin destroyed it all. He never really said how it happened, but Narvin's been searching for things ancient ever since."

Toric harrumphed. "Does this story have a purpose?"

"Course it does! See, I told Narvin I heard a story about a mountain carved with faces. I told him I was headed west to investigate. I think he sent those men to find my treasure."

"So they did follow you here?"

"No, don't think so. I left a full year—I mean annum ago. I got hurt, and Zacar had to nurse me back to health. I think Narvin sent these men when I didn't come back. If those men don't come back, he'll likely send more."

"Comes to the same thing. If you hadn't told him about the temples, those men wouldn't be here."

"Don't be so sure about that. I heard it from a man most folks thought was crazy, but I still came to check it out."

Toric spat, "You've been a whole lot of trouble since you knocked on our door. I've a mind to end this here." He bounded toward Trep, fists in tight balls.

Zedic stepped between the two men. "We'll find these men and then go to the city and eliminate any tales about the Godstones."

Toric grudgingly lowered his fists. "You're a good boy, Zedic, but it's dangerous to step between angry men."

Zedic acknowledged the warning with a nod. "If we do catch these men, we should make sure no one else wants to investigate our mountain."

Collin said, "I don't think we can threaten a whole city. Trep needs to convince Narvin there's no truth to the rumors about the mountain."

Trep agreed, but added, "That might buy y'all a few years, but eventually, someone's gonna find y'all."

Zedic ran a hand through his dark hair and grimaced. "Hopefully we'll have better defenses by then."

The next day, the river turned east and Trep worried that he'd missed the crossing. He didn't want to say anything that would worry his companions, so he told them tales of the places he'd been and watched for signs. The river widened as two more streams added their spring runoff to the flow. "We should cross over now. The river gets swifter and much deeper around the bend."

The men removed their moccasins and forded the shallow river. The bluffs on the other side told the story of heavy rains and fierce winter snowmelt. They made camp about a mile down river. After an evening meal prepared by Naturi, Collin and Trep hiked to the top of the bluffs looking for the light of a campfire to the east. The sun painted the sky with streaks of bright orange and pink as lavender clouds drifted by aimlessly. On better days, Trep would have enjoyed the beauty of the sunset, but he was beginning to worry he'd missed the trail and led his team too far north. Eleven days out and they were no closer to completing their mission.

Collin twisted a lock of hair between his fingers as he stared off to the east, and then asked if there was another way to the city. "Maybe they didn't have to cross the river at all."

"Don't really have to cross it, but it's a long way around the lake. Don't make sense that they wouldn't."

They sat there until it was dark. The moon was a sliver and gave no light to climb down the bluffs. Collin's cloak caught on the prickly spines of a thistle, making him stop and turn around to untie it. As he did this he saw a light far to the west. "Trep! Look over there! Is that what I think it is?"

Trep turned to look where Collin pointed. "Gods, I think it is. I was sure they would reach the river before us. Must have had a hell of a time getting around the peak and back to the plains. I know I got lost every day in those mountains."

"What should we do?"

"First we need to let the others know, and ditch our fire. We don't want to give away our position."

Once back at camp, they doused the fire. Trep's group was below the bluffs to the west, so it was unlikely the Madics saw the fire, but it only made sense to keep a low profile. Toric grumbled something under his breath about Trep's parentage, but helped put out the fire. Toric was actually much relieved at having found their prey, thus saving him the obligation of having to kill the obnoxiously friendly traveler. The camp was cleaned up and the group moved to the top of the bluffs where they could see farther. The wind had come up, chilling the night air, and the clouds began to drift in, putting out the light of the moon as Trep and Toric began to form a plan to eliminate the enemy.

Zedic suggested taking them head on. "We outnumber them. They wouldn't last ten minutes."

Trep frowned. "They have two karracks. They can do a lot of damage in ten minutes. No, the plan is that none of us gets dead. That means we have to come up behind them, or let them get close enough that we can take them out with arrows."

Toric scowled. "What about your karrack? Why do we need arrows?"

"I can take out one man, but by the time I reload, I'm afraid the other man will kill one of y'all."

Toric nodded. "We need to set a trap."

"My thinkin' exactly."

The night slowly deepened as each man was assigned his part. There were arguments as to whom would play what part, and whether or not Trep needed someone with him at all times. Toric grudgingly accepted the plan and acknowledged Trep's lead. It was too dark to put their plan in motion so while Naturi and Zedic watched for movement, the rest of the group drifted off to sleep. Toric and Trep weren't friends yet, but finding the Madics went a long way toward mending a serious rift between the two men.

At sunrise, the group studied the western skyline for signs of movement. Noisy geese honked overhead, returning from their long winter sojourn to the south. Being quick with his sling, Zedic took advantage as the V of birds passed low over their heads in search of the river. Angst rippled through the air like ozone after a lightning strike. It was the need to take action that prompted him to kill the bird. The sun rose higher in the sky as Zedic cleaned the bird, hoping it was a good omen. The Survinees rarely had goose. The big birds flew too far to the east to be hunted with regularity.

By mid-morning it became apparent why they'd seen no riders: the men were floating down the stream on a bundle of logs tied together to form a raft. The lone horse was trailing beside the river. Toric motioned for everyone to move out.

Trep pulled Naturi and Zedic aside. "Naturi, Zedic, remember, this won't work unless y'all can keep their attention. If you're not in karrack range, they won't see y'all as a threat, and might see Toric and Collin. Ya understand, don't you?"

Naturi nodded. "I will do my best to see that Zedic does not get shot."

"Y'all take care of yourself, and let Zedic take care of his own hide."

Toric walked up to Naturi, hesitated, and then threw his arms around his son. "I'm damn proud of you, boy. Don't get killed."

Naturi choked back a hard lump in his throat. "Thank you, Father. This will work, and I'll see you on the other side."

Toric backed up just far enough to give Naturi a playful jab on the chin. "Stones, when did you become a man?" He turned away quickly and grabbed his supplies.

Trep hid behind a stone pillar about six feet from the water's edge. The raft came around the bend and began moving faster in the fullness of the river. Using a log stick to control it, the man standing on the raft tried to stay near the gentler shoreline. As it neared, Trep could see a second man, his skin pale, lying under a mound of blankets. *Must be the man who got shot. They're missin' a horse too, but dead to right, that's the men we saw at the temples.*

Trep watched the raft come near, but it was still out of kill range. *He should a put a rudder on it. That thing's goin' all over the place.* He looked to the east where Zedic and Naturi stood by the water's edge. *Hope you're ready, boys! Good luck.*

Suddenly the small raft pulled up short and moved to the far side of the river behind a large rock outcropping. "Damn," Trep said, lowering his karrack. *If he had only come a little closer, I coulda ended this. He must have seen the boys already.* The sound of a karrack split the silence, and Trep saw Zedic and Naturi dive into the water. Trep fired once and turned to look down to the left, where Collin and Toric were sliding into the cold water. *That should get their attention.* Sure enough, a bullet chipped a nearby rock, followed by the unmistakable sound of a karrack. Trep ducked down from his stone perch, thankful the shooter had been facing into the sun. The Madics fired down river again and Trep watched the two boys disappear under the water once more. Across the river, the thin tether attaching the horse snapped the lone horse bolted and headed east. *Damn, could've used that horse. It'll be half way to Peireson Landin' by nightfall.*

Down the river, bullets zipped into the water at incredible speeds, followed by the unnatural sounds of the karracks. The water was cold, but warmer than the mountain streams they swam in as children. Naturi and Zedic had to surface often enough to keep the shooter occupied without getting killed. They didn't head in a straight line from shore to shore; instead, they bobbed and weaved back and forth so the shooter couldn't anticipate where they would surface next. Hearts racing as the eastern shoreline drew near, the two young men swam faster and straighter. Although they carried a bow and sling, they were out of range for their own weapons and had to depend on Trep to keep the shooter off balance until they could find cover. They saw Trep try to move west, closer to the raft, but the shooter, seeing him move, fired a round at Trep, forcing him back to his hiding place. The rocky bank was a little more than an arm's length away when Naturi felt the burn slice across his back and heard Zedic yell, "You've been hit!"

Trep tried to lure the man away from the boys. *If I could just get a clean shot at him.* He moved out from the rock and was greeted by the frightening sounds of bullets hitting nearby. *Whatever kind of karrack*

he has, it shoots farther than mine. Sorry boys, you're on your own. He hunkered down and debated whether he should waste more precious ammunition. *One way or another, we have to stop these men. Not that they deserve to die, but it's the only way to protect Survin. So why am I here? If I'm honest with myself, I don't know if I'm protecting these folks, or if I want to keep Survin secret because I don't want to share the discovery. And if it really is the Star of Genesis, why, that's the biggest find possible.* He fired once more to let the shooter know he was still there. *How do I get myself in these messes?* Reloading his karrack, he saw the water near Naturi turn red.

Using long reeds to breathe through, Collin and Toric slowly made their way across the swift-moving water, fighting the current with each step. The rocks that Trep had them tie to their belts held them below the surface well enough in the deeper channel, but there was a sand bar in the middle of the river that, even crawling, couldn't hide them completely. At this close range, the shooter would have no trouble hitting them. They waited for the sounds of karracks firing, hoping that meant the shooter was aiming down river at Naturi and Zedic. For the plan to work, they had to go now, hoping the battle would last long enough for them to reach the other bank and steal away behind the boulders they'd picked out earlier this morning.

They made it across the sandbar and waded through the eastern channel. There was a pause in the shooting and Toric held Collin back. Time slowed to a crawl as they sucked air through the now water-soaked reeds. They wouldn't be able to stay under the water for long once the reeds gave out.

A bullhead fish began to nibble on the feathered arrows in Toric's quiver. Collin brushed the fish away, but it came back again. Toric's bow was the largest in Survin. It took a strong man to wield it, and because of its size, Toric could shoot farther than anyone else. Collin's bow was pretty standard, and although he was a good shot, Naturi was more accurate with the weapon. As Collin brushed away another fish, he wondered if Naturi should have been here, waiting to surprise these strangers.

The sounds of karracks once more filled the air and the two men raced for the shoreline. The feathers of the arrows would need time to dry slightly. Taking them out of the quivers, Toric and Collin gently rapped them against the rocks, shaking the water out. The sun was nearly overhead now. That would make sighting easier. They crawled around the sandstone outcropping to the north. Coming up on the summit, they could make out the edge of the raft. The Madics were still hidden between the rocks. Silently, they snaked their way across the rocks. The dirt and sand were sticking to the wet suede on their bellies.

Toric pulled ahead slightly and motioned for Collin to stop. Like a stone, Collin paused in the process of reaching the next handhold. His right leg began to shake, supporting all his weight in this odd position. Thankfully, Toric waved him on, and he slithered up beside the older man. Below, the two Madics were reloading their weapons.

Toric pointed to the man standing and then to himself, and then pointed to the man crouching on the raft and back to Collin. Toric mouthed the words as they notched their arrows. "On my mark."

Collin nodded and raised his bow taking aim, as Toric did the same. A quick nod and two arrows sliced through the air gracefully. Before they hit, Toric had already notched another arrow.

Collin's arrow fell short of its mark, but Toric's second arrow completed the job. Animals don't die quickly unless the arrow pierces the heart or the brain. Men are no different, and Toric used two more arrows before the men on the shabby raft were lifeless. Collin had fired once more, but the arrow went wide, hitting the crouching man in the leg. He felt embarrassed by his poor marksmanship, but Toric clapped him on the back and said, "Well done, boy. I can't tell you how much better I feel knowing it's over."

Collin stared at the dead men for a long time. "We should bury them. It wouldn't be right to just leave them here."

"You're right, son. They didn't ask for this. They just stumbled into the wrong valley." Toric began to make his way down the rocks toward the raft. "Signal the others. Let them know it's over."

Collin stood on top of the rocks and waved to Trep. He could see the man race toward the place Zedic and Naturi were supposed to be, and he felt his gut tighten. "Toric, I think something's happened to Naturi or Zedic. Trep went racing toward them the moment I gave the *all clear* sign."

"This can wait! Let's go!" The two of them hurried around the bend where Naturi lay face down in the sand, his back red with water and blood. Zedic leaned over him, cutting away the leather vest. There was small hole in the back of the garment, near Naturi's shoulder blades.

Naturi moaned and Toric dropped to his knees. "You're going to be all right. Zedic's here."

The wound was shallow, only grazing Naturi's muscular back, like a knife slicing through the deltoid and across the trapezius muscles. The cold water had helped slow the bleeding and Zedic was able to stop it completely using Naturi's vest to put pressure on the cut. "I think he needs to lie here for a while. If someone could bring our things over, I might find a better bandage."

Trep offered to go. Toric suggested Collin go with him, not only to help carry things, but to make sure he came back.

Once Naturi was resting comfortably, Collin and Zedic went to bury the Madics. In a small, narrow ravine, they found several loose stones to build a cairn over the dead men. As they gathered rocks, Collin was very quiet.

Zedic thought he understood what was bothering his friend. "Don't take this personally, Collin. You did what had to be done."

"I didn't do it," he said flatly, "I missed." He laid one of the dead men in a shallow grave.

"Still, the men had to be stopped. If it makes you feel any better, they fired on us first." Zedic helped Collin move the other man to the grave.

"I know. I just hope this is the end of it."

"We still have to stop the rumors about the Godstones."

"Do you think that will be enough?"

"I don't know. We'll see."

After placing stones over the dead, Zedic recited the words he'd heard said on similar occasions. Collin was sad, but not overly morose. He knew Zedic was right. His duty was to Survin and that meant making hard decisions. It helped to think of these men as the ones who killed his brother and sister. He didn't know what happened to those men, but he knew he would recognize their faces if he ever saw them again.

Naturi rested while the other men set up camp. The snow goose Zedic killed earlier in the day made a magnificent meal. The fire crackled, sending sparks like fireflies into the dark. Toric relayed the story from his and Collin's point of view.

Zedic looked over at his best friend. "Weren't you scared, waiting in the water like that?"

"Probably less frightening than having someone shooting at me."

Zedic laughed. "Yes, that was rather terrifying, now that you mention it. It all happened so fast. Before I had a chance to think about it, it was over and I was dragging Naturi to the shore."

Naturi mumbled a thank-you to Zedic for saving his life.

Zedic shook his head. "It wasn't that bad. Might have hurt like the devil, but it didn't hit anything vital, just made a long cut."

Toric leaned down so he could see Naturi's face. "You'll have a fine scar to show everyone how brave you were. A day or two and we can go back to Survin where Isontra can take a look at you."

"I am going on to the city, Father."

Toric harrumphed. "But you've been wounded, son."

"It is a small thing, really. I will not change my mind."

Lying there, his back stinging from the medicine Zedic had applied, Naturi wondered if he would have been able to draw his bow if he'd been in Collin's place. He would not have missed and he recoiled at the thought of taking a man's life. Watching Collin, who was eating heartily on the other side of the campfire, Naturi wasn't sure if he were more appalled at, or leery of, Collin's ability to kill without remorse.

Chapter 23

The following morning, Collin and Zedic examined the raft. It was too small to hold more than three men and not very well constructed. Zedic was convinced he could make it larger using some of the cottonwood logs near the river, but at his suggestion to use the craft Trep shook his head. "If I didn't have Belle, we could ride most of the way on the river, but since Belle's gotta walk, I don't wanna add the extra miles."

Collin looked up from the karrack he'd appropriated. "Extra miles?"

"Yeah, the river winds back and forth on itself a couple dozen times. We're already far north of the city. I walked dang near every step of the river comin' west, so I wouldn't miss any possible towns 'long the way, but I can assure y'all, there's nothing on the river worth seein'. If we stick to the plains, close enough to see the washes, but not next to the water, we'll cut the miles nearly in half."

"I'm all for doing that," Zedic said.

Toric picked up the other karrack and asked Trep to show him how to load it.

"I don't wanna waste a lotta powder, but I think we could have a few shootin' lessons while Naturi mends." After Trep demonstrated how the karracks worked, they spent the remainder of the day practicing with the new weapons.

After two days of recuperation and arguments, Naturi insisted on moving again. Toric wasn't happy with the decision, and although he made several pointed remarks, he trudged on with the party toward the east.

Like an endless sea of grass, the plains rolled on ahead of them, never changing. The afternoons in the mountains were usually overcast and damp, but here on the vast plains the sun ravaged their skin and drained their spirit. Graceful hawks drew lazy circles in a sapphire sky, while rabbits and small foxes darted out of their sight. Occasionally patches of Shasta daisies and wild roses broke up the endless prairie as they swam though the tall grasses and prayed for shade. Slowly the stream they were following began to grow and take on the appearance of a river, and lavender and daylilies dotted the steep banks. Although huge cottonwoods appeared on the riverbanks, the trees were so close to the river that they offered the travelers little relief from the blistering sun.

As the days slipped by, they were all weary of traveling but found comfort passing the evenings with conversations about their cultures and beliefs.

Collin was curious about everything beyond Survin, badgering Trep with questions about his life and the places he'd seen. "Were you born in Peireson Landing?"

"No, I was born in a city down the great river. Town called Charltown. I left when I was sixteen, after my ma died. Wasn't easy, as we was the property of a wealthy Bear."

All faces turned to him, but it was Zedic who asked, "What's a Bear? I'm guessing you don't mean the kind that roam the mountains and eat all the good blackberries."

The corners of Trep's lips rose, and then he looked thoughtful. "No. How do I explain this? Ya see, where I come from, in Charltown, there're some folk who look a lot like y'all do. Ya know, they're really big and strong. Most have dark hair like you folks. We call 'em Bears. The smaller people, like my ma, we're called Innates."

Naturi looked up from the rabbit he was preparing for supper and asked, "Why do you call the others Bears?"

"Well, look at y'all. Y'all are big and strong as bears. What should we call ya?"

Naturi's back straightened, pulling on his recent wound—obviously offended. "We call the small ones Madics, and ourselves Survinees."

"I'm sure there's lots of different names for different people. The Survinees have different names for almost everythin'. That's one of the things that make y'all so interestin' to me."

Zedic was filling a black pot with water. "But you're not small and you're not as big as us. What are you called?"

Now Trep laughed out loud. "I'm what y'all would call *a bastard*."

Naturi's eyebrows shot up. "Why do they call you that?"

"Aside from the way I act sometimes? Well, see my pa was actually the Bear who owned us. So I'm not really a Bear, and I'm not really an Innate."

Collin interjected, more vexed by the thought of being owned than by the silly names they used, "I don't understand. How can someone own you?"

"That's the way it is in some places." Trep's voice became bitter. "The big guys own the little guys. It's what we call slavery. There are a lot of Bears in Charltown. Since the beginning, they kept the smaller, Innate people as workers in their fields and homes. They use and abuse 'em as they please."

Collin didn't think he would like Charltown. "Why don't the Innates just leave? Why do they keep being owned by the Bears?"

"It's not that easy to leave. There are laws. Kinda like your laws about leavin' the mountain."

All four Survinees nodded in understanding.

The weeks of camaraderie seemed to make the reclusive people more open to discussing their lives, and Trep was fascinated. Naturi explained how the leadership of the colony had always passed from mother to daughter and how long the colony had lived in their secluded little valley. Collin told chilling stories about the infamous White Ones who haunted the caves around their valley. But it was Toric who relayed the legend of the angel of Genesis who chose the Survinees, above all other races, to carry on Nor's mission.

"*Charles,* the embodiment of evil." Toric slammed his fist on the makeshift table they were using for the evening meal.

"That's y'all's belief. Other people have their own devils, but they use different names for him." Trep baited Toric with a wry grin.

"But how can that be?" Toric growled. "It is written in the Word of the Ogs that his name was Charles. Why would others call him by a different name?"

Trep leaned back casually. "Well, not everyone has heard of y'all's Ogs, or y'all's Charles. They have very different ideas about right and wrong, and what constitutes the truth." Trep enjoyed these heated discussions with Toric. Trep often started out asking a benign question he knew would lead to one of these more interesting topics. It was a great way to learn what made these people tick, but mostly it seemed to bring Toric out of his shell.

Toric sounded frustrated. "How can there be more than one truth? Surely if they were to read the Word they would see that it is the *one* truth. The Truth is the Truth."

Trep winked at Collin and Zedic, who were listening intently to the argument, and then smiled at a red-faced Toric. "Well, they would tell y'all the same thing. If y'all would only read their *history*—as I refer to their religious works—then you would see that theirs is the only possible truth. It would appear, the older the writin', the more *truthful* the words, and after a while that truth becomes a way of life, and then the law of the land. Or you might say—one's religious philosophy."

Toric shook with anger. "But the words in the scrolls *are* the only truth. They tell us we came from the angel of Genesis. The angel fought with Charles so that Miral Amanda could complete her mission to safeguard us and lead us to Nor."

Trep cocked his head to the side. "Then what happened?"

Toric swallowed the dried meat he was chewing. "Well, they fought off and on for several annums, and when Miral Amanda died, she passed the mission to her daughter Belendra, who eventually passed it on to Crysten."

Trep nodded, and then asked, "So whatever became of Charles?"

"He came back many times trying to destroy our people. I don't think he can find us now that we've reached the sacred Mountain of Nor. That's why we have to stay hidden, so Charles can't find us. The mission was to come to the Mountain of Nor, to this land that was set aside for us. This isn't only written in our Ogs, but it also says this on the Statue of Nor. That's how we know Survin is where we belong."

Trep was quiet a long time as he ate his supper. His forehead crinkled slightly as he thought over Toric's words. "Lemme get this straight. The angel gave you folks a mission—told y'all to go to Nor—and then she went away. The evil Charles kept y'all from completing your mission for hundreds of years, but eventually y'all found the Mountain of Nor. Mission complete, right? Yet, he still keeps botherin' y'all. Why? And ain't he kinda old by now?"

Toric wasn't swayed from his faith. "Charles never dies. He's like the angel, only he's bad instead of good. The gods of Nor Mountain protect us from his evil ways. I'm not very well versed in the teachings. The Miral could answer your questions about Charles and his disciples."

"Charles has disciples? Now, that's interestin'. But ya still haven't answered my question. If y'all completed your mission, settled on Nor mountain, why is he still after y'all?"

This was the one question Toric couldn't answer. Not because he didn't know, but because Trep couldn't be told about the Crystal. Instead, Toric got up from the meal and stomped away. At the mention of this legend, Trep almost asked about the Crystal, but held his tongue with much more difficulty than he'd thought possible.

Trep came to realize that the mystical Star of Genesis, or *Healing Crystal,* had always belonged to these people, and because of their fear of strangers it had never been found and never been taken away. What he didn't understand was how the legend had spread so far when these people were so reclusive. Unless the legend had its beginnings in a time when the Survinees still mixed with other races. As far as the powers it was said to have, Trep hadn't seen any. In fact, the Survinees were some of the most primitive people he'd ever met. It would take no little time to verify that this actually was the revered Star of Genesis, and the only way to do that would be to return to the mountain after this trip, preferably in Isontra's good graces. It didn't hurt that he really liked these people. Trep didn't want the power of the Star for himself. Like so many things he studied, he just had to know what it was and how it came to be.

Time passed, and as the men grew stronger they covered more ground each day. The miles fell behind them, and the black hills to the west disappeared from view. The first morning they could no longer see the mountains brought an unexpected wave of distress to the Survinees.

Chapter 24

At the end of the third week, the river widened into an immense winding lake. Huge bluffs engulfed the travelers suddenly and the return of hills and forest made the Survinees rest easier. On the expanding bluffs across the vast inland sea, they could make out several large valleys filled with emerald-green trees. Here they turned to the south.

Toric, the oldest of the group, was holding up well because he was used to hunting trips, but the weeks of constant travel had taken their toll. He walked behind the others, hoping they wouldn't see him occasionally limp or stop to rest. He was a proud man, so secretly he was glad when Trep said it was less than three more days to the city. Toric wasn't a man for idle chatter but found himself caught up in the talk of horses, karracks, real beds to sleep in, and the strange people they would soon meet. Such talk often helped him forget his weariness.

Trep, apparently eager to get home, moved quicker and his voice filled with playfulness. "We have to go south for two days and then turn east again. Cain't follow the river here. All these hills would jess wear us down, and we wouldn't get nowhere. The land to the south is much flatter—soft rolling hills instead of the sharp bluffs near the water."

As the wide river wound its way back toward the south, the fatigued travelers could see large homes in the distance. Huge buildings with fences and livestock dotted the hillside, and the houses bunched closer together as they neared the city. The local Madics waved uncertainly as they walked by.

Naturi shied from the press of strangers, but Collin seemed to immediately warm to the oddly dressed men and women, his curiosity unmistakable in his voice. "I didn't expect them to be so friendly. It's odd, though, everyone here is so much smaller than us."

Leading the disheveled travelers down a narrow street lined with ocher brick-faced buildings, Trep said, "That was probably the single most interesin' thing I learned about y'all's little village. I'd seen tall, well-muscled people in my travels before, but never a whole city of Bears together without any Innates. I'll admit, I was a bit intimidated at first, most of y'all being almost a head taller than me. Never considered myself short, before. Y'all won't see any Bears here." He smiled and nodded to a petite blond girl as she walked past, and her eyes were wide with wonder at the sight of the tall dark man.

Zedic stared as she scooted quickly by him. Backing up automatically to give her space, he almost stumbled into a creaking wooden cart being pulled by two odd-looking animals.

Naturi caught him by the arm, pulling him back onto the wood walkway, giving him a reproachful look. "Pay attention to where you are going."

Zedic nodded, and a little of the excitement leached from his face.

Enthusiasm oozed from Collin as he danced out of the way of another wagon, whispering breathlessly, "We should bring the rest of the Survinees to Peireson Landing. Look at how prosperous they are, and there must be hundreds of people living here. Look at the size of their homes."

Naturi frowned. "Remember the reason we keep to the mountains. Contain your excitement. Do not draw attention to us."

Trep told the Survinees he had a friend he wanted them to meet, and they needed a place to stay—preferably a room with a hot bath. "We can do some sightseeing in the mornin', but we jess spent weeks walkin' across God's prairie and I'm in sore need of a bath and a soft bed." He pointed down a street wider than the one they had just traversed. "See that big red buildin'? That's gonna be our new home for a while." The hotel was larger than the temples and its magnificence only slightly shadowed by the ostentatious building across the street from where they stood.

As they walked, Naturi studied the structures and listened to the buzzing of strange voices speaking words he couldn't understand. He felt uncomfortable among these small, colorfully dressed people. The experience was overwhelming, and he longed to be back in the safety of the forest he understood.

Naturi was painfully aware of the way the Survinees were dressed. Obviously, they were dusty from the long trip and much of their clothing showed signs of hasty repair. Looking closer at the men and women darting in and out of buildings on some unknowable mission, he realized that very few people wore leather and fur with the exception of what appeared to be an overcoat. None of the women he saw on the street wore skirts, but instead they wore long, very loose-fitting pants. The men had closely cropped hair on their heads and lots of hair on their faces. A good many wore a hat with a large, flat bill in the front that shaded their eyes. They were wearing some kind of lightweight fabric that moved easily when they walked. He made a mental note that he must buy new clothes, becoming increasingly uncomfortable with the way people stared at them as they made their way up the dusty street. Through all this Toric said nothing, and Naturi was sure his father felt the same apprehension.

Collin walked into Zedic who had stopped dead in the street and Naturi stumbled into them, almost knocking the young men over. Toric actually guffawed loudly as Naturi tried to recover his composure.

Startled by the sound, everyone turned to look at Toric and then began to laugh as well. Pure joy raged through Naturi. It had been annums since he had heard his father laugh like that. *Even if we bring nothing back, this one moment has made every risk, every uncomfortable night, and every cold meal, well worth the trip.*

When Naturi smiled, his sharp, perfect features made him look like a fairy-tale prince—a fact noticed by a couple of young women exiting the bakery to the right of him. He beamed at them. The girls blushed bright red as they hurried away, although they turned several times to look back, smiling and whispering to each other.

A quick walk brought the men to the loading area of the White Dove Hotel, where Trep tied up his horse next to several wooden and metal carts of all shapes and sizes. The hotel was formed of huge, red quartzite stones, cut roughly square. It had the appearance of being a remnant left by the gods, or *Ancient Ones* as Trep so often referred to them. The superstructure was five stories high and dominated the street. The midday sun glinted off the rows of windows that circled the third, fourth, and fifth floors. White marble stairs led to a set of six doors at the center of what appeared to be the front of the massive building. Above the wide entry was a carved sculpture of two white doves, their necks intertwined in an embrace. The hotel had all the grandeur of the Temples of the Godstones, and it wasn't the only edifice of its kind here in this amazing city. The four strangers stood on the walk, not daring to speak.

Like showing a child a magic trick, it tickled Trep to be the one to introduce these quiet people to the amazing sights of Peireson Landing. His dark eyes sparkled as he unloaded the horse and handed gear to Zedic and Naturi to carry. "Don't be shy now. Let's see if they have a room for us." Quietly, to each of his companions, he warned, "Don't let 'em see your gold, let me handle the negotiations." He thought for a moment, and then his lip twitched. "Never mind, they probably couldn't understand half of what y'all said anyway."

He led them up the stairs and through the large doors into a room with gold carpeting and intricately carved walnut chairs covered with bright jade cloth that glittered in the sunlight—furnishings that made their own look primitive. Although the Survinees were skilled wood carvers, suede and fur coverings didn't compare to the deep sapphire and garnet satin pillows on the benches and the velvet draperies that lined the walls.

A couple of men who were standing in the corner of the ornate room looked over when the Survinees came through the large double doors, and their curious stares followed the Survinees as the dusty travelers made their way to a long wooden counter.

Misha Dove, an energetic young woman with dark brown eyes and light blond hair that swirled about her waist, looked up. She smiled brightly as she came from behind a lavishly carved walnut counter and approached Trep. They could see the tiny woman was wearing an embarrassingly short red dress of a clinging fabric, leaving little question about her flawless figure. Around her long slender neck hung a necklace of shiny red stones that glittered brightly in the light from the lanterns about the room, and a matching red ring decorated her shapely right hand. Collin thought she was quite possibly the most beautiful thing he had ever seen. Zedic had no doubt.

As Collin started to walk around Trep to see her better, a man grabbed him and pushed him back toward Zedic, cursing at him. Although he didn't really understand the language, he understood the look and the tone of voice. Toric started to react, but Naturi held his arm. "Let it be. We do not know their customs. Maybe Collin erred." Pulling Collin to the side, Naturi said, "Let us follow Trep's lead here. Let him explain what is customary before making any rash moves."

They stood in a tight circle, trying without success, to blend in. There was a long discussion before Trep gave the woman one of the smaller gold nuggets. Her eyes widened and a look of amused delight crossed her face as she looked around Trep at the scraggly dressed men from the hills. Beaming, Misha took the stone and left the room. After a few moments, she returned and led them up the stairs to a suite of elegantly appointed rooms.

Trep set his pack on one of the beds in a small room off the main gathering area. "I'm gonna rinse a full moon's worth of dirt off me and then take a little nap. I suggest y'all do the same."

Collin and Zedic and even Naturi went from room to room exploring all the amenities, many of which they didn't understand at all. Toric followed Trep's lead and as soon as the young men vacated the bathing room, Toric staked his claim to the lavish tub of hot water, and soon various sounds of pleasure emanated from behind the door.

While Trep and Toric dozed, the other travelers bathed and put on somewhat cleaner clothing.

Later that afternoon, Trep changed clothes and looked elegant to the Survinees. "Let's start out at the assayer's office," he said. "We need to turn some of y'all's gold into money." Buttoning a pale yellow linen shirt, Trep motioned for Collin to wake Toric.

Naturi unpacked his things and stared at the clothes he had brought with him. Turning to Trep he asked, "Where can I get clothing like I see people here wearing? I feel very conspicuous in our usual dress." Zedic and Collin looked at each other and grinned, not surprised that clothing would be the first thing Naturi would want to obtain.

"We'll go to the mercantile where y'all can buy most anythin' ya want." He stopped and looked hard at the unusually tall young men in the room with him. "Not entirely sure they're gonna have anything that will fit y'all, though."

A short walk down the dusty street brought them to a small two-storied building, and Trep led the group into the office of the local assayer.

The workplace was narrow, with wooden walls whitewashed to lighten the room. A few small windows sat high on the wall, adding to the meager lamp light. On the main floor, just inside the door, was a wooden counter, and behind the counter were shelves of assorted jars, scales, and several tools the Survinees had never seen before. A small stairway led to second floor where the assayer lived.

A small, very dark-skinned man looked up as they came through the door. He wore a cap with a wide brim on the front that seemed to smash down lots of exceedingly curly black hair. Trep stepped to the counter and the man greeted him, "Lo, I'm Bassen. What can I do for you folks?"

"Name's Trep, and these are friends of mine." Trep pulled out two small piece of gold. "Like to turn these into bank notes if we could."

The assayer looked the stones over closely and whistled appreciatively. "Looks like pretty good quality, but I'll have to run some tests. We don't get much raw minerals here. Most of what I test is ancient coins and assorted metals. Most of those don't have much real gold or silver in them." Bassen looked over the odd-looking tall men standing behind Trep. "Where'd you say you found this?"

Trep stepped into the assayer's line of sight. "Didn't actually say where it come from. Ya think ya might exchange 'em for bank notes? We'd like to pick up some supplies here in town, and these things are a little awkward to spend."

The assayer grabbed a set of scales and placed it on the counter. His eyes kept darting back to the unusual men who accompanied Trep. Having never seen a man with skin that dark, the Survinees were as curious about Bassen as he seemed to be about them.

After a few minutes, Bassen made Trep an offer. Trep shook his head. "Might get a better offer from Samuel at the mercantile."

Bassen put both hands up and shook his head. "Oh no! This is just a minimum offer. I can guess this much just from the weight. To really know what you have here, I need to run some tests, and that'll take several days. I can give you thirty notes today, and give you the rest when I have a more accurate figure. Say the end of the week?"

Trep looked relieved. "Okay, we have a few more pieces." Bassen's eyes widened as Trep turned to his friends and whispered, "I'll only give him a few now. We'll see what he's offerin' at the end of the week. If it's a good deal, we'll give him the rest."

When Trep returned to the counter and placed additional stones on the scale, Bassen again glanced at the odd-looking strangers. Trep showed Bassen some of the jewels they carried. "Could ya give us an estimate on these too?"

"I could, but it's pointless 'cause Aterin's downriver till mid-month, and he's the only jeweler we have 'round here." He looked at the pieces of blue agate, garnet, and purple amethyst closely. "But I'm sure he'll be interested in these."

Trep turned to the Survinees behind him. "Looks like we'll be in town awhile."

The assayer pulled out a ledger and turned it toward Trep. "I'll have to give you a letter to take to the bank. Sign this here note accountin' for what you gave me and I'll write up the bank draft."

Zedic was standing close to Trep and looking at the writing of odd-shaped pictures and slash marks. "I wish I could read. How did you learn?"

Trep folded up the assayer's draft and put it in his pocket. "I learned when I was a boy. My ma taught me to read. She was the teacher for our master's brats so I attended lessons with 'em."

They were making their way down the dusty street to the bank now. Zedic was keeping pace with Trep as the others gawked at the fascinating surroundings. Zedic pointed to a large sign over the door of a building across the street. "What does that say?" The sign had an image of a sack, a jar, and a boot, followed by an X.

"That's a general mercantile store. If it's for sale there's this"— he crossed his fingers to make an X—"after the picture. If they buy somethin' you'll find this"—he drew a U in the air—"before the picture, and if they repair it, you'll find an upright line with another line across the top. If it's a doctor, the line goes through the middle."

Trep pointed to the left. "This way to the bank. I find it odd that y'all don't know how to read."

Zedic shook his head. "I find it odd that you do."

A few small businesses lined the wide street. They passed the livery where several men were working with horses and wagons. Across from the livery was another tall stone building covered with intricate carvings. Huge white pillars framed an immense doorway, holding up a second floor balcony. Multicolored flags hung from the rails of the balcony, fluttering gaily in the light breeze. Trep indicated this was the home and office of his friend, Narvin.

When they reached a large gray granite building at the end of the next block, Trep motioned them through the door. While Trep redeemed the assayer's draft for silver coins and bank notes, Collin stood in the doorway, opening and closing the heavy wooden door. He looked at the hinges and felt the weight of the door, marveling at the way the hinges were attached to the frame. *I carried that silly alloy piece with me for annums and never understood what it was. Kairma looked at it for a few minutes and guessed.* He smiled to himself. *Wish she could have seen this.*

The bank was even more elegantly appointed than the hotel. The Survinees stood in the middle of the room trying to look inconspicuous as a few locals came and went from the bank, not hiding their curiosity in the least. Trep joined his friends in the middle of the room. "Y'all will feel better once we get ya into clean clothes. Don't let their stares shake you. They jess never seen such good-lookin' folk before."

He led them out the door and back up the street. Across from the assayer's office was the mercantile store. They had to pass Narvin's office on the way and were, once again, awed by the sheer grandeur of the building.

The mercantile was impressive as well. Peireson Landing's general store was three stories tall and ran the length of two city blocks. Several people stopped and stared when Trep walked into the store with four curious Survinees in tow. Some of the store's patrons pointed and made rude comments about how savages and filth should be kept outside.

Trep wagged his finger at the people who stared at the Survinees men. "Don't let their appearance fool y'all. We plan to buy enough goods to supply our own small town." He laughed at his own joke.

The storeowner, Samuel Mories, escorted them to the back where they stood in front of a small dressing room. Trep pulled Samuel to the side and showed him several silver coins and a few bank notes. As had happened at the hotel, when Trep had showed the clerk a piece of gold, the merchant became very helpful in choosing respectable clothing for the Survinees.

Minutes turned into hours as the Survinees looked at everything from common rope to rhinestone jewelry. They picked up metal pans and metal tools for friends, and Zedic picked out gifts for his sisters: a silk scarf the color of sunset for Kairma and a red jewel necklace, like the one worn by the girl in the hotel, for Kinter.

Collin couldn't make up his mind what to get. Every time he thought of what Kairma might want, his stomach tied in knots since he knew what she really wanted was to be there with them. She would have loved to see the tall buildings, the strange clothes, and the vastness of this store that almost overwhelmed him. He was about to settle for a small gold chain set with a stone the color of her eyes, but he saw some wide, blue satin ribbon and knew it was perfect.

Naturi picked out four new outfits including a very nice wool hat. He selected a set of ink pens and a small stack of tablets, two small sacks of seed, and a silky blue dress for Kairma. Zedic caught Collin's eye and grinned. Kairma hated dresses.

Zedic filled a basket with shirts and pants, fabric, jars for Isontra, and carved wooden horses for the triplets.

Toric felt the clothes he had on were good enough and it took no little persuading to change his mind. After a while he gave in and picked out a dazzling midnight-blue satin shirt with shiny white stones on the cuffs and collar, but refused to give up his buckskin leggings. Seeing a display of hats, Toric walked over and picked out a bright red cap. Turning to Trep he handed back the cap he had been wearing and said, "I believe you're going to give this to me, are you not?"

Trep's lips curled in a friendly smile. "Yes, of course I will. I do owe ya a hat, and if that's the one ya want, it's yours."

Naturi was pondering a display of food in glass jars. "Where does the food come from?"

Trep explained. "Ya see, there are farmers here who grow more food than they can eat. The farmers then sell the extra food to the packers, who put the food in jars. The packer then sells the food to the storekeeper, and the storekeeper sells it to folk who don't grow gardens."

Toric scratched his scruffy face and thought about this. Trep was just about to walk away when Toric stopped him. "Wouldn't it make more sense for the farmer to give the extra food to the person who's going to end up with it anyway?"

"I suppose, but maybe the farmer needs somethin' from someone who doesn't need food. This way he gets money and he can buy whatever he wants." Trep's mouth fell open. Only then did Trep realize the Survinees didn't really understand what money was. They lived in a closed community where absolutely everything was shared. He never would've believed it possible to live without money.

Trep thought hard about the two different ways of living. There were benefits and drawbacks to each. "I think the biggest difference here is that wares are so much better when ya have people dedicated to producin' only one or two things, instead of tryin' to do everythin'. By competin' with each other to sell the best product, everyone gets better stuff." Trep realized the Survinees had changed very little over the years and knew they were going to be bringing home more than a few karracks and some pretty trinkets.

Collin picked out some new clothes but soon saw what he had traveled more than one hundred and fifty miles to find. On the wall in the back, behind some outdoor gear and saddles, was a large glass case filled with different kinds of karracks.

In his hurry to look at the guns, he almost knocked down a young woman who was studying a dark plaid horse blanket. He mumbled an apology toward her and stepped back. She said something he couldn't understand, and, when he didn't answer, she became indignant and walked away.

Collin called to Toric, and soon Naturi and Zedic had joined him. Samuel Mories came over to the counter with Trep and proceeded to make arrangements for the purchase of several karracks. Trep pointed to the case. "We're gonna need at least four of those long barrel ones and let's say, six, maybe seven of the short ones."

Trep looked at Toric, who shook his head and said, "I think we want all of those, and those." Toric pointed to another display case.

Trep translated the message, and the shopkeeper was visually shaken. "There are more than thirty weapons in that case!"

Naturi leaned toward Trep. "Is there a problem?"

"No, guess he ain't used to big sales." To the shopkeeper Trep explained, "These are gifts for their family and friends. There are many folk like these out west of here."

"But why do they need weapons all of a sudden?"

"Because they don't have any, they want 'em, and they have the money to pay for 'em. Now, you gonna sell us the goods or not? Y'all don't have a thing to worry about with these gentle folk. In a short while, they'll be on their way home, and you'll never see 'em again."

Samuel looked uncomfortable, "If I sell all of these to you, I'll have nothing for my other customers."

Trep explained the problem to Toric and the older man settled for all but five of the long barrel karracks and ten of the handheld models.

Once the subject of karracks had been taken care of they moved on to the saddles and horse gear. Trep said, "We're gonna have to purchase an ox or a mule." When the four Survinees looked at him with blank faces, Trep explained, "Those beasts you saw pulling the cart that almost ran over Zedic this morning are mules, but oxen are easier to handle. To pull the weight of the weapons, we'll need somethin' a might stronger than a horse." Trep shuttered, "Cornfeathers! Was it only this mornin' we got here?"

The owner had promised to store the majority of their supplies and the karracks until the Survinees were ready to leave town. The exception to this was a few small items and the new clothing. They would be celebrating tonight and they were going to look good doing it.

The livery stable was two blocks away, but since everyone was hungry, Trep suggested they go back to the hotel to have an early dinner. The purchase of horses and a wagon could wait until tomorrow.

It didn't take long for word to get around town that these strangers were spending a very large amount of money. Misha Dove, the pretty woman who had escorted the visitors to their rooms when they'd arrived, met them at the door of the hotel. She directed Tarl, one of the hotel workers, to take their things up to their rooms and told Trep how nice she thought they would look in their new clothes. Trep translated her comments, and being much more comfortable now, the Survinees smiled and gave her the traditional Survin greeting followed by the formal bow Trep had taught them.

Misha was a bit startled by this fervent display of courtesy. "Trep, whatever did you tell these lovely men?"

"I only said ya approved of their purchases. They come from a society where the rulers and lawmakers are always women. Naturally they think you're a powerful leader here in the city and offer ya their respect."

"It sounds like an interestin' culture, I'd love to hear more. Tell me, can they understand everythin' we say?"

"They can understand 'bout half of it, that is, if we don't talk real fast. They do learn pretty quick though, and I don't doubt they'll be able to understand a great deal more before we leave to go back home."

She walked them to the bottom of the wide staircase. Toric, Naturi, and Zedic went up to change clothes while Trep and Collin stayed behind. Trep would be dining dressed as he was, and Collin would be relieved by Zedic in a few minutes. Because Collin had a better command of the language, it was decided he should accompany Trep everywhere while they were in the city. Misha smiled at Collin. "Aren't you going to change?"

"Zedic will be down in a few minutes, and I will go up to put on my new clothes."

Misha's smile grew. Collin's accent was charming, though hard to understand.

Trep looked back at Misha, his eyes hopeful. "Tell me, how is Lysara?"

"Well, I don't know if she's quite forgiven you for takin' off." A gentle smile played on her cherry lips. "But she's well."

Collin stood in the doorway as Misha led Trep into the dining room, taking the seat to the right of him at a long lace-covered table.

Trep's voice was wistful. "I missed her."

"I'm sure she missed you too. Tell me, was it worth it?"

Trep couldn't help but laugh. "Ya saw what I found. You tell me."

"Yeah, you're right. Where did you ever find such wonderful examples of manliness? And rich too, from what I hear."

"It's a very different culture. Their wealth isn't in the gold they brought. Y'all should see the way they live." Zedic came to relieve Collin, and Trep turned back to Misha. "They have something else I want."

Misha toyed with her bracelet. "Really? What might that be?"

Trep looked around the almost empty dining room and made sure

Collin and Zedic were involved in their own conversation. "There's a girl there who can read the ancient writing."

Misha almost choked. "Trepard! Are you pullin' on my saddle?"

Trep watched Collin dash up the stairs. Turning back, he lowered his voice. "I saw it myself. She was readin' the words written on an ancient statue. I swear to ya. I'm not makin' this up."

"I know how much that means to you. Kind of your lifelong mission, isn't it? You really believe this?"

Trep was adamant. "I *saw* it."

"So, am I to understand you'll be returnin' with 'em then?"

Trep paused for a moment as the serving girl set a plate of rolls in front of him. "I've given it a great deal of consideration and, yes, I'll be goin' back with 'em."

Misha shook her head, and a halo of blond hair rippled softly. "Lysara isn't gonna like this at all. You broke her heart, you know."

Before Trep could say anything more, four striking men came in and found seats at the dining table. In turn, each of the Survinees thanked her for her hospitality in a fair execution of her language.

Misha, who was usually quite at ease around men, felt the blood rise to her cheeks when Zedic continued to stare into her dark brown eyes. She looked away and mumbled something to the young, black haired serving girl who was setting steaming bowls of soup on the lace-covered table.

The beef and onion soup tasted wonderful and was almost gone by the time Tarl joined them, taking a seat on the other side of Misha. She turned to Toric, put a slender, ring-bedazzled hand to her chest, and said, "I am Misha. I own this hotel." She waved an arm to suggest the room and the building. Pointing to Tarl, she said, "This is Tarl. He works for me at the front desk." She pointed through the elaborately carved doors to the lobby of the hotel.

Trep cleared up a little confusion on the point of owning the hotel. The Survinees families had homes, and there were public buildings, but true ownership wasn't something they readily understood.

"The young lady who is waiting on us is Dianay." The girl with the dark, almond-shaped eyes and pale skin bowed to the guests.

Taking her lead, Toric stood, and introduced himself and his companions. Each person stood up as he was introduced, bowed deeply, and then sat back down. Collin was the last to be introduced and—more by habit than anything—he winked as he bowed to her. She felt the heat rise to her cheeks again, and that made his dimples deepen as his smile swelled.

Throughout the meal, Misha tried to bring the Survinees into the conversation, telling them about all the things they should do and see while in the city. With the help of Trep, they found enough similarities in their respective languages to have a truly enjoyable meal.

After a delicious apple pie and several cups of tea, Trep suggested that they retire early so they could tour more of the city tomorrow. They would start by picking out some good horses in the morning. Then, as he headed for the front door of the hotel, he explained that he had to meet with a friend and would be back in a short time. Collin was by his side in a heartbeat. "No need for y'all to come with me. I know you're tired. I'm going to tell Narvin the stories about the carved mountain are false."

"All the same, I'll go. I don't want to miss the chance of meeting someone new."

Trep shook his head but relented. As he was about to walk out the front door, he saw her come in through the kitchen and quickly disappear up the back steps. There was no doubt in his mind; it had to be her. Not many women had ever turned his head, but Lysara was not like other women he had known. His heart caught in his throat for a moment. He desperately wanted to call to her, but they hadn't parted on the best of terms, and he didn't have time right now to patch things up the way he would have liked.

Three small chandeliers lit the long and narrow cocktail lounge of the Belle Lodge Hotel. A dark intricately carved mahogany bar ran the length of the room. Smoke, mixed with the scent from the oil lamps, filled the air. Several patrons conversing in low tones were scattered among the small tables. In a back corner, three men sat on red-velvet covered chairs. In front of the men, crystal glasses filled with an amber liquid sat on the table.

Trep's voice carried over the sounds of other conversations. "There is no great carved mountain. I found a natural formation that kinda looks like a man's face. That must be what the old trapper was talkin' about."

"Trep, I'm responsible for this entire city. Certainly you can understand why I'd like to know a little bit more about these people." Narvin was agitated, not by what Trep was saying, but more because of what he wasn't saying. "Come on, Trep, the gold you have is unprocessed. That means you, or they, have access to a mine that hasn't been played out."

Trep sipped his drink slowly. "I cain't tell ya more. What I am tellin' ya is"—he nodded to Collin—"they usually kill strangers. It took all the persuasion I could muster to get 'em to allow me to tell ya what I found. They're gonna let me study 'em, but even that has to be done from a guarded distance. The gold we brought is everything they had. They don't use money. To them, those are just rocks."

Narvin motioned to the bartender to refill his drink. "Look, I know you came in from the west."

Trep looked over the top of his glass. "It's a pretty big west."

"So what's to stop me from followin' you back?"

"I'd have to kill ya, and neither one of us really wants that."

"Good God, Trep, what's the big deal? They're a bunch of backward savages. This town could really prosper from the influence of a new gold mine. I'm only tryin' to do what's best for Peireson Landin'."

Trep's jaw tightened. "There ain't no mines. We brought everything they had with us."

Narvin rubbed the finely manicured beard on his square chin as he considered the word *mines*. His shrew-like eyes glinted in the soft lantern light. "Of course, I'd never allow the takin' of their property. My police force is quite good, you know. I hired and trained them myself. I'd just like to know as much about them as you."

Trep relaxed hearing this. "Like I said, I plan to go back to study 'em. I can return in a year or so with all the information ya want. I just don't want folks here to get it in their heads to come after us. They like privacy."

Narvin sipped the amber-colored brandy, feeling the liquid warm his throat. "So, Trep, I hope you have some kind of plan as to how I'm supposed to stop half of the city from tryin' to follow you when you leave here. I'm not the only one who knows they have raw gold."

"For starters, y'all can let everyone know that's the last of the gold and jewels, then they won't be set on followin' us. If they do, well, you got your lawmen, don't ya? We can discuss the details at another time."

Narvin didn't miss the word *jewels*. Trep hadn't sold those yet. He motioned toward Collin. "Does he understand everything you're sayin'?'

"Yep."

"I see. So you're tellin' me there's nothin' to be had there, but you're going back?"

"Yep. It's just a little secluded village that hasn't been influenced by the outside world. Real interestin' folks."

From across the small table Narvin eyed the golden band on Collin's little finger and made calculations of his own concerning the secluded village.

Chapter 25

Collin woke early the next morning, anxious to see more of the city. He pulled on his worn leather moccasins. The long trek from the mountains had taken its toll, and he decided he needed new footwear as well as a horse.

A few minutes later Zedic rolled over on his bed and stretched out. "Isn't this the most wonderful place? I wish Kairma could have come. She would love this hotel. And this bed is amazing."

Collin got up and walked to the window to stand in the sunlight streaming in on the soft mint-green carpeting and reflecting gently on the ivory-colored walls. Pulling the satin drapery aside, Collin looked out onto the quiet street. "Yes, but she'll come with us next time."

Getting up to dress, Zedic said, "You really think there'll be a next time?" Zedic joined Collin by the window. "I'm glad you've decided to come back with us. For a while, I thought you might want to stay here."

A lopsided grin crossed Collin's face. "It's really tempting, but someone has to keep you in line." He playfully punched Zedic a couple of times. "Besides, we still have a room full of mysteries to show Trep, then maybe I can come back here to stay."

From his stack of treasures he'd bought the day before, Zedic pulled out a tiny box tied up with a fragile pink bow. Collin didn't miss it and couldn't pass up the chance to tease him. "Let me guess: there's a lady who's caught your fancy here, isn't there?" He leaned over Zedic's shoulder to get a better look at the gift. "We've really only met a couple, so it must be that cute little serving girl who was waiting on us last night. Don't think I didn't notice that she gave *you* the largest steak."

Zedic laughed and tucked the gift in his pocket. "You would do good to catch that serving girl, my rogue friend."

"Zedic, is that a challenge?" Collin took a boxer's stance and jabbed at the air a few times.

Zedic didn't rise to the taunt. "If you must know, this is for Misha, something to thank her for her hospitality."

"Oh really?" Collin was a little surprised but quickly recovered. "Now that's a fine lady. And I hear her sister, Lysara, would do a man right proud too. Makes me wish I could have two mates, maybe three. Is there another sister?" Collin flashed a brilliant display of perfect white teeth in a mischievous grin. "How will I ever have enough energy left for your serving girl? She looks like she could be quite a handful."

Zedic rolled his eyes and tried to hide the smile that threatened to break through and destroy his resolve. "You can chase around if you want. As for me, I think I'll see if Misha will go to the Music Hall tonight. It sounded so interesting." Zedic walked toward the door.

"I think that may have to wait a day or two. We're going out to see something called a *museum* today and a *sawmill* tomorrow. Trep said it would be late when we get back. Maybe we can ask her to go next week?"

Zedic's eyebrows shot up. "We? I was actually planning something a little more private." He laid the topcoat of his new indigo suit over his arm and stood by the door, waiting for Collin. Standing tall, Zedic looked regal in the white brushed-linen shirt. His ebony hair waved slightly, setting the background for his prominent cheekbones and deep gray eyes. Until this moment, Zedic's birthright as a member of the Healing family had never really occurred to Collin. Although they would always be close friends, Collin felt a subtle change in Zedic, or at least in the way he saw him today.

For a moment he chided himself for having the audacity to wink at Misha yesterday, but his chagrin passed quickly. After all, she did smile back at him. He slipped on his new coat and followed Zedic down to the dining room for breakfast.

When Zedic and Collin reached the dining room, Misha was helping Dianay set out covered dishes. She turned and smiled at the tall young men. "Welcome. You're here just in time. Take a seat. The eggs are hot."

Collin gave her a formal Survin greeting followed by a deep bow. She smiled brightly and returned his greeting.

Zedic made the same gesture and then handed Misha the small box.

She eyed him suspiciously. "What's this?"

"I would like to thank you for your hospitality."

"This isn't necessary. Trep paid me well for your rooms."

"It would please me for you to have it."

She opened the small box and gasped. "This is too much. I can't accept this." The box held a small, expensive broach.

Zedic looked hurt, and she was immediately sorry for what she had said.

"Please keep it."

"Zedic, it is really beautiful. Thank you."

"It doesn't even compare to you."

Collin rolled his eyes but thought he should be taking lessons. Misha was totally captivated by Zedic at that moment. He pulled out a chair and offered it to Misha. She thanked him and sat down. As the others came into the dining room, Dianay began to place food on their plates.

The Survinees were used to eating grouse eggs, but the large chicken eggs Misha prepared were wonderful. She mixed them with fried pork bits, peppers, and onions. Fried potatoes and hot rolls accompanied the egg dish. Apple juice and hot tea were served in delicate pottery cups that matched the plates and serving dishes.

Indicating the beautiful tableware, Zedic said, "Mother would love to have a set of dishes like these. I think we should see if they have any at the mercantile."

Misha dabbed her lips with a linen napkin. "These have been in my family for years. On occasion, traders bring pottery goods up river, but this set is quite rare."

Lysara joined the assembly for breakfast, and it was quickly apparent that she and Trep knew each other rather well. Her soft golden curls fell scarcely past her shoulders, surrounding an angelic face. Her unrestrained friendliness was powerfully sensual, and when she laughed it seemed to exude from every part of her curvaceous figure. She dominated the conversation for most of the morning, and by the time the meal was over, it had been decided that she would not be going to the office where she worked as a city planner and a schoolteacher, but would be leading the visitors on tour of the museum.

After breakfast Misha took care of a few hotel duties, and then she and Lysara led the Survinees down the main street of Peireson Landing.

The stately museum that housed Narvin's collection of antiques was located next to the overseer's office. The two-story, tan brick building was attractive, and encircled by a lovely garden of flowering trees and roses. A trellised arch and gate opened to a flagstone path that led to a wide set of stairs. A broad porch, decorated with hanging pots of flowers, ran the length of the face of the building.

Zedic marveled at the hanging flowers. "Are these used for medicine?"

Misha's forehead crinkled delicately as she said, "No. They're just here to look pretty."

"How odd," Zedic replied.

Misha shook her head and led them inside. Gesturing to the room before them, she said, "These glass cases house most of Narvin's collection."

Looking at cases displaying the odd items, Zedic was suddenly acutely aware of how naive his people were. Turning to Collin he whispered, "Glass. Look at the cases here. The cases in the vault are made of glass. I thought some kind of magic created it, and these people have been making it for annums. Maybe Trep wouldn't have been all that impressed by what we found. After all, they can make glass here. They can sail boats on the river and make things from alloy too."

In the cases they saw artifacts resembling those they had found in the Temples of the Godstones. Although the ones here on display were not in as good condition, it was easy to see that they were considered very valuable. A broken cup with a picture of a cat, a chipped plate, and blackened metal spoons littered the floor of the display case.

Collin pointed out a ring similar to the one he was wearing and quietly suggested to Zedic that the vault had much to offer. "The glass in our vault is different. See all the bubbles and wavy marks in this? The glass at home is perfect and feels warmer to the touch." He ran a hand over the case. "All these things in here are old, really old, but they're rusted out and damaged. The stuff in the vault is still perfect."

"What are you men whispering about?" Misha stood by the door of the long room.

Zedic quickly closed the space between them and took her hand. "We're in awe of our surroundings. We didn't mean to be rude."

She looked up at him. He was so tall she almost had to step back to see his face. A smile played on her lips. "It is something, isn't it? Narvin buys most of these artifacts from traders who come up river."

Collin had joined them. He bent down and kissed Misha on the cheek, making her blush. "I wanted to thank you for bringing us to this wonderful place. Very impressive."

Zedic slipped an arm around Misha, and Collin laughed. Misha looked confused for a moment, and then laughed too. It was obvious to her now that the two young men were competing for her attention. She looked flattered.

Her dark brown eyes sparkled. "Have either of you seen my sister recently?"

Collin went back to case he had been studying. "I believe they're in the garden. Trep said he had something he wanted to discuss with Lysara. Naturi is with him."

"No matter," she said blithely, "you still haven't seen the upper floor. We'll join them later."

The smell of roses and lilacs mingled with the scent of leather and horses flooded Trep with pleasant memories. He was relieved to see that Lysara harbored no ill feelings and contrived to get her alone for a while. Naturi wasn't likely to let him wander far, but maybe he could convince the young man to give him a moment of private conversation. As they walked through the garden, Trep said to Naturi, "I would like to speak privately with Lysa. I haven't seen her for two years, and there's a lot of things I need to apologize for, least of which is leavin' her for so long. Ya understand, don't ya?"

"I do. Are you going to ask her to come back to Survin?"

"That all depends on how mad she is."

Naturi looked past Trep at the woman now sitting on a bench. "She does not look angry to me."

"Funny thing about women, sometimes ya cain't tell how mad they are till they steal your horse or poison your friends."

Naturi looked alarmed, and Trep laughed. "Don't worry, she ain't gonna poison none of ya, that's jess an expression. But ya really cain't tell always tell when a woman is mad. They can act pleased as pie to your face, and then refuse to talk to ya for weeks."

Naturi looked as if he were filing away this nugget of information. "I will wait for you over here. Have a pleasant talk with her."

In the shade of a flowering pear tree, Trep brought Lysara's hand to his lips and kissed it. She smiled, her eyes dancing about his face, remembering the months of romance they had enjoyed before he left so suddenly two years ago.

He sat next to her on a small rose quartzite bench and put his arm about her soft shoulders. From his vantage point he could see down the valley of her breast revealed by the azure ruffle of her blouse fluttering in the warm breeze. Gently pressing his nose to her hair, he said, "At the moment, I cain't remember what was so all-fired important that I had to leave ya two years ago. I'm sorry I was away for so long. Hope things have been going well for ya here."

Lysara understood Trep. He had come into town riding the wind, and like the scent of wild flowers he would drift away again, leaving nothing in his wake save the fond memories of a girl's first true love. But now he was back, and something in her soul needed Trep, needed him like roses needed sunlight. She dreamed about him. She could see the two of them wandering about the country, caught up in the currents of adventure. Her heart ached, and she was powerless to resist him. Logic told her to run, run as fast and as far as she could. But she would not.

She didn't feel like talking right then, content to be in his virile arms and wishing this moment would last a lifetime. After a long silence, she asked how long he would be staying.

"A few weeks at most. We've got to be back before the snow comes."

Lysara's heart clutched in her chest, and she fought back tears. "I was hopin' you might change your mind and stay." She knew he wouldn't. "I've been workin' for the overseer's office the past year. You remember Narvin Parns. He was elected overseer last fall and he mentioned the possibility of hirin' a full-time curator for the museum. I cain't think of anyone more qualified than you."

Trep stared at her, considering what she had said, his finger slowly tracing the curve of her cheek. "I saw him last night. He didn't mention anythin' about it, but then I really never gave him the chance. Ya know how I get when I start talkin'. Sometimes ya have to pour a bucket of cold water over my head to shut me up."

Lysara's breath caught from his touch. She smiled and nodded in total agreement. "I think I'll ask him about it tomorrow, just to see if the position is still available."

"He must be a hard man to work for. Kinda demandin', ain't he?"

She reflected on the past few months. "Yes. I'd say he's about the most demandin' son of a dog I've ever had the pleasure of bein' abused by." They both laughed. She went on, "I don't know what bee got in his bonnet the last few days, but he has been positively *evil*. At times, I think he absolutely hates me."

"Oh, great. And ya want me to go to work for this dragon."

She looked up as innocently as she could and batted her long lashes. "Yes, I need someone to protect me from the ogre."

Trep kissed her gently on each eyelid. "I've seen ya in action, lady, and I cain't see ya needin' protection from anyone. Except me!" He bent down and began to chew playfully on her neck.

She giggled and pushed him away. "Behave yourself, people will talk."

"I don't care what people say. When we're gone they can talk all they want."

Her heart was breaking again, but she wasn't going to let him see it. "Well, I have to hear it, Trep."

"Funny thing about the mountains, ya won't hear a word. And in a few months, ya won't even remember what ya were so all-fired worried about."

Her lips parted into a slow smile as she realized that he was asking her to go with him when he left. Her heart began to beat wildly. A myriad of sensations engulfed her: fear, joy, distress, delight, sorrow, and, as he kissed her moist lips with uncontrolled passion, she was lost in the feeling of utter happiness.

Chapter 26

Kairma was never allowed to leave the canyon alone and there was no one she could trust with the secret. Isontra was still angry with her for not telling anyone that Naturi had gone with Trep. But the draw of the vault was strong, and Kairma constantly devised new ways to get to the temples alone. Unfortunately, every idea she had come up with had its crucial faults, and had to be abandoned before she had the chance to put it into action. She wasn't even sure she could open the heavy door by herself, but it was a challenge she longed to meet. As the days slid by, Kairma became almost obsessed with desire. Isontra attributed her inattention to her lessons to worry about the men who'd been gone so long. In trying to assure Kairma that things would be fine, Isontra only succeeded in reminding Kairma how much she missed her brother and friends.

The safety of the men plagued her thoughts as Kairma carried the heavy basket of corn down the steep stairs to the cellar. Helping Isontra prepare the corn mash to make antiseptic was heavy work, but a fairly simple task that took the early hours of the morning.

Isontra explained the process as they worked. "We need to convert the corn into sugar by *sprouting* the corn. We'll place the corn in this shallow pottery dish and cover it with warm water. See the little hole here on one end? That lets the water drip out very slowly." She showed Kairma the hole. "I hear you've been spending time teaching Kinter to read. How is that proceeding?"

285

Kairma shrugged. "She's getting faster every day. At the rate she's consuming them, she'll be through all the Ogs by the harvest."

"I seriously doubt that. There are several thousand Ogs. I hope she doesn't forget to eat." Her tone sounded concerned, but a smile danced in her eyes as she continued explaining the fermenting process to Kairma. "Cover the corn to keep it clean while we wait for it to sprout." She poured warm water over the corn in the dish. "You'll need to check this a few times a day and add water if it gets too low."

Kairma did as she was instructed. "How long will this take?"

"In three or four days the corn should be sprouted and once it's dry we'll grind it into meal, and then add boiling water to make a mash. The mash must be kept warm to start the fermentation process, which could require more than ten days. You'll know it's ready when it stops bubbling."

They walked up the stairs from the cellar where they had set up the sprouting trays. "I'm proud of you," Isontra said. "I know it isn't always easy to assist your younger sister. She can be quite a handful at times, but you're doing the right thing."

"She gets mad at me when I correct her, but she doesn't make the same mistake twice."

"I'm sure Kinter is reading through the old Ogs this morning. Why don't you see if she needs your help?"

Kairma shrugged and went to the sitting room where they usually studied the old records.

Kinter looked up when she came in the room. "You didn't think to bring any terrid with you, did you?"

"You didn't think to help us carry all that corn to the cellar this morning, did you?"

Kinter blushed. "Sorry, I know I should have helped. I'm trying really hard to catch up with you on the colony's history."

A small smile danced briefly across Kairma's lips as she turned to go to the kitchen. She wouldn't have done that if Kinter hadn't said she was sorry, but Kairma thought she actually meant it this time.

While Kairma was standing by the hearth, filling the kettle, Loren came in with his hand wrapped in a blood-soaked rag.

He looked around the room nervously. "Where is the Healer? I've cut my hand cleaning a hide."

Kairma set the kettle down and went to check his wound. Loren backed up, holding his injury possessively out of her reach.

Loren shouted, "Don't touch me! I want to see Isontra."

Kairma nodded curtly and went to find her grandmother.

When Isontra came in, Loren unwrapped his rag. The hand would need several stitches. She turned to Kairma. "Go get my box. I will show you how to mend a wound. It's very much like mending clothing. Get some antiseptic while you're there."

Once Kairma had left the room, Loren said, "I don't want Kairma touching me."

Isontra looked disapproving at Loren. "Why ever not? She's a very bright Healer."

"You know. She looks like one of them—like a Whitey."

"And what's wrong with that?"

"They're evil, you know that. They kill people. I don't want the white witch near me."

Isontra's brow furrowed with anger. "Loren, you weren't even born the last time there was a real problem with the White Ones. Kairma is a good Healer, and as you can see, the White Ones didn't kill her either."

"My father has told me the stories. I can't have her taking care of me."

"Once she passes her Seridar, she will be the Vice Miral. What will you do when I'm gone?"

"I'll go to Jettena."

"You're being foolish. You've known Kairma all of her life. You know she isn't wicked."

"If it's all the same to you, I'll not have her treat me."

"Well, it isn't all the same to me, and she will treat you, or you won't be treated at all."

Loren paled. "You don't mean that. You would refuse to heal me?"

"Yes."

Isontra turned to see Kairma standing in the doorway. By the pained look on her face, Isontra was sure she had overheard the entire conversation. She motioned for Kairma to come into the room and prepare the wound for stitches. Loren's mouth turned down in a grimace, but he allowed Kairma to clean the cut.

Later in the evening, when Kairma was alone with Isontra, cleaning bottles to be filled with antiseptic, she brought up the conversation between her grandmother and Loren. Isontra patted Kairma gently on the arm. "The White Ones have been our sworn enemies for as long as we've lived in these mountains. Some superstitions are hard to overcome."

"I know, but I don't think the community will ever accept me as the Miral because, even though we no longer battle with them, the White Ones are hated."

"You have a difficult lot in life. You'll have to make them see that you're a good Healer, but before you do that you have to convince yourself that you can do this." Isontra paused thoughtfully. "I wish I could ease your burden, but I only seem to add to your tribulations. Some of the decisions I've made over the annums have been unorthodox to say the least. Many will hold you responsible for my poor judgment."

"I can accept that, if they can accept me, but Loren's apprehension isn't unusual. How can I ever convince people to trust me when they won't talk to me?"

"We made progress today. Loren let you treat his wound. When it heals—and it will heal cleanly, I'm sure—he'll realize his fear of you was baseless."

Kairma blew out a sigh. "That's one. Only one hundred more people to convince."

Isontra smiled widely. "That's the spirit. We'll turn them one at a time."

Kairma forced a smile, but thought her grandmother was entirely too optimistic.

The wound did heal cleanly. A little more than a week later when Loren returned to have the stitches removed—although he wasn't particularly happy about it—he allowed Kairma to treat him without dispute. She clipped and removed the gut strings, checking him for any signs of infection. As she finished, Tristan came in with a sore hip. The elderly man hobbled over to take a seat by the hearth, watching the interaction with concern.

Once Loren had been dismissed, Kairma turned her attention to Tristan. "You look like you're in pain. Is it your hip again?"

Tristan searched the room, his eyes wrinkled and mouth pursed in distress. "Where is the Healer?"

Kairma fought back a nasty retort. "Isontra is out in the garden with Kinter. They're harvesting herbs. Can I help you?"

Tristan got up to leave, and Kairma stepped into his path, blocking the door. "Let me help you. The last time you were here your hip was bothering you. Isontra gave you some willow bark terrid. I have some on the shelf."

Tristan eyed her suspiciously. "Did Isontra make it?"

Kairma wanted to tell him Isontra had prepared the terrid, but it wasn't true. If she lied, Tristan would take the terrid and leave happily. If she told him she had mixed the potion, he would most likely balk and return when Isontra came back. She thought about it for a moment before saying, "Tristan, I have been helping Isontra prepare terrid since I was seven. I understand why you would rather Isontra treat you. It's difficult for you to see me as your great-great-granddaughter—now that my hair has lost its color—but I am still of your blood. I'm not a White One—I only look like one."

The old man looked her over for a while, and then slowly nodded. "I'm sorry, I lost my father and many close friends to the battle with the White Ones. It's hard to look at you and not see those ones who hurt me so many annums ago."

"Let me get the terrid. If it doesn't help, come back this evening. Isontra will be here then."

Tristan nodded, and Kairma went to the shelf where she pulled out a leather bag of dried herbs. Filling a smaller bag carefully, she said, "You know, you're welcome to stay in Zedic's room. He may be gone for several more weeks and even when he returns there's an extra bed. We hate to see you all alone in that house now that Great-Gramme has passed on." She brought the leather pouch to him, careful not to make contact. "Mother is an excellent cook too."

He stared at her for a moment. "I'm trying to remember what you were like before the fever. Your hair was sawdust brown. You were such a pretty little girl. Thank you for the terrid."

He hobbled out the door and up the canyon to his empty home.

Tristan was alone, and it broke Kairma's heart to see him wander away as if no one cared.

Her great-great grandfather didn't come back that evening so, bright and early the next morning, Kairma took some of her mother's best pan breads, fresh fruit, and a new batch of willow bark terrid to him. He was surprised by her visit, hesitant to let her in. She showed him what was in her basket and after a bit of coaxing, he allowed her to come in and set the table for his breakfast. He hadn't asked her to come back, but by the end of this moon, she knew he would. As she walked out the door she thought, *That's two—only ninety-nine more to go.*

Chapter 27

The sun was shining brightly on the river down the hill from the
White Dove Hotel as white gulls squawked noisily overhead. Trep
had another surprise to show the Survinees, so they piled onto a large
wooden wagon.

Driving the team of horses over the rutted dirt road, Trep explained
the layout of the town dropping behind them. The road winding up
the steep hill to the northeast of the town provided an expansive view
of the city. Twenty-eight neat blocks of buildings and houses spread
before them. Docks and warehouses lined the curve of the riverside,
while on a slightly higher plane the main street of town could be seen
with its taller and more ornate buildings. East of Parns Street, houses
of all sizes fingered their way up the bluffs and into the forests beyond.
The bluffs around the city were towering and the road wound back and
forth until it reached the summit. From this vantage point, the view
was breathtaking. The large lake to the north stretched out before them,
dotted with small boats and rafts. Pulling the horses to a halt, Trep let
his companions gawk. He said, "If I time our return from the mill jess
right, y'all will have an even more spectacular memory to take home."
The wind was stirring enough dust into the air to create a beautiful
sunset.

The box elder and bur oak trees to the east of the city were tall with
massive trunks. The broad leaves created a subdued rustling sound

very different from the higher pitch of the singing pines and aspens the Survinees were used to hearing. The road was fairly straight once they crested the bluff, and after a few miles they came to a building next to a fast-running stream. Rushing water poured over the top of a big wheel and turned it with a loud creaking noise. Bright colored rainbows danced in the mist.

A small man with sandy red hair came to greet them at the end of the drive. Halting the wagon, Trep motioned for the men to disembark. The strangeness of the landscape and the odd mechanical sounds of the great wheel left the Survinees awed and slightly uncomfortable. Getting out of the wagon, they bowed courteously to the small red-haired man and lined up like ducks behind Trep.

Trep waved his hand, indicating the Survinees with him. "These are my friends. They ain't never seen a lumber mill before. I was hopin' I could show 'em 'round a bit."

Conrad Hipptem, a round-faced man in his late forties with crooked teeth, was happy to have visitors, even ones as strange as these. Because his mill was well outside of the city, he seldom saw anyone outside of his immediate family. "Glad to have you folks. I don't get many callers." He reached over and vigorously shook the hands of each man. "Now don't be shy. Come on in. Jess stay clear of the saw." His laugh was deep and throaty. "When you see it cuttin' through a log, you'll know what I mean."

The Survinees looked a little confused. Conrad spoke very loud and fast with an even stronger inflection than Trep. Trep repeated the warning as he led the way into the stone building where they witnessed an enormous metal disk slicing through timbers almost as big around as a wheel on the wagon that brought them to the mill. As men pushed the huge timber past the spinning blade, the loud and painfully grating noise from the saw hurt their ears. It was obvious why Conrad spoke loudly. Annums of listening to the giant saw had deafened him.

Naturi wandered over to the gears that turned the saw blade. He marveled at the sheer ingenuity of the mill. Taking out a pad and one of the quills he'd purchased a few days before, he quickly sketched the working of the gears.

Conrad led his tour out the back of the building where huge stacks of cut boards were stored. "Folks come up from the city to get wood, for everythin' from buildin' a house to keepin' their fires hot." He pointed to piles of smaller limbs and branches. "This here's the easy part. Cuttin' 'em down out there and haulin' 'em here is what takes most of the work." Across the field of cut wood, two mules pulled a wagon loaded with heavy logs.

Collin sat beside Trep, listening to the two old friends gossip about everything from the selection of the new overseer to the winner of last night's card game—two subjects which Conrad apparently had sour feelings toward. Collin was able to discern a mild distrust of the new overseer, but Conrad's description of the many things Narvin was trying to do sounded advantageous to the town. Collin couldn't understand why Conrad didn't want the city to manage the docks and warehouses. It seemed only natural to him, coming from a place where every job and duty was handled by the entire colony. So while Zedic and Toric investigated the yard, and Naturi made more quick drawings of the fascinating lumber mill, Collin tried to understand the political landscape of Peireson Landing.

Collin understood the Peireson family was the largest and most powerful family on the river and Grant Peireson owned most of the riverfront and all of the docks. In the last fifty years, more and more riverboats came upriver from distant towns. Merchants traded unusual and unique items for the grain and lumber the city provided. Grant Peireson made a good living as the dock master. He scheduled ships and rented warehouses and storefronts, but Narvin insisted the city should manage such an important part of their economy. After all, if Grant were to mismanage the docks, everyone would be deprived of the goods that regularly came upriver.

Although irritated by this proposal, it was the changes in the overseer's power that seemed to bother Conrad the most. Apparently the overseer's power had always been pretty limited and the man could be tossed out with no regard to procedure if a small number of citizens felt he wasn't doing the job properly. But over the past several years, more procedures had been established and the job had grown in scope. As it was, the current overseer wasn't really retiring now, but was moving into a newly established position as past overseer, a deputy of sorts to the new overseer.

Collin listened and marveled at how simplistic Survin was compared to the greater world. Peireson Landing was complicated with ownership, designated duties, and money. There were so many choices—it required a person to think all of the time.

On the way back to town, Trep told the Survinees about the flour mill located a little farther down river. "It works a lot like the saw mill, but I don't find big stones grinding wheat and corn nearly so much fun to watch as them big logs bein' cut up."

Naturi showed a drawing to Toric. "We can build a mill. We would need to get some of the parts before we leave, but think of all we could accomplish with a mill."

Toric looked at the drawing thoughtfully. "Our stream isn't as big as that one. We'd have to put it on the east side of the lake and even then there wouldn't be much water to turn the wheel. Maybe if it was a little smaller?"

Naturi beamed. "We will make beautiful things for Survin."

Trep sat on the buckboard seat, reins in hand, listening to the excited chatter. "Wait till I show y'all how we work metal. That's really somethin' to see." He made a soft clucking noise at the horses pulling the wagon. "We can do that in a few days. I want to show y'all a real cattle ranch tomorrow. We're gonna need horses, and Acton Peireson has the best breeds around."

Trep had been right about the sunset. It was glorious. The soft pinks and oranges, reflected off the now still waters of the lake, doubled the splendor of the sight.

It was dark when they reached the hotel, and Tarl stood at the main door, waiting to lead the tired men to dinner. Opening the huge wooden door, he motioned them through. "Misha is waitin' dinner for you. This way. We have roasted pig tonight."

Misha got up from the table as they entered the dining room. She wore a silky white blouse and long black velvet pants, and although the Survinees preferred the short dresses she usually wore, they kept their thoughts to themselves.

As the men filed past, they bowed graciously and offered the traditional Survin greeting. Misha's dark eyes sparkled as she returned the greeting. Zedic was the last to come into the dining room. He reached for Misha's hand, and as he bowed he lightly kissed her fingertips. Her eyes widened, and she smiled brightly. As Zedic sat down, he glanced at Collin, who answered his challenge with dimpled cheeks and a subtle nod.

As the Survinees told Misha and Tarl about their visit to the sawmill, and their plans to see the blacksmith, Misha reached over the end of the table and patted Trep on the hand. "Don't forget tomorrow is Market Day." She turned to the Survinees. "Market Day is fun. People from the small farms in the area bring goods into town to sell and we always have a dance in the evening."

Collin smiled at her. "Misha, tonight, you are as lovely as the sunset we just witnessed. I would be honored if you would save a dance for me."

Zedic almost spit out the water he was drinking. Not only was Collin sounding suspiciously like Naturi, but Zedic had never seen Collin dance.

Misha beamed. "Of course I'll dance with you." She turned back to Trep. "I forgot. Lysa will be late tonight. Narvin has her workin' on some garden he's buildin' for the new town square." She shook her head. "As if renaming the main street of town and the bridge after himself ain't enough, he wants a big garden where the livery is now. He's askin' the Bowart boys to move out of town. Claims the smell of horses is hurtin' the city somehow."

Trep swallowed a tender piece of roasted pork. "The man's been busy since I left."

Misha grimaced. "He got himself elected overseer, and hired his personal tax collector. We might well name the town Narvin soon."

A moment later Lysara came bounding into the room. Her green eyes flashed with obvious pleasure when she saw Trep. She took off her light jacket, revealing a short pink dress—very much approved of by the men at the long dining table—and hung the jacket on a wooden post by the door.

Trep jumped up and wrapped his arms around her curvaceous figure, kissing her like he was never going to see her again.

When he finally let her go, she saw the looks on the faces of the diners and blushed. "Dang! Trep, I'm glad to see you too."

Laughter rang from the table as the others welcomed Lysara to dinner.

The conversation once more turned to tomorrow's agenda, and dances were promised to all of the tall, dark strangers.

Chapter 28

Although Survin sat high in the western hills, the next morning was very hot. It hadn't rained in several days, and the small creek that meandered through the canyon was almost dry. Water had to be carried from the lake north of the village for anything more than drinking.

The spring sun was baking the rocks outside, but the cellar below the Chancery remained an almost constant temperature of fifty-nine degrees. Kairma added water to the corn mash, enjoying the reprieve from the unusually hot weather. The musty smell of earth reminded her of rare canned goods and preserves. Covering the corn mash with a buckskin cloth, she couldn't help thinking about the vault for the hundredth time since Zedic and Collin left. The vault had a dry, almost brittle air when they opened the doors the first day and she thought about the difference. The air was cool, but it lacked the smell of moist earth. Suddenly her desire to investigate the vault again became almost overwhelming. The solstice was still weeks away, and even if everything went as they planned, Zedic and Collin wouldn't be back until high summer at the earliest.

She finished her work and made her way up the stairs. The cellar stairs were directly below the stairs leading to the upper floor and opened into the middle of a long hallway, separating the kitchen, dining, and great room from Isontra's suite of rooms. At the main level she turned right and walked down the hall to her daily lessons.

Isontra sat at the wooden table in her sitting room with Kinter. Kairma wasn't paying attention to the details of the history they were discussing. It had something to do with a Comad she didn't know. Her mind was up at the Temples of the Godstones, mentally exploring the clear cabinets filled with silver tubes.

The little silver box that contained so many fascinating items lay open on the table. Walking over to it, Kairma began to investigate its contents. Inside the box sat a sack of soft suede and a clear vial inside. She asked, "Is this used in the Blood Rite?"

Isontra looked up from the Og she was reading. "Yes, when the Crystal is passed from mother to daughter, the Healing power of your Efpec blood is also passed. When you give birth to your first daughter, a cine will be made from your blood and put in a small cut on her shoulder to pass the power of the blood."

Kairma pulled her blouse off her shoulder and looked for a scar.

Isontra smiled. "You were very young. The scar has faded by now. I was going to go over the Blood Rite tomorrow, but we still have a little time this morning. I'll get the rest of the items needed for the procedure."

In the corner of the room was a door that led to a large closet lined with wooden shelves. The girls were familiar with this room since they spent one day each week dusting the hundreds of canvas, leather, and golden scrolls stored there. Many words were faded and hard to read. Sometimes she and Isontra would take whole paragraphs and try to decipher their meanings, only to end up setting them aside as useless. At times like these, Kairma's mind wandered. *How does one decide what is important and what is not? Centuries of the daily writings of one Miral after another contained every decision made, every person born, and every idea tried, That is a lot of information to digest.*

Isontra came back a few minutes later with a leather cord and tied it around the lip of the glass vial. She then showed Kairma a long, thin clear tube that was very sharp on one end and hollow through the middle. "Let me see your arm," Isontra said.

Kairma reached across the table. Turning her hand up, Isontra tied the other end of the cord just above her elbow. Tapping the light blue veins that began to emerge from the crook of her arm, she showed Kairma where the sharp end of the long clear tube should be placed. "The other end of this tube is attached to a reed and the blood will flow through the reed into the vial as we loosen the cord from your arm." Isontra untied the cord, and Kairma could feel the blood flowing back to her hand. "Once the vial is filled, we'll spin it by the cord over our heads until the liquid separates into layers. The top layer will be clear. This is the cine, the part of your blood that contains the Healing power."

"Doesn't it hurt to poke your arm with that sharp stick?" Kairma asked, examining the crook of her arm.

"Yes, it hurts a little, but only for a moment, and it's a very important ritual."

Kinter looked up, her nose wrinkled in distaste. "Glad it's not my blood they need."

Isontra smiled. "You have very powerful blood too. Someday, we might need it."

Kinter cringed. "Kairma's the next Vice Miral. She can give up her blood."

Setting the items back in the silver box, Kairma said, "I'd really like to go down to the lake for a swim today." Using the hem of her skirt, she wiped sweat from her brow. The room was stifling and not only from the heat. "Would you mind, Gramme?"

"Put your skirt down, dear," said Isontra as she shook her head. "You've been studying hard the last few weeks. Go have a swim."

Kinter looked up wistfully. A swim sounded wonderful, but the look on Kairma's face told her she wasn't invited. Her lower lip puffed out, and she turned back to her studies.

Kairma could see Kinter's disappointment and as much as she really wanted to be alone, she asked, "Kinter, do you want to come with me?"

Kinter looked up in surprise. "Yeah. It's really hot today. Help me put these things away." Kinter gently stacked the Ogs. "Are you going to find one of the men to escort us? You know Mother doesn't like us to go to the lake alone."

"Dillon and Siede were carrying nets this morning. They'll be there if we need them."

Kinter said, "As long as we're at the lake, we should take some laundry."

"You put those away, and I'll be right back," said Kairma as she left the room.

Kairma climbed the stairs leading to the upper floor. She and Kinter shared the west bedroom directly above Isontra's rooms. The room had two narrow beds and a large chair. Wooden shelves lined walls paneled with pine and trimmed in oak. Kinter's clothes were neatly folded on the shelves next to the hearth, but Kairma's were casually tossed on the other shelves or laid over the chair. Kairma sighed. It was so like Kinter to suggest washing her clothes was more important than swimming.

Kairma picked up a basket from beside the hearth that heated the room in winter. It was directly above Isontra's hearth and shared with the bedroom where her parents slept. The east end of the Chancery's upper rooms shared a hearth and chimney with the one in the great room below.

After gathering up the girls' clothing, Kairma went to the opposite end of the upper floor where her three younger brothers slept at night. Picking up a few items that needed cleaning, Kairma walked to the small window between the beds and looked to the east. She wondered how much longer it would be until she could see the inside of the vault once more. Leaving the room, she walked past Zedic's room once more, but there were no clothes to be gathered there, and it made Kairma sad.

Meeting Kinter in the Grand Hall, the two girls walked down to the lake. As often happens with people who share a small community, the girls gossiped about the latest trysts and arguments. As Kinter slipped out of her dress, she swore Ember was infatuated with Efram.

Kairma's nose wrinkled. "Yuck. He's mean and he drinks too much."

"No more than Collin does." Kinter stepped gingerly into the cold water.

"Yeah, but Collin is fun, not mean like Efram." A pain struck her deep in the chest as she realized how much she missed Collin and Zedic at that moment.

Kinter rolled her eyes when she saw the look on her sister's face. "Kairma, you're pathetic. They've only been gone one moon."

Kairma stepped into the water beside Kinter. "I know, but it seems like forever some days. Anyway, I think Ember's just trying to be nice to Efram. He's her cousin, you know. I saw her dancing with Siede a lot at the Awakening."

"Siede is nice. He should cut his hair, though. I think he's trying to see how long it will get." With those words Kinter ducked her head under the water and suddenly jumped up, splashing Kairma.

Kairma gasped as the cold water hit her, and in return she splashed water at Kinter. Soon the girls were laughing and playing games in the icy waters of the mountain lake.

Coming in from the lake, the girls ran into their great-great grandfather, Tristan, in the hospital. Kairma was fluffing her wet hair to dry it as she greeted him. "Lo. Do you need some more terrid?"

"Yes, I finished the last of what you gave me, last night."

"Did you think about coming to stay with us?" she asked as she filled a small pouch with terrid.

"I did. I think I'll stay with Noah. He has no living relatives, and as elders we have much more in common, but I thank you for the offer."

"It's not good to be alone all the time," she said, handing him the pouch.

"I realize that now. I hope this doesn't mean you won't bring me breakfast any more. Noah's a terrible cook."

Kairma's smile showed her perfect white teeth. "Of course I'll bring you breakfast. I really enjoy our talks."

Since Kairma began taking breakfast to Tristan every other morning, the man had slowly opened up to her. Their talks covered the history of the village and regular gossip that Kairma wasn't usually privy to. She was learning who was most intolerant of the White Ones, and who didn't have a strong opinion either way. Now she would be able to add Noah to her list of morning visitation. He was old enough to have strong feeling regarding the White Ones, but changing the attitudes of Grimly's family would be her toughest mission. Not only was it the largest family in Survin, but one of Grimly's grandsons was Efram, and Efram openly despised her.

Chapter 29

arket day was important to the citizens of Peireson Landing. Running a hotel required a constant supply of goods and traders meant rented rooms, so Misha was up early, taking inventory of supplies. The market was held along the wide river, one block west of the main street, near the warehouses that lined the riverbanks. On the street directly in front of the river, dozens of wagons and tables were being set with food, clothing, and other wares. A large warehouse that backed to the mercantile store housed tables, chairs, a dance floor, and a huge stage. Across from the dancehall, a fence enclosed cattle, sheep, and pigs. Boats lined the docks and brawny men unloaded crates and sacks in the hot sun, while lively people arranged their goods and chatted gaily with each other.

Leaving the others to their own pleasures, Naturi wandered off to spend his day drawing pictures of fascinating buildings, while Trep and Toric headed to the livery to see about acquiring some horses. Lysara walked with her arm in Trep's as they passed wagons and tables and described the goods to Toric.

Meanwhile Misha was entertaining Collin and Zedic. The young men were delightfully curious about things. Their easy laughter and charming remarks made her feel beautiful while she enchanted them with strange food and unusual merchandise.

People couldn't help but stare at them. At five feet, nine inches, Misha's head came to the center of Collin's broad chest, and Zedic was an inch taller than Collin. Like towering bronze guards, they walked on each side of her, attending to her every need.

They spoke with several merchants in their search for boots, but within a short time it became apparent the boots would have to be specially ordered. Choosing a popular vendor, Collin and Zedic had their feet measured for boots. "We have two more people who'll be needing boots. I'll send them this way when I see them."

Byran Heston was a round man with large front teeth that covered his lower lip when he concentrated. Laying out his tools to measure the men, the boot maker told them it would be at least two days before the first pair of boots would be done.

Ordering ladies boots for Kairma, Collin said, "That's something I know she'll wear." When the boot maker asked what size to make the boots, Collin replied, "She's about your height, maybe a bit taller. If you make the boots big enough for you, I think they'll fit okay."

Misha looked up at the boot maker—who wasn't a small man—and her dark eyes went wide as she turned back to Collin.

A broad smile split his face as he explained, "Kairma is Zedic's *little* sister. I suppose we should get a pair for Kinter too."

Looking back at the boot maker, he said, "Make Kinter's boots the same size, but pretty like the ones Misha's wearing. Kairma's should be tan like mine."

As the hot day turned into a warm night, people began moving toward the dancehall. Misha excused herself to change into something more appropriate.

In the dancehall, Zedic and Collin found a large table near the stage. Candlelight glittered over the tabletops and oil lamp chandeliers lit the hall's wide stage at the front of the dancehall. Along one wall was a bar offering several different kinds of liquor, and on the opposite wall one could purchase assorted prepared foods.

After a few minutes, Zedic went to watch the band tuning up their instruments. One of the men on the wide stage said something to him. He thought the man asked if he played an instrument, but he wasn't sure, so he bowed politely and went back to the table.

Collin had returned from the bar with an assorted array of drinks. The containers were odd-sized and although some were made of glass, most were clay cups.

Zedic laughed. "Leave it to you to find the closest source of wine."

Collin's cheeks dimpled. "I didn't know what anything was, so I pointed to several different bottles and held out my money for the man to take what was needed."

Zedic pulled his favorite lightweight mug from his pack and poured a dark red wine into it. The mug was very old and the paint that once designed its surface had long washed away, leaving roadmaps of minute fractures on the now white mug.

Trep and Toric joined Collin and Zedic at the table, and immediately began to show off their purchases. Toric was unusually talkative this evening, telling everyone how much he enjoyed watching the men working with the horses and wagons. It was obvious the hours spent at the livery had warmed Toric toward Trep. The two men discussed the needs for the trip back to Survin while the smell of baking breads and sizzling meats wafted across the room, awakening their appetites.

Naturi came in a few minutes later with Tarl. Pulling up another table and more chairs, Zedic told Naturi about the musical instruments. "I can't wait to hear them. I wish Kinter could be here. She would love this dance." Naturi looked around the room filled with men in fine clothes and women in long, pretty dresses and agreed with Zedic.

Exotic people filled the dancehall, while the six men enjoyed sampling the drinks that Collin brought to the table and waited for the ladies to return. They were laughing about an entertaining story when Trep suddenly stood up. He waved, and the rest of the men stood as Misha, Lysara, and Dianay came to the table.

Lysara was a goddess in flowing jade velvet. In her hair were emerald rhinestones, accenting her dark green eyes and forming a crown in the golden curls piled on top of her head. Matching stones in a necklace gently lay on the upper curves of her breasts.

Misha was not to be outdone. Her dress was also of velvet in the shade of crimson. A deep V in the front was laced together with gold string, offering an enticing view of the cleavage of her full breasts. The sides of the long dress were slit to the thigh, showing off her long, shapely legs. Tonight, she wore gold around her neck and in her hair.

The surprise of the evening was Dianay. Her cobalt satin gown shimmered in the soft candlelight. The dress fit tight in all the right places, covering her from neck to toe, but leaving little to the imagination. Clear stones, like dewdrops, glistened in her long dark hair.

The ladies sat down after the appropriate amount of flattering comments, each taking seats between two men. As Collin took Misha's hand, she had no choice but to sit between Collin and Zedic, Lysara was flanked by Toric and Trep, and Dianay was pleased to find herself between Naturi and Tarl.

The music started and people began to dance. Not waiting for an invitation, Lysara grabbed Trep and led him to the dance floor. Before Collin could say anything, Zedic nearly carried Misha away. Naturi intently watched the dancers, and listened to the music for a while before asking Dianay to dance.

The Survinees were so tall, it almost looked like fathers dancing with young daughters, but the women didn't look anything like children. Collin commented to Tarl about how regal the women of Peireson Landing seemed to him. "I'm sure it has a lot to do with the jewelry and the fabric of their dresses, but I find it hard to look away."

Tarl laughed. "I think that's the point of it."

"Do they dress like that for every dance?"

Tarl took a drink of his wine. "No. Tonight the overseer will be appointing city positions and giving out awards and commissions."

Collin looked across the room at a stocky man with salt and pepper hair. His clothing was meticulous and he was flanked by two men in black. "Isn't that him?"

Tarl nodded. "Yeah. Don't care for the man myself. Makes my skin crawl, but most folk adore him for some reason."

Collin recalled the distrust the lumberman had voiced. The first night Collin met Narvin at the Bell Lodge, he got the impression of a man used to getting his own way. His eyes slid to the dance floor where Naturi spun the beautiful Dianay in graceful circles, and Collin immediately decided he didn't like the overseer either.

After about an hour of music and dancing, the band stopped for a break and Narvin took the stage. He was energetic, smiling generously at the crowd. As the people found their way to their seats, Narvin said, "Good evenin', ladies and gents. For those of you who don't know me," he smiled as if that was something unheard of, "I'm your current overseer, but I've been making this city strong for years, and now, with your help, I can do even more. I hope you like the new name for the bridge I built. I'm having the bridge named Narvin's Pass. A bridge should have a name. Without a name you won't know where you're goin', right?" He laughed gently at his little joke.

Tarl whispered to those at the table, "Narvin didn't build the bridge. It was an ancient structure in bad shape, so about fifteen years ago Grant Peireson hired builders to make the repairs because he owned land on both sides of the river and that bridge is the only way across the river other than by boat. Narvin wasn't much more than an errand boy on that crew. While working there, Narvin learned a lot about architecture, and since then he's worked hard to make sure his name is associated with any new structure."

Naturi ignored Tarl's comments as Narvin continued. "I bring your attention to the following projects now in the process of completion." He pulled out a large drawing of the main street of town, recently renamed Parns Street. The Bell Lodge, the bank, Narvin's office, and the museum were clearly marked. What was missing from the picture was almost all of the other businesses that stood between Narvin's office and the river. Where the livery, the bakery, the doctor's office, and fifteen other small businesses and warehouses sat was a huge park called Narvin's Garden. "This is gonna be great for us. Folks will move here and bring new jobs and more money to Peireson Landin'." He beamed at everyone. There were a few quiet hisses from a neighboring table, but most of the crowd applauded loudly.

"Now for the awards and honors today. My first appointment goes to Artuk Masin. He will serve as our new tax assessor."

Soft applause followed Artuk to the stage. "I've spoken with a great many of you, and our desires are mutual, but with all new advances there is a price. We have been very prosperous over the last several years and now we can afford to move forward with our dreams." Again there was loud applause and a few stifled catcalls.

Narvin smiled widely at the crowd. "My next appointment is a reassignment actually. Since the current sheriff has apparently moved away—he really should have given us more notice—I've decided to appoint Rorey Bainser to the position of sheriff." There was more applause as Bainser took his place beside Artuk. "Now I have a surprise for everyone. I know you've seen them all over town this week. You can't miss them. My friends from the west have been helpin' out our economy all week. I heard the Mercantile's sales are up 300 percent this month." Narvin pointed to the table of stunned Survinees. "They're a little shy, so I won't make them come up on stage and make formal introductions. But please, welcome my friends." The applause was slightly louder this time, and the Survinees stood and bowed to the overseer.

Trep sounded surprised by Narvin's announcement and said, "Why, he hasn't even met y'all yet." As if on cue, Narvin stepped up to the table to meet the Survinees.

Naturi stood, and being just less than seven feet tall he towered over Narvin, making the smaller man look uncomfortable.

Narvin motioned for everyone to stay seated. "Please don't get up. I wanted to welcome you to Peireson Landin'. If there's anythin' I can do for you, jess ask."

Trep started the introductions with, "Ya know my girl, Lysara, and her sister, Misha. This other pretty little thin' is Dianay. She works for Misha, and so does Tarl here." Tarl reached over and shook the hand of the overseer as Trep continued. "This is my friend Toric and his son Naturi." Narvin's finely manicured hand was engulfed by Toric's broader hand as he repeated the gesture he saw Tarl make. A moment later Naturi was shaking Narvin's hand and openly scrutinizing the older man's posture and attire, obviously impressed.

Trep waved a hand, indicating the remaining men. "Ya met Collin the other night, and this is Zedic. Zedic's a member of the royal family."

Narvin's brow lifted slightly as he reached over and shook the hands of the young men, pausing a little longer on Zedic. "Welcome, Sir. As Overseer of Peireson Landin', your needs are my concern."

Assuming a regal air, Zedic stood gracefully. "You have a magnificent city, and we are enjoying our visit immensely. I have seen wonders beyond imagination—and tonight—I have the pleasure of being accompanied by Peireson Landing's most beautiful women." He smiled, indicating the ladies at the table.

Narvin's smile was smooth as he pulled up a chair and sat next to Zedic. "Yes, these ladies are my dearest friends. I know they'll take excellent care of you."

Zedic sat back down, but before he could say more, Naturi said, "Your festival is splendid. You must be proud."

"I do what I can. Tell me, what sights have you seen? Anything of interest?"

Entertaining Narvin with stories about the marketplace, Zedic and Naturi drank the dark red wine from their personal cups, which gave Collin his first chance to dance with Misha. Before Naturi could ask more about the city, Narvin stood up. "Now I really must go. There's so much to do when you're responsible for a whole city." He bowed curtly and left the dancehall.

Naturi was very impressed with Narvin. "The man is responsible for a vast city filled with more than a thousand people, and he took the time to personally welcome us to Peireson Landing." Although Narvin was much older, Naturi could see himself as the overseer of a city like Peireson Landing one day. He was so wrapped up in his thoughts that he didn't see the woman approach his father.

A small, attractive woman tapped Toric on the shoulder. "I couldn't help but notice you're the only one at this table who hasn't been dancin'. Could I invite you for a whirl?"

Toric shook his head, about to say he didn't like to dance, when Trep said, "Course he'll dance with ya, Tatiance." He pushed Toric toward the dance floor and said, "Don't disappoint the woman. Tatiance is the owner of the bank here." He winked at Toric. "And she's used to gettin' her way."

Naturi could remember his parents dancing often and wasn't surprised by Toric's hesitance. What did surprise him though, was after the first song, Toric danced several more times with different women, including Misha, Lysara, and Dianay.

Chapter 30

While the politics of Peireson Landing were starting to get interesting, at home, Kairma found politics excruciating. The Nor Day rituals were the same from week to week, but the discussions varied widely, sometimes becoming quite heated. Grimly and his followers had made dreadful accusations at the last meeting. Much to her chagrin, Isontra had asked Kairma to lead the discussion at this week's service. She had recited the Naming ritual and the Thirty Blessings, but she had never tried to control the business of the day.

Kairma was nervous, but Isontra was firm, insisting, "You will have to do this regularly after your Seridar. Do you remember the rules of order we talked about?"

Kairma squared her shoulders and nodded. Taking a deep breath, she called the meeting to order. After a short prayer, Kairma reported on the progress of the fields and the current batch of antiseptic. Noticing several people were not in attendance, she worried that it was a reflection of her ability to run the service. *Maybe the poor attendance has more to do with the heat. I hope that's it. I'm getting better at this. At least I don't panic every time I have to stand up here anymore, and I don't think my voice cracks nearly as often.*

Sharra and Jerman announced that Sharra would have a child before winter and children were precious to the small village. The fever that swept though the colony six annums ago took the lives of almost every child under the age of ten and most of the elderly. Forty-eight annums earlier, a similar plague left many dead and several families sterile, so any news of fertility was welcome indeed.

The meeting was short. There were a few comments about the upcoming hunt and the duty lottery was drawn. Everyone appeared to leave the meeting in high spirits.

Kairma stayed behind to prune some of the wild roses that grew around the monument. She liked to keep the vegetation back, and since Isontra didn't have any chores for her today, she took a few hours to tidy the area. Nearby, Siede and Canton cut wood for the cleansing rooms.

Kairma's mind drifted to days when Zedic and Collin took her to the caves and dared her to go inside. As frightened as she was, she never let the boys know of her fears for the greater fear was that they would never invite her to play again. In the early days, she'd never noticed the White Ones anywhere near their playgrounds, but lately the creatures seemed to be stalking her. They had come to the temples the day she delivered the Awakening tribute and again the day they showed Trep the ancient buildings. She knew they had been there the day Collin and Zedic left to hunt the Madics, but she was at a loss to explain why. Having Siede and Dillon nearby was comforting.

After finishing her gardening, she walked alone down the path from the monument to the Gathering House. Her daydreams wandered from the vault to what the city might be like. The sun was hot and her buff-colored buckskin top stuck to her back, making her uncomfortable.

When she entered the south door of the Gathering house, Efram stepped in front of her. "You thin yur reelly someem special. Ba I know wha ya are. If ya din't have tha sack roun yur neck. Sumbody would probly breck id, yur neck I men." He stumbled, and put a hand on the wall behind Kairma to keep his balance. She cringed away from him. His breath reeked of alcohol. "I be happy da do tha onors, ba I know bedder than a touch ya. Ya'd make me sick wid yur curses."

Kairma tried to slide past him, saying, "Efram, you're drunk. Let me go."

He spit on her as she moved, and she wiped spittle off her neck. Efram was too drunk to aim well, but the sticky slime made her want to retch. She was angry now. Her breath came faster and her voice was loud. "Let me pass!" She put both hands on his chest and took a step forward, pushing him away.

His hands flew up, knocking her hands away as he stepped back, almost falling over a chair. "Whoa. Don touch me, witch!"

Her jaw clenched and the words came out even more menacing than Kairma had thought possible. "If you don't get out of my way—*right now*—I'll beat you to a bloody pulp, you drunken sloth!"

Efram laughed in her face and as she balled up a fist she said, "Efram, I'm going to tell you one last time. *Get out of my way!*"

Diakus, sitting at a table not far from the commotion, yelled, "Efram! Let the girl go. You're drunk, and she hasn't done anything to you."

Efram turned, grabbing a chair to keep from falling. "Yur jus dfennin her 'cause yur son luuvs her. Well, how'd tha do fer ya, Di'kus? He's jus as gone as yur other kids. Loss em all, ya have."

Diakus was out of his seat in a flash, grabbing Efram around the neck and shoving him against the wall. "You don't say nothing about my children! Ever! You understand? One more word out of you, and Kairma won't be the one beating you to a bloody pulp."

Kairma was embarrassed that Diakus had been drawn into the fight, and tried to pull him away from Efram. She pleaded with Diakus, "It's okay. He's just drunk. I wasn't really going to hurt him."

Without looking at her, Diakus said, "Just get out of here, girl. This is between Efram and me now."

"He's just a mean drunk. He won't even remember what he said tomorrow."

Diakus spit an angry profanity, but loosened his grip on Efram, who immediately slid to the floor in a sloppy heap.

Efram looked up and tried to focus on Kairma. "I stil gadda score ta seddle wif yur lover. I rememer wha he dun at tha Wakinin ceremony."

Kairma stood with her hands on her hips, desperately wanting to kick him. "He's not my lover! He's my friend!" Tears stung her pale eyes and raced from the room. She was so angry that she tore one of the leather hinges that held the door in place as she shoved it open and fled to the privacy of the nearest cleansing station.

She sat there in the dim light and cried. Efram's words had hurt her, but it was more than that—she really missed Collin and Zedic. They had never been separated before now. Even when she was sick with the White Fever, Collin had come to visit her, and Zedic rarely left her side. *Great Nor, I wish I knew what to do. I feel this darkness seeping into my heart like a summer storm and there's a growing shadow of doubt that you won't come back to me. I miss you. I miss your laughter. I miss your teasing. Please. Come home soon.* The men had only been gone for a little over five weeks, and at the rate she was going, she felt sure she would kill someone before the summer was over.

Pulling herself together slowly, she went to the shower room. She paid special attention to where Efram's spit had landed. The cool water felt good on her bare skin as, along with the sweat and tears, it washed her embarrassment down the stone gutter. Pulling on the rope again, she rinsed her hair and stepped out of the gutter.

The day was warm, so without drying off she pulled on her thin buckskin top and the long suede skirt, relieved to find the building vacant. No doubt everyone in Survin had already heard about her fight with Efram, and she really didn't want to talk about it. It seemed to her that for every advance she made with people like Loren and Tristan, she lost ground with Efram and Grimly. The fact that Diakus had come to her defense wasn't lost on her, although she wasn't sure if it was a good thing or not. Did he defend her because he thought Efram was drunk and in over his head, or because he didn't think she could take care of herself? She fought the urge to hunt Efram down and show him that she was very much capable of taking care of herself.

Chapter 31

The river had large boats that hauled trade goods from large cities downstream, but on the big lake to the north the boats were mostly used for fishing. As they rode past in the creaking wooden wagon, they saw a number of rafts and canoes bobbing haphazardly along the shore, tied to stakes and small docks. Seeing one of the smaller sailboats skimming faster than a fish across Lake Peireson, the Survinees stared in awe.

Toric looked back over the long curving road that led to the upper lake. "These roads are something here. No place wide enough to drive a wagon near Survin."

"I was jess thinkin' we might need to do some tree cutting on the way back to Survin." Trep slowed the wagon as they neared a small log cabin. "We won't have much trouble till we get to Zacar's place, but from there, we're gonna have to clear some land. Best we plan on a few more days added to the trip back."

"We didn't buy a saw," Zedic said.

Collin stepped out of the wagon and stretched his back. "We didn't buy a wagon yet either."

"When the jeweler gets back from his trip, we'll have enough money to get a wagon and the tools we need for cuttin' trees." Trep assured them.

Naturi said, "It is very hard to know what to buy. Survin could benefit from a mill, but I would need to study them awhile longer to

315

know what parts I need to purchase here, and what could be made in Survin."

Trep shook his head. "We don't have time for too much manufacturin'. Have to be gone well in advance of the snow. The plains ain't no place to be caught when winter comes. Best y'all try to make what ya can when y'all get back to Survin."

"Can we do that? Make the things we need?"

"Y'all saw how the blacksmith works metal. With some practice, I think y'all could learn."

Toric grunted. "I'd like to learn a little more about that. Can we stop there again tomorrow?"

"Certainly. Uri Giman would be happy to show you more."

The next day Trep walked into the assayer's office and the coolness of the dark room felt soothing on his face. Bassen looked up from his desk. "Lo, Trep. Good to see you. I have a total on the gold you left with me." He pulled out his ledger. "See, here. That was mighty pure stuff you brought in."

Trep whistled as he read the numbers. "That should be almost enough to get us the wagon we need and maybe two or three horses. Ya know anyone who has a wagon for sale?"

Bassen started filling out the bank draft. "Cain't say I do. Wagons are mighty valuable, don't none of 'em stay on the market too long."

Trep folded up the note and put it in his pocket. "Ya know anyone who'll build one?"

"You might try Serges or Yemmat. Seems they had some parts laying 'round for a while."

Trep tipped his head to the small dark man and said, "Thanks. Worse comes to worst, everybody has a price." He stepped out into the bright sunshine.

Trep led Collin and Zedic to the warehouse of the wagon master.

The large building was made from various materials, the majority of which were different colored bricks. When Zedic commented on it, Trep said that they often used the bricks from old buildings for new ones, because bricks were hard to get. "There's a few folks that bake brick, but the labor makes 'em expensive so we reuse 'em when we can."

Inside the dark building were several wagons and parts of wagons. Serges, the warehouse owner, came out from behind a large wheel and put out his hand. "Thought I'd see you folk here. I heard you was lookin' for a wagon to take out west."

Trep shook the wagon builder's hand. "I've been told ya don't have any finished wagons for sale. Who do all of these belong to?"

Serges' amber-colored eyes swept over the room. "Well, these here," he pointed to five wagons in the back, "are harvest wagons. Cain't sell 'em. Those two b'long to old man Peireson. I'm reworkin' the floor on one, and the other has a bad wheel."

"What about that one?"

"B'longs to Derbin. Got a bad axel."

"Well, I guess we need to order one then."

"I got lots of parts, but I need another wheel. Go see Uri Giman. See if he's got any hoops ready. He lives just south of Loric Neismen's place. You know where that is?"

"Yeah, up by the big lake. What do ya need in way of payment?"

"I'm a pretty busy man, you know. If I have to stop workin' on Peireson's stuff, he'll dock my fee."

"I'll talk to him and see if we can work somethin' out."

They haggled over the finer points of the wagon they needed and then went back to the market place. Collin spotted the boot vendor setting up his table and hurried over to it.

"Lo. Remember me?"

Byran Heston smiled. "You're pretty hard to forget." He reached in the back of his covered wagon and pulled out a pair of scarlet boots with a flowered vine tooled into their shafts. "Still workin' on the tan ladies boots."

Eying the shiny black boots, Trep whistled appreciatively. "Who'd ya buy those for?"

Collin gathered up the boots and looked them over. "Kinter will love these."

Byran pulled out the boots he made for Collin and Zedic and they immediately put them on. Trep paid Byran for the boots, telling him Naturi and Toric would be by in a while to get measured for their boots.

Later that week, at the dance, Collin and Zedic had to take the boots off and put their soft moccasins back on. The boots had a small heel and the Survinees weren't used to heels. It would be several more weeks before they would get used to the new footwear.

Lysara saw little of Trep during the next week. Most of the supplies had been purchased, and they were waiting for the wagon to be built. Serges had promised them results in just over a week, but Lysara had been kept away from the hotel until very late most nights. Working on Narvin's garden plan required her to meet with business owners seeking their support, but she still didn't have the cooperation needed from everyone who would be affected by the new city center.

Jake Bowart and his brother Carl were the last holdouts. They refused to move to the edge of town, stating that their family had lived and worked at that location for more than seventy years. They blithely suggested that Narvin locate his garden somewhere else—a place that would be very dark and uncomfortable for Narvin.

She sighed as she filed the deeds she had received to date. *I hope he's right about this garden. There are an awful lot of folks I've made mad the last three weeks.* Narvin was applying pressure to the business owners by suggesting that their property was hurting the progress of the city, thus hurting everyone. Narvin guaranteed the new location for the livery would be much larger and more prosperous. He appeared very generous—often making elaborate promises he couldn't keep. Lysara had worked with him long enough to know Narvin was only generous with other people's money, and only when the gift would benefit Narvin and his vision.

Narvin came into her office so quietly that she let out a small scream when she turned around to find him sitting on her desk. Although he apologized profusely for startling her, she thought Narvin enjoyed making people uncomfortable.

"I came in to see if we got all the properties we need to begin construction." He slid off the desk and came to stand close to her.

Lysara took a step back, and then quickly moved to put the desk between her and the stocky man who was her boss. "I still don't have the deed for the livery. The Bowart brothers aren't interested in moving."

"I don't care if they're interested or not. This is what's best for the city." He leaned across the desk and looked her up and down as if he were appraising a piece of property. "Sometimes, I don't know why I keep you here. If you really wanted to do your job, you could have gotten that deed a long time ago. They're a couple of single, old men and you're a woman. Now get me that deed." He turned and walked out of her office.

Lysara sat down hard on her chair. She knew what he expected her to do, but she would help the Bowart brothers *relocate* Narvin's garden to their suggested place before she did anything like that for the man.

The Survinees had been in the city for almost two weeks— already a week longer than they had planned to stay. The wagon was part of the delay. Pan Aterin hadn't returned to purchase the gemstones they carried so Zedic and Collin spent a lot of time with Misha. They were fascinated by the workings of the hotel. Travelers were not that common in Peireson Landing because the plains to the east were vast grasslands with scattered farms, and few people traveled across the land on a regular basis. By land, the closest city, Wauke, was more than six hundred miles to the east. Peireson Landing had a fairly large port, but it was over nine hundred miles by water to Charlton, the next town of more than five hundred people.

Charlton was the only city within fifteen hundred miles to have a salt mine so traders came up river in the summer bringing salt, spices, and luxuries like coffee and chocolate. Peireson Landing traded fur, grain, and lumber to Charlton, whose surrounding land was almost non-arable.

Zedic and Collin trailed behind Misha as she walked down to the docks looking for prospective boarders. She would offer housing in exchange for items she needed for the hotel. Today, she was looking for cloth, soap, and salt. She could get locally made soap and cloth, but the White Dove Hotel was known for its expensive linens and soaps.

The sun was hot and Collin and Zedic had opted for wearing the sleeveless buckskin vests that were common summer clothing for Survinees men. The vests laced loosely up the front, revealing their powerfully built, hairless chests. "I really don't mind carrying this back to the hotel," Zedic said as he picked up a large sack of salt, the muscles of his deep, bronze-colored arms rippling in the sun.

Misha looked at him, appreciating the gesture and the view. "Nice," she said. "Thank you, but we could rent a cart for these things."

Collin picked up three large bolts of fabric. "Don't be silly. When you have two capable men to do your bidding, why would you not want to use them?" He adjusted the bolts on his shoulder and reached out to take her hand. As he helped her up from the lower dock, he winked at her. "It would please me greatly, if you would bid me to do much more for you."

Heat came to her cheeks as she thought of what he was insinuating. "I'll keep that in mind," she said, grinning.

Zedic stepped beside her. "Surely you would rather have an older man of stature." He bowed slightly to her.

Collin laughed. "Zedic, you're only fourteen moons older than me.

Not what I would really call an *older* man." He turned and smiled at Misha. "Though he is a member of the royal family, where I am no more than a humble Survinees hunter." His dark green eyes crinkled at the corners and his cheeks dimpled.

For the first time since the strangers had arrived, Misha wondered about their ages. She knew Trep was about thirty-five and guessed that Collin and Zedic were maybe ten years younger. The suggestion that Zedic was only a few moons older had her curious so she asked, "Just how old are the two of you?"

Collin switched the bolts of fabric to the other shoulder and brushed back a dark lock of hair. "I'm seventeen annums and Zedic is eighteen. Naturi is twenty, almost twenty-one."

"Annums? Is that the same as years?"

Zedic nodded as he led her gracefully past children playing in the street. "Every harvest is the beginning of a new annum."

Misha was startled. Their large stature and polite manner had her believing they were much older. "I never would have guessed that you were that young."

Zedic looked wounded. "We aren't children. My father was mated when he was fifteen annums."

"Oh. Of course. I know many women who marry at sixteen and seventeen. It's just that you seemed so much older."

Zedic slowed his pace. "Why? How old are you?"

Misha turned away but couldn't help smiling. "You're not supposed to ask a woman how old she is."

Now it was Zedic's turn to blush. "I meant no offense."

"It's really okay. I don't mind," she said, "It's more like a silly superstition." Reaching over, she gently stroked is forearm. "I'm twenty-five." But she felt ancient at that moment.

Collin asked, "Have you ever been mated?"

"By that, I assume you mean—have I ever taken a husband?"

Zedic and Collin looked at each other, brows furrowing, obviously hearing another word they didn't know.

Zedic asked her, "Is a husband a mate?"

"Yes, a husband is a lifetime mate. And no, I've never found the time to take a mate."

Zedic smiled.

Collin said, "It's interesting that the people of Peireson Landing mate so late in life. When Trep told me that he never had time for a mate, I thought he was unusual, but now it appears many people in the cities wait until they are much older. Maybe it isn't odd that Naturi is twenty and still waiting to mate."

Misha didn't know the cause, but Collin suddenly looked very uncomfortable.

As they walked the five blocks to the White Dove Hotel, both young men thought the cart would have been a good idea. Zedic's sack was quite heavy and Collin's bundles were unwieldy. Misha smiled at them—happy to carry her small basket of perfumed soaps.

Collin's boyish playfulness and endless energy renewed her spirit, while Zedic's regal manner and disarming integrity impressed her deeply. Collin was the embodiment of adventure, and Zedic was safety and security. The rivalry between them was never bitter or envious. The two men obviously loved each other like brothers, but someday soon she would have to make a real decision, and she didn't think it was going to be easy.

Chapter 32

Naturi stood on the top step leading to the door of the overseer's office and tried to organize his thoughts. He hoped the overseer wasn't too busy to see him. He had so many questions about Peireson Landing and how one man could lead so many. Although the position of Comad seemed similar to that of overseer, it was folly to think their positions were actually anything alike.

Stepping through the large doors, Naturi found himself in a small foyer where a plain dark-eyed woman sat behind a pine table sorting some kind of ledgers or tablets. She looked up at him. Her soft auburn hair was gently caressing her shoulders. Standing, she reached out a hand to him. "Lo, I'm Yevve. Are you here to see Lysara?"

Naturi took her hand, shook it gently, and then bowed to her.

Yevve's eyes widened a little as she smiled and said, "I'm sorry, but Lysara is out of the office at the moment."

"Actually, I was hoping I might have a moment with the overseer, if he is not too busy."

"He's in a meetin' right now. I don't think it will be a long one. Would you like to wait?"

"Thank you, I will wait."

Yevve pointed to a small sofa against the wood paneled wall. "Have a seat. Would you like somethin' to drink?"

"Thank you, no, I am fine."

Yevve went back to her sorting but soon asked, "So, how long will you and your friends be stayin' in Peireson- Landin'?"

"We are waiting for a wagon to be built. I believe we may be here for another week."

"What is your home like? Do you miss it?"

"I do miss my home and my friends there, but your city is so interesting, I would like to stay a long time."

"I heard that the young man with the black hair is from a royal family of some kind. What do you do there?"

Naturi was cautious in his answer. "I am a member of the community like many others. I am planning to become a leader, much like your overseer. This is why I have come today. I would like to learn more about being a great leader."

A wide staircase led to the upper floor where Narvin had his office. Webster Herborn, the other wagon master in town, came down the stairs looking very upset. He glanced at Naturi, and then quickly left the building without a word to anyone.

Yevve got up and went up to Narvin's office. A moment later she came back down and said, "The overseer would be glad to meet with you. Right this way." She led him up the stairs and waved him in to meet with Narvin.

Naturi thanked her and walked into the elaborate office suite.

The first thing Naturi noticed about the office was the expansive view of the river beyond the livery stable. The room was nicely appointed with finely carved furniture more elegant than the White Dove Hotel.

Narvin stood up from behind his desk and walked quickly across the room to greet the young man. Shaking Naturi's hand vigorously, Narvin said, "It's great to see you! What can I do for you?"

Naturi disengaged Narvin's grip and bowed. "If I could have a moment of your time, I would like to know more about leading a great city. I am to be a leader of my own community one day soon, and I wish to learn what I can from you."

Narvin preened. "I have lots of time," he said. "I'd love to share any meager leadership skills I might have."

"Thank you, Sir." Naturi bowed again.

"Sir? Call me Narvin. Your name is Naturi, right?"

"Yes, Sir." Naturi bowed again."

"First, the bowin' is okay when you meet with me, but others should be bowin' to you. It's important to be friendly, but always let them know you're the boss." Narvin motioned to a plush leather couch. "Have a seat and let's get to know each other."

Naturi sat, and Narvin pulled up a chair beside him. "Before I can teach you much, I need to know a few things about you and the place you will rule. How large is your village?"

"It is much smaller than Peireson Landing."

"How much smaller?"

"I'd rather not say, Sir."

Narvin pointed to a bowl of candies on the table. "These are excellent maple toffees. Try one."

"Thank you." Naturi tasted the sweet toffee. It was wonderful.

Narvin helped himself to a piece of candy and said, "So, what kind of industry do you have?"

Naturi didn't understand the question. "Industry? Sir."

Narvin pointed out to the warehouses by the wide river. "Businesses. What do you make in your village for money? We make wagons here among other things. We sell them to folks down river. What do people do to earn a livin'?"

Naturi smiled. "We hunt and fish. We have a large garden to grow many foods."

Narvin nodded. "How many folks live in, what do you call your home?"

"I'd rather not say, Sir."

Puzzled, Narvin cocked his head and for a moment, a frustrated look flashed in his eyes. His charming smile quickly returned and he said, "I was thinkin' of sendin' some gifts to your village— maybe some of this candy. I won't know how much to send if you don't tell me how many folks live there."

"I'd really rather not say, Sir."

"What did I tell you about calling me *Sir*? Please, call me Narvin. We're friends, ain't we?"

Narvin helped himself to another candy and said, "As a leader, you must be well respected. Are you well respected?"

"Yes. I am."

"Are you well liked?"

"I believe so."

"Do you have any enemies?"

"No, Sir."

Narvin looked incredulous and said, "It's rare for a man to attain power without creating enemies."

Naturi was quiet, thinking about how Collin's father, Diakus, made his ill feelings regarding Isontra quite clear, as did Grimly and Hiram. Naturi understood now what Narvin was asking. He realized his friendship with Collin had soured over the last year and hoped it wasn't too late to mend the rift. Naturi didn't like conflict.

After a moment Narvin said, "As a leader, you're responsible for the defense of your folks. What kind of defense does your village have?"

"I would rather not say, Sir."

Narvin's lips formed a hard line. Getting up, Narvin walked to the window and stared out at the river. Turning back a few minutes later, he said, "Leadership is about relationships. Folks will do almost anythin' for a friend. It's a good thing you don't have any enemies. That puts you ahead of the others."

Narvin walked over to a set of glasses and a pitcher on a beautifully carved bureau. He poured a glass of water for himself and offered one to Naturi. "Let's try a little exercise in buildin' relationships. There are a couple of men in town who don't want to be involved with the more excitin' events of Peireson Landin'. As a foreign dignitary, I'm sure you could entice them into joinin' the fun. Carl and Jake Bowart never come to the Market Day Dance. The next dance will be the High Summer Dance, an important event for the city. All the best folks attend. I think if you asked the Bowart brothers to attend, they might have a real good time. What do you say?"

"I have met both men. They are quite nice. I will ask them to join us at the next dance."

"Wonderful. Tell me as soon as you get their answer." He took Naturi's glass. "Now, I have much to do. We'll talk again soon." He motioned to the door and Naturi quickly got up and left the room.

After a few minutes, Narvin went down the stairs and asked Yevve to find Jaimer. "I have an important job for him. Don't let him stall."

Naturi's whole life had centered on mating with Kairma and becoming the Comad of Survin. He had once thought it was a lofty goal, but now the world was so much larger. He wanted to bring home all the luxuries he'd seen here in the city. He envisioned Survin becoming a great trade center like Peireson Landing, bringing wealth to his people. They would build hotels for the people who came to sell them goods, and factories to make their own goods to sell. He saw a lumber mill and a flour mill nestled in the granite hills. Survin would have pens of cattle and sheep to feed an expanding city. The people of the plains would make pilgrimages to the Godstones.

Then he saw the Crystal in Kairma's hand and knew it could never be. An unaccustomed frustration surged though him. To invite hordes of strangers to buy and sell goods in their hidden valley was to invite someone to steal the Crystal. He had made a vow, as all Survinees did, to keep the Crystal safe, hidden from the unworthy. It was his reason for being. It defined who they were. What was a monarchy without its crown jewel?

Naturi became more reflective over the ensuing days. Toric's unwillingness to accept new ideas had often irritated Naturi, but now he found that his father's pious nature was an anchor in the swirling winds of change. Sitting alone in their hotel room, Naturi asked his father what he thought of the city and all the marvelous things it had to offer.

"I think we are a very lucky people. I listen to the conversations around me and I hear stress, and ambition, and envy. It seems, with all they have here, it still isn't enough."

Naturi said, "I see the endless food, the wonderful tools, the luxurious fabrics, and I want to take it all home."

"This life isn't well-suited for us. We're a quiet people. We've lived without all these comforts for centuries. I don't pretend to know all about the Crystal, and what makes it so important that our ancestors died to keep it hidden, but I know we can't bring this world home with us."

Naturi grimaced. "Isontra has made many unorthodox decisions, but never has she said we must not protect the Crystal."

Toric stretched across the comfortable hotel bed. "We're the gods' chosen people. We have but one real task in our lives. Let us not fail that mission for want of hot and cold water or,"—he patted the feather pillow—"for want of soft beds. We have done well for over seven hundred annums. With the gods' help, we'll last another seven hundred."

"Collin told me that Isontra asked him to find people of Efpec blood to return with us, but we have seen no one."

Toric's eyes widened. "People of the blood? But strangers are forbidden."

"Our people are dying. There are too few young people to mate."

"Is that so?" Toric was quiet for a long time. "I guess I've been so angry over the past annums—the annums since your mother left—I didn't realize you had so few choices for a mate." He stared across the hotel room for some time before saying, "I know you have your heart set on Kairma, and it makes me uncomfortable. She isn't like the other young girls. Her sister would have been a better choice for Vice Miral." Naturi's mouth turned down angrily, but Toric went on. "I never told you I had once thought to mate with Jettena, but I fell in love with your mother before Jettena came of age. As it was, Tamron stole her away from everyone almost two annums before she was eligible to pass her Seridar. It rankled the elders something fierce, but by that time we had you, and it didn't matter much to me or your mother."

Naturi said, "I never thought much about my choices. From the time I was small, you insisted I prepare myself to be the Comad. You said you wanted me to mate with Kairma. That is, until…" He couldn't finish.

"I guess I did want that for you at one time, but the girl really bothers me now. She doesn't look right, and anyone can see her sister has more willpower in her big toe than Kairma has in her head."

"I think Kairma has a lot of willpower, it is just that she is very quiet and selective about its use. Kinter is a little volatile."

"Maybe, but in time Kinter would be a strong leader. She's pretty bright."

Toric began to dress for bed. Naturi took this as a sign the conversation was over and turned to leave.

"Son?" Toric said.

Naturi turned back. "Yes, Father?"

"I'm glad I came here."

Naturi smiled, and Toric added, "I'm also glad you're not planning on taking the entire city home with us. Good night, sleep well."

Over the next several days, Narvin invited Naturi to join him for dinner several times and let the young man sit in on city meetings concerning everything from the planning of a new building to neighbors arguing over a fence. As time passed, Naturi became more comfortable with the overseer and learned a great deal about making people feel important and well-cared for. Narvin was generous with his time and knowledge. Naturi liked the man's easy nature when dealing with his supporters, and grew to respect his ability to take a hard line when someone was in the wrong. Narvin was a strong leader and, more than once, Naturi was glad he was Narvin's friend and not his enemy.

Chapter 33

Collin enjoyed Misha's company, but he realized that it had become a real competition between Zedic and himself, and he was afraid of unintentionally hurting someone's feelings. If Zedic had said the word, Collin would have backed down in a moment. It was merely a game with Collin—the flirting came natural—but he was beginning to think Zedic might have stronger feelings. Unfortunately, asking Zedic to voice his intentions toward Misha would invariably get a thoughtful pause that could last until they were safely home in the mountains again. Zedic could take forever to make a life-altering decision, so it was up to Collin to force his hand. Over the next few days, Collin found other interests to occupy his time.

Seeing Toric heading toward the stables, Collin called, "Toric, wait for me. Are you checking to see if they have any new horses?"

Horses fascinated Toric and he spent hours watching the livery men take care of the animals and tack. Toric waved and said, "Come on. Jake said that they were going to break some two-year-olds today."

Collin laughed as he matched step with the older man. "Hope they can fix them again."

"It's an odd thing to say. If you're teaching a horse to accept a rider, I wouldn't call it broken, but these people have a funny way of saying things."

When they reached the livery, five men were getting into a big wagon. Jake called to the Survinees. "Jump on. We're headed out to Peireson's ranch to see the new colts."

Toric and Collin climbed over the side of the wagon and met the other men. Three of these men worked at the livery and already knew Toric and, although they had seen Collin a few times, this was their first formal meeting.

Carl shook his head sadly. "Bad news about Conrad, ain't it?"

Toric looked over at the older livery owner. The Survinees had met Conrad when they visited his lumber mill. "What happened to Conrad?"

"Guess he got kicked in the head by a horse yesterday. Said it killed him. I hear he was out in the woods by hisself, so when he got kicked, weren't no one to take him to the doc."

Another man said, "That's awful. Was it a wild horse?"

Carl replied, "Don't know the details. Jess what Sheriff Bainser told me."

Collin and Toric looked at each other, remembering Trep's warning about respecting the powerful animals.

Acton Peireson's ranch was about five miles south of the city, high on the flat top of a bluff overlooking the river. The house, made from red brick, gray stone and rough-hewn logs, gave the appearance of being thrown together without thought. Most of the materials had been scavenged from old ruins, years ago. It was the oldest working ranch in the area, and Peireson bragged that his ancestors were here before the curse.

According to local religious history, God set a worldwide plague upon mankind to exterminate man's evilness. God had only saved the most pious of men to repopulate the earth. Because the Peireson family could trace its history back to the beginning of the millennium, many of the town's people thought the family was beyond reproach. Both Grant and Acton Peireson always tried to live up to their own notoriety, and each did his best to raise his children to be worthy of the town's admiration.

Behind the Peireson house was a barn of apparently new construction. The sides and roof were made from milled lumber and painted a dark brown. A corral to the side of the barn held several horses of varying ages, some no more than a few weeks old. A small pen was behind the corral. The split-rail enclosure was roughly circular and about thirty feet across. A lone black Arabian stallion, with a white star-shape marking on its head, paced inside.

The men climbed out of the wagon and made their way to the corral. Acton Peireson greeted them, and introduced himself to Toric and Collin. "Nice to meet you boys. They wasn't jerkin' my saddle when they said you was big." He tilted his head back to look up at Toric. "I hear you would like to learn how to break a horse." He grabbed Toric's hand, shaking it vigorously.

Toric smiled and nodded. "They're quite amazing animals. I'd like to know more about them."

"You come to the right place, friend. Narvin tells me you're in the market to buy a few too."

"Yes, we've been talking with the liveryman, Jake Bowart, and he says you have the best horses in the area."

"That I do. Family's been in the business since the beginning of recorded time. Named the town after my greatest great granddad. Cain't beat a Peireson horse. Come on over here and let me introduce you to my men."

Four men sat on the fence rails of the corral like crows on a clothesline. Starting with the man on the left, Acton said, "This is Rocky Tomsman, Hans Harbed, and my sons Richard and Patrick Peireson. They'll show you how it's done with the first one, and then if you want, we can let you have a go at one of the others. I got three here ready to break."

Richard, an auburn-haired man with a stocky, muscular frame, jumped off the fence and slipped into the pen with the sleek black horse.

The horse shied away as Richard spoke softly to it. A rope hung gently at his side in his left hand as he closed in on the frightened horse. Still speaking gently, Richard began to stroke the neck of the horse. After several minutes, he slipped the rope over the head of the animal. The rope halter was slowly tightened on the horse's head. He held the halter with his right hand and the lead with his left.

Peireson explained, "Richard has been workin' with Midnight for several weeks now. He's been teachin' the horse to respond to his touch by pokin' him to make him move. Then if the horse moves, Richard stops pokin'. That way, Midnight learns to move away from pressure."

Richard was leading the horse around the pen. He picked up a blanket and saddle off the rail and placed it on the horse's back. Midnight jumped a little but settled down as Richard soothed him.

Richard quickly tightened the cinch and Midnight began to buck wildly. Toric and Collin got off the fence. When the other men began to laugh, Toric got back up on the fence, but Collin merely shrugged and leaned against it.

Peireson said, "Richard has been here before. Midnight'll settle down in a minute. It takes a good three weeks to break a horse right. You can push it by being demandin', but I think it's best to go at the horse's speed. Makes him a better friend."

Midnight stopped bucking and Richard talked to him for several minutes before trying to mount. The first time Richard got on the horse, Midnight nearly threw him off. Richard dismounted and soothed his horse again. He repeated this several times before Midnight would let him sit in the saddle for more than a few moments. Soon Richard was walking the black stallion around the ring easily.

Richard smiled as he rode up to where Toric sat on the fence. "This is Narvin's new horse. He paid top dollar for it."

"Looks like a really fine animal."

Peireson led the men to the corral to choose the horses they were interested in bidding on. Jake helped Collin and Toric select five horses. The first was a russet thoroughbred mare. Something about the way the young mare nuzzled Toric's hand made Toric choose this one first. Collin bid on a muscular chestnut Morgan stallion, but a man named Vaden outbid him, so Collin chose a buckskin stallion. Toric looked over the animals closely, wanting a really nice one for Naturi. It was a gift. He'd learned to respect his son's decisions and wanted to apologize for the annums he'd been so angry. He was about to bid on a dun-colored stallion when Jake stopped him. "It's best to have only one stallion in your herd. They have the tendency to fight, and one might be injured. That buckskin is a nice horse, and one good stallion can father several colts."

Toric understood. There was only one alpha in a wolf pack. He bid on a tawny mustang mare, an appaloosa mare, and a feisty black and white pinto.

As the next week passed, Collin and Toric spent more and more time with the horses. Toric was a natural rider, seeming to have a way with young horses that rivaled the regular trainers, and Collin shared Toric's enthusiasm.

Chapter 34

Kairma's enthusiasm was at an all-time low. Aside from making soap, making antiseptic was her least favorite duty. It was too hot to stand over a fire, but unfortunately this was Kairma's chore today. The second batch of corn had fermented and was ready to boil. In a stone building near the center of the valley hung a large copper pot with a tight lid. Under the kettle a fire blazed. Like the tradition of making antiseptic, the pot had been passed down from time immemorial. Once used, the pot was dried, covered with bees wax, and then wrapped tightly with layers of hides. Over the annums, bits of blue and green decorated the copper pot.

Kairma carefully put the sour mash into the pot and hung it over the fire with a heavy rock on the lid to keep it tight. A long copper pipe extended from the top of the lid and was connected to a copper coil that was as old as the pot. The coil sat in an earthenware container that had a small hole at the bottom that drained into another container. As the sour mash cooked in the kettle, Kairma poured cold water over the copper coils to condense the vaporized alcohol. At the end of the copper coil, Isontra set several pottery jars to collect the alcohol. The liquid was translucent, and the color of dark terrid.

Isontra tossed out the first jar of liquid. "The first run has a lot of contaminates in it. We'll collect the rest of the jars and set them aside to be reheated. Once we get near the end of the run, we'll check to see if the antiseptic will burn. Once it refuses to light, we'll take the mash off the fire and let it cool." Isontra set more jars near the opening of the copper line. "We'll use the leftover mash to start a new batch of cornmeal fermenting."

"How many batches will we make this annum?"

It was very hot in the little room, and Isontra wiped her dripping brow. "Five should be enough. That will give us about twenty jars."

"Is Kinter preparing more corn?"

"She started the sprouting a few days ago. It's drying now." Isontra handed Kairma another pitcher of cold water.

"So why isn't she helping us here today?"

"She'll be along soon. I have her getting more water for the barrel."

Kairma thought Kinter had the better job. The water was heavy, and the lake was a good distance from the Still House, but Kinter wasn't melting into the dirt like Kairma.

Kairma's lessons were becoming much easier now, and the weekly meetings were almost a pleasure to run as long as Grimly and Efram didn't attend, which was usually the case.

She hadn't heard anyone comment on the fight she'd had with Efram last week, and was glad she hadn't lost her temper with him. Isontra had often advised her, "Always look like you're in control on the outside, no matter what is happening to you on the inside."

As she worked in the heat, Kairma mentally listed the community members who had begun speaking to her. Even with all her work and early morning visits, fewer than twenty people were friendly toward her. Trying to change the bigotry of a people was difficult, but Kairma had her own bias when it came to the White Ones. How could she convince others to accept her, if she couldn't accept herself the way she looked? It was because of the White Ones that she couldn't step easily into her position as Vice Miral. It was because of the effects of the fever that the few choices she might have had for a mate were drastically reduced, and because of the reduced number of possible mates, her grandmother had sent her brother and best friend to the city, leaving her here, feeling lonelier and more insecure than she ever imagined possible.

Kairma knew a lot her troubles were caused by Grimly and Hiram's obstinacy. Somehow, Grimly was key to winning back the community. If he would acknowledge her as the Vice Miral, many others would follow his lead. The problem was that Grimly denigrated her with almost as much zeal as Efram.

Kinter came in with a large bucket of water and placed it at Kairma's feet. She stretched her back and picked up the nearly empty bucket from which Kairma had been dipping water. She took one look at the sweat running off Kairma and almost ran out the door to go after more water before Isontra could suggest they trade jobs for a while. Kairma sighed and began to pour more water over the coils. She smiled to herself. *At least I'm not making soap.*

The next morning, the great doors to the north and south of the Grand Hall stood open, allowing the summer breeze to freshen the air. Kairma was mixing herbs for medicinal terrid at the long conference table when she saw Grimly's mate, Saffron, come racing down the canyon shouting, "Miral Isontra! Vice Miral Jettena! Come quick! Something has happened to Diakus and Massie!" Saffron was shaking and her brown eyes were puffy and red from crying.

Jettena came to the door, holding Sonty on her hip, surrounded by three little boys. From the flour spilled down the front of her blouse, Kairma could tell her mother had been baking and found herself wondering how the woman could stand to bake when it was so hot in the valley.

Getting up from her chore, Kairma heard Saffron say, "I don't think you will want to bring the little ones. It's much too unpleasant a scene."

Jettena nodded. "I'll send Kairma. She has a good head on her shoulders."

Saffron's face pinched.

Kairma said, "I'm right here, Mother. I'll go with Saffron."

Grimly's mate scowled for a moment, but accepted Jettena's decision with a curt nod.

Isontra came to the door with her medical pack in hand. Looking at the pack, Saffron burst into a new deluge of tears. Isontra wrapped an arm around the woman's shoulder and asked her what was wrong, but Saffron shook her head mutely and turned to go back the way she had come. Isontra and Kairma followed her up the canyon as quickly as their feet would carry them. Curious people began to gather around the door of Collin's family's home.

Saffron refused to go back inside. Pausing at the door and trying to gain control of her weeping, she said, "I found Diakus on his bed. He had been stabbed in the chest several times with his own hunting knife." She sat heavily on a stool by the door and put her head in her hands.

Isontra slipped into the house and studied the scene in the bedroom for a while before returning to the little front porch where Saffron sat dejected. Placing a comforting hand on Saffron's shoulder, Isontra said, "It appears that he was unconscious from the drink when the attack began. He didn't put up a fight. Where's Massie? Is she okay?"

Saffron shook her head, unable to hold back a powerful sob. Her voice was raspy with emotion. "No, I found her in there." She pointed, and Isontra and Kairma walked into the back room where dry goods were stored. There, hanging from the rafter, was the frail body of Massie. She still wore the most recent bruises from Diakus' last temper tantrum. Kairma's stomach cramped as she raced to the door and retched, barely missing Tamron and Siede as they came in to take down the cold and stiff body.

In the hours that followed, Isontra and Tamron tried to piece together what had led to the tragedy.

Siede was one of several witnesses who claimed the couple had been drinking at the Gathering House when an argument about Collin's leaving began. Diakus hit Massie and she fell to the floor. Siede pulled his long dark hair back from his face and tied it with a strip of leather and regret bled through his words: "Massie shocked everyone when she got up and spit in his face. Diakus hit her again and again until Canton stopped him. Massie got up, wiping her bloodied nose, and left." Siede clearly felt guilty for not foreseeing the events that would follow. "Diakus drank until Canton and I had to help him home. From there, it was assumed he would pass out like so many times before."

Saffron's voice shook as she spit an accusation toward Isontra. "She lost all three of her children to strangers. Diakus succeeded in driving off the last one. How could you let this happen? How could you let Collin leave?"

Siede came to Isontra's defense. "Massie must have taken all she could take. How could anyone have known Massie would do this?"

Turning away and sitting beside the body of her oldest daughter, Saffron's curse was heard by several distraught neighbors. Real tragedy seldom visited the small mountain community, but when it did, it was felt deeply by everyone.

Kairma instinctively knew Grimly would use the death of his daughter to further alienate Isontra and her family, but couldn't help wondering why Grimly hadn't stepped in before to protect his daughter. Surely he knew what kind of man Diakus was—everyone knew.

Seeing Grimly coming down the valley toward the tragic scene, Kairma fled before the old man could corner her. There were tears in her eyes, but they were the hot tears of anger. Anger, because it was the Miral's job to mend rifts in the community and heal those who suffer. Anger, because the responsibility of her family was so heavy. Anger, because the colony would bear the guilt for this slaughter, not Grimly—when he could have prevented it. Her heart went out to those around her who loved Massie and Diakus, but who would be there for Kairma? Who would whisper the words of comfort and compassion that she longed to hear? Who would hold her when she grieved?

Finding a vacant house, Kairma slipped into a dark room and tried to make sense of things. She was painfully aware of her mixed feelings about the deaths, and it appalled her. She hated the way Massie and Diakus had treated Collin, growing more cruel over the annums, but she knew Collin loved his parents. She truly regretted the pain he would feel when he returned. It was heartrending how tragedy seemed to haunt Collin.

Sitting on the stone floor of an empty house, Kairma rocked back and forth in her grief. She longed for strong arms to hold her—arms like Zedic's or Naturi's. She thought of Collin, and fresh tears streamed down her cheeks. She missed his smile, and the way he coiled the dark curls of his hair around his long fingers. She wanted to hear him call her a *tag-along* and pull on her braids. She ached to hear the excitement in his voice when he told her scary stories about the White Ones, but today, she wanted to be there for him as he grieved. A darkening cloud of worry beckoned to her, and she cried for her loss as well as his.

Hours later Kairma made her way back to the Chancery. Isontra was waiting in the great room for her, a hot cup of terrid and some warm spice cake in her hand. Her gentle grandmother led her to an overstuffed chair and plied her with the alms. Kairma's eyes were red and puffy as she accepted the food. She thought she had cried every tear available to her, but when Isontra wrapped her arms around her and said, "Oh, my dear child," a fresh stream poured from her, and her body was once again wracked with violent sobs. Holding her, Isontra let her cry for a long time. As Kairma came back to herself, Isontra suggested plans for the service could wait another day. Not wanting to wake Kinter, Isontra led the broken child to her suite and put her in the large feather bed, tucking the blankets tightly around Kairma as she fell into a fitful sleep.

That night, standing in a clearing, with the long shadows of evening spilling across the faces of the crowd, Hiram swore the responsibility for this tragedy lay on Isontra's shoulders. "We all know Isontra chose to mate with the outsider, Petar, even though the elders had barely considered him eligible to become Comad, and she allowed her daughter, Jettena, to mate with another outsider two full annums before her scheduled Seridar." Hiram paced, his old and wrinkled hands clenching into tight fists. "Then, when Kairma was sick with the White fever, Isontra refused to take her to the Godstones, risking every member of Survin. I can't even look at that child without being reminded of those vile cave dwellers." Anger and grief bled through his words as he met the eyes of the audience surrounding him. "And now, we have a ghastly murder and suicide caused by allowing our men to leave Survin."

Hiram wasn't a particularly affable man, but his list of atrocities was impressive and several new people from the crowd joined his growing rebellion.

Chapter 35

Kairma woke to the smell of frying meat and sunlight streaming through an unfamiliar window. It took her a moment to remember where she was and why. Her heart ached and she felt exhausted as she made her way to the kitchen. Afraid to meet anyone's eyes, afraid to see the sorrow she knew would be there, Kairma took a piece of fruit and went to sit on the front porch. Knowing she had a duty to perform, her feelings were packed away deep within her as she planned the words she would use to ease the pain of Massie's family. Isontra would do this, but it was important that Kairma prove to Massie's family that she was capable of fulfilling even the most difficult of her duties. And Massie was Collin's mother, so Kairma felt an obligation to him as well.

To complicate matters, Massie's sister was Efram's mother. Consoling her would be hard. Like Grimly and Saffron, Efram's mother, Ambrie, never cared for Kairma and her family. Although Efram was the only one who openly harassed her, she could feel the loathing of the rest of the family. She couldn't help noticing how the light bands of color around them grayed whenever she walked nearby.

Kairma considered what Isontra had done for her the night before, and with fear making her heart pound she put together a basket of food and drink. Many people would look to her family for guidance and support, but Efram's family was her mission today.

She collected her courage and knocked on the door. Hearing Ambrie bid her enter, she stepped inside. The woman was sitting at the table staring out the window. She turned, and a look of surprise suddenly changed to anger. "Why are *you* here?"

Kairma set the basket of food on the table and began to pull out sandwiches and fruit. "I didn't think you would feel like cooking and you need to eat. I have rolls and spiced meat pie."

Ambrie stared at Kairma, saying nothing.

Kairma poured a cup of juice for Ambrie and handed it to her. "I have some spice cakes as well, if you like. Jettena made them last night. She likes to bake. Sometimes I think that's all she does. The honey on top is fresh, and there's some goat cheese and apples in here. Can I slice these for you?" Although Ambrie didn't answer, Kairma sliced the apples, topping them with thin strips of cheese, and handed the food to the silent woman staring out the window.

After several minutes, Ambrie said, "Massie liked spice cake. She made the best cakes in Survin. We learned to make them when we were only eight annums old, but Massie always made better cakes than me."

As the morning slid away, Kairma listened to Ambrie talk about her sister. Some of the stories were sad, but many of the memories were happy. When she fell silent, Kairma encouraged Ambrie to continue her reminiscences by mentioning things she remembered Massie doing or saying.

While Kairma consoled Ambrie as best she knew how, Efram listened from the back room. He was surprised to see Kairma there when he got up from a restless night of sleep. His mother had cried all through the night, and Efram was at a loss as to how to console her. When he saw the white witch sitting at the table with his mother, he wanted to scream and toss her from the house, but his mother was opening up to the girl. Efram felt anger that she was doing what he could not. As he listened, he heard Kairma gently drawing out his mother's happier memories, even hearing his mother chuckle on occasion.

He stood hidden behind the doorframe, listening, and through the tender words the women spoke he felt his own grief assuaged.

A new, intense feeling of shame swept through him as he realized he had been cruel to Kairma over the annums. His mother had made disparaging remarks about her and her family as well, but today the girl was sitting in the next room, helping his mother deal with her grief.

As children, before Kairma was bitten, they played together and Efram realized he had been cruel even then. In those days, it had been fun to make her mad, but now the teasing was hurtful, and although he still thought she was peculiar, he was sorry for the incident at the Gathering House. Rueful, but afraid to say anything, he stood silently in the dark and watched Kairma bid good-bye to his mother.

The meeting with Grimly was far more difficult. Grimly refused to let her into the house until she had convinced him she needed his help with the funeral service she was preparing. He was bitter and short-tempered, often making obscene comments about the White Ones and Isontra's decision to let Collin leave the mountain.

Kairma couldn't help judging him; he sounded so much like Efram. She wanted to rail at him for not protecting Massie, and for allowing Diakus to hurt Grimly's own grandson. She blamed Grimly as much as Diakus for Collin's desire to leave Survin.

It was hard to be civil, but she kept her comments and questions to the business of the funeral service. After several exchanges, Kairma was thankful Grimly was the kind of person who fell back on his work when his emotions became too strong. The discussion was stilted and detached, so she was startled when Grimly commented on how much his daughter had loved Diakus. After a while, Kairma came to understand that it had been Massie's choice to stay in the relationship, not her father's. Grimly had tried several times to convince Massie to leave Diakus, but Massie refused to leave him when he was in so much pain. Massie had believed her love was enough for both of them.

The only thing Kairma said personally, concerning the recently deceased couple, was, "Love can be so very cruel, can't it?"

Grimly regarded her thoughtfully as he walked her to the door. His voice was quiet and trembled slightly when he said, "Thank you for coming today." Dropping the hide door cover, he disappeared into the house.

Eventually Kairma made her way to the homes of everyone who was close to Massie and Diakus. She realized that her best tool was her ability to listen. She had no magic that could heal them, but expressing their grief and anger seemed to help, so she continued to encourage people to talk. By nightfall of the second day, she had met with all of the immediate family members and had learned the strength of their love for each other. As she made her way home, she realized how much she had lost by never truly knowing the family until now.

The funeral service for Collin's parents was held the following day. The entire village walked the four miles to the Temples of the Godstones to bury Massie and Diakus, as Kinter led them in a sweet song of mourning. Traditionally it should have been the Miral to lead the procession, but Isontra was having a difficult time dealing with the loss. She explained that she felt responsible for not seeing how depressed Massie had been.

Vice Miral Jettena never felt comfortable stepping into formal occasions and she encouraged Kairma to lead the procession. Knowing Kinter was more talented and how much it would mean to her, Kairma asked Kinter to do the honors. For a moment, Kinter looked unsure, but Kairma said, "There are things I'm meant to do, and there are things you're meant to do. And Kinter, you're meant to sing."

At the base of the mountain, below the carvings of their gods, were piles of stone ranging from very small to quite large. Massie and Diakus were laid out on one of the tiers of the great amphitheater and each member of the village picked up a stone to place over the dead. As they did this, Isontra led them in prayer, and then turned the service over to Kairma for the eulogy.

Kairma was afraid her grief would make the words garbled and incoherent. She looked up at the carved faces of granite and began. "Sometimes it feels like the gods have deserted us in our times of greatest need. We wonder how this could have happened to us. We are a good people, and we know Massie and Diakus didn't deserve the pain they endured. I don't pretend to know how it is to lose a child, though many of you have suffered this loss.

"I can't pretend to know how desperate a person has to be to take his own life. I can only imagine it has to be the greatest pain. As much as I'm angered that they would hurt those who loved them, I'm not sure it isn't selfishness on my part that expected Massie to go on living with her pain.

"Massie and Diakus were a part of the body Survin, and like all bodies, Survin has grown older. As we age we stumble, and sometimes we fall. Our body has cuts and scrapes that have left it scarred. We have painful wounds that never seem to heal. Today we do our best to close a long festering wound that will leave Survin scarred deeply.

"Diakus and Massie had more than their share of pain, but let us not dwell on the hurt. If they have done wrong, let us forget that, and remember the good. Let us remember the laughter.

"While we look for our own place in this life, in their name, let us vow to never take more than we give. As long as we remember them with a good deed and a kind word, they will live forever among us."

Everyone in the small village knew Diakus and Massie, but no one felt more guilt about the deaths than Efram. He had encouraged Collin to leave the mountain on several occasions over the annums. Efram had often been cruel, accusing Diakus of being a poor father, implying that that was the reason Cody and Ellen had been killed. Efram didn't understand why he felt the need to be callous and, only now, realized how damaging his actions could be.

As the villagers left, Efram stopped in front of Kairma. "Those were wonderful words. Even though they were part of my family, I wasn't that close to them, recently. It was good to hear the nice things you said."

Kairma looked surprised by his words. "Thank you, Efram. I know they were your aunt and uncle. You lived with them for a while, didn't you?"

"Yeah, back before Cody and Ellen were killed. My parents were really sick for a while, so I stayed with them for a few moons. Collin and I didn't get along very well, but it's too bad he couldn't be here today." He turned to walk away, but stopped and added, "Hey, I'm sorry for what I said the other day."

Kairma nodded. "All's forgiven."

Efram shrugged and moved away from Kairma, allowing others to speak with the Healers. He wanted to say more but his feelings were too confused.

Chapter 36

As he walked away, Kairma realized it was impossible to stay angry with someone who was in obvious pain. Kairma didn't know all the reasons for Efram's pain, but from the time he was little it had been apparent to her. In the last two days, there was a new shade in his aura and she thought it might be remorse, but for what, she wasn't sure.

The service for Massie and Diakus was completed in a little over an hour, and the members of the fractured community filed through the wide archway and returned to their homes. Kairma remained behind with Isontra to complete the burial, placing the last few stones over the bodies of their friends and neighbors. Before leaving, Hiram had vented angrily, and Isontra had barely defended her position. Kairma wondered if her grandmother would have made the same decision had she known the outcome.

The village was in tatters now, with many people openly rebelling. Looking around the ruined temples, Kairma wished she knew how to repair the damage. It seemed everything was falling apart around her.

Kairma wanted to see the vault again, with its pristine interior. She desperately wanted to see something whole and undamaged again. Her thoughts drifted to the last day she was here with Collin and Zedic. They had been gone for weeks now and Kairma was worried something had happened to them. She berated herself for allowing Naturi to go. Looking back, it seemed a foolish thing to have done. She wondered if

Collin had taken the assorted items he'd found in the vault and suddenly recalled the picture of the boy and girl Zedic found. The picture was similar to the one she'd seen in her grandmother's room.

Walking over to where Isontra was picking up the last of her things, Kairma said, "Hiram was pretty hard on you."

"I'm unconventional, and I think it scares him."

"Maybe I shouldn't have let Kinter lead the singing today."

"Kinter was perfect for the part—and she truly enjoyed the honor."

Kairma ran her hand over the stone parapet. "She does have a beautiful voice."

Isontra smiled as she gazed out at the hundreds of graves at the foot of the mountain. "The death of any community member is difficult to bear. I wonder how things would have been, had I not made certain choices? I can't see the future." Isontra was quiet for a long time.

Kairma pulled Isontra from her rumination. "Since we've been talking about things that aren't orthodox, I have a confession to make. I saw the picture you have in the box in your room—the picture of the temples. It looks like a very old picture." She sat back on the aged and broken parapet overlooking the once grand amphitheater.

Her grandmother sighed and sat next to her on the low wall. "I'm sure you have questions about it. It has been passed down for several generations. I look at it often now. You might have noticed the difference in the temples." Her long fingers pointed to their surroundings. "I ask myself if it is a picture of what used to be, or what it should become."

Kairma turned toward Isontra. "The temples look new in the picture. The people look very much like us with the exception of what they're wearing."

Isontra cooled herself with a fan made from braided vines. "You noticed that. When Trep came to our village that first morning, I saw the coat he wore, and that's when my nightmares began."

Kairma's forehead wrinkled in puzzlement. "I don't understand. What did his coat have to do with your dreams, or the picture?"

"It was the pockets in his coat. I knew I had seen pockets like his before, but I couldn't remember where." She laid the fan down, placed her hands together as if in prayer, and gently tapped her lips. After a moment Isontra went on. "It was while we were going over the history of the Crystal Wars that I ran across that picture again. I took it out and studied it."

Kairma's eyebrows shot up. "Trep's pockets are like the ones in the picture!"

Isontra nodded slowly. "That's when the dreams began in earnest."

"How can that be? Is he one of the people in the picture? Could he be one of the ancient ones? No. He would have to be ancient. Do you think he found the coat? No, his coat is too new and the only thing that's really the same is the pockets." Kairma's face twisted in frustration. *I should have seen the similarities of his coat and shoes with the statues in the hidden vault.*

All this time, Isontra had been studying her granddaughter closely. "That's when I knew we had to understand this man. I knew he was from a different world, and we needed to know about that world. If his world is like the one in the picture, maybe this is a sign of what is to come. The picture shows us hundreds of people at the temples worshiping the Godstones. The buildings are whole and clean, and the grounds well-maintained. To have that would be glorious, wouldn't it?"

Kairma hesitated before speaking. "Gramme, I think it's a picture of the past, a picture of those who lived before us. I don't know if they're gods or magical people, but they left something else behind." She very much wanted to share her secret, but felt like a traitor for doing so. She fidgeted with her hair, debating whether she should break her promise to Collin and Zedic.

When Kairma didn't say more, Isontra prodded her. "You know something. Go on, dear."

The words came out in a tumble. "Collin and Zedic found another temple behind the Godstones. It's full of amazing things: statues, and silver scrolls, and things I don't understand at all. I want to show it to you."

Isontra's lips curled slightly at the corners. "Collin found it. Now why doesn't that surprise me? The laws are clear about taking things from the temples, and I know Collin understands this. But you, Kairma, I'm quite surprised that you would do such a thing."

Kairma felt shame color her cheeks. "I'm sorry, Gramme. I know I shouldn't have followed them, but I really think this is important."

"Then I guess you'd better show me."

After the last of the villagers left the temple grounds, Kairma led Isontra to the stairway leading to the top of the monument. It was a challenge to ascend the eight hundred stairs, and climbing over the boulder was even more difficult. Kairma wondered at Isontra's ability to scale this with so little trouble and reassessed her opinion of her grandmother's health.

The two women made their way to the ancient vault, and it took both of them to move the heavy door. The sun was dropping quickly, leaving only minutes to examine the tomb. With some trouble, they were able to light one of the torches that Collin had left in the mouth of the tomb in anticipation of further exploration.

The light was meager, but enough to reveal the treasures before them. It looked the same as when Zedic and Collin were there and Kairma felt a familiar tightening in her chest as she thought of her friends again.

After walking around the huge room, Isontra sat on the leather chair and pinched the bridge of her nose.

Kairma knelt down beside her. "Are you okay? Can I get you some water or something?"

Isontra shook her head. "No, dear, I'm fine. Well, maybe just a little overwhelmed at the moment." Again, she pressed her hands together like she was praying and lightly tapped her lips with her fingertips. "I'm sorry, Kairma. I wish I had answers. I know there is something I'm missing here. Something major, but I just can't see it. I've spent the last forty annums of my life trying to figure out why the Crystal hasn't brought us peace and health." She looked into Kairma's worried face. "Every time I think I'm on the right track, I get a new surprise." After a moment, she seemed to pull herself together. "Who else knows about this place?"

"Only Zedic, Collin, and me."

"There is so much here. It will take annums to understand this, if we ever will. We need to tell the elders what you have found."

Kairma wrung her hands. "Please don't tell them. I promised Collin and Zedic I wouldn't tell anyone. I only told you because I saw that picture. That, and I really wanted to come up here again, and I knew I would have to give you a good reason for coming to the temples so often. I promised Collin I'd give him until the Harvest Seridar before sharing the secret with anyone."

"This the largest discovery of our lifetime. We shouldn't keep this from them."

"Please, Gramme. Just wait until the harvest." Kairma blotted out the fear they would never return. "*Please*. Collin and Zedic should be there when it's announced. It is their discovery."

Isontra looked at the room thoughtfully, and after a long while said, "I suppose we can wait a little longer. Have you spent a lot of time here?"

"I haven't been here since Collin left." She moved quickly to a cabinet of silver scrolls. "There're lots of things with script written on them and I really want to know what they say, but there's more than I could ever read. I don't read very well."

"Nonsense, you read quite well."

"I was hoping you could help me."

Isontra nodded in agreement. "Kinter can help us too. She loves to read the Ogs."

Kairma blanched. "I can just see that now."

"Give the girl some credit. She really is quite bright. And you know how much she likes to be part of a secret."

Kairma cringed. *Collin is going to kill me when he finds out.* But she knew that when Isontra had made up her mind there would be no changing it, and at least Kairma would have a chance to explore the vault. She really didn't want to wait until Zedic and Collin came back to open all of those silver canisters. At the thought, she felt horrible. Collin would be so hurt.

Two days before the solstice, Isontra asked Kairma and Kinter to retrieve a few silver scrolls. This would be the first time Kinter would see the vault. That night after dinner, Isontra and Kairma explained what was hidden behind the great carvings. Kairma thought Kinter would be excited, but instead she seemed afraid. Kairma had never thought of Kinter being particularly pious, but the discovery had unnerved her younger sister. Kairma didn't know if Kinter was uncomfortable because the vault was found in a cave, and White Ones usually occupied caves, or because it was another temple and they had somehow desecrated it by rummaging through it uninvited.

Kinter said little to Kairma as they made their way down the worn path, and Kairma found herself wishing Zedic and Collin were there. Kinter had been easier to get along with lately, but she wasn't fun. She primped and preened, and made Kairma feel even more clumsy than usual. Today she was wearing a long, freshly cleaned skirt while Kairma's skirt had a tear in the hem. Kinter was growing so fast that Kairma thought she could actually see her getting taller.

When the young women made their way between the two great temples and onto the terrace, Kairma said, "Well, it's time to see what's up there. Are you ready?"

Kinter nodded sullenly. "Let's get it over with."

"Honestly, I don't know why you're so reluctant to see this. I'd be happy if you didn't want to come, but Gramme's dead set on having your help reading these records or whatever they are."

From the bottom of the stairs, Kinter watched Kairma begin the ascent. "Looks like a long climb," Kinter said.

"It's not so bad. There is a rock you'll have to climb over. I hope you don't tear your skirt."

"Is that how you tore yours?"

Kairma shrugged. "I don't know when I did that."

Kinter blew out a sigh. "Kairma, you're supposed to be the leader of Survin. You really should care about the way you look. If you want people to respect you, you need to respect yourself."

Kairma thought about this as she crawled over the boulder that blocked the path. Kinter sounded so much like Isontra in that moment that it made Kairma shudder. But Kinter was right, and Kairma knew this. Unfortunately, being a clumsy mess was who Kairma was, and she didn't know if she could change.

Kinter gracefully stepped down from the huge rock and looked at the brass-colored doors. Seeing the beautiful carvings above the door, Kinter's eyes went wide and her mouth made a tiny O. Kairma smiled, happy to see a little awe on Kinter's face. Maybe she would enjoy this after all.

Lighting two torches and handing one to her younger sister, Kairma led Kinter into the room.

Even in the scanty light of the torch, Kairma could see delight on Kinter's face. Kairma whispered, "Isn't it beautiful?"

Kinter ran a hand over a display case, shaking her head. "It's absolutely astonishing. Look at those carvings along the ceiling, and the statues. They're perfect. I wonder if this is what the Godstones looked like when they were built?"

"I think they did. Look at this statue. The god on the left probably looked like this one."

Kinter came over to examine the statue. "It does look like him. Most of the nose is missing and some of the chin is gone from the mountain carving, but I think it's him."

She looked down the long line of statues. "Here is the one on the right too. On the mountain he has no hair here and here." She pointed to places where time and weather had worn away the finer details. Maybe they weren't giants after all. Maybe they were little, like the Madics."

Opening a case, Kairma pulled out a few silver scrolls and handed them to Kinter. Kinter began to cry.

"What's wrong? Did it cut you?" Kairma examined her sister's hand.

"No. It's just so perfect in here—the carvings, the furniture, the cases." She ran her hand over another display case. "And the scrolls. Look at the perfect letters on the scrolls. I think this is the way the world is supposed to be."

Kairma sat on a small chair and rubbed the armrest. "Do you really think this was meant for us?"

"If not us, then who?"

"I don't know, but sometimes I don't think we're worthy of all of this." Kairma waved a hand around the room.

"Of course we are! We're Nor's chosen people. I just can't believe it took us so long to find this. How many annums have we wasted, rewriting all the old records, when all that time they were right here in perfect condition?"

"These aren't the same at all. That's why Gramme wants us to bring some home today. She wants to see if we can figure out why they were written, and who left them behind."

"Well, let's gather a few and get started. The smoke from the torch is burning my eyes and I'm hungry."

Filling their arms with silver scrolls, the two young women left the vault.

❧

Feeling horrible, Kairma took her seat at Isontra's large pine table. It had only been a little over a moon and she'd already broken her promise to Collin. But, by telling Isontra about the vault, she would have the whole summer to figure out what was in there. She justified her actions by thinking of all the interesting things he would be seeing in his travels, places she would never see. She knew it wasn't right, but it made her feel better all the same. She sighed. "I miss them."

Isontra nodded. "I know you do, but they'll be home soon."

Dejected, Kairma began to read a scroll.

> National Aeronautics and Space Administration - NASA, an agency of the United States government, responsible for the nation's public space program. NASA was established in 1958 by the National Aeronautics and Space Act. It is also responsible for long-term civilian and military aerospace research. Since 2006, NASA's mission statement is to "pioneer the future in space exploration, scientific discovery, and aeronautics research." NASA's motto is "For the benefit of all."

Kairma rubbed her temples and said, "This would make a lot more sense if I knew what *Aeronautics* or *Aerospace* meant. Everything we read has an administrator of some kind, but why would you have one for space? What kind of space are they talking about? It could be the space around a house or around a table. Maybe it's the space under a bed. This makes no sense at all." She crossed her arms and laid her head on the table.

Isontra sighed. "I don't know what to make of it either." She pulled the scroll over to her side of the table and studied it for a long time. "I think the numbers are a way of dating things or marking time."

Kairma sat up again. "Our date is ATD 794-6-17. Are 1958 and 2006 annums? No. That doesn't work. We're only in the 794th annum."

"I don't understand it any more than you do."

"It says, 'pioneer the future.' Do you think they went into the future?"

Isontra shook her head slowly. "That's an interesting thought."

Kairma and Isontra spent the rest of the day trying to make sense of the NASA.

Chapter 37

Four hundred miles away, Naturi's thoughts were also consumed with the upcoming Solstice Celebration. It made him feel good to know these odd little people celebrated in much the same fashion as the people of Survin. The dance here was called the High Summer dance and when Naturi had asked if it was a solstice dance, no one knew what he was talking about. He walked into the livery stable and looked around. The smell of horses and hay was strong in the afternoon heat. The powerful animals were beautiful, and Naturi stroked the noses of each horse that he walked past. In the back, Jake was putting a new shoe on one of the geldings. He looked up when Naturi approached. "Lo, Naturi. What can I do for you today?"

Naturi patted the nose of the rust-colored horse. "I wanted to see if you and Carl would like to join us later this week at the dance. I hear this is your High Summer festival. It should be very enjoyable."

"Well, I don't know. In a hundred years, I would've never guessed you would stop by to ask us to the dance." Suddenly, Jake looked suspicious. "Why is it you want us to join you?"

Naturi smiled as amiably as he could. "You and your brother have been friendly and gracious to us since our coming to Peireson Landing and your dances are a wonderful tradition. I thought you might like to have some fun with us. Please say you will be there."

Jake nodded slowly. "I'll need to talk to Carl. We ain't been to a dance in years. They still got lots of pretty girls there to dance with?"

Naturi's smile was genuine. "They have the prettiest girls I have ever seen."

Near the center of the long canyon that made up the walls of Survin was an informal garden. In the middle of the garden stood a very old bur oak tree, with its thick branches stretching nearly twenty feet across. Over the annums, the Healers cultivated their perennial herb garden near the great oak, and in summer the ground was beset with bright yellow golden seal, purple lavender, and blue lobelia. Pink yarrow bushes lined the cliff wall behind the great oak, and creeping over a large boulder to the right of the tree was a wild rose bush covered with dark red blooms. In the deep shade of the tree, dangling from a thick branch, was a wooden swing. Someone had added a back to the bench seat, and time had made the wood smooth. It was a favorite place for Kinter to play her pipes, and friends often sat on nearby logs or rock outcroppings to hear her play, but today she was alone.

Kairma had come looking for Kinter to see if she would accompany her to the vault. As she rounded the bend she could hear Kinter singing. She stood for a moment to listen. It was a haunting melody. Kinter had played it at the Awakening, but now her sister had added lyrics. Kairma remembered Naturi had danced with her during that song, and Kinter had been so very angry. The lyrics explained much.

> With her stolen powers she's taken you from me.
> She has blinded your eyes and has bound you falsely.
> I swear to the gods something is wrong, it can't be,
> As I kneel to fate's might—All alone in the night,
> In the soft candlelight—I see your face forthright.
> But something is forever wrong, can't you see?
> I know in my very soul you belong to me.

Kairma turned and went back home, feeling bad for Kinter. A part of Kairma was angered by the accusation that she had done something to cause this triangle. Kairma had never done anything to encourage Naturi, but she had never discouraged him either. Walking back to the Chancery, she tried to remember Naturi's face when he left for the city. He had told her how he would make her proud, and that he would come back to fulfill his duty. The thought made her sigh. The handsome and impeccably dressed Naturi would always do what was right.

At the Chancery, Kairma found Jettena sweeping the wide porch while her younger brothers played catch-me in the bushes. They tried to involve her in their game as she walked by, but Kairma didn't feel like playing. Kinter's song had hurt her and she really wanted to be alone. She nodded to her mother and slipped into the semi-darkness of the house.

In the room where she studied, the table was littered with scrolls. Picking a random scroll, she took a seat by the window where the light was better and tried for the fifth time this week to understand its meaning. It aggravated her that so much writing was concealed in the tomb, and yet so little of it made sense. The language, although the same as hers, was filled with strange words that meant nothing to her even when reading them in the context of the rest of the scroll. She read:

> These events are controlled by valves, often working inside a steam chest adjacent to the cylinder. The valves distribute the steam by opening and closing steam ports, communicating with the cylinder ends, and are driven by a valve gear of which there are many types.

How could she ever understand anything if she didn't know the meaning of the words *valve gear*? All she knew was that it applied to something called an engine. She threw her hands up in frustration and let her mind wander to more pleasant thoughts.

The Solstice Celebration was tomorrow. It was the highlight of the summer. When her thoughts drifted to Naturi, she realized how much she wanted to dance with him again. As she stared out the open window, she was so lonesome she had to fight back the tears.

Music filled the summer air, and the Solstice Celebration was well underway when Kairma arrived. She'd spent the morning helping Jettena prepare food for the gathering. Watching Alyssum and Rose dancing in the square with Jared and Noah made her smile. Noah was about a hundred annums old and Rose was seventeen, but they were enjoying themselves. Kairma wasn't much for dancing, but every slow number reminded her of Collin and Naturi. Collin had never asked her to dance, but if he had been there, Kairma would have asked him. She moved around the buffet tables, looking over her choices of partners. Her eyes met Efram, and she shuddered. She couldn't be sure, but she felt they had been discussing her. She turned and walked back to where Isontra sat at the head table.

When Kinter finished her song, she joined her family. After a few minutes, Siede asked her to dance. Jettena leaned over and whispered something to Tamron about Siede being several annums older then Kinter, but Tamron didn't sound worried when he replied, "He's ten annums older, but in a few more annums it won't seem like such a large discrepancy."

Jettena looked around the gathering and sighed. "I suppose. There really aren't many choices, and maybe this will take her mind off Naturi. I know she thinks she's in love with him and I hate to see her heart broken come the harvest."

Tamron reached over and held Jettena's hand. "It seems the men should have been back by now. I know Trep said it would be mid-summer before they returned, but I can't help worrying about them."

"I'd like to strangle Naturi for going with them. How could he have been so thoughtless?"

Tamron smiled. "When I was younger, I would have wanted to go as well. I think we're lucky Kairma didn't try to run off."

Jettena touched her forehead, and then the four corners of an imaginary table. "Nor be thanked."

As the day wore on, people began to bring up new household items to be judged. Someone had entered a terrid pot that had small holes in the spout to strain the leaves. Kairma thought this was quite ingenious. The winner, however, was an oak butter churn. Made by Canton and demonstrated by Ember, the churn was truly an amazing device.

After Kinter announced the winners, Kairma presented them with a beautifully carved plaque, and then the girls went on to enjoy the rest of the evening eating and singing. And, for a while, Kairma almost forgot to worry.

Chapter 38

Celebration was in the air in Peireson Landing where the market was booming. A new ship had arrived with unusual spices, and Misha was in heaven as she sampled the interesting wares. She saw Narvin buying several bottles of spices as well. Nodding politely to the overseer, she looked to see if Lysara were nearby. Instead she saw Toric coming down the street. Waving to the big man, she scampered back to the hotel—excited to try her new spices.

Toric went to check on the boots he had ordered, and when Byran saw him walking down the dusty street, he called, "Lo, Toric. I have your boots ready." Reaching inside the wagon, he pulled out a pair of shiny black boots.

Toric took the boots, and looking them over carefully, he said, "They look really nice. Hope they fit as good as they look." He sat down on the small table in front of Byran's wagon and pulled on his new boots. "They feel kind of odd. I'm not used to the heel."

Byran smiled sheepishly. "I kept your heels really small on account of you bein' so tall already."

Toric laughed. "Guess that makes sense, but even this little heel is more than I'm used to wearing."

Byran took another pair of boots from the wagon. "These are Naturi's. Could you take 'em to him for me?"

"I'd be happy to. Thank you for getting these made so fast. You do fine work."

Byran smiled happily as Toric walked away, a little uneasily in his new boots.

Lysara spent the week planning the summer festival, but by the end of the week she was almost too tired to enjoy it. As she dressed in her favorite black gown and added jewels to her hair, she worried because Narvin still hadn't received the deed to the livery. She hoped she wouldn't have to answer for that in front of her friends. She knew Narvin could be really cruel in that way. She slipped out the door and called to her younger sister. "Misha, are you ready to leave?"

Misha was in the dining room putting linens away. "I'm down here, and yes, I'm ready."

Lysara came down the stairs gracefully with her black gown flowing about her curvaceous figure. Meeting Misha by the door, she asked, "Is that a new dress? You look wonderful."

Misha nodded. "A girl cain't have too many pretty dresses." Her gown, a deep blue that accented her long blond hair, was sleeveless and almost backless. She laughed as she said, "Ever since those young men came to town, I feel like dressin' up."

Lysara agreed enthusiastically, and looping her arm in Misha's they walked out the wide doors of the White Dove Hotel.

The dance hall had been decorated with flower garlands, and huge bouquets adorned the tables. Trep, along with the rest of the Survinees, were drinking spiced apple wine at their usual table near the stage so Lysara and Misha were able to find them easily.

Trep's face was grim, and after a moment he said, "I'm glad I have you all here. We've spent most all the gold we brought with us and unless Pan Aterin gets back soon, we'll be broke."

Naturi took a sip of his wine. "Do you expect him soon?"

"He was supposed to be home for the Summer Festival, but his boat wasn't docked this mornin' when I went down to the river."

Naturi checked the bank notes in his pocket. "Will we have to leave the city?"

Trep shook his head. "We paid for lodgin' for another week. We just can't buy any more extras until I can meet with Aterin."

The Survinees looked relieved. Collin went to get drinks for the ladies. He returned from the bar with Carl and Jake, who were looking a might uncomfortable.

Naturi stood up. "Lo. Are you looking for our table? I had hoped you might be joining us. Please take a seat."

His broad smile eased the apprehension in the older men as they made their way to the front of the long table. Dianay and Tarl had joined the table while Collin was gone, and the seating grew crowded and the conversations lively.

Shortly after the Bowart brothers were seated, Tatiance and two other women came looking for dance partners. Naturi suggested they join the group, and by the time the band took its first break, they were forced to pull up an additional table to seat everyone.

The music was so loud it was some time before anyone heard the alarm. There was a fire in one of the warehouses and everyone raced to form a bucket brigade, but it wasn't a warehouse burning—it was the livery. Black smoke curled around the burning timbers, and the hay burned so quickly that it was nothing but ashes before they could get water on it.

Jaimer had relocated the horses to a corral a block away. He said, "I saw the fire, and all I could think of was *save the horses.* So, I grabbed 'em as quick as I could."

Carl and Jake were furious about the fire but thankful Jaimer acted so quickly. "We appreciate all you done," said Jake. "First time we go to a dance in twenty years and our business burns to the ground. How's that fate for you?"

When the fire was finally out, the sun was coming up. Sheriff Bainser walked the ruins of the stable. "Looks like one of the horses got out and knocked over a lantern. Could have happened to anyone."

Lysara sat on a dirty wagon wheel. Her dress was ruined, and her hands were covered with blisters, but that wasn't what had her so upset. She didn't want to think about how convenient this fire was for a certain person who had aspirations of obtaining this property. She felt sick—glad this would be her last week working for Narvin. She couldn't prove anything, but something told her to get out now.

Chapter 39

Narvin met with the Bowart brothers the following day. "That was a damn shame, what happened last night at the High Summer Dance."

Jake grunted. "Mighty inconvenient for us to be at a dance."

Narvin nodded gravely. "I was so surprised to see you there. You hadn't been to a dance in years."

"That tall stranger, Naturi, asked us to join him at the dance."

Narvin studied his fingertips. "That's interestin', isn't it?"

Jake paced. "We was wonderin' if you still have that piece of property you offered us before. Could we still make the trade?"

Narvin looked up. His eyes were sorrowful. "The original deal included a livery building, but I think I could work something out, for a smaller price of course."

Jake's mouth turned down. He knew he would have to agree. They wouldn't have money to rebuild if they didn't take the deal Narvin offered.

Down the street, the kitchen of the White Dove Hotel was warm as Misha went about her preparations for the evening meal while thinking about the two young men who had become enamored with her. Collin had been spending more time with Toric training the new horses, and he didn't seem as infatuated as he'd once been. It didn't hurt her feelings, as she had grown very fond of Zedic. Zedic enjoyed helping her at the hotel and accompanying her to social functions. He was gifted at socializing, and ever so polite. It didn't hurt that he was quite good-looking too.

She saw Lysara come in through the back door and head up the steps to her room. "Hey Lysa, are you in a hurry?"

"I'll be right down. I need to change clothes." Misha poured them each a cup of tea and set out some sweet rolls. They hadn't had much time to talk in the past few weeks. Lysara spent most of her time with Trep, or at the office, and Misha suspected that Trep was with her there too.

Lysara came into the kitchen wearing a long, forest-green velvet dress and looked as if she were walking on air. Noting the dress, Misha said, "Does this mean you won't be havin' dinner with us again?"

Lysara nodded and sat at the cozy little kitchen table. "Don't get me wrong, I love your cookin'." She took an exaggerated bite out of a roll. "It's just that Trep has offered to take me to the Music Hall and then to eat at the Bell Lodge. You know how much I like the Music Hall."

Misha laughed. Lysara would have been just as happy sitting in a cattle pen as long as Trep was with her. "So when did you become a music devotee?"

"When did Trep get back into town?"

"I thought as much!"

Lysara sipped on her tea, staring into space.

Misha cleared her throat. "Hello? Are you gonna let your little sister know what's happening in your world, or am I gonna have to grill Trep's friends for the information?"

Lysara sighed. "Speaking of his friends, I think Naturi and Dianay are joining us tonight. I love them to death, but I haven't had a moment alone with Trep since he's come back. I really don't know what's goin' on. It seems to me that you've been spendin' an inordinate amount of time with his two friends."

Misha felt a little silly. She had been as obvious as her sister in her revelry. "They're fun. They make me feel like I can take on the world. I get swept away in their enthusiasm for life." She set the dish she was preparing aside. "You know, it's been eight years since Father died and I guess I jess wrapped myself up in this hotel and stopped livin' in the real world."

Lysara touched her sister's cheek. "It is good to see you smilin' again."

Misha nodded. She would have been devastated by her father's death if it hadn't been for Lysara. It was Lysara's belief in Misha that had sustained her through the worst years, and convinced her to take over the hotel. "What would I do without you?"

"You know, I've been thinkin' about that very thing for a while now. Trep has asked me to go with him when he leaves." Misha tried to hide the anxiousness she felt as Lysara continued. "You know I really love him. Besides, Narvin has become a genuine ogre to work for. Oh, I suppose I could endure him until another overseer is selected, but there is a part of me that really wouldn't mind seein' a little more of this world."

"When are they leavin'?"

"Four, maybe five days from now. It depends on when Pan Aterin gets back. They have to sell some gems to pay for their horses and the wagon."

Misha's heart stopped. "That soon? I'm gonna miss 'em terribly when they go."

A moment later, Trep came in the main door and Lysara beamed at him. After kissing her lightly on the top of her golden curls, he lifted her head to meet his eyes. "You look ravishing tonight. I'm the luckiest man in Peireson Landin'."

Lysara closed her eyes. "Thank you, Trep. I'm ready to leave when you are." He cradled her arm in his as they floated out the door, and Misha realized that Lysara had already decided to go with Trep when he left. She wept.

The little bluff overlooking the lake was picture-perfect, with cool shade under a large oak tree and a gentle breeze scented with wild daisies. As Misha climbed out of the buckboard, she thought Zedic looked unusually nervous. He paced back and forth a moment and then said, "Thank you for joining me here. I wanted to discuss something important with you where we wouldn't be interrupted."

Misha gazed at him thinking he had never looked so beautiful. *Is it right to call a man beautiful? Zedic is, with his soft ebony hair, and those mesmerizing dark gray eyes.* At the moment, Zedic looked vulnerable and yet determined.

Zedic grabbed a blanket from the wagon and spread it on the grass. He looked up at her and said, "In Survin a man does not own buildings the way he does here. Traditionally, when a man chooses a life mate he moves into her family home. Sometimes the home is enlarged, or cottages may be added. As the eldest male of the Healing family, I have my choice of moving into the home of my mate or building a brand new home. The rest of the community would help build it, of course. I could always choose to move into an empty home." He took a deep breath before continuing. "There are some truly fine homes there that have been empty for many annums. Nothing to compare to your hotel, but they are very—comfortable." He stopped and gazed at the river.

Misha waited for him to continue, and at length she said, "I'm sure you have lovely homes in Survin." When Zedic still didn't reply, she asked, "Was there something else you wanted to say?" He smiled at her and then went to the wagon to get the basket with their lunch. Misha just shook her head and spread out the dishes for their picnic.

Halfway through their lunch, while discussing the rudiments of running a hotel, Zedic reached over and took Misha's hand. He searched her eyes with a passion that Misha had never seen before and his words fell out in a tumble. "I am leaving here in three days. I would be honored beyond words if you would come to Survin with me."

The joy Misha felt when Zedic asked her to be his wife surprised her. Her breath caught and her heart raced. She hadn't realized until that moment that she really was in love with him. Not the kind of love her sister found with Trep—that all-consuming passion—but rather a deep bonding that would be missed when he left. She was truly torn between losing Zedic and losing the life she knew.

Remembering the day Trep arrived in town with four dusty and savage looking men trailing behind him, she found herself fearing what could lay ahead should she decide to join him. "Zedic, I don't know what to say. I'm so happy here with you. I just ..." Her voice trailed off. *I can't leave. Who will take care of the hotel? But Lysara is goin', and my life will be so empty without her.*

"I understand," he said. "This is rather sudden. I don't mind if you need time to consider it." Dropping the entire matter, Zedic bit into his lunch with gusto, and an instant later he was asking about the hotel as if the subject of marriage had never been brought up. Misha wasn't as good at changing the subject, and she had trouble talking about one thing while thinking about another.

Chapter 40

A cross town, a wide porch lined with ornate chairs ran the length of a pink sandstone home. Trep knocked on the expensive, beautifully carved door with a glass window. A small round man with a crooked smile on his thin lips opened the door and said, "You must be Trep. Heard you've some stones to sell."

"I am, and I do. This is Naturi. I hope ya don't mind if he tags along. He wanted to see how y'all cut stones for jewelry."

"Come on in. Show me what you have."

They stepped through the door and into a pleasant sitting room boasting expensive furniture. Looking around, Trep noted, "The jewelry trade must be good."

Pan Aterin nodded and led the two visitors to a small room in the back. "The harvest has been good the last few years, so folks have the money to buy extras."

The workspace in the well-lit room was covered with assorted cutting tools. As Aterin cleared a space, he held out his hand to see what Trep was selling. The stones Trep emptied from a small sack glistened in the bright light of the room. Trep sat on a wooden stool and Naturi leaned against the wall while Aterin, taking out a tiny magnifying glass, looked over the stones.

He weighed them and poked at them for the better part of an hour before saying, "I think you have some quality stones here. Not that much call for the quartzite, but the green tourmaline is interesting. The garnets have exceptional color too. I can get a good price for those and I haven't seen amethyst or jade of this quality in many years."

After another twenty minutes, Aterin made an offer.

Trep looked upset. "Not sure that's worth the effort to carry 'em across the country."

"It's a fair price for uncut stones. It will take me weeks to get these ready to set. I'll give you a little more for the cut ones." Pan looked over at Naturi. "You said you wanted to see how I cut stones for jewelry, but several of these gems are already cut. I hope you came by these honestly."

Naturi was incensed. "We brought them from home! Of course, we come by them honestly."

Pan Aterin made a mental note of this very interesting fact. Knowing that Trep was friends with the new overseer, Pan decided to speak with Narvin to see what he knew about the jewels. He didn't think the strange young man knew the true value of the cut jewels. They had to have come from an impressive archeological dig.

He turned toward Trep and asked if the price was satisfactory. Since they still had to pay for the horses and wagon and there wasn't another jeweler in the area, Trep agreed to the price. Aterin wrote a bank draft and handed it to Trep. "If you come across more of these opals, I'll take all you have."

Trep shook his head. "Ain't no more."

Once they had reached the street, Naturi asked Trep if the price was really fair. Trep rubbed his hand over his stubble of beard. "Well, I guess it's worth whatever he was willing' to give us. I'd hoped for more, but it's not like I could go to another jeweler. We might get more if we took the jewels to another city, but the cost of traveling would likely eat up all the profits."

Naturi asked, "Will we have enough money for everything we need?"

"We'll be okay."

The next stop was the bank, and then the Peireson ranch to pick up their horses. At Trep's insistence, Naturi had spent the last week getting to know his new horse. Trep had named her Miss Nosey because she had a habit of trying to stick her nose inside his jacket, looking for snacks. From there, the two men would see if the wagon was ready. Serges promised it would be finished by the end of the week. Excitement was evident on Trep's face as he talked about leaving. He told Naturi that although he enjoyed the city, he was never more content than when he was traveling, and he had some really interesting things to study back in Survin.

Later that evening, in the privacy of their hotel room, Collin was happy when Zedic told him he'd asked Misha to come to Survin, and chided himself for thinking Zedic wouldn't make up his own mind. "You had me worried for a while. I was beginning to think you were gonna let her get away."

"I don't tell you everything, you know."

Collin laughed. "I'll say, and I've been meaning to talk to you about it." His look softened. "She's a wonderful woman. I truly hope she says yes."

"So you really don't mind. I thought you were going to ask her yourself."

Collin made an act of fluffing his pillow. "I suppose the thought crossed my mind, but truth be told, I'm still partial to your serving girl."

Zedic threw his pillow at Collin. "She's not *my* serving girl!"

"Yes she is. You just haven't taken advantage of it— so I guess I'll just have to do it for you."

Zedic rolled his eyes. "You do that!" An instant later he added, "You'd better hurry—you've already wasted four weeks chasing after my girl."

Collin shook his head and pretended to go to sleep. All of a sudden, he realized how much he was looking forward to going home.

Chapter 41

Trep, and the others were due home any day, and Kairma had trouble concentrating on the silver scroll she was reading. She knew there were a dozen possible reasons the men might be delayed, but each day it grew more and more difficult to think of anything else. Taking a drink of cold water, she tried once more to apply herself as she sat with Kinter at Isontra's large wooden table, trying to decipher the latest scroll taken from the tomb. She read.

> "Admiral: derived from the Arabic *amir-al* or *emir-al*, is the title of the officer who commands a fleet, a subdivision of a fleet, or of the head of an important naval administrative activity on shore.
> Commodore: is a commissioned naval officer who ranks above a captain and below a rear admiral; the lowest grade of admiral, usually commanding a squadron or naval station.
> Captain: is a naval officer in command of a military ship."

Kinter rubbed her temples. "Does *shore* mean *to strengthen* or is it like a lake shore? The previous word is *on*. That leads me to believe it must be a noun, not a verb."

"Fleet is another noun then, and not meaning *fast.*"

"There's that navy/naval word again."

Kairma got up from the table and began to pace. "We know that the word *title* means *label* in this sense, and we know *Admiral* is a label." She spun around to face Kinter, her eyes were wide as she almost shouted, "*Admiral* is a title—like *Miral!* And *Commodore* is a title like *Comad!*" A shiver ran down her back as the epiphany overwhelmed her. "It can't be a coincidence. They're describing a chain of command like ours! But they command something called a *ship*, a *station*, or a *fleet.*"

Kinter leaned back in her chair, exhausted. "Well, that only took us three weeks to figure out. We should know the meaning of the rest of these scrolls by the time we're Gramme's age." She rolled a kink out of her neck. "Let's quit for a while. I'm hungry, and I haven't gathered the lavender I promised Gramme."

"Yeah, I think we did enough for today. I can't wait to tell Gramme what we learned! This is amazing!"

Kinter carefully put the silver scroll into its case and set it on the shelf in the records room. "They probably put the records in a certain order. We need to find the beginning."

Kairma handed her another scroll to place on the shelf. "I think each case is a different subject matter."

"So, do you remember which case we took these last scrolls from?"

Kairma wrinkled her nose. "I think we took a couple from several cases."

"That's great. As if this wasn't hard enough, we just made it a lot harder."

"Tomorrow, we can take these back and figure out which case they belong in. From there, we'll choose one case and go all the way through it before going on to the next one."

"How will we know where these scrolls belong?"

Kairma pointed to the first scroll on the shelf. "There are numbers on the outside of the canister. I think there must be an order to them. If nothing else, that one contains the words *navy* and *naval.* We just need to find a case with more words like that."

"Well," Kinter sighed. "Let's go pick some flowers before it gets too dark to see them."

The next day, Kairma and Kinter were excited to pick up more scrolls. Having learned something important, they were convinced they could understand everything if the scrolls were read in order. They spent a long time trying to figure out the system of arrangement. After deciphering the words *admiral* and *commodore*, they hoped the rest of the scroll would be easier to understand, but after a morning of searching, it was clear they didn't have the background to comprehend the majority of the words here. The reason why these scrolls were written was still well beyond them.

They put back in the cabinet a scroll with the following text. They would try to understand it another day.

> Photography is the process of creating still or moving pictures by recording radiation on a sensitive medium, such as a film, or an electronic sensor. Light patterns reflected or emitted from objects activate a sensitive chemical or electronic sensor during a timed exposure, usually through a photographic lens, in a device known as a camera that also stores the resulting information chemically or electronically.
>
> The word *photography* comes from the Greek (phos) "light" + (graphis) "stylus," "paintbrush" or (graphê) "representation by means of lines" or "drawing," together meaning "drawing with light."

Drawing with light sounded very interesting, but words like *electronic, sensor, radiation,* and *chemical* were mystifying.

Kinter sat cross-legged on the floor of the tomb where she opened silver cases and looked for words she recognized. It wasn't easy. After several attempts she found *medicine* and set the scroll aside. Kairma was busy doing the same on the other side of the large room.

Kinter stretched her back. "This is such a beautiful room. How do you think they carved this stone?"

Kairma turned to her sister, and also stretching like a cat said, "I wish I knew. Could you imagine living in a place as wonderful as this?"

"I think I would live here if I were the Vice Miral."

"That would be crazy—there's no fireplace. How would you stay warm or cook your food?"

"I would build a fireplace."

"How would you vent the smoke?"

Kinter was getting annoyed with Kairma. "I'd figure something out."

"What would you use the side rooms for?"

"What side rooms?"

"The rooms with the long counters on the wall. They have all those tiny rooms with doors and big white bowls on the floor."

"You never showed me those rooms." Kinter was miffed that Kairma had withheld something for her.

Kairma got up. "Come on. You have to see this. I didn't find it the first time we came up here. There was so much to see in the main room I didn't think to look farther, but last week when I was here with Isontra I pulled on that bar on the wall over there, and it opened to a smaller room."

She led Kinter to the door and opened it. Inside there was a long counter along the left side of a large room. Inset in the counter were four white bowls with a hole in the bottom that led to a long tube of metal that curled oddly and then disappeared into the wall.

Behind the counter was the largest looking glass the girls had ever seen. Age had blackened the edges of the glass, but the vacuum of the tomb had preserved it well beyond its natural age.

Kinter looked into the glass for a long time, her eyes wide with wonder, as she absentmindedly straightened her hair and brushed dirt from her cheek. Kairma smiled behind her because of all the things they found in the vault, she knew this would please Kinter the most. Isontra had once given Kinter a small looking glass, and she carried it everywhere.

An archway led to another room with eight doors on each side of a long hall. Behind each of the doors was an even larger oddly shaped white bowl on the floor. The bowls couldn't hold anything because there was a hole in the bottom of every one of them.

Kairma led Kinter out again and pointed to another door. "That room is a lot like this one except it has strange white bowls mounted on the walls too." As Kinter went on to investigate the bizarre rooms, Kairma packed up their selected scrolls and prepared to head home.

Kinter joined her a few minutes later saying, "I will definitely figure out a way to move here. If you want to stay in the canyon, that's fine. I'll stay here and learn to read all these scrolls."

"I think Isontra may have something to say about that."

"It only makes sense for us to use this space. It would save a lot of time if we didn't have to walk back and forth all the time."

"Don't you think you would get lonely up here all by yourself?"

Kinter seemed to consider it for a moment. "I would wait until I took a mate. Then we would live here together."

Kairma grinned. "I'll miss you,"

Kinter rolled her eyes. "No you won't. You'll probably be glad to be rid of me."

"Sometimes, you're okay," Kairma said as she picked up her pack and walked out the door.

Kinter hurried to catch up. "I can't believe no one had discovered this before now."

Kairma nodded. "It's incredible, isn't it?"

"Do you think those Madics were searching for the vault?

"I don't see how they could know about it. It was partly buried under a rockslide until Collin and Zedic dug it out."

"I hope Zedic catches them. I hate Madics." Kinter's chin jutted out as she squared the pack on her shoulder.

Kairma kicked a small rock in the path and watched it skitter over the cliff edge. "You know Collin and Zedic are going to kill those men."

"Of course. That's why they went after them."

"But, Kinter—what if we're wrong?"

Kinter stopped and looked at her sister. "How can we be wrong? The Law of Fontas clearly defines our duty."

Kairma chewed her lower lip. "But, what if Fontas was wrong?"

Kinter abruptly turned away. "Frankly, Kairma, your lack of faith frightens me. How can you become the Vice Miral if you don't believe what you're teaching?"

Kairma had no answer. It was the very question she'd asked herself for annums.

The summer heat had returned, and the valley had seen little rain over the last few weeks so Kairma was carrying water to the herb garden when Isontra stopped and asked, "Could we make another trip to the Godstones tomorrow? I'd like to take a closer look at the small rooms Kinter mentioned this morning."

Kairma sat down her bucket and rolled a kink out of her shoulder. "I was planning to go anyway." She looked over at Kinter, who was filling a bucket at the stream. "If I know Kinter, she would rather go to the vault than carry water too."

"Good. Let's leave early—before it gets too hot."

Isontra was about to walk away when Kairma stopped her. "Why don't we live in the temples? It seems like a waste of a perfectly good building."

Isontra pondered the question for a while. "I think it has more to do with defense and this garden."

Kairma nose wrinkled in puzzlement. "I don't understand."

"This valley has steep cliff walls on all sides. It's easy to defend and good shelter from winter storms. The land by the Godstones is too open. The temples could house maybe fifteen families, so there isn't enough room for everyone. Where would you build more houses? Where would you grow food? Here we have a lush valley with a good stream running through it."

"Kinter wants to move to the vault."

Isontra smiled. "Our princess. I can understand why she would like to live there. It's really beautiful inside. I think she would miss her family after a few moons."

"She's planning to take her mate to live there with her."

"I wonder how her mate will feel about that."

Kinter was approaching the garden so Kairma didn't respond.

Later that afternoon Kairma wandered into Isontra's suite looking gloomy.

"What's wrong, dear? You look like you lost your best friend."

Unintended tears sprang to Kairma's eyes and she quickly brushed them away. Isontra's words had hit their mark. She did feel as if she had lost her best friend. She wanted to show Zedic and Collin the small rooms she'd discovered in the vault. She wanted to tell them about the *admiral* and *commodore*. She wanted them to come home. They were a full moon past due and Kairma was frightened for them.

"I miss them, Gramme. I hope they come home soon. They've already been gone for three moons. I thought they were going to be home in two. Do you think they're okay?"

Isontra put down the lace she was working on. "If I know those young men, they won't miss your Seridar. Any number of things could be keeping them." Secretly, Isontra was as worried as Kairma. The early August moon was nearly full, and the men of Survin were preparing for the last extended hunt before the Seridar. The community was becoming more agitated every day, and Isontra worried there would be open rebellion soon.

Kairma set her cup of terrid on the table and went to the storage room to get another scroll. "Has Kinter come in? I didn't see her at lunch."

Isontra opened the thin metal scroll in front of her. "She stopped in for a few minutes but went out to help Tamron pack gear for the hunt. She'll be along in a moment."

Kairma said, "I think the hunters should go east tomorrow. Maybe they can see Zedic and the others."

"That's an excellent idea. I'll tell Tamron tonight."

Kairma set a silver scroll on the table and unrolled it. A frown crossed her face and Isontra reached over and patted her hand. "I know this is hard. It's even more frustrating that you can't share it with Zedic and Collin."

Kairma blew out a sigh. "How do you do that? You always know what I'm thinking. Earlier, I was worried about the men getting back before the harvest and you knew I was thinking about that. Now you know I want Collin and Zedic to see these."

"Your thoughts are usually pretty plain on your face. Also, we are enough alike that if I put myself in your position, I can usually guess what you're thinking."

"That's eerie."

Isontra smiled. "You do it too. I don't think you do it consciously, but you're very empathetic. You adjust your emotions to suit those around you, often anticipating another's response, before he has a chance to act. You have trouble with Kinter because you envy her."

Kairma looked up sharply. She didn't realize her emotions were *that* transparent.

"Don't worry. Most people can't see it. As a matter of fact, most people are so caught up in their own point of view that they never see anyone else's perspective.

"I don't want to envy Kinter, but she's so pretty. She's really smart too."

"You are just as smart, and beauty is quite subjective. I happen to think you're a very beautiful girl, and I know at least two young men who would agree with me."

Kairma could feel her cheeks warm. She studied the scroll in front of her and began to read aloud: "Personal Computer: A small, single-user computer based on a microprocessor. In addition to the microprocessor ..."

Chapter 42

The five rooms directly above the kitchen and dining room of the hotel were private quarters belonging to Misha and Lysara. The only access to the suite was through the kitchen. Often the two sisters would share a cup of tea and something sweet at their private table before retiring for the night, but the past few weeks had been a whirlwind of activity and their little ritual was overlooked. Misha had already gone to bed when Lysara crept through the back door of the kitchen. For a moment, she thought she saw Misha slip into the dining room, but, when no one answered her call, she passed it off as her imagination and went up to bed.

A few minutes later Lysara awoke choking on thick black smoke. Her room was on fire and it took a moment to realize that she wasn't dreaming but was in danger of being cut off from her only escape route. Wrapping her blanket around her body to keep from being burned, she ran for the door. The carpeting under her bare feet was on fire and she grit her teeth to keep from crying. Once out in the hallway, she could see that Misha's room was also blazing uncontrolled. Screaming for help, she thrust her way into Misha's adjoining room. Misha wouldn't wake up and Lysara was forced to pick her up and carry her out of the inferno. When she had reached the stairs to the kitchen, Misha came around, coughing and gagging on the smoke that encircled their heads. Lysara's eyes burned so badly that she couldn't see, and it was Misha who led them safely down the stairs.

Trep's room had been the closest to the kitchen and he was there to lead the frightened women out into the night. By this time, the rest of the hotel was awake and scrambling to safety. The volunteer fire department arrived within minutes, but it was obvious that most of the hotel would be ruined.

Dozens of volunteers carried bucket after bucket of water from the river, but it was a long way between the water's edge and the flaming building. The residents gaped in horror as the magnificent curved stairway leading to the second floor burned with a passion. Not having any way to reach the upper floors, the residents of Peireson Landing watched one of their most beautiful buildings burn uncontrollably. The wind was threatening to spread the fire west where several fine homes were located. Unable to save the hotel, they concentrated on keeping the flames from spreading.

Lysara watched Naturi race to the northwest storage room where the Survinees had placed several of their purchases. She was thankful he was able to save a few items before the upper floors came crashing down in a thunder of noise and heat. The hotel supply rooms were also buried under a mass of broken and burning timbers, and the private quarters belonging to her and Misha became nothing but ashes and twisted metal.

As the flames were slowly brought under control, Lysara found a dazed Misha sitting on the walkway across the street from the inferno. Lysara was amazed how different it was to fight a fire in a strange place as opposed to fighting your own. It was the most personal violation she'd ever felt.

Hugging her arms to her chest, she watched Zedic frantically fight his way through the melee of people and noise and race to Misha's side. His voice was choked with worry. "Are you okay?" he asked as he swept her into his arms—thankful she was alive.

"Yeah, my head and my throat hurt, but I think I'm gonna be okay." She tried to pull away, but Zedic held her tight. "Really, Zedic, I'm gonna be fine. The Bell Lodge will put us up for a while and I can always buy new clothes."

She didn't have to add there were hundreds of other things that could never be replaced, because it was evident on her face as Zedic held her, and stroked her soot-blackened hair.

Lysara looked for Trep and found him shoveling dirt over the sizzling coals that used to be a beautiful attached sunroom. He dropped the shovel, and taking her into his sweat and ash covered arms, he held her as she wept.

The next morning, as they picked their way through the remnants of the burned hotel, Collin suggested that the fire started in both of the rooms at the same time. "But that seems unlikely. What're the odds of both lanterns falling over at the same time?"

Lysara shook her head. "I put the flame out in my lantern before goin' to bed. I passed Misha's room on the way to mine, and her room was also dark." Lysara didn't voice her suspicion, but the fire at the livery had her concerned that their current difficulties might have a sinister founding. But she was at a complete loss as to why someone would want to hurt her or Misha.

Sheriff Bainser was eager to get started on the investigation. Two fires, only days apart, was a lot of excitement for Peireson Landing. When he arrived on the scene of the gutted hotel, with four new deputies in tow, he gave the appearance of having the situation under control. He took statements, made measurements, and nodded his balding head often when he reached various conclusions. His mud-brown eyes twinkled in his cherub face as he directed his deputies here and there.

Lysara picked her way through the blackened carcass of the hotel as she looked for anything salvageable. She watched Bainser as he directed his men through the rubble. She didn't care for Bainser. He smiled too much and laughed too easy for her taste. She didn't mistrust the man, but neither was she confident that he could find his way home, let alone get to the bottom of an arson investigation. She shook her head and wondered why Narvin had appointed him sheriff.

Two days following the fire, Bainser concluded that the cause of the fire had been accidental and the case was closed. The hotel had been constructed of large rose-quartzite stone and while the outer walls gave the appearance of little damage, the inside was beyond repair. The upper floors had been completely destroyed, but some of the dining room remained standing. Misha was able to find the dinner service she had inherited from her mother. Several of the pieces were broken, but she packed away what she could save. Her expensive linens were gone. Her clothes and her keepsakes were nothing but black, soggy ash.

While Misha was trying to clean off a pan that still looked useable, Nixon Blong, the city treasurer, approached her. "I'm sorry for your loss," he said. "It was a terrible fire."

Misha looked up at the thin man. His almond-shaped eyes were dark and sad. She stood up and grimaced. "Yes, it was. What can I do for you?"

"It's more about what I might be able to do for you."

"I'm listenin'."

"I know you ain't in a position to rebuild your hotel, and I was wonderin' if you might want to sell the land and the remainin' stone?"

Misha's laugh held no humor. "Why would you want this?"

"The land is in a convenient location to the docks, and you know how hard it is to find stone blocks like these." He waved a soft hand toward the outer walls of the structure.

Misha deliberated for a moment. She had lost everything, and her sister was leaving for the west in a few days. The decision to accept Zedic's offer was forced on her like an unwelcome storm. She looked over the ruins of her life and began to cry again. When Nixon put a consoling arm around her, she pulled her thoughts together and wiped the tears from her cheeks, leaving long streaks of black across her cheeks.

"How much are you offerin'?"

"I can give you enough to replace most of the clothing you and your sister lost. It might cover some of the goods the strangers bought too."

"I don't think they would hold me responsible for their loss, but it's the right thing to do."

"Do we have a deal?"

"I need to have a word with Lysara first. Come by the Bell Lodge in the mornin' and we'll talk."

The following morning was hot and muggy and it would be raining by early afternoon. The Bell Lodge was comfortable, but it wasn't as elegant as the White Dove had been. The Dove sisters were sipping a cup of tea in the dining room of the Bell when Narvin entered.

"Mornin', girls."

Misha nodded. Lysara said, "Sir."

"I spoke with a few folks around town. I was able to raise a little money for you girls." He laid a few bank notes on the table in front of them. "With Nixon's offer to buy your land, you should have enough to build a small house."

Lysara looked up into his light brown eyes. "Thank you, Sir. That was very kind of you."

"I'm so sorry about your hotel. The city lost a wonderful landmark."

"Yes, it did," Lysara said curtly.

He patted her on the head. "Now you girls take care." And with those words, he turned and left the room.

A few moments later Nixon walked into the dining room. He told the waitress to bring him a cup of tea as he sat down across the table from the Dove sisters.

After they came to an agreement on the price, Misha went to the bank and drew out enough money to replace much of what the Survinees lost in the fire. She would spend the rest on travel supplies since Trep had insisted the Peireson Landing bank notes wouldn't be good where they were going. The thought sent a shiver down her back.

Chapter 43

The carriage house hadn't suffered from the fire, and the Survinees were busy packing what was left of their belongings in the new wagon. Luckily, the majority of their goods had been stored at the mercantile. The Dove sisters owned a small buckboard and a pinto mare, so while Zedic prepared it for travel, Lysara and Misha spent the morning at the mercantile replacing what items they could. By early evening they were ready to leave.

The last night in Peireson Landing was cheerless as Lysara and Misha visited with friends and said their good-byes. Returning to the room they shared, Misha told Lysara about her apprehension of leaving the city.

Lysara tried to reassure her sister. "We're gonna be fine. Trep has told me a lot about Survin. It really sounds like a very friendly place."

"I don't know. It's sounds pretty primitive, but it's more than that. I don't really know if I love Zedic enough to marry him."

"You don't have to marry him. You're goin' to Survin as my sister. You can decide what to do about Zedic later." Her green eyes twinkled. "If the men that came here with Trep are an example of Survinees men, you might find someone else when we get there."

Misha shook her head. "I'm not sure that I want to marry anyone."

"No need to decide now. Let's get some sleep. We're leaving at dawn."

The morning sky was a dark gray as they packed their last items into the wagon. The seven travelers waved to the friendly people of Peireson Landing and headed west into a drizzling rain. The weather was warm so, although they were wet, they weren't cold.

The newness of the experience kept Lysara and Misha from dwelling on their recent losses. As they rode through the bumpy fields, Trep regaled them with stories of adventure. They stopped for the night in a large grassy field, where the men laid out bedrolls under the wagons and the women curled up inside. The space was tight between the supplies, and the floor of the wagon was hard, but the canvas tarp kept the women fairly dry.

The next evening, about twenty-five miles west of the city, they came across Narvin and about ten men sitting around a large campfire. Lysara's gut tightened. Turning to Trep, who was riding beside the buckboard, she asked, "What's he doin' here?"

Trep said, "It's okay. I told Narvin to meet us here. I wanted 'em to misdirect any people who mighta had plans to follow us."

As they set up camp for the night, Narvin assured Trep that his men would turn back anyone who thought to follow the Survinees. Several of Narvin's men would leave a false trail leading to the north, giving the appearance of crossing the river, while the Survinees headed west. The wagons couldn't negotiate the steep riverbanks, forcing them to cut across the open prairie where the heavy wagons would leave a conspicuous trail for weeks. So Narvin promised to do his best to erase the trail marks before he headed back to Peireson Landing.

Although Lysara didn't know why it was important to hide their trail, she was feeling better about the man's appearance, and silently chided herself. *I don't like the man, but do I have reason to think he had something to do with Conrad's death or the fires?*

While bands of pink and lavender colored the sky as the sun set in the west, Lysara and Misha prepared a hot meal, and Trep shared more stories about traveling to distant places. Trep was a wonderful entertainer. Eventually the conversation turned to celebrations and the many different ways people celebrated the same thing. Narvin asked Trep how many different autumn celebrations he had attended. Trep mentioned several. Turning to Naturi, Narvin asked if his people had an autumn celebration.

Naturi grinned. "We have a Harvest Celebration where everyone brings food and drink, and we have contests of skill. We hope to be home several weeks before the last harvest. "

"Sounds like fun. When's it held? Is it always the same time?"

"Usually the last full moon of the summer, or the full moon closest to the autumn equinox."

Narvin raised an eyebrow as he looked over at Trep, but Trep shrugged. "Equi … Equo …?"

"The equinox is the day when there is exactly as much dark as there is light. It signals the change of the annum."

Narvin nodded sagely. "Smart! You folks always surprise me. Oh, by the way. I have a special gift for you." Turning to Artuk he asked, "Where's that box I asked you to get from my office?"

Before Artuk could answer, Jaimer jumped up and went to his saddlebags. "It's right here, with the other things you wanted."

Taking the box from Jaimer, Narvin said, "I brought somethin' for you to share with your families." Narvin pulled out a large sack of maple toffees and handed it to Naturi. "They're just like the ones you had in my office the first day we met. I thought you'd like to take some home with you. Save 'em for somethin' really special, like your Harvest Celebration. They're very expensive candies. I hope I brought enough."

Lysara had been with Narvin the day he purchased the candies, and they were indeed expensive. She was quite surprised the man had offered them to the Survinees, and again admonished herself for mistrusting him.

Naturi thanked Narvin, who assured him there would be plenty. Toric wanted to taste one then, but Narvin insisted they wait for the harvest party. Putting a friendly hand on Toric's shoulder, Narvin said, "Pack them away and forget about 'em. That way they won't tempt you all the way home. I wouldn't want your friends to miss out on the treats."

Once the candies were put safely away, Jaimer began telling an involved story about a celebration where he had apparently lost several things, including his virginity, and the rest of the night was spent trying to top Jaimer's story.

The next morning, the Survinees packed up their camp, saying good-bye to Narvin and his men, but before they rode off Narvin reached into the box where he had found the maple toffees and pulled out two small satin pouches. "I almost forgot. I brought these for the girls. Kind of a remembrance of Peireson Landin'." Pulling open the drawstring so that the women could see the golden hair combs, he advised, "Keep 'em in this powder at night and they will stay clean and shiny." He handed a pouch to each of the ladies, who immediately put the trinkets in their hair. Narvin smiled. "Have a safe trip."

They made poor time due to the slow moving oxen and heavy wagon carrying their supplies. The landscape was rough, and in many places they were forced to go around gullies or steep hills. At the end of the third day, Collin, Toric and Trep rode to the river to refill their waterskins while the others made camp.

It was after sunset and the fire and smell of roasting meat was a pleasant welcome when the men got back. The moonlight leached the color from the landscape, leaving silver gray in place of the colorful prairie flowers, and the heavens were bright with stars. A waning moon hung low in the eastern sky, marking over eight weeks that the Survinees has been away, and it would be another three before they saw the granite carvings that marked their home.

Misha and Lysara took some of the clothing and fabric from the supply box and created a makeshift mattress. It wasn't as restful as their beds at home had been, but it was a vast improvement over the hard floor of the wagon. The men were used to sleeping on the hard ground, but, with the exception of Trep, none of the men were used to riding all day on a horse. By the end of the first week, each one was walking a little slower and with a slight shuffle.

Keeping the river in sight, they made their way across the rolling plains. Trep and Naturi rode a short distance ahead, looking for the best route for the wagons, while Collin and Toric hunted for small game, leaving the two women to drive the wagon and buckboard. Zedic rode his horse next to the buckboard Misha was driving and described every facet of Survin to her.

The wagon stalled in a rut. Zedic and Misha stopped to free the wagon. It was hard work and Misha wondered if she would have agreed to come at all had the hotel not been destroyed. The village of Survin sounded quaint—maybe a little too quaint. After all, Misha was a big city girl used to running a hotel, not fighting her way through thistles. Although she was in her mid-twenties, marriage hadn't been a serious consideration and now the thought of being a wife frightened her. Trying to imagine what her new life was going to be like, she asked, "Zedic, what do women do in Survin? I know your Miral is the leader, kind of like our Overseer, right?"

Zedic put his shoulder to the back of the large wagon, and with Misha's help they pushed it through the deep rut. "They're the religious leaders of the community. The Comad is sort of like your Overseer in his duties, but he is second to the Miral."

She absently rubbed her arm where the wagon had scraped her. "So if your sister is the new Vice Miral, what will you do? What's your job?"

Zedic looked piqued. "Why, I'll take care of you, of course."

"Oh, I know that, but how will you make a livin'—pay for food and things?"

Zedic thought for a very long time. Misha had almost given up on getting an answer when he said, "Everyone contributes to the welfare of the village. Each week, there is a drawing for duties. Sometimes I chop wood, sometimes I build new homes, and sometimes I work in the cleansing stations." When Zedic explained what the cleansing station was, Misha's face turned a bit green. "All the men hunt and the game is shared throughout the village. Everyone works the fields, although Naturi is the most gifted."

"What will I do there?" Misha asked.

"The same. Everything." Zedic helped her climb back onto the buckboard.

"I don't know how to do everything."

"Don't worry, I'll teach you."

She thought about making hotel beds and cooking meals for guests. She did know how to do a lot of things. Suddenly, Misha thought of all her pretty clothes she'd lost in the fire and realized sadly that she wouldn't have much need for them now.

Seeing the sadness on her face, Zedic reached up and lightly stroked her cheek. Leaning toward her, he whispered, "I promise, I will make you happy."

Resigned, she considered what he said. *Well, maybe I won't miss the stress of running the hotel.*

Chapter 44

The morning sun stirred in the east, creeping through the shutters of the south window in Isontra's suite as she pulled out her charcoal and yesterday's Ogs. The hunters had come back from a long hunt yesterday with a fresh supply of game and Isontra could hear the sound of Survin pitching in to help clean and cure the meat. The usual celebration that followed the hunt only reminded Isontra how long Naturi, Zedic, and Collin had been gone. Worried that Toric was hurt, she sent the hunting party east to look for him, only to become more frustrated when the men—thwarted by several White Ones—were forced to turn south. Permanently losing Survin's best hunter and best gardener would be a major loss to the community. The hunt had gone well, but the dry summer was taking its toll on the fields. The crops weren't as strong as they should be this late in the season, so men cleared new canals to water the fragile plants.

The evening before, Isontra had seen Hiram and Grimly standing near the canal, deep in conversation. Hiram took every opportunity to criticize the Healing family for any difficulties, and she could imagine him blaming her for the hot weather as well. Over the two moons Trep and the others had been gone, before his death, Diakus had also become very vocal in his protests, and had managed to persuade several Survinees to renounce the weekly services. If Grimly and Hiram were more charismatic, the split would be especially decisive. There was nothing she could do about the heat, but the loss of Diakus weighed heavily on her mind, and she blamed herself for not seeing that Massie had been so terribly depressed. Writing in her daily Ogs, she asked that future Mirals not judge her too harshly for her actions and inactions.

Later that day, as the sun was low in the western sky, Kairma and Kinter packed up new scrolls to study and headed back the village. The title of the scroll Kairma was carrying was something called *Molecular Virology, Molecular Evolution, Pathogenesis, Host Immune Reponses, Influenza Research, and Epidemiology.*

Unfortunately, only three words in the title were familiar: *Host, Responses,* and *Research.* The work had been so difficult. It had been more than a week since they had learned anything new, and they were frustrated to have all this knowledge in front of them and not understand it.

The scroll she now carried had been found in the same cabinet as a scroll that mentioned *antiseptic,* leading Kairma to believe it had something to do with medicine. She tried to make sense of the other words, but only managed to figure out that the scroll referred to a study concerning something called an *influenza virus.* The text said, "Improved influenza countermeasures require basic research on how viruses enter cells, replicate, mutate, and evolve into new strains and induce an immune response."

One phrase played on Kairma's mind as she and Kinter walked down the worn path from the temples. *"Only one therapeutic measure, transfusing blood from recovered patients to new victims, showed any hint of success."* Kairma understood this to mean a formerly sick person's blood could help someone who was sick or might get sick. From the text she read, Kairma knew the Ancient Ones wanted to understand what made one strain of the virus more lethal than another. The text claimed genetics might have had an impact on those who survived and those who did not. *Is my family stronger than other families because Grampe Petar and Father were outsiders? That might explain why I've never lost a sibling to a fever when so many others have died.* She turned to look at her sister, who was quietly humming an unfamiliar song, and then looked down at the silver scroll in her hand. *Could Father have given me something to protect me from the White Fever? What if my blood could protect others?*

As they walked, Kairma noticed the frown on Kinter's pretty face. "What's wrong?"

Kinter sighed hugely. "I'm just getting so bored with all this. We're never going to figure out what it means." The book they had found in the desk was simply list after list of words and different ways to say the same thing. The reason for the book was still a mystery.

"How can you be bored? This has to be the biggest mystery of all time."

"But I am bored. It's the same thing every day. It's not like reading the Ogs. The Ogs are like reading the story of someone's life. These are just lots of strange words, and I'm getting really tired of reading."

"See that field over there? Life is like a field. At first glance it's only a meadow of grass, but if you look close, you'll see different colors of grass. Then you'll see a few yellow flowers, and look, there's a butterfly and a rabbit. Suddenly the whole meadow is alive with excitement. See? When you're bored, you're just not paying attention."

Kinter rolled her eyes. "Ugh, you sound just like Gramme."

Kairma laughed. "That's because that was exactly what Gramme said to me yesterday, when I told her *I* was bored."

Kinter wrinkled her nose at Kairma. "Did it help?"

"Yeah, it kind of did help. That's not to say I won't be just as bored as you tomorrow, but I feel better today."

Kinter rolled her eyes again, but Kairma continued. "I know most of what we read doesn't make any sense, but I think this one might help us. When we get home, could you find all of the Ogs that mention the Blood Rite? I may know why I didn't die when the Whitish bit me."

"Sure, *that* won't be at all boring."

As the full moon began to wane once more, and the long days of summer became shorter, Kairma and Kinter slowly grew closer, now rarely snipping at each other as they had done in the past. Kairma continued to study everything she could find concerning the Blood Rite, and the regular practice of reading the ancient scrolls helped improve her confidence. She could now read faster than Kinter or Isontra. The meanings of many of the writings were still unclear, but little by little she was understanding the importance of what they'd found.

The summer sun was tanning her pale skin, and with a dark scarf over her hair she didn't look all that much different from the others, making her morning visits a little less objectionable to the members of the community. Before setting out on her rounds, and because Zedic was away, she brought in wood and started the morning fire. Mornings were warm, so the fire Kairma built was small, only large enough to heat water for terrid and cooking breakfast.

Sitting by the fire, sipping a cup of terrid, Kairma thought about how she'd broken her promise to Collin. *I'll have to tell him about his parents as well. Maybe he'll be sorry he came back. He better come back.* She chewed on a day-old biscuit. *I wonder how much they'll change over these long weeks? If I'm honest with myself, I know I've changed a lot. It's really scary how much Kinter has changed. The hardest thing to get used to is how tall she's grown. Never thought I'd be jealous of the girl, but she's really something to look at now with her dark blue eyes and beautiful chestnut hair. She rarely fights with me anymore, almost treating me with respect—curse the thought. I used to know her, and now she's like a stranger.* A grin played across her pink lips. *Maybe the Whitish took my sister and left a copy of her.*

Kairma turned a small log in the fireplace, the smell of burning pine relaxing her. Kairma had to admit that even if Kinter hadn't blackmailed her into their current situation, she liked having Kinter attending lessons with her, *if it wasn't for the way Kinter was always showing off for Isontra.*

Kinter had an uncanny ability to remember things. Having seen things once, Kinter had almost total recall, whereas, Kairma had to study her lessons over and over again.

The sun was peeking over the eastern tree line when Kairma returned from a brief visit with Tristan and Noah. The men seemed to enjoy her company more each day, and that had Kairma feeling particularly happy this morning. She put a few blackberry cakes on a plate with some fresh apples and refilled her cup of terrid. Since Isontra would be awake by now, she poured another cup for her grandmother and headed to the west wing of the house.

As she walked through the lavishly carved doorway to the room, she saw Isontra pulling leaves from the bush that had been drying by her small hearth, and putting them into a large pottery bowl. Isontra's long white hair wasn't yet pulled up into her customary braid. Kairma wondered if she would look the same in a few annums. Her grandmother was a pleasant-looking woman with eyes that flashed darkly when she was angry. Laugh lines crinkled her eyes when she was happy, and her smile was almost too wide for her face.

Kairma set the cups of terrid and the plate of cakes on the table and then went to help Isontra with the herbs. She was familiar with these bushes that grew wild anywhere there was good sunlight. The best plants were from Naturi's fields and were used for any number of things. Their most common use was for pain relief. The smoke from the leaves, or pills made from the pollen, could relieve most headache pain, arthritis, rheumatism, muscle spasms, and sleeplessness, and to cure an unruly stomach. The harvests had been good, but like willow bark terrid it was a much sought after medicine, so the stores were low.

Isontra looked up at Kairma and smiled. "Where is Kinter this morning?"

"She didn't want to get up." Kairma looked at the pile of plants to be processed. "Sometimes, I think she knows when there is real work to be done." Kairma smiled widely, much like her grandmother. "Can't blame her there." In a gentler tone she said, "Kinter read late into the night. I asked her to research the Blood Rite for me. She'll be here soon."

Isontra nodded knowingly. Kairma and Kinter still competed fiercely, although the girls had grown closer in the absence of Zedic and Collin. Isontra asked, "Would you get the safety box from under my sleeping cot, dear?" She put the stem of the plant aside to be used later, and while Kairma was off on her errand, Isontra took the time to braid her hair and wrap it in a neat coil on her head.

Kairma found the box and brought it back to the sitting room. She loved to look in the strange cache made of a thin alloy like the silver cylinders they found in the secret vault. And like the vault, it too was filled with the most fascinating objects. Many of the items were made by means no one could explain. She carefully put the box on the table and turned the dials on the handle until the symbols matched the code she had been taught and, with a click, the box opened.

Kairma took out a square of loosely woven alloy and handed it to Isontra, who laid the screen over a flat earthenware tray. The plant was harvested before the buds could flower and the sturdy stems were stripped of leaves and buds.

As Isontra rolled the buds over the square, covering it with brown sticky pollen, she said, "I've been giving a lot of thought to the last writing we brought down from the vault." She rolled the pollen into small pills and dried them over a low fire.

Kairma was breaking the stalks down to make rope and canvas. The canvas was used for making clothing or the sacred scrolls on which the Healers recorded the daily lives of the Survinees. Without breaking the rhythm of her work, she said, "It would be so much easier if we understood the things they were describing. Really, what's a *hard drive?* I know what *hard* means and I know you can *drive* a stake into a hole, but together I don't understand." Frustration saturated her voice as she placed the stems in a pot of water to soak overnight.

Isontra agreed. "I've been studying a silver scroll that reads, 'Before World War II, blacks were not allowed to enlist in the United States Navy,' and I'm not sure if it means there were eleven wars fought by the entire world, or the name of the war was II. I can't figure out what *blacks* are, or the meaning of *States Navy*."

Kairma set seeds to the side to be replanted. "By cross referencing some of the words that show up often, I think the people who wrote the scrolls wanted to list everything they had studied and everything they accomplished."

"That's a good thought. I think this work is very important. I wish we had more time to dedicate to it."

Kairma gathered the ingredients for making soap. It was a job she really hated, but the village depended on the Healing family for soap, canvas, and medicine. "The last scroll I was reading mentioned something called a *vaccine*. Do you know what that is?"

Isontra placed the bowl of ingredients on the table. "I've never heard the word before. How did they use it?"

"It has something to do with healing a virus. I think a virus might be the name of a disease. In the text, they said genetics might make the difference between someone who lives through the illness and someone who dies. I was wondering if the genetic pool has to do with the number and combination of people mating, would my genetic blood be sufficiently different from, say Collin's, to have kept me from dying when I came down with the White Fever?"

Isontra stood absolutely still, staring at her granddaughter. "That's it! Kairma, that's why you lived, when everyone else died from the fever! I wonder if your blood could pass the healing power to the rest of our people?"

"It could also give them the fever, couldn't it?"

Isontra chewed her lip. "I don't know. More importantly, I don't know how to find out without risking someone's life."

Kairma stretched her back and shifted position. "We need to know. I'll keep trying to understand that scroll until I know if my blood is the curse or the cure."

Isontra patted Kairma's arm. "One miracle is enough for today."

The two women worked through the morning as Isontra instructed Kairma on the proper way to add the lye water to the melted oils. It was hot in the room and Kairma's arm ached from stirring the soap.

Kinter rapped on the door and stepped into the room, rubbing her eyes as if she had recently woken up. Isontra motioned for Kinter to take a seat next to Kairma. "I do wish you would arrive a little earlier for these lessons. I hate to repeat myself so that you may sleep longer. Kairma has been here for quite some time already." Her words were stern, but her eyes were friendly. "Kairma tells me you were reading all night."

Kinter smiled sheepishly and took her place at the table. "Yes, and I was reading for her." She jabbed a finger at Kairma. "Next time, she can do her own research." Kinter resented Kairma's relentless initiative almost as much as Kairma resented Kinter's perfect memory.

Isontra was cleaning up the screen she had been using and asked Kinter to stir the soap for a while. "Kairma, you can help me put these things away."

Kinter frowned. The leverage she'd once held over Kairma to avoid making soap had disappeared when Isontra was shown the vault.

The mountain was alive with color. Delicate Venus slippers dotted the deep ravines and sawsepal penstemons bloomed in huge lavender bunches, complimenting the bright yellow and pink yarrow bushes. Colorful coneflowers danced in the light breeze. Kairma and Kinter were returning from one of the many trips to the vault with their packs loaded with silver cylinders filled with ancient writing.

After walking for a long time, Kairma noticed Kinter seemed unusually melancholy, so she asked, "What's bothering you? You're being awfully quiet."

"I was just thinking." It was almost a whisper. "You know, I really don't want to be a bad person. It's just that sometimes I get so mad about the way things have turned out."

Kairma was guarded, waiting for Kinter to spring some new accusation on her. "Is there something in particular you're upset about now?"

"It's silly, really. I don't know why it bothers me, but you remember the Awakening Celebration?"

"It was only three moons ago—of course I do."

"I did something bad."

Kairma couldn't think of anything Kinter had said or done at the celebration. "Go on."

"Mother told me you were going to enter your blackberry preserves in the contest and I was so mad. I thought you were doing it to spite me." Kinter's full lips made a thin line. "But you didn't enter the blackberry preserves. You switched to the apple preserves, even though they probably weren't as good."

"I still took second place to you. That's better than I've ever done before. It really doesn't matter."

"The thing is ..." She paused. "The thing is, I thought the blackberry preserves were yours and I ..." Kairma stopped walking and looked at Kinter with concern. Kinter went on to say, "It was stupid, and now I feel really awful, but I put some dirt in the blackberry preserves."

"You did *what*? Kinter, that's positively evil!"

"I know it was a horrible thing to do. I was so mad; I wanted to get you back for showing up my blackberry biscuits. But then you had to be the better person and not bring your best entry. So I ended up destroying Lakisha's entry. I didn't want to hurt her." Kinter did shout now, "Don't you see? Because you did the nice thing, you made what I did all the worse."

"How could ruining someone's entry be made worse by it not being mine?"

"I don't know. It just feels worse." She began to walk again. "We always fight, so I guess it feels different when it's you I hurt."

"Oh, that makes me feel *so much better.*"

"Kairma, you have everything. You're going to be the next Vice Miral and you're going to mate with Naturi." Tears flooded her cobalt eyes, and she quickly wiped them away. "What will be left for me? I'll probably end up with Efram and have mean, ugly babies."

Kairma grabbed Kinter by the arm and spun her around. "Kinter, look at me! My hair is almost pure white, and my skin is so pale I look like I'm going to faint! Half of the colony believes I'm a Whitey who should be sent to the Godstones! Don't you see the way people avoid me like a plague? And you know how Toric feels about me! And this!" Kairma wrapped her hand around the leather pouch that held the Crystal. "This is nothing but an albatross around my neck!"

Kinter was stunned by Kairma's outburst. Kairma was always so reserved. Kinter choked on her words. "I just feel like I'm always in your shadow."

Kairma put her hands on Kinter's shoulders. "You have an outstanding memory. You write script better than anyone other than Gramme. You have gorgeous, thick chestnut hair." She ran a hand through the thick tresses. "Your eyes are the deepest shade of blue. You're already taller than me. And your figure is perfect. How can you be envious of me?"

"I guess I'm just made that way," Kinter stammered angrily.

Kairma shook her head sadly. "I'm sorry. I know it was hard for you to admit what you did at the celebration, and I didn't react very well."

Kinter threw Kairma's hand off her shoulders. "You're doing it again! I tell you I did something horrible, and you apologize for *your* reaction." She stomped away.

Kairma raced to catch her. "Kinter, you don't make any sense. How can this be *my* fault?"

Kinter was actually running now, trying to get away, but Kairma could hear her curses. "You always have to be the good one. Even when I try to do the right thing, you always come out looking better. I hate you, Kairma."

Kairma ran after her. She had enough trouble keeping up with her own volatile feelings, and she resented Kinter's constant play for attention.

She saw Kinter near the edge of the trail, running, careless of the drop of more than ninety feet. Kairma had noticed loose stones earlier that day, but before she could shout a warning Kinter's foot caught on a root. Kairma screamed in horror as she saw Kinter disappear over the edge of the cliff.

Chapter 45

As Kinter fell, her hands scrabbled to catch hold of a branch, a root, a shrub, a bit of rock—anything to break her fall.

Kairma cursed herself for upsetting the girl. Her heart pounding, she raced to the place where she saw Kinter fall. In her mind, she saw her baby sister broken and mangled on the rocks below.

Crawling to the edge of the cliff, mindful of the loose stones, she peered over the precipice. Her heart clenched, and her eyes filled with tears when she saw Kinter clinging to the side of the rock face, standing on a narrow ledge about three feet below her outstretched fingers. "Hold on, Kinter! I'm coming. Just stay still."

Kairma looked around for anything that could help her. Pulling her knife from her belt, she looked for something to use for a rope. There was nothing. Frantically, she stripped out of her skirt, and using the long knife she cut it into strips. Braiding the strips of soft leather, she was able to make a sturdy rope. Kinter had gone quiet and Kairma called out, "Kinter! Are you still there?"

"Yesss," she sobbed.

"Don't panic. I'm right here. I'm going to make a rope to pull you up." The sobbing got quieter and Kairma worked as fast as she could.

"Kinter, sing to me. Sing something pretty." Kairma hoped to distract Kinter. She also needed to hear her sister's beautiful voice again, praying it wouldn't be for the last time.

"What?"

"Sing a song for me."

"I don't feel like singing," she wailed.

"Please, I love the way you sing. Sing an old song for me. Sing the one about the flowers."

Kairma leaned over the edge and dropped the rope. It would reach her sister, but it wasn't long enough to secure her. "Kinter, I want you to take your skirt off and tie it to this piece of rope I'm holding. Can you do that?"

"You want my skirt?"

"Yes."

"Why? It's just like yours."

"I'm going to make the rope longer." As she lay there, helpless and alone, Kairma could feel the eyes of the White Ones watching her. The familiar dull ache wrapped itself around her heart. *Not now. Oh, please, not now.*

"Kinter, I'm going to make the rope long enough that you can tie it around your waist. Then I can pull you up without having to worry about you falling farther if the ledge breaks."

"Is the ledge going to break?" Kinter's voice rose several octaves.

"I think you're safe for now. Just give me your skirt."

With one hand, Kinter untied the belt holding her skirt and let the fabric drop around her ankles. She gingerly stepped out of the skirt, and catching the band of the garment with her foot, she lifted it to her hand. Not letting go of the rock face with the other hand, she slipped the skirt over the end of the homemade rope and loosely tied the rope back on itself. She couldn't get it tight with one hand and couldn't reach it with her teeth. "Okay, pull it up slow. It's not very tight."

Kairma pulled the rope up. "Please sing to me, Kinter."

Her voice was shaky and barely loud enough for Kairma to hear, but grew stronger as she sang.

Where have all the flowers gone, long time passing?
Where have all the flowers gone, long time ago?
Where have all the flowers gone?
Young girls have picked them everyone.
Oh, when will they ever learn?
Oh, when will they ever learn?

Where have all the young girls gone, long time passing?
Where have all the young girls gone, long time ago?
Where have all the young girls gone?
Gone for husbands everyone.
Oh, when will they ever learn?
Oh, when will they ever learn?

Where have all the husbands gone, long time passing?
Where have all the husbands gone, long time ago?
Where have all the husbands gone?
Gone for soldiers everyone.
Oh, when will they ever learn?
Oh, when will they ever learn?

Where have all the soldiers gone, long time passing?
Where have all the soldiers gone, long time ago?
Where have all the soldiers gone?
Gone to graveyards, everyone.
Oh, when will they ever learn?
Oh, when will they ever learn?

Where have all the graveyards gone, long time passing?
Where have all the graveyards gone, long time ago?
Where have all the graveyards gone?
Gone to flowers, everyone.
Oh, when will they ever learn?
Oh, when will they ever learn?

Where have all the flowers gone, long time passing?
Where have all the flowers gone, long time ago?
Where have all the flowers gone?
Young girls have picked them everyone.
Oh, when will they ever learn?
Oh, when will they ever learn?

"Kairma?"

"Yes. Kinter."

"What's a *husband?* And why do they become *soldiers?*"

"I don't know. It's a very old song. The oldest one I know of. I think a *husband* might be the same as a *mate.* I'm not sure what *soldier* means, but I think it means someone who dies."

"Oh. How sad. Every one of them dies."

Kairma agreed—it was a very sad song. As she cut and braided the last strips together, she tried to imagine the reason it had been written.

When she finished the rope, she had left just enough skirt left to cover the most important parts of their bodies. A sound in the bushes made her jump, and she turned in time to see a White One disappear into the trees. Her hands were shaking as she prepared to lower the rope over the precipice once more. The presence of the White Ones grew stronger, and her hands began to sweat. Not trusting the slickness of her hands, she searched for something to tie the rope to. She went from shrub to shrub, trying to pull them out of the ground. She finally found a sapling that would hold her weight—one that was close enough to the edge to reach Kinter below. She tied the rope at its base and dropped the other end over the cliff.

"Can you tie this around your waist?"

Kinter felt the rope hit her on the top of her head and slide down over her back. "I can't tie a knot with one hand."

"Wrap the rope around you with your free hand, and then you can use the other hand to help you tie it tight."

"I'm afraid to let go."

"It's okay. Just hold on to the rope."

The murmuring of voices behind Kairma grew louder. *Am I going to save Kinter from a fall only to sacrifice her to the White Ones? Go away, monsters. Please, go away.*

Kinter began crying again, so Kairma sang to her as she lay on her belly, looking over the cliff. "Where have all the flowers gone ..."

Kairma wanted to cheer when she saw the look of relief flood Kinter's face when Kinter was finally able to get the rope tied. She knew if the ledge broke now, she wouldn't fall.

"I want you to hold on to the rope and wrap the slack around your wrist. Lean back and walk up the cliff."

"Are you crazy?" Kinter wailed.

"No, Kinter. It will work. I've done it dozens of times with Collin and Zedic. You don't have any place to put your feet and no hand holds, unless you can swing over to the rock outcropping." Kairma pointed to the right.

"I'll never make it."

"Trust me, Kinter. You can do this. Lean back and walk up the wall. I'll pull you up from here."

Vertigo set in when Kinter tried to lean back, and Kairma reassured her. "You're doing fine. The rope will hold you."

Marshalling her courage, Kinter leaned back again and began walking up the wall. It was a scant ten-foot walk, but the longest walk of her life.

Kairma pulled the rope gently, slowly raising her sister to the top. She was surprised to find Kinter wasn't as heavy as she thought she would be. The feel of the White Ones around her was like the annoying buzz of mosquitoes. She tried to shrug off the feeling and concentrate on the plight of her little sister.

As she saw Kinter rise over the edge of the cliff, Kairma pulled faster—almost causing her to lose her footing. Kinter's eyes were wide with fear, and her mouth was caught in the act of screaming, but no sound came out. Kairma jerked on the rope once more, feeling all of Kinter's weight, and relief swept through her as her sister nearly flew into her arms.

Brushing the hair from Kinter's tear-streaked face, Kairma asked, "Are you okay? You're safe now. I knew you could do it."

"Whitish! There were so many behind you. I thought they were going to attack you, but when I came over the top, they ran." She curled into Kairma's arms. "You saved us both when you pulled me over the top so fast. It must have scared them away."

Kinter was right. The feeling of loss and pain she that usually felt in the presence of the White Ones was gone now.

Kairma reached down and picked up what was left of Kinter's skirt. "Here, I know it's ruined, but at least it will get us home should we run into anyone on the road. Kairma's hands were still shaking slightly as she untied the rope from the small pine tree. "I think I'll keep this with me. You never know when you might need a rope and don't have a skirt to cut up."

Walking carefully yet quickly toward home, Kairma searched the trees for signs of the White Ones. It seemed as though they had left the area, but Kairma's mind raced with scary images of what might have happened on the cliff. The familiar sight of the hospital door strengthened her. Still shaken, the two girls made their way to the Chancery.

Jettena's mouth dropped when she saw the state of her two eldest daughters. "What in Stones happened to you girls? And *what* have you done to your skirts?"

Before Kinter could say anything, Kairma made up a story about trying to make a new style of skirt.

Later, she explained to Kinter that telling their mother the truth would frighten her needlessly, and neither of the girls would ever be allowed to leave the canyon again. "We don't need to worry mother. She has enough to think about without adding near-death experiences into the mix."

Chapter 46

Large expanses of flat land crisscrossed with deep river valleys forced them to go several miles out of their way. Although most of the riverbeds were dry, years of spring floods had cut deep channels into the landscape, leaving serrated gullies too difficult to cross with a loaded wagon. Trep and Toric started ranging farther ahead to find the most direct route across the prairie, and there were many days when the main river was too far away to see.

Misha felt little control over her new life on the prairie. It was hot and dry and the creaking wheels of the wagons grated on her nerves. She wasn't usually a person of short temper, but the heat and the uncomfortable bed made her irritable and her head ached daily. Although she liked Zedic well enough, and she knew he was a good man, his constant attention annoyed her. She found herself snapping at him when he was only trying to make her happy.

Lysara seemed to be happy with the travel. She was tired and complained of headaches, but she was looking forward to seeing Survin. Lysara had little opportunity in the city to do anything really exciting and was drawn to this adventure. Both of the girls missed the luxury of a hot bath and soft bed.

The Survinees were anxious to get home, but the wagons were slowing them down and it would only get worse when they entered the mountains.

Toric had always enjoyed hunting trips, but the long distance he'd traveled this past summer had shown him sights he never could have imagined. As the days went by, he found himself thinking about seeing more of the world. The laws of his society forbade this and he became increasingly uncomfortable in his thoughts. He had promised Isontra that he would bring Trep back to Survin and Toric was a loyal man, but hunting trips would no longer be limited to the three days of the full moon.

Trep's mind was on the artifacts he'd seen in Survin. He was looking forward to getting a closer look at them. He still wasn't sure if the Healers could read script, but that was a mystery he longed to solve. Once he was truly a member of the village, he would be able to study the Crystal. His mind was obsessed by the possibility of the Crystal actually being the legendary Star of Genesis.

Renewed excitement filled the party as Trep pointed out the barren hills of the desert to the south and told them they would reach the river crossing soon. Collin and Toric had discovered a natural affinity for the horses, and their travel skills were improving quickly as the scouts ranged wider every day. The wagons were another matter. The prairie was difficult to negotiate, but it would be nothing compared to pulling wagons through the steep mountains with their thick forests.

Eleven days west of Peireson Landing, the western mountains could be seen in the morning sunlight. Collin whooped and got everyone out of their bedrolls. He pointed to the west. The hills were just a faint glimmer, a hazy deep green that looked almost black. This would be a good day to celebrate.

Trep put more wood on the embers from last night's fire and prepared a spindle for roasting meat. Toric had killed a large pronghorn buck the day before and they spent most of the evening cleaning and salting the meat. It was Toric's first time using his new karrack. Remembering the first time he'd met the stern man, Trep marveled at how easily Toric had taken to the horses and karracks.

They planned a small celebration marking the sighting of home. Collin was helping Toric and Trep dress the meat and cut it into manageable pieces, while Naturi was frying a little bit of the fresh game and it smelled heavenly. Misha and Lysara had been feeling tired, but the sight of the mountains raised their morale considerably. Zedic had collected a few rose hips and red clover near a small stream for making a flavorful terrid, and everyone was in good spirits as they ate their morning meal.

After a delicious breakfast of fried meat and a porridge made from pine nuts, chokecherries and wild oats, the party began to break camp.

Misha and Lysara suddenly became violently ill. They had complained of headaches days before, but now they retched several times. Trep gave the women some biscuits from the night before, but it was useless. They couldn't keep anything down.

Holding Misha's hair away from her face as she continued to retch, Zedic asked, "Collin, do you think you can find some wood sorrel or mint leaves? Chewing the leaves may help relieve the nausea."

"I'll see what we can find. Naturi, come help me."

While the men searched for herbs, Toric and Trep loaded the gear in the wagon.

As the days passed, the two women became steadily weaker. Each morning was a struggle to get up and they soon lost their appetite, subsisting on boiled water alone. Trep suggested they set up an extended camp in hopes of letting the women regain their strength. It wouldn't hurt to rest the horses too.

Once they reached the river, they found tall cottonwoods and willows for shade and an abundance of dead logs of varying sizes with which to build a small lean-to. Firewood was plentiful and dry. Using some of the materials purchased in the city, the temporary home was made comfortable.

Collin and Toric gathered clover, lamb's-quarter and wild carrots. They came across a large bed of wild strawberries. "Look, Toric, strawberries. I can't believe the birds haven't eaten them all. This will make the girls feel better."

"I sure hope so. I'm really worried about them." Toric began to pick fat red berries. "Wish we had a Healer with us. I've never seen the likes of this."

Collin placed the delicious fruit in the sack with the clover. "It's driving Zedic crazy. I can see it in his eyes. He thinks he should know how to make them well because he comes from a family of Healers."

"I would never have thought we would need more than a bit of willow bark myself. I wish we could do more."

Adding the fresh greens and fruit to the evening's meal, Naturi said, "I am making a broth with garlic and wild onion. I hope the girls might be able to eat it. They have lost too much weight." His voice sounded sharp with frustration.

Going to the wagon, Toric pulled out the blankets and rope. "Collin, give me some help here." Collin was at his side in a flash. "See those logs over there? Find about six more like those. I'm going to build bed frames. I don't think it's good for the girls to sleep on the hard ground. I'll use rope to tie the joints together. You can punch a few holes along the side of the blankets so we can tie them to the frames."

Toric and Collin spent the evening making cots for Misha and Lysara while Trep and Zedic tried to force the warm broth into the two pale women.

"Ya have to eat somethin'!" Trep's forehead was creased with worry. "Ya have to get your strength back."

Lysara was curled in a ball in the corner of the lean-to, wrapped in a blanket even though the afternoon had been sweltering. "I just cain't keep it down. Please, I wanna sleep."

Trep refused to leave her, and she managed a few sips before she began to retch again. Tears swelled in his eyes as he rocked her gently until she fell into a fitful sleep once again. He was still holding her, his eyes never leaving her face, when Toric and Collin brought in the new beds. "Thank you," he whispered as they set the beds in place.

Trep lifted Lysara up and placed her on the cot. She was so light. He looked over at Zedic, who was tending to Misha in the same fashion, brothers in misery. "She'll feel better soon enough," he lied. "Let's make the girls as comfortable as we can."

Zedic's face was closed and hard. He was trying to remember anything he may have heard about this kind of illness. Nothing came to him. After a while, he turned to Naturi, who had been tending to the cleanup of their supper. "I'd like to heat some water. Maybe Misha would feel better if we washed away some of this dirt and sweat." He got up and walked to the stack of supplies. "Don't we have a large pot in here somewhere? I thought I picked one up for Isontra."

Naturi said, "It is still in the wagon. I will go and get it for you."

Zedic nodded. "We'll need a bigger fire too."

After the water was warm, Zedic gently removed Misha's clothing and began to bathe her, gently washing her hair and twisting it into a braid, much like he had seen his sister do. Once dry, he dressed her in clean clothes and covered her with a fresh blanket. He slept on the ground next to her bed in case she might awake and need something.

Misha was quite beyond feeling any embarrassment about her nakedness, and the warm water and clean clothes felt heavenly. She slept better than she had in several days.

Seeing how much better Misha looked, how much better she seemed to sleep, Trep bathed Lysara the following morning.

When Trep tried to place the golden combs in her hair, Lysara shook her head. "Let's save them for a special occasion. Middle of a dusty field ain't the place for fancy combs."

"Of course. We're gonna have a big celebration when we get to Survin." He tried to sound light, but his eyes were dark with distress.

Chapter 47

Kairma rubbed the sleep from her eyes as she padded down the stairs to the kitchen. Jettena was already heating oatmeal for breakfast while her little brothers played hide and seek. Taking an overturned chair from Taren, she sat down and grabbed an apple from the pottery bowl on the table, making Tadya squeal with delight when Kairma revealed Taren's hiding place. Soon the boys were chasing each other around the table and, as Jettena set a bowl of oatmeal in front of Kairma with her right hand, she stilled the boys with the other.

Isontra came into the sunny room. Pouring a cup of terrid for herself, she offered one to Jettena, but Jettena shook her head. "No. I've had several already. The boys were up just after dawn. I swear, I try my best to wear them out at night and they still wake me at an unearthly hour every morning." Bit by bit, the boys returned to their game.

Isontra smiled. Jettena was usually an early riser too. "Speaking of wearing someone out, I'd like to go to the temples today with Kinter."

Kairma's eyes shot up to her grandmother. "I was planning to go this morning."

Jettena sat a bowl on the table for Isontra. "You spend a lot of time at the Godstones anymore. This is the second trip this week. Whatever has you so preoccupied?"

Isontra took a bite of the warm oatmeal. "I've had the girls studying the buildings. A few things came to my attention after the funeral service." She looked over to Kairma. "It's been a while since I've looked at things. I'd like you to stay here because I have a few patients coming by this morning." She reached out a hand and snagged one of the young boys. Seeing the look on her face, he immediately went and sat down again. Turning back to Kairma, Isontra said, "I'm expecting Loella to come by today to have her dressings changed. That's a nasty burn she got last week. Please give her another horsetail and slippery elm poultice, and she'll need plenty of terrid made with rose hips, white oak bark, and blackberry too." Isontra nibbled at her breakfast and thought for a while. "I'm also expecting Sharra to come by. She's in her fifth moon and is having trouble with heartburn. You'll also need to go over those exercises we discussed the last time she was here."

Kairma nodded. Her mother could have handled both patients, but it would soon be her responsibility and Isontra was testing her. Kairma often wondered what their lives would have been like if Jettena had not given the Crystal back to Isontra. Her mother claimed she'd been too busy to take on the duties, but Kairma knew there was more to it. Invariably, when the subject came up, Jettena would get despondent and refuse to discuss it. Kairma finished her meal and placed the bowl by the large pot used for washing dishes. Turning to her mother, she asked, "Would you like me to wash these for you, today?"

"No, go to the hospital. You have more important things to do."

Jettena watched Kairma leave the room.

Isontra's eyes followed Jettena. "She's an unusual child, isn't she? Sometimes it's easy to forget how young she really is. The Vice Miral needs many annums to train. It's good to know if something happens to me, you have enough training to continue in my place."

Jettena frowned as she sat down across from Isontra and said, "Never in our history has a Vice Miral abdicated her position. It's little wonder Grimly hates me the way he does."

Isontra reached out, touching Jettena's hand. "He doesn't hate you. He's afraid of the changes we've made. Adjusting to change can be difficult."

"But what if we're wrong, mother? What if she is too young? What if Zedic never comes back?"

"Let's not borrow trouble yet. We often worry about a great many things that never come to pass."

Kinter came into the kitchen yawning hugely. Walking to the hearth, she spooned out some oatmeal and added dried blackberries from a covered dish on the shelf. Without a word, she sat down at the table and began to spoon the hot mush into her mouth. The room was too quiet, and it made her look up. Her mother and grandmother were staring at her, and Kinter immediately sat up straighter.

Isontra said, "I think I'll go to the temples with you today, Kinter. There're some things I'd like to look over."

Kinter swallowed the tasty oatmeal. "I thought Kairma was going with me?"

"I asked her to stay here and take care of a few patients."

Kinter finished her meal quickly, placing the dish in the washtub before going to get her travel pack. "I'll be ready to go in a little while."

"Good. Jettena, would you pack us a small lunch? We'll be gone for most of the day."

Jettena got up and started placing some carrots in a basket. "Why are you traipsing off to the temples again? For weeks, you've had those two girls going up there every other day. When you and Hestra were teaching me healing, we rarely went to the temples."

Pulling unleavened bread from a drawer, Isontra said, "There were a lot of things we didn't take time for, and we should study the Godstones. You aren't so busy with Sonty and the boys these days. Maybe you should resume your studies as well."

Jettena spun around furiously. "Mother, how many times do I have to tell you? I'm not a Healer!"

Isontra pulled back at Jettena's words but recovered enough to say, "You could be. I know it was difficult for you, being so young, but do you think this will be any easier for Kairma?"

Angry tears sprang to her eyes as Jettena slammed the basket on the table. "Don't you understand? She was *my daughter*, and I would have let her die!" She choked back a sob and added bitterly, "I wanted so badly for the colony to respect me—I would have done anything! What kind of Healer would kill her own child because of what others might think?"

Isontra went to comfort her, but Jettena pushed her away. "I'm not fit to be a Healer."

"You were placed in a very difficult position while you were suffering from the weeping. The boys were but a few months old. When a mother gives birth, a part of her is lost, and she longs to replace it. You didn't know enough to see how it was affecting you."

"But you had the strength to defy the elders. You changed the mating rites for Tamron and me. You kept Kairma alive while I would have let her die, and you let my son leave. I don't have that kind of strength." Before Isontra could say another word, Jettena stormed out of the room.

Kinter stood in the doorway as her mother passed. Isontra's eyes glistened with unspent tears as she placed the last of their lunch in the basket. Kinter, never having seen her grandmother that close to crying, was at a loss to know what to do or say. Pillars of strength never shed tears where others might see them, so Kinter stepped back and, and making more noise this time, she re-entered the room. She knew the tears would be gone now, but the memory of her grandmother's vulnerability would be with her forever.

Later that morning, Kairma was lying on a thick mat to show Sharra some stretching exercises when Martena came rushing into the room. "Where's Miral Isontra? We need help right away!"

Kairma jumped up. "What's wrong? Miral Isontra is at the temples."

Martena wrung her hands. "How can she be away at a time like this? They're going to die."

Kairma placed her hands on Martena's shoulders. "Please. Tell me what's happened."

Tears streaked down Martena's sun-darkened cheeks. "Kaiden and Rhylee. It was a huge bear. I can't get Rhylee to wake up. Kaiden tried to save her from the bear and got torn up really bad. We need Miral Isontra."

"Where are they now?" Kairma asked as she packed bandages and assorted bottles in a leather basket.

"They're up by the Nor Monument. We have to get the Miral."

"We don't have time. Take me to them now. Every minute we waste is a minute we'll never get back." Inside where no one could see, Kairma was shaking, and her stomach tied in knots. She would have given anything to have Isontra beside her.

Martena surrendered and led Kairma out the door.

Word had spread through the small village and several people followed Kairma and Martena to the monument. When they got there, Kairma saw Tristan holding Kaiden. His arms were badly clawed and his head was bleeding at an alarming rate. Kairma tossed a several rolls of bandages to Tristan and told him to try to stop the bleeding. "Apply steady pressure to the wounds. Don't move him if you don't have to." Dessa was standing nearby, so Kairma enlisted her help as well. "Dessa, see if you can help him. Don't worry about cleaning the wounds. We need to get the bleeding stopped first."

Moving to where Rhylee lay sprawled in the churned-up dirt, she checked the injured woman's pulse and lifted her eyelids to see how badly she was hurt. Rhylee's hands were clammy and she had lost a fair amount of blood. "Martena, hold up her legs and wrap that blanket around her. I'm going to bandage these cuts."

Kairma took antiseptic from her pack and went to work on the woman's injuries. She felt a lump behind Rhylee's left ear. "She must have hit her head. Probably saved her life. The bear would have sensed she was no longer a danger." She made a pillow with another blanket to cradle Rhylee's head and moved to see what she could do for Kaiden. As she checked his head wound, she asked Kaiden what happened.

"We were looking for berries over on that ridge." Kaiden pointed to a small rise several feet away. "We must have startled the bear. It took a few swings at Rhylee, and I tried to save her, but I was knocked down the hill. When I got back here, Rhylee was just lying there. Is she going to be okay? Where is the Miral?"

Kaiden's strong voice was a good sign he hadn't been hurt as badly as Kairma had first suspected. Kairma explained, "Miral Isontra is up at the Godstones. We didn't have time to fetch her." He winced as she cleaned the blood from a deep cut on his arm. "I'm sorry. I know it hurts." Her hands shook slightly as she wrapped the wound with a clean bandage and moved on to another cut, praying she was doing everything correctly.

His face was puckered with pain, but his concern was for his mate. "How's Rhylee? I can't see her."

He tried to sit up, but Kairma gently held him in place. "I won't know for a while. I think she was knocked unconscious. Right now, we need to keep her warm. We can't move her until I know how bad her head wound is and you'll only reopen your own wounds if you try to move again. We'll know more by sunset."

The cut on Kaiden's head needed stitching, and reaching for her pack, Kairma found the items she needed. Taking the catgut sutures from a pottery jar filled with antiseptic, Kairma threaded the thin cord through a small needle made from bone. She leaned over to Kaiden and warned him. "This is going to hurt, but I promise it is necessary."

Kaiden nodded and grit his teeth as Kairma carefully closed his wounds. Kairma's stomach was filled with warring butterflies. She knew if something went wrong, the colony would never forgive her. In her mind she replayed every healing lesson she could remember— desperately hoping she hadn't forgotten something crucial. She had just finished closing the last of his cuts when Martena called her name.

"Kairma, Rhylee is waking!"

Kairma went to the young woman and checked her pulse again. It was much stronger, and Rhylee's skin was regaining its color. Placing a hand over Rhylee's eyes to shade them from the sun, Kairma asked, "Rhylee, can you hear me?"

Rhylee opened her eyes and looked confused. "Where am I?"

Kairma smiled softly. "You got into a fight with a bear over some berries and lost, but I think you're going to be okay."

Kairma held her down firmly as Rhylee panicked and tried to sit up. "Where's Kaiden? Is he okay?" The jerk of Rhylee's knees as she tried to get up told Kairma there had been no spinal injury.

Kairma soothed her, and gently turned Rhylee's head to the side so she could see her injured mate. "He's right here. He's going to be fine. He'll have lots of interesting scars to show his grandchildren someday, but right now you need to rest. I'm going to have some men go to the hospital and get a litter. In the meantime, we'll make a small shelter to keep the sun off you."

Several villagers had gathered to witness the magic of healing, which made Kairma even more nervous now that the emergency had passed. Under her instructions, a few men quickly made a crude shelter while others went to fetch the litter.

The change in attitude was subtle, but Kairma noticed people actually looked her in the eyes when she spoke to them now, and they followed her orders without question. Although she understood what she had done here today wasn't terribly difficult, she was the only one present who would have known what to do and felt a wave of pride for having handled it well. Healing a few cuts wasn't the same as leading a community, but it was a good beginning.

That night, when Isontra and Kinter returned, Kairma told them what had happened. Isontra looked over the two injured patients and praised Kairma. "You did a very good job today. I'm proud of you. I know it was frightening, but sometimes it's good for us to be tested."

Kinter looked over at her celebrated sister and felt an all too familiar wave of envy. Kairma didn't do anything terribly difficult—it was nothing that she herself couldn't have done. Kinter sighed heavily and walked out the door. *Timing, Kairma! The glory is only yours by a matter of timing. If you had gone to the temples with Isontra, it would be me wearing the laurels of success today.*

Chapter 48

Out on the plains, Misha and Lysara were deathly ill. The bath seemed to help them rest better, and the girls managed to sip a little broth this morning, but they still slept most of the day. Trep and Zedic were relieved to see that the girls were able to eat something for the first time in days, and they stayed with the two ailing women throughout the day while Toric, Collin, and Naturi foraged for food and generally tried to stay out of the way.

By the third day, Lysara was eating solid food and sitting up again. Misha was also improving, though not as quickly. Ever vigilant, Trep and Zedic never left their sides except to relieve themselves.

After six days of rest, the women had regained enough strength to continue on. They found a shallow place to ford the river. Staying to the west, close enough to see the river, but up on the higher, flatter land, they continued the hard journey. It was a solemn party that made its way to the narrow stream that led into the heavily forested hills.

They were but days from their convalescence camp when Trep pointed to the craggy rocks in the distance. "We'll stop for a visit with Zacar. It's gonna take us some time to cut a way through those hills big enough for the wagons. We can let the girls rest again."

Passing the first range of steep hills, the Survinees felt an overwhelming joy. They were home. It would still be some days before they would see the valley of Survin, but these hills were familiar—these hills were home. If it weren't for the wagons, they would be sleeping in their own beds by nightfall four days hence.

Zacar's cabin was in sight by dusk the following day, and Trep rode ahead to see if the large man was home. The cabin was nestled in a broad gap between two stone cliffs, where huge ponderosa and spruce trees gave shade in the summer and blocked the worst of the winter winds. Zacar sat in an oversized rocking chair on the wide porch of the large stone and pine-log cabin, whittling on a substantial piece of wood.

A large mountain lion, lying in the shade of a massive pine tree, opened one eye as Trep came up the road. The man didn't look interesting to the cat, so Purder rolled over and went back to sleep.

Zacar's big black dog ambled up to Trep with his tail whipping back and forth frantically. Reaching down, Trep patted Jesse on the head as he walked through the small yard. "Lo, Zac. Told ya I'd be back."

"Good to see you. Where're the rest of your friends? Didn't you have some of those canyon people with you?"

"They're on the other side of the hill. We have a couple women and two wagons with us now."

Zacar whistled softly. "How do you plan to get wagons through these hills?"

"Guess we're gonna have to cut down some trees, starting with that one up there." Trep pointed to a huge blue spruce at the top of the rise.

"Trep, I like that tree."

"That's the flattest ground over the pass. It's the only place to bring the wagons through."

"Hate to lose it, but you're right there isn't any other level ground close to this canyon." Zacar looked at the tight canyon winding to the west. "You got your work cut out for you. Even if you can fell ten trees a day, it will take you at least four days to reach the lake."

"I guess we need to work a little harder."

Zacar got up from his comfortable rocking chair and went inside. A few minutes later he returned with an axe. "Well, let's go."

Leading Zacar back to their camp, Trep introduced the tall man to Misha and Lysara. Both women's eyes widened as Zacar approached. He was at least two feet taller than Lysara. Standing next to him, her eyes were level with his belly and she had to back up to see his face. Misha was at eye level with Zacar as he came to shake her tiny hand, but Misha was standing in the back of the wagon at the time.

"Nice to meet you, ladies." Turning to Trep he said, "Cute little things, aren't they?"

Trep laughed. "Only because y'all are so big. They're just the right size for me!"

As Trep took the saw from the back of the wagon, Zacar warned the women about Purder and Jesse. "They're nice pets. Might get a little excited on occasion, but they won't hurt you."

Naturi and Toric pulled out another saw and Collin grabbed his axe. Trep put a hand on Collin's shoulder. "Cain't all of us cut down the same tree. Don't worry. Y'all will get lots of chances to cut down trees before we get to the lake. Zacar and I will cut this one down now and then we can have a bite to eat. We'll work on the road beyond his cabin in the afternoon.

Zacar hacked a large wedge shaped section out of the tree and then, grabbing the other end of the two-man saw, he helped Trep cut through to the other side. The tree fell loudly, breaking many branches as it dropped and rolled a short distance from the pass. The wagon axle didn't quite clear the stump and they were forced to cut it down a little further. Zacar smiled as he rubbed his big hands together. "Best measure a little closer from here out. Don't want to have to cut 'em all down twice.

They had to cut down four more trees before the wagons could be parked in front of Zacar's cabin. Once settled, Zacar led them inside for lunch. Misha and Lysara helped the giant man prepare a meal as the others went out to mark additional trees to cut. An hour later they called to the men and then sat down to eat. Misha and Lysara were grateful to have an actual table to sit at, even if it was so tall they had to sit on pillows to reach it comfortably.

The women tired easily, and Zacar showed them to a small room with a large bed. "You two can sleep in here. I often sleep outside when the weather's nice."

"Thank you," Misha said. "We don't want to put you out. It was kind enough of you to give us lunch."

"Nonsense. I love having company. Don't get much out here, you know. You look like you need some rest. Go on now, before I have to sic Jesse on you."

Misha and Lysara crawled into an oversized bed that felt like a little slice of heaven and they were asleep in minutes.

The next two days were spent clearing the road to the lake. They opted to leave the women at Zacar's to rest. Each night the men would come back to the cabin, have a quick meal, and fall soundly asleep.

On the morning of the third day, they decided to move the wagons and set up camp at the end of their new road. They still had about six more miles of forest and rock to clear before the wagon could be brought home, but being this close to home rejuvenated their spirits in an essential way.

Once they reached the campsite and set up a crude shelter, they made plans to take the women on to Survin the following morning. Stirring a venison stew over a low flame, Naturi said, "We could reach Survin by midday if we leave the wagons here. We will ask for help from the village to cut down the rest of these trees."

Zedic wrapped an arm around Misha. "That's a great idea. We can get the ladies home, and let Isontra observe them, since they're still not feeling very well."

Misha looked up at him. "That sounds wonderful, but what about all the supplies in the wagons?"

Zacar sat by the buckboard with his broad back against the wheel, petting his dog Jesse. "I'll stay here with the wagons. I know you all want to get home to see your families. I don't think three or four more days out here would be good for you and your sister. You ain't nothin' but skin and bones now."

"Thank you so much, Zacar. How can we repay you?"

"I've lived out here for about twenty annums, and you all are the first friends I ever had. That's worth more than you can imagine. I never realized how much I missed talking to people until everyone came through here last spring looking for those Madics."

Lysara's forehead crinkled as she looked at Trep. "What are Madics?"

"Jess some folks we had to find before we came to Peireson Landin'. Nothin' for y'all to worry 'bout." Trep clapped Zacar on the shoulder. "I think you should come to Survin with us. Meet the rest of the village."

"Maybe after we finish the road. Until then, I'm happy to watch your goods for a few days."

Zacar was awkward around strangers because he was so large. The Survinees were bigger than most people and that made Zacar more comfortable, but all the annums of being alone left him unsure of himself. He was fine in his own home, but meeting others in their home was a step he wasn't ready to make right now. Even though he was well aware of the Survinees, he had purposely avoided meeting them over the annums. Just knowing they were three days walk from his home was enough to ease much of the loneliness he felt. As luck had it, the game was better to the south and west of the canyon, and on the few times hunters had come east, they'd never seen his cabin nestled deep in the trees.

Misha and Lysara wanted to make a good impression on their new family so the following morning the women put on clean clothes. After combing their long hair, they pulled it up with the beautiful golden combs.

The hunting party was the first to see the travelers return. A messenger was sent back to Survin to let the others know. "I saw them! I saw them! They've come home!" Dillon couldn't control his excitement as he ran through the canyon yelling. "They have horses! They're home! Toric, Naturi, Collin, I saw them all! Everyone has come home!" Excited people poured from their homes and out of the canyon toward the lake.

The travelers were tired and worn, but it felt good to see the lake that was so familiar. Collin wanted to kiss the ground, but restrained himself, unsure what the others would think if he did. It had been a hard trip, physically and emotionally.

The Survinees gathered around the returning explorers and took many of their burdens, and although they shied from the horses, they were obviously curious. The travelers were nearly carried the remaining steps to the Grand Hall by a throng of excited people.

Kairma met them at the north doors. When she looked at her friends she was amazed at how old they had become over the short summer. She could see new lines on their faces, now darkened from the long days in the sun. Toric seemed gentler than she remembered. He held his head high, and a shadow of a smile played on his lips, even though he was grousing about all the things that would need to be put away.

She saw Zedic just past the stocky Toric, and her eyes lit up. She noticed the pretty little blond woman who hung on his arm. The girl looked very weak, as if she were about to faint, and a grayish-green light played about her. There was another woman with dark gold hair being supported by Trep who had the same gray-tinged light hovering. Something was wrong, and Kairma's heart went out to the women. It didn't take much imagination to see that Zedic was in love with the poor sickly creature he almost carried. He seemed to feel Kairma's stare and turned to her as she ran and hugged him hard. She had missed him so much.

Zedic didn't have time to make introductions before Collin came barreling past him, almost tripping over his feet to get to Kairma. He picked her up and spun around and around.

She noticed Collin had grown stronger since the spring as he lifted her off her feet and hugged her tightly. She could scarcely get the words out: "Collin, I … can't … breathe. Please …put … me … down." Collin set her down, but he didn't let go, making Zedic laugh for the first time in weeks.

Kinter came out and stood in the north doorway, watching as the throng of people made their way up the narrow path. Her deep chestnut hair was twisted up in a complicated swirl of braids with white pearls winding through it in a dream-like dance of light against the dark. She was taller now, taller than Kairma, and decidedly more feminine. As they arrived, Zedic noticed the change in Kinter first and whistled appreciatively, which made Kinter blush a deep scarlet. That was the moment Naturi looked up from the bundle of goods he'd been struggling to carry. He stopped and stared—almost dropping the package he was holding. While Kairma had always been pretty, Kinter was absolutely breathtaking.

Isontra hurried down the steps past Kinter to meet the returning men, and Zedic went to her at once, hugging her. Looking over his grandmother approvingly, Zedic said, "You look wonderful. I can see you've been getting more sun too."

"The girls and I have a regular exercise ritual nowadays." She gave him a private wink. "We'll talk more in the morning. At the moment, there's too much I want to hear from you." She looked around, and Zedic led her to meet the new arrivals.

While introductions were made, and villagers helped unpack burdens, Isontra joined the homecoming men in the conference area of the Grand Hall. She was eager to learn what happened to the Madics they'd been sent to stop. Trep and Toric made them all sound brave. Collin wasn't so sure about his part in the action, and he told Isontra that he'd missed his shot, an easy shot at that. "If Toric hadn't been so quick to fire another arrow, we would have been killed."

Kairma led the two ailing women to comfortable beds close to the hearth because, even though it was late summer, the women were cold. While lighting a fire, she asked simple questions to see how long they had been feeling sick.

Misha was almost too weak to talk, but Lysara was feeling a little stronger today. Lysara told Kairma everything that had transpired during the long journey. "We started gettin' sick about six days after we left the city. I thought we were jess not used to all the hard walkin' and ridin'." She smiled humbly at Kairma. "Well, that was true enough. We're pampered little city girls, and ridin' on a wagon for days at a time, and gettin' blisters from walkin', was somethin' completely out of our reckonin'."

She struggled to sit up and take a drink of water from the cup Kairma offered. "I have to admit, it did my heart good to see that most of the men folk had saddle sores too. Trep is used to ridin' horses, but the other men got a valuable lesson those first days out." She sighed and laid her head back on the down pillow. "It was odd the men kept gettin' stronger while Misha and I got weaker."

Isontra and Zedic joined them bedside where Isontra checked for fever and listened to their hearts. The darkness in Isontra's steel gray eyes told Kairma she was worried about Misha. The women needed rest and quiet, so Isontra cleared the room quickly, insisting all the travelers needed rest. She assured everyone that they would have plenty of time to hear stories and see gifts in the morning.

Kairma stopped Collin as he headed for the door. "Can I talk to you for a moment?"

Collin's head jerked up when she said his name, and her slightly husky voice sent a thrill of joy through him. He was tired, but he had time for Kairma. He had really missed her. "Sure, let's go out back. I want to check on the horses anyway."

They walked through the north doors and down the path toward the lake, watching ribbons of color waltz across the sky as twilight set. "It's so beautiful here," Collin said, almost reverently. "I really missed this." Not thirty steps from the door Collin turned to Kairma, and was about to ask her what she wanted to talk about, when he put both hands on her cheeks and kissed her. He had never kissed a girl before and didn't really know why he did it now.

Intense, unfamiliar, raw emotion swept through Kairma and she reacted without thinking. She'd been so shocked and confused by her feelings that she punched him in the arm. *Hard.* Then suddenly she began to cry big tears—tears she couldn't stop. Kairma rarely cried unless she was angry or frightened, and she wasn't sure what she felt at this moment.

Collin held his arm. "I'm so sorry. I don't know why I did that. Did I hurt you?"

Kairma shook her head, but the tears wouldn't stop. She hated not being in control of herself or her feelings, and it made her cry even harder.

Collin turned away. "I'm such an idiot. Really, Kairma, I'm so, so sorry. I don't know why I did that. You can hit me again if you want."

Again, she shook her head, the tears less intense now, and she was really sorry she'd hit him. She put a hand on his shoulder and he flinched. Now she *really* felt bad. "I'm sorry. I think it was just all the stress from today. We'd been so worried about you. And with Misha and Lysara being so sick, and everyone needing something from me. I'm sorry I hit you."

Collin turned to face her again. "Are you sure you don't want to do it again? I hardly felt the first one."

The corners of her mouth lifted, and she shook her head. "I really didn't bring you out here to beat you up. I needed to tell you something before you went home."

"Okay. Is it about my folks?"

For a moment, Kairma wondered if he already knew what had happened. "Yes. When you left last spring your mother was very angry." Collin nodded, but didn't say anything. "She was so mad she fought with your father at the Gathering House. It was very bad." She could see Collin picturing it in his mind. He had seen their fights all too often. "This time Massie didn't back down. It took four people to get her home. Your father stayed and drank until he also had to be taken home."

Kairma closed her eyes; she couldn't look at Collin now. "It appears your mother killed your father while he was passed out, and then she hung herself. Collin, I'm so very sorry."

Collin said nothing. He just stood there looking at her. She wanted to put her arms around him, to comfort him, to kiss him on the forehead, to mend his heart that was surely breaking. As she watched him, his body slowly stiffened, and his eyes grew cold as the words registered.

After a moment, he thanked her for telling him and then turned and walked away.

Fresh tears came to Kairma. Not like the ones from moments ago, but deeply felt nonetheless. She would cry for Collin since he couldn't cry for himself.

Chapter 49

The next morning Trep and Toric gathered several men to clear the road for the wagons. Even though Collin and Naturi had only been home for a night, they went back to help the men cut trees. Kairma wanted to go with them, but Isontra insisted she help with the homecoming celebration plans. It would be three more days before the wagons would roll up to the north door of the hospital.

Isontra was standing by the basin in her suite, cleaning her teeth with a carved wooden stick, when Kairma come in carrying two cups of terrid. "Bless you, dear. You're always so thoughtful." She chewed on some mint leaves to freshen her breath and took a seat at the large central table. "You're here very early today. Is there something on your mind?"

Kairma sat at the table and sipped the hot drink. "It's Lysara and Misha. They're so sick and nothing seems to be helping them. I was thinking about the Blood Rite. If Mother's blood is really strong, maybe it could help the women."

Isontra nodded slowly, thinking about the proposal. "Your blood might be even stronger than your mother's blood."

"I can't risk it. What if I give them the White Fever?" Kairma frowned and chewed on her lower lip. "We don't know what causes the fever. If it's one of those things the Ancient Ones call a virus, my blood might be the cure, but if it isn't, I might kill them."

Isontra's brow wrinkled in frustration. "You're right. We'll ask Jettena to do the Rite. Go see if she has time to come by my room this morning."

Kairma slipped out of the room to find her mother and as she walked down the hall, the smell of frying meat made Kairma hungry. The kitchen was warm with the morning fire and the early morning sunlight streamed through the east window.

Jettena turned as Kairma came into the room. "Morning. You're up early."

"I was worried about Misha and Lysara. Gramme and I talked about performing the Blood Rite, hoping it might help them." Kairma sat at the large dining table, taking a piece of bread from the plate.

"You could be right. The blood of the Healing family has always been strong. I think the elders would agree to allow you to perform the rite."

"I can't do it myself. I had the White Fever, so we can't be sure it would be safe."

Jettena set the hot plate of meat on the wooden counter by the hearth. "Of course. Isontra will do it."

Kairma's nose wrinkled ever so slightly. "I was hoping you would do it. Your blood has been passed from Grampe Petar. If it's blood from outsiders that kept me from dying when I had the White Fever, your blood might be stronger than Gramme's blood."

Jettena stared into the fire. After a moment she said, "I'll do it. Let me call a meeting of the elders. They'll want to have a say in this. We should include Trep in this too. After all, he has decided to become a member of our colony." Jettena went back to preparing the morning meal.

"I really don't want to wait until Trep gets back. I'm afraid the women are too weak now. Can't we give them the blood today and save the rest of the service for when Trep gets back?"

Jettena frowned. "What is a ritual without the service and prayers?"

"Yes, I know it's a very important part of the rite, and we should say the prayers and read the sacred script, but they're too weak to make the trip to the altar of the Godstones. Could we do it in private, this evening, in the hospital?"

Jettena handed Kairma a plate of food. "I suppose we can do this today. I'll go to the elders and let them know what we've decided, but I expect you to come with me. They'll want to know why we're doing this without waiting for the Harvest Festival."

Kairma ate her breakfast and mentally prepared the speech she would give to the elders. It would have to be strong enough to convince them to break another tradition. After placing her plate in the washtub, Kairma fixed a plate for Misha and Lysara and then went to the hospital to explain what they would be doing later that day.

Kairma found the two women conversing quietly by the hearth. They looked a little stronger today and they had a little more color in their cheeks. Setting the food down on a small table between the women, Kairma checked their vital signs.

Misha sighed heavily. "I'm sorry to be so much trouble to you and your family. I really don't know what has come over us."

Kairma smiled. "The look on my brother's face when he sees you is all the thanks I will ever need."

Misha took a bite from the plate of food. "He really is something. I can't believe he hasn't tired of taking care of me."

"Speaking of taking care of the two of you ... We have a procedure that may help make you strong enough to fight this illness. We call it the Blood Rite. It's a ceremony where the healing power of a mother's Efpec blood is passed to her daughters. A cine, made from the Miral's blood and put in a small cut on your shoulder, will pass this power to you."

Kairma poured each of the women a cup of water. "I'm going to get the things needed for the procedure and I'll explain more then."

Kairma came back a few minutes later with the small silver box. Once she was certain everything was there, she explained the procedure. "Vice Miral Jettena will be the one to give you the cine of her blood. A small cut will be made on your shoulder and a tiny bit of clear liquid, the cine, will be forced into the cut." Seeing the ashen looks on the two

Madic women, Kairma assured them, "This is the same procedure we use on all of our children when the are only a annum old. I promise you it's safe." Kairma laid out a very old Survinees scroll. -"The Miral will read from this, saying the sacred prayers to the gods of Nor. Usually we do this at the altar of the Godstones, but I'm afraid to have you walk that far."

Kairma got up to leave. "I'll be back in a few hours. I need to speak with the elders before we do this."

Jettena and Kairma went from home to home seeking elders who might wish to be a part of the ritual blood service. Kairma put emphasis on the need for new blood, reciting the oldest Ogs that stressed the necessity of keeping the colony's numbers over one hundred and fifty. "We are below those numbers now and are in need of these women. They have promised to remain with us until the end of their natural life. These women are of childbearing age. We need them to be healthy. I don't know if this will help, but I see no reason to wait." To Kairma's great relief, Martena and Grimly both agreed to attend.

That evening Isontra, Kairma, Jettena, Martena, and Grimly sat at the large conference table in the center of the hospital where the various items had been sterilized and prepared for use.

Misha and Lysara were dressed in traditional white suede shirts that dropped just below their knees. They sat in tall chairs facing the open north doors and the sight of the Godstones filled the opening.

As Isontra said the sacred words, Kairma reached across the table and took her mother's hand. Turning it up, Kairma tied the other end of the cord just above her elbow. Tapping the light blue veins that began to emerge from the crook of her arm, Kairma placed the sharp end of the long clear tube against the vein and pressed. Jettena flinched ever so slightly as Kairma pierced the skin and the blood flowed slowly through the reed and into the beeswax-sealed vial.

Once the vial was filled, Kairma swung it by the cord over her head until the liquid inside separated into layers. As she did this, Isontra read from the ancient Ogs. "The power of the cine that is created from the blood will bring health to the community. It will guard us from the ruses and other ailments. Use only the top layer. The clear cine contains the power to protect."

Jettena held a small bandage to her arm until the bleeding stopped while Isontra showed Kairma how to draw off the clear fluid. The clear tube was then inserted into a shoulder of each Madic woman and a small amount of the clear liquid was forced into the skin by blowing on the attached reed.

Isontra said a closing prayer and then the women lay down to rest.

It would be days before the healing power would manifest the desired effects.

Chapter 50

Excitement swept through the village at the sight of the wagons, and while men marveled over the construction of the vehicles, the women looked over all the packages inside. A great feast was prepared and held at the Gathering House. Several large tables displayed the gifts and supplies brought from the city, and one by one the items were held up and explained. The karracks were issued to those who had expressed an interest, and the metal tools were distributed according to the jobs they would improve.

Kinter went wild when Zedic gave her the red rhinestone necklace, but looked a little less excited about the boots—until she saw Kairma's boots. Kinter's black boots had delicate red flowers climbing up the sides, while Kairma's boots were tan and plain. But that didn't stop Kairma from kicking off her moccasins and pulling on the stiff boots. Lifting her skirt to show everyone, Kairma stomped around the room gaily. Her new scarf the color of the inside of a ripe cantaloupe was her second favorite gift. All the women were impressed by the metal cookware.

The evening was spent examining the pictures of the buildings Naturi had drawn, listening to Toric describe the perils of a boat ride, and hearing Collin explain the details of breaking horses. Zedic hadn't let go of Misha, and Trep kept close to Lysara. The women were still feeling poor, but they wanted to meet the many Survinees who welcomed them to the village. On the far side of the Gathering House, about twenty

438

people sat quietly talking among themselves. They pointedly refused to meet the newest Survinees members.

Zedic asked Kairma, "What's going on? Why are those people being so unfriendly?"

"That's Hiram's group. They believe it's wrong of us to invite strangers to Survin. I've tried to explain how important it is for us to have new members, but I think they're still angry regarding Isontra allowing you to leave."

Zedic shook his head. "It worked out well. Why can't they let it go?"

"I was quite surprised Grimly came to the Blood Rite we held for Lysara and Misha. Could have knocked me over with a feather when he said he would witness."

"I never did thank you for pushing the Blood Rite." He reached over and caressed Misha's cheek. "Well, we're home now, and everything is fine." He kissed Misha lightly on the neck. "Everything is more than fine."

Kairma smiled enviously. Zedic looked so happy.

Zedic looked back to Kairma and said, "I noticed Grimly is cordial to Isontra now."

Kairma nodded. "I've made a few friends over the summer. Well, maybe not friends, but you know how Efram was always saying horrible things about me? After the service for Diakus and Massie, he apologized to me."

Zedic's eyes bugged out, and Kairma laughed. "It's a start. Also, Martena has started to treat me more like a Vice Miral. We had a little accident with a bear while Isontra was away. I guess Martena and a few others have learned to trust me where healing is concerned."

"How do you have an accident with a bear?"

Kairma relayed the story of the incident with Kaiden and Rhylee. It was easy to laugh about the sheer luck involved now that everyone was safe.

Jettena called to Kairma, who stood up to see what her mother needed. Before she left, Misha and Lysara thanked her again for her kindness.

Kairma nodded. "You're very welcome."

Gracefully, she made her way through the various tables, greeting people as she headed toward her parents' table.

The evening was wearing down and Collin nudged Zedic. "I didn't see Naturi give Boo the dress he bought for her. Do you think he changed his mind?"

"You're right. I was counting on seeing the look on her face." Zedic had his arm draped casually on the back of Misha's chair. He looked over the crowded space and picked out Naturi at a long table against the rough stone wall. His lips lightly brushed across Misha's ear as he whispered, "Don't go anywhere. We'll be right back."

Collin and Zedic casually ambled over and sat down at Naturi's table. Collin took a long pull on his wine and caught Naturi's eye. "So, what about the dress you bought for Boo? I didn't see it come out tonight."

Naturi squared his shoulders and brushed back an annoying curl from his forehead. "I plan to give it to her after we are mated. It is a gift for her Seridar next moon."

Collin's voice was light, but his eyes were on fire. "Pretty sure of yourself, aren't you?"

Naturi drew back in surprise. "Yes. I am." His words were calm and sure. "I was not aware of any other contenders for the position. Could it be that you might be thinking of becoming the next Comad?" His tone was incredulous. Naturi had returned with gifts and a war wound. Collin was not a credible threat to his standing in the community. Now that Naturi had come back a hero, even Siede would be foolish to challenge him. Collin would have to win at least one physical challenge, and Naturi knew Collin couldn't best him at the bow and had never beat him in hand–to–hand combat. Collin claimed no skill with a sling or a knife either. Seconds ticked past as Naturi's handsome face showed his clear disregard of Collin.

Collin had had just enough to drink to want this to escalate. His mouth twisted slightly, biting back the scathing words he thought. He stood quickly, and Naturi mimicked his move. The sound of chairs scraping the floor filled the room, and all eyes went to the two tall young men as conversation died.

Zedic put a hand on Collin's arm. "Hey, let's go see how Trep's doing with the karracks. I heard we might not have brought as many as we needed."

Collin saw this as the distraction it was meant to be. He also knew Naturi was right. He was rogue, not the kind of man usually chosen to lead the Survin people. Stepping away from the table, Collin said, "Sure, let's go. Later, Nate." And then he smiled as Naturi bristled at the nickname.

Sometime later, Collin saw Kairma leaving. "Hey Boo, wait for me. I'll walk with you." He said good-bye to Zedic, Misha, Lysara, and Trep.

He had to hurry to catch up with Kairma, because she had long legs and walked more quickly than most people. The night air was warm and the stars were plentiful as they walked in comfortable silence. As they came to the village center gardens, Collin motioned to her to sit by him on the old bench swing by the wild roses. She sat down and pulled off the silken scarf Zedic had given her, and her long braids fell down her back in a river of white. As Collin watched, Kairma unbound her hair. The braids left soft waves from her crown to the bench she was seated on. With an exaggerated sigh, Kairma said, "What? What are you staring at?"

"Your hair. It's beautiful, Boo." Suddenly, he felt awkward. He handed her the ring he had found in the vault. "I was wondering if you could read what it says on the inside of this."

Her mouth twisted into a wry grin. "You're teasing, right? I can't even see your ring in this light."

Collin felt a little foolish. She was right. It was much too dark here to read the script on the inside of the ring. He put the ring back on his little finger and said, "I've waited all summer to find out what it says. What's a little longer gonna hurt me?"

Kairma sounded nervous. "Speaking of reading script, I have an awful confession to make." She paused. "There's only one way to say this, and that's straight out. I told Isontra about the vault."

Collin really wasn't listening. He was daydreaming about how it would feel to run his hands through the soft silver of her hair. It took a moment for her words to register. After she had told him about his parents, he didn't think she could shock him more. He was wrong.

"You told Miral Isontra about what we found? *Why?*"

Kairma's face was hot. Collin sounded so angry. She had been expecting this, but it still made her cringe. She could see fire burning in his expressive green eyes and his mouth formed a hard line as she explained. "You see, I found a picture like the one Zedic has. It was in Gramme's things. We were talking about it when she pointed out the pockets on Trep's coat."

Collin's face went from angry to thoroughly confused. "I'm not understanding what Trep's pocket has to do with telling Isontra about the vault."

Kairma carefully explained how Trep's pockets were the same as the pockets in the pictures and on the statues in the vault. "This is why Isontra felt it was important to know more about the people who live in the city. Why she let you go there. When I saw the similarities of the pictures, I had to show her. We've been bringing home the silver scrolls and trying to understand them."

"Well, have you gotten anywhere?" he asked curtly.

"We've made progress. There was a scroll concerning something the ancient ones called a *vaccine*. It comes from the blood of someone who survived an illness. It's very similar to the Blood Rite we do for babies after they reach their first annum."

"Okay, go on."

"It might mean my blood can protect others from the White Fever."

The significance of this wasn't lost on Collin. "I guess I understand why you did it." His voice still sounded hurt and angry, and his eyes wouldn't meet hers.

Kairma hated to upset him like this. "We still have tons of things to learn. We just got a little bit of a lead on it while you were gone. Kinter is really pretty good when it comes to reading and cross-referencing notes."

The swing jerked violently as Collin stood up in a flash. His jaw tightened and the hurt in his voice cut her like a new blade. "Tell me you didn't tell Kinter about this!"

"I had no choice. Isontra insisted on the additional help in reading the scrolls."

"Kairma, you had no right to do this. *Any of this.* That discovery belonged to Zedic and me. You should have waited. You promised!"

Bracing herself against his anger, she said, "It was the right thing to do for Survin. I had to tell Isontra, and now we need to tell the elders about the vault. This is far too valuable to keep from them. We need to show the people of Survin how important it is to let strangers join our community. They need to understand how much we don't know about the world around us."

Collin turned to see she was crying now. Fat tears streamed down her ivory cheeks, glistening silver in the moonlight. He was torn between wanting to hold her and wipe away her tears, and wanting to stomp away, never speaking to her again. He stared down at her. Several minutes passed as he deliberated.

She sobbed quietly, "I'm sorry, I never meant to hurt you, Collin."

That was all it took. Hearing her say his name in that deep and sultry voice mesmerized him in ways he couldn't understand. Her honesty had honored him, and he was beside her again, holding her and wiping away the wetness from her pale and beautiful cheeks. In this moment he was sure. Naturi would never mate with Kairma if there were any way he could prevent it.

Collin was sitting there, content to hold her in his arms when he saw Trep, Zedic, Misha, and Lysara making their way north toward the Chancery. Although Trep had been offered the home he had used during the spring, he spent most of his evenings in the hospital with Lysara. Kairma, Kinter, and Isontra did their best to help the two new Survinees, but every time they thought the women were improving, one of the women would have another relapse.

Collin and Kairma joined the others in their walk through the canyon. They sang silly drinking songs and laughed, happy to be home and safe once more. Collin still had his arm around Kairma's waist, glad she didn't seem to mind. When they reached Collin's new home, the others left Collin and Kairma alone.

Since the death of his parents, Collin had moved to a smaller home closer to the Chancery. It was more of a cottage built to accompany the family home of a lineage that had died out annums before. Collin pulled Kairma toward him. "I won't keep you long." He kissed the top of her head softly. "I still want to know what it says inside the ring."

"Oh," was all she said, but she looked flustered by the kiss.

Collin pulled aside the heavy hide that covered the doorway and led Kairma inside. The room was comfortable, clean, and well-maintained. In the style of most of the Survinees homes, there was a large fireplace in the center of the building. Several walls, like the spokes of a wheel, radiated out from the fireplace, making up the different rooms of the house.

Collin lit the lamp that hung on the wall just inside the doorway, leaving most of the room in shadow. The home wasn't terribly large, but it was empty, and Collin was lonely here by himself. It felt good to have company. He handed Kairma the ring from his finger and waited.

Holding the ring to the lamp, she studied it for a moment. The writing was small and delicate. She looked up at him and said, "Forever Yours," as she handed the gold ring back to him.

He was thunderstruck. It was the way the words sounded as she said them. They were perfect. It was everything he wanted to say and everything he felt for her. "Again. Say it again, please."

She smiled a curious smile. "It says, 'Forever Yours.'"

He took the ring and placed it on her finger. "I am," he said.

Kairma staggered. Her eyes widened, and her soft lips formed an O, making him want to kiss them. He leaned toward her, but before his lips met hers, she pulled away. He had said too much. She was going to be the next Vice Miral. She had no choice in these matters. He watched in horror as tears flooded her eyes once more. Before he could apologize, she hurried out the door.

Collin berated himself. *Of course that was the reaction I should have expected. What was I thinking? It doesn't matter. I only told her the truth. No matter what happens at her Seridar, I will be* forever hers. He threw himself on his bed without taking off his clothes. *I know she doesn't have the same feelings for me. Holy stones! She punched me when I kissed her, and then she cried. I always make her cry. What's wrong with me? I'm such a fool. I should leave. No, I should fight Naturi for her. No, the elders will never select me. No, I should leave. I can't stand by and watch Naturi take her. No, I can't let Naturi win. No, No, No!* He slammed his fist into the wall. *Life is so utterly unfair.*

Chapter 51

The morning after the celebration, noise and laughter spilled from the doorway of the Gathering House as people excitedly showed off their new gifts. When Kairma entered the large room several people greeted her. It was such a strange feeling. Thinking back over the past couple of annums, she asked herself if the people of Survin had partially avoided her because she had always shied away from them. Now that she felt better about herself, it seemed others thought more of her too. *Isn't it odd how a little confidence can change your entire perspective?*

She was looking for Collin. She wanted him to be the one to announce the discovery of the vault to the remainder of the elders, but he hadn't come by the house that morning and that was unusual. She hoped she hadn't hurt his feelings last night when she left so suddenly. Not finding him there, she went back to her studies.

Later that evening, when Kairma was returning from the cleansing station, she saw Collin across the small field. "Collin, wait for me. I need to talk to you."

Collin paused. He looked a little embarrassed.

Kairma came to him. "We need to have a meeting with the elders.

You should tell them what you found." She looked at the dirt on his face and his clothes. "That's where you were today, isn't it?"

"Yeah, so?"

"Just asking. No need to get mad about it."

"Sorry, I guess I'm feeling a little defensive lately. Didn't mean to snap at you." Collin walked with her toward the Chancery.

"It's okay, I'm really tired myself. I've been up with Lysara and Misha for days now. I just can't seem to help them."

"You were saying something about the vault."

"Yes, we have a regular service in five days, and I'd like you to announce the discovery of the vault. Maybe you could show everyone some of the things you found." They reached the Chancery, and Kairma sat on a chair on the large porch.

Collin stood near her chair, poised to bolt. "How do you think they'll react?"

Kairma put a hand out, pulling Collin into the chair next to her. "I think they will be very impressed. Once they learn how much knowledge is in the silver scrolls, they'll understand exactly how valuable your discovery is. I wouldn't be surprised if they didn't look at you in a whole new light."

"Zedic helped me find it, you know."

"Zedic never would have been anywhere near there if it hadn't been for you. You're always the one willing to take chances. Right now, I want everyone to understand how important it is to take risks." She hadn't let go of his hand. "I need you to help me in this. We've broken a lot of rules lately, and I need people to know some good can come of this. Are you with me?"

Putting his arm around her shoulder, Collin said, "Boo, I'm always with you." The words were sweet, but there was a slightly bitter undertone.

Zedic rose early the next morning to find Kairma sitting by the fire, sipping a cup of terrid. He noticed she was wearing Collin's ring. He wondered briefly what it meant. "How are Misha and Lysara today?"

"They're sleeping now. They're better, but very tired. I sincerely hope the Blood Rite will help them. Misha may be slipping a little. We'll keep her close now. No big parties for a while." Her smile was gentle and understanding.

Zedic poured a cup of terrid for himself and joined her at the hearth. For a long time neither of them spoke, content just to be near each other and listen to the sounds of the mountain as it came to life.

Zedic was fondling a small satin pouch; Kairma noticed and put her hand on his arm. "She's very pretty."

It was uncanny the way Kairma always seemed to know what he was thinking, and Zedic had missed this closeness. His eyes met hers and misted ever so slightly. "No. She's *beautiful.*" It was an undisputable fact. "She reminds me of you sometimes. She's strong and always knows what she wants."

Kairma shook her head ever so slightly, not seeing herself that way at all.

He paused for a while and then took a sip from the pottery cup. "Almost everything she and Lysara had was destroyed in a fire just days before we left. They must have suffered more from the smoke than we'd first thought. They seemed fine when we first set out from the city, but after a few days they began to suffer from dizzy spells and gradually grew weaker and weaker." He sighed. "We really didn't think we would make it back. Those were the hardest days of my life. Every time she went to sleep, I worried, afraid she wouldn't wake up." He blinked back a tear that threatened. "She's going to get better, isn't she?"

Kairma stirred in her seat. "I don't know, Zedic. We don't know what's making them sick. What is that you're playing with?"

Zedic opened the satin pouch and showed her the little gold and jeweled comb. Kairma had seen it in Misha's hair last night. "It's a little keepsake from a friend Misha knew in Peireson Landing. It reminds me of her. I like it when she wears it in her hair. I always tell her how beautiful she is." Kairma reached out for the comb, and Zedic handed her the pouch, saying, "I should have come and gotten you or Gramme. Maybe they wouldn't have gotten so sick if I had." Looking back into the fire, he fell silent, regretting his inaction.

Kairma opened the pouch and took out the golden comb. "What's this powder for?"

"That keeps the gold shiny."

Kairma rubbed the powder between her fingers and sniffed the powder. "It has no discernable scent." Curious, she dabbed a small bit of the white powder on her tongue. "It's tasteless as well. Odd. I wonder what it is."

Kairma greeted Isontra as she came into the great room and joined them in front of the fire. It wasn't unusual for the influential Miral to be silent for a good part of the morning. Isontra used this time to plan her day, though she rarely wrote anything down until after at least two cups of steaming hot terrid.

The tall, thin woman sat at the hearth, sipping her terrid and studying her two grandchildren. She looked as if she hadn't slept well. The way in which she rubbed her hands said her arthritis was particularly annoying this morning, and Kairma instinctively knew her grandmother wanted her pills. When Kairma stood up, a wave of nausea came over her and she quickly sat back down.

"Is something wrong?" Isontra queried.

"No, just a little lightheaded. I think I need something to eat." She stood up again and the nausea struck her once more, though less violently. After a moment, she seemed to be fine. She put the comb back in the satin case and handed it to Zedic. She hurried to her grandmother's room to get her medicine. Reaching for the ceramic canister of pills, she saw the fine white powder on her fingers. A wave of terror engulfed her, and beads of sweat formed on her upper lip. Running from the back room, she screamed, "Zedic, don't touch the comb! I think it's been poisoned! Great Nor! I think someone is trying to kill them!"

Zedic dropped the satin pouch and stared at it in disbelief. "I have to tell Trep."

As the two women watched him bound out the door, Isontra looked up. Kairma said, "I think I had better explain."

Isontra nodded.

"It has to be the combs. Zedic told me each of the women had received a comb as a parting gift from a friend. They both wore the combs at first, but when they became so ill it seemed pointless to wear trinkets in their hair so they took them out." Kairma sat down close to Isontra. "That must have been when they stopped and made camp. Zedic said both women began to recover after a week or so. This morning, Zedic said he sometimes gives the combs to Misha to wear in her hair because they make her feel pretty. That must be why she is so much weaker than Lysara."

Isontra paled visibly. "Where did the combs come from?"

Kairma shrugged. "Zedic said they were from a friend—someone they met in the city."

Isontra rose from her chair and took the commanding posture that Kairma recognized as the Miral. "I think the impact of this may well reach much farther than the death of two innocent women. Go quickly, child. Bring the others to my planning room. We have much to consider, and I don't want to have this conversation in the hospital where the women might overhear."

Kairma nodded and ran out the door.

Chapter 52

Later that night, seven people sat around Isontra's table and watched as a violently angry Trep paced the brightly lit suite of rooms. His broad shoulders shook and, like a trapped animal, he circled the table until Miral Isontra demanded that he return to his seat. As the leader of the community, the tall thin woman sat at the head of the table, her steel gray eyes following his every movement. Trep grit his teeth tightly and looked at her, then at the others— all powerful members of the small community he had so recently joined. Seeing the expression on Zedic's face, he realized he didn't have a monopoly on anger and went back to his place next to Toric. As he did, he couldn't help but say it one more time. "I'll kill him! I swear if it's the last thing I do in my life, I will hunt him down and I will kill him!"

Isontra raised her voice just over Trep's mutterings. "I am deeply troubled by something else you revealed about this man Narvin. You mentioned that he's a great collector of artifacts and might do anything to discover our location if he knew about the great carvings. Do I understand correctly?" Isontra folded her long fingers and placed them in her lap. Her face was stern with sixty annums of responsibility etched in fine lines around her down-turned mouth.

Trep blanched. "I'm afraid so. But that don't explain why he would kill Lysa. I told him there was nothin' here. I said I wanted to study your village and that I'd return in a year or two with my findin's." Trep shook his head in dismay. "I'm really sorry. Truly, I am. I honestly thought he'd believe me." He pinched the bridge of his nose between his thumb and forefinger.

Isontra asked, "What makes you think he didn't believe you?"

"He's a very powerful man in Peireson Landin'. He's the Overseer— that's kind of like y'all's Miral or a Comad. He practically owns that city. We used raw gold as well as cut and uncut gems for tradin'. He guessed there were gold mines here that ain't been played out yet. I told him there weren't any, but he might suspect me of lyin'." Worry lines danced across Trep's face. "Narvin mentioned needin' the gold mines for his city." Trep's fists were in tight balls. "I'm not sure he would actually travel this far for a few artifacts, but I hate takin' the chance. If somehow, we could slip into the city and quietly eliminate him …"

Zedic stood. "I'll go. I'll take care of him." His dark hair was unusually messy and his mouth was a hard line. He put his hands on his hips, his voice bitter. "I can be gone by sundown."

Collin stood beside him to show his support and then Toric rose as well. Isontra waved her hand for them to be seated. "That is a noble gesture, but I am afraid winter is too close at hand. Although you might make it to the city before the first snow came, you wouldn't be able to make it back, and in the spring you would find yourself faced with the same problem of being followed." Realizing she was right, the would-be heroes took their seats and tried to come up with an alternative plan.

Kairma caught her grandmother's eye. "Yes, Kairma?"

She stood up and clasped her hands behind her back as she had seen Isontra do many times. She searched the faces of everyone in the room, looking for something that felt like it was just beyond her reach. "You told Narvin there was no gold or artifacts here in our valley." Trep nodded and she continued. "You also said you would return in a few annums with information—information you were forbidden to share."

Again Trep nodded. "Yeah, but I only said that to keep him from askin' more questions." Trep felt Kairma's ice-blue eyes looking right into his soul.

Then Kairma turned to Isontra. "If Narvin believed Trep, he wouldn't have him followed, but if he thought Trep would be returning with Lysara in two annums, he might have reason to fear that." She looked at Trep. "Does he have reason to fear Lysara and Misha? Lysara worked for Narvin in the city. Do you believe he would poison them?"

Isontra looked over at Trep. "I'm not sure if one thing has to do with the other. But Kairma's right. If Narvin thought you were hiding something, he would have followed you. Were you followed?"

Trep grimaced. "I didn't see any signs, but in all honesty I was so worried about the women, I really didn't pay attention."

Naturi said, "Miral Isontra, my father and I watched for signs but saw none. I spent many days with Narvin, and his city is most important to him. He is a well-respected man, and very generous. I do not believe he would hurt someone who was leaving. Blaming Narvin does not make sense. Could it be that another person poisoned the combs without his knowledge?"

Trep began to pace again. "The night before he gave the girls the combs, he gave Naturi a sack of candies."

Naturi swallowed and then looked cautiously at Isontra. "I was saving them for the Harvest Celebration. He gave me over one hundred pieces. I really want to trust Narvin; he seems so genuine in his charity."

Zedic grabbed Trep's arm as he paced by and forced him to sit again. "I remember the night Narvin gave Naturi the candies. He asked his servant, a small, dark man named Artuk, to get the gifts, but it was the man they call Jaimer who handed the box to Narvin."

Isontra asked, "Did any of these men give you reason to believe they wanted to injure these women?"

Naturi looked uncomfortable. "Not really, but Narvin did ask a few odd questions about the size and defense of Survin. I told him nothing, and that seemed to upset him, but only for a moment. I did not even think about it, until now."

Collin twisted a dark curl of hair at his neck. "Several people knew about the gifts. At least three of the men who were there that night had access to the combs. My theory is that someone wanted to make sure the women would never return. Perhaps they know something he or she wishes to be kept secret."

"She?" Trep leaned back in his chair, his eyes suddenly brightening. "Ya know, Collin may be right. Narvin had a woman who helped him 'round the office. Think her name was Yevve. What if she was jealous of one of the girls? She woulda known 'bout the combs, and poison's always been a woman's tool. Men are usually more hands-on than that." He chewed on a nail, his eyebrows knitted in thought. "I don't know anythin' about Jaimer or Artuk, but Narvin is a very prideful man. I have no idea what lengths Narvin would go to in order to keep somethin' secret, but murderin' helpless women seems a little harsh, even for a man as ambitious as him."

Kairma, who had remained standing, looked at her grandmother. Isontra nodded for her to continue. Her voice was soft and husky. "Zedic tells me Narvin wanted to buy a piece of land for a garden of some kind. As I understand it, the owners of the livery didn't want to sell." She paused for a moment and then turned to Zedic. "How did Narvin get the land he wanted?"

Zedic pondered the question a long time. "There was a fire. The livery was burned to the ground and the Bowart brothers didn't have enough money to rebuild. Narvin was able to buy the land for much less than his original offer." With Trep's help, Zedic spent the next few minutes describing money and private property.

Kairma turned to Trep. "That sounds like a man with incredible luck, or absolutely no scruples. How much does this man know about us?"

Trep answered, "Not much, really."

Kairma didn't like the sound of this man, but everything she knew was circumstantial. "If Narvin could burn a man's business to acquire the land, or kill someone he'd worked with, how hard would it be for him to kill strangers? I think this man would go to any length for something he really wanted, and Collin has told me about the museum that houses his vast collection of ancient artifacts."

Her heart was heavy with guilt. It had been at her insistence that Trep was spared and then allowed to take four Survinees men to the city. This new peril was her doing. "I believe we are left with two choices. We can move Survin as has been done many times in the past, though not for almost five hundred annums, or we can post rangers at the edge of the forest and kill *anyone* who approaches. I hate to do either of these things. We need new blood, but I'm afraid of the people who might come here." Sitting back down, she rubbed her eyes and chewed her lower lip in frustration.

While Toric spoke of defensive measures, Kairma toyed with the sleeve of her blouse. The soft lightweight fabric, so unlike the usual leather most Survinees wore, was from Peireson Landing. She briefly wondered if the goods brought from the city would be worth the price they may have to pay. She turned to Toric. "How many karracks did you bring back?"

"We have thirty-six if you count Trep's karrack."

"With any luck, that will be enough."

Toric looked hard at Kairma. "You're so certain Narvin's coming?"

Kairma looked at her grandmother and then back at Toric. "No, I'm not certain of anything—I'm afraid. Men from the plains killed Collin's sister and brother. Others will certainly come and—whoever is coming is probably not very nice."

Naturi's eyes darted away when Kairma turned to him and said, "Tell me what you know about Narvin."

Naturi took a deep breath, forcing his voice to sound more confident than he felt. "He is powerful, yes, but he is loyal to his people. I saw him doing many wonderful things for his city. I cannot believe he would hurt those women or come here to hurt us." Shaking his head caused a stray curl to fall over his eyes, and he flipped it away. "We cannot be sure we are in danger until we check the candies. Even then, the poison may have come from someone who had access to the gifts, someone else who may have wished us harm."

Kairma nodded. "We'll test the candies. If they're clean, someone meant only to hurt Lysara and Misha. If not, we'll need to arm ourselves."

Toric sighed heavily. "We can post rangers around the walls of the canyon. They can guard the approaches to the north and south of us. We met a friend of Trep's about three days east of here. Slightly past his place, you can see a lot of the eastern plains."

Kairma said, "I want to meet with him, the man you call Zacar."

Trep shook his head. "Zacar will let y'all pass, and he might even offer y'all a meal, but don't expect him to join the fight."

Kairma said, "I wasn't planning on asking him to fight, but it'd be handy if he would warn us if he sees something."

Isontra grimaced. "Kairma, I don't want you away at a time like this. It's too dangerous."

Kairma looked at her grandmother and grimaced. "This is my doing. If we're going to form an alliance with this man, Zacar, I'd like to be there. I want him to understand what's at stake and the danger I've put him in."

Isontra rubbed her tired eyes. "Your mother is going to be very angry with me."

Chapter 53

The sun was shining in the southern door of the Grand Hall as Kairma was preparing to meet the man they called Zacar. She felt better knowing Lysara and Misha would be getting stronger now that the poison had been discovered. While Kinter helped prepare herbal teas and medicines, Kairma set a small pack on the large conference table in the middle of the room and added a few common health remedies.

Misha lay back on a cot, her long blond hair fanned out haphazardly around her head. Her eyes were closed, but as the Healers worked, she pleaded, "Please take Zedic with you. He comes here and paces for hours." Her lips lifted at the corners. "Really, I'm getting better as fast as I can. I know he wants to spend time with me, but sometimes he just needs to go away for a while."

Lysara sat back on her cot, sipping her warm terrid. "Yes, take Trep with you too. He needs to find another interest, even if it's just for a day or two." She smiled, reaching over and taking her sister's frail hand. Lysara whispered, "A couple more days and we'll be strong enough to run away from them." Misha laughed quietly, and Lysara turned back to Isontra, saying, "No offense, but I really can't wait to get out of this hospital."

Isontra laid a blanket over Misha and smiled. "If it's nice tomorrow, we can go for a walk."

Kairma set a few small packages containing supplies next to the travel pack. "Where are Trep and Zedic now? I thought they would be here. I was planning to take Trep with us because he's Zacar's friend."

Laying out the makings of a medicinal terrid, Kinter said, "Trep drew water hauling in the work lottery yesterday. Zedic went to help him finish up this morning. They should be back soon."

Although Trep enjoyed more freedom since his return, Zedic and Collin usually accompanied him in his duties to appease the less welcoming Survinees. After feeding some of the candy to a captured mouse, news of the poisoned candies swept though the small village like a brushfire, and the tension regarding the newest members of Survin grew even more uncomfortable. Hiram continued to berate the Healing family for placing them in such danger, and Kairma could only agree with him.

Looking at her grandmother, Kairma saw new lines had etched her once pretty face, and her hair seemed thinner. Isontra wasn't particularly old as Survinees went, but the weight of the decision made over the summer had taken its toll.

Helping Lysara into a clean blouse, Isontra said, "Kairma, I need to speak with you privately for a moment. Please take that basket of lavender to my rooms. I'll be there in a moment."

Kairma picked up the small bundle and headed past the kitchen to Isontra's suite of rooms, certain her grandmother would be giving her a strong lecture regarding the dangers of meeting with Zacar.

As she had been taught, Kairma was gently removing the tender leaves from the stems of the lavender when Isontra entered the room. Her grandmother looked tired and worried as she placed a soft hand on Kairma's shoulder. "You must leave the Crystal here. It's against my better judgment to let you go at all, but Collin and Trep have both promised to keep you safe. I'll feel better if I know the Crystal is safe here with Kinter and me."

"Of course." Kairma took the suede sack from under her blouse and handed it to her grandmother.

Isontra sat in the chair across from Kairma and pinched the bridge of her nose. "May the gods forgive me for the danger I've incurred."

"Gramme, this is not your fault. If we've learned anything from the great vault, it is that we really don't know anything, and ignorance is the most dangerous handicap of all. You said men would come eventually, and that they would have the weapons Trep showed us. If we hadn't allowed our men to purchase karracks, we would be helpless now. We can't hide forever. The world is too small."

"I was hoping to spare you this battle, but yes, I knew it would come eventually."

"We don't often get to choose the battles we fight, do we?"

Isontra's smile was wry. "I always knew you were a brave girl, but I want you to be very careful. We have a lot invested in you."

"I need to get back."

"Of course, you need to be ready when the men return." The two women stood and hugged briefly. Kairma's eyes misted slightly. "I'll be very careful, Gramme. Toric said he would go with us as well."

"That makes me feel better." Isontra studied Kairma for a moment as they walked down the long hall to the hospital section of the building. "Hiram and his followers are still upset about Trep. He believes bringing the women to Survin was a mistake too. What will he say when he learns I've let you go meet with this Zacar person?"

"If we want him to help protect us from those who would seek us out, we need to meet with him. Hiram must understand this."

Isontra nodded slowly. "I hope we can convince him of the necessity of our actions, but it won't be easy."

Kairma hugged Isontra once more. "I'm going to grab something to eat and I'll see how Zedic and Trep are doing."

Collin was just returning from one of the four public cleansing areas where the duty he'd drawn required him to check on the flush water and rebuild the central hearth fire. He'd raced through his chores, eager to make the trip to Zacar's. He still couldn't believe Isontra was allowing Kairma to go with them, but the old woman was always surprising him.

He walked into the Chancery much the way he had for the last eighteen annums of his life. The difference now was that instead of looking for his best friend Zedic, he found himself looking for Kairma.

She was there, sitting at the table, finishing what looked like a mixture of grains and fruit. He saw she was wearing the gold ring he had given her, and his heart skipped a beat. Pulling out a chair and sitting next to her, Collin said, "Hey, Boo, that looks good." Kairma looked up at him. Her ice-blue eyes sparkled, and her smile was warm. *How does she do that? I know she isn't meant for me, but every time I see her smile at me like that, I start thinking she should be.* He picked an apple from a bowl in the center of the table. His dark hair, grown longer over the summer, curled around his collar and fell in soft waves over his forehead. He brushed the hair back, and his dark green eyes fastened on Kairma. "Are you ready to go, or has Isontra changed her mind?"

Kairma swallowed her food and took a sip of terrid. "We can leave as soon as Kinter gets back."

"Where'd she go?" He took a bite out of the sweet red fruit.

"She went to get some herbs from Naturi's garden. Gramme said something about needing some bergamot this morning—for Misha, I think." She looked down at the ring on her finger nervously. She hesitantly said, "You look like you're in a really good mood today. I was afraid after I left your place so suddenly the other night you might feel—*uncomfortable.*" She was afraid to meet his eyes until Collin reached over and lightly traced the edge of her ear. Looking up, she saw a wicked smile played across his mouth.

He said eagerly, "It must be the thought of another adventure that has me so excited. I can't believe Isontra is letting me take you away."

"It's only for a couple days." Kairma's voice cracked as his touch gave her goose bumps. She couldn't decide if she wanted him to stop or not.

His cheeks dimpled, and his green eyes flashed mischievously. "A lot can happen in a couple of days."

She quickly finished her breakfast and called to Isontra, "I'm going now. Collin is here." She picked up her bowl and rinsed it in the large alloy pan on the hearth. Collin jumped up and followed her out the door.

When they entered the hospital, Kinter was just finishing her work. She looked pleased that Kairma was going away and leaving the Crystal, *and Naturi*, behind. She smiled brightly as they entered the room. "Have a good trip. I'll be sure to take care of things while you're gone."

Kairma and Collin both thought, *I'm sure you will.*

Zedic had finished his chores and was sitting beside Misha, holding her hand. As Kairma gathered the packs of supplies, she looked over at her brother and Misha's dark brown eyes pleaded with her. Kairma's mouth twitched into an almost smile. "Hey, Zedic. Are you coming with us? We could really use your help."

Zedic looked up and smiled lamely. "I'll stay here with Misha, but please say hello to Zacar for me."

Kairma watched Misha roll her eyes, and she added, "Come on, Zedic. You need to get away for a while."

Zedic looked thoughtful, so Kairma said, "Grab some fruit from the table, and get your things."

Zedic slowly shook his head. "Maybe next time."

A moment later Toric came in with a large pack on his back. "Let's get on the way," he said, and then he looked over at Zedic. "Aren't you going with us?"

"Not this time. Trep will be back in a little while. He's planning to go with you. Did you ask Naturi if he wanted to go?"

Collin made a big deal of helping Isontra fill a pottery jar with leaves, not meeting Zedic's eyes. Collin had avoided Naturi since the exchange at the Gathering House concerning the blue dress purchased for Kairma, and Zedic was determined to patch things up between his friends.

Toric set his pack on the table. "He'll be along. Had to finish some instructions for taking care of the new plants he brought back from the city."

Collin's mouth hardened, and Kairma couldn't help but notice. She was about to say something to him, when Trep walked in with Naturi. She saw the look on Naturi's face when his eyes met Collin's eyes. She noted their silent exchange—a challenge never voiced, but fully understood.

Kinter looked up at Naturi briefly, and then quickly left the room. Kairma stared after her. *Poor girl. Every time she thinks she's getting something she wants, it slips away.*

Chapter 54

As long as they were going to make the trip, Trep had suggested they make the road between Survin and Zacar a little smoother, so the small buckboard was loaded with gear and a few gifts for the big man. Naturi helped Kairma onto the seat. He took the seat next to her and grabbed the reins. Toric, Trep, and Collin mounted their horses and led the way east around the lake. The sky was a deep blue with sharp-edged cumulus clouds creating interesting shapes above the travelers. The newly cut trail was rough and Kairma had to hold on with both hands to keep from being bounced out of the wagon. A huge smile lit her face as one of many dreams had finally come true. She was actually going to meet someone new.

They were about a day away from Zacar's cabin when they stopped for the evening. The men, well-practiced at making camp now, had a fire built in a short time and while Naturi prepared a meal of venison and stewed vegetables, Collin and Toric erected a tent of hides to sleep in.

Taking the bedrolls out of the wagon, Kairma asked, "What is Zacar like?"

Collin took a bedroll from her and placed it in the tent. "He's big. Never seen anyone as big as that. Compared to a Madic, he's a giant."

"Why does he live alone? Doesn't he like people?"

"He says people don't like him, but I think he's a pretty nice person."

Kairma handed Collin the last bedroll. "Do you think he'll be willing to help us?"

Collin said, "That, I don't know. He seemed pretty friendly when we came through here, and he helped us make this road. I guess it depends on how involved he wants to be."

Kairma sat down on a stump conveniently close to the fire Naturi had built. "Does he know very much about us?"

In unison the men said, "Of course not!"

Kairma nodded. "Do you think he would like to join our village?"

Shocked looks crossed the face of every man there, and Toric spoke from across the fire. "I think he likes to be alone."

"So you don't think he would be interested in fathering any children?"

Toric's brows knit together. "Kairma, where is this line of questions coming from?"

Kairma took a drink from her waterskin. "When you set off after the Madics last spring, Isontra asked Collin to bring back karracks and Trep's mate. She'd also hoped he would find people of Efpec blood to augment our genetic pool."

Toric said, "We've already added Trep, and two new women."

"Yes. We didn't expect you to bring back a lot of people, only one or two, which you did, but I was just wondering …"

Collin laughed. "I can just see Rose and Ember now if we brought Zacar back with us."

Kairma cocked her head toward Collin. "You do realize that Rose and Ember are related to Siede, Efram, and you? Alyssum is related to Zedic and Jared. Any one of those women would benefit from the introduction of another man. Unfortunately, Trep is already taken." Kairma nibbled on a biscuit and said to Trep, "We will definitely prosper from any children you and Lysara have, but in the meantime, several women are very limited in choices for mating."

Naturi handed Kairma a bowl of stew. "All we can do is ask."

Collin grinned. "Maybe we should have brought some eligible women with us."

Toric and Trep laughed.

The next day was hot. The sun was near setting when Collin announced they were almost there. Coming around the last bend, Zacar's large stone and log cabin came into view. Kairma was impressed by the home, but it was the large tawny cat on the porch that held her attention. "That must be Purder," she said with wide eyes.

Pulling up beside the wagon, Collin said, "You should have seen us the first time we met that cat. You could have knocked us over with a breath."

Kairma's eyes were wide. "I can see why. That's the biggest cat I've ever seen."

Toric pulled his horse up to the other side of the buckboard. "I think we should wait until Zacar comes outside. I wouldn't want to upset Purder." He whistled and waited for an answer. When no reply came, he whistled again. After a moment a reply came, not from the cabin, but from somewhere to the east.

Toric rode toward the sound. "I think Zacar must be on the other side of that hill to the east. We should ask if he'd allow us to stay here tonight."

Naturi clicked his tongue, and the horse pulling the buckboard lurched ahead. Kairma grabbed the seat before she could be thrown into the back of the small wagon.

On the other side of the hill they found Zacar staring off to the east. "Nice to have visitors again so soon. It's only been a few days since you all came through here last. Where are you going now?"

Toric dismounted and walked over to the giant man. "We came to visit you. We have a little problem we were hoping you could help us with."

Zacar pointed out to the east. "Does it have something to do with that?" At the end of his thick finger was the dark smoke of a campfire near the river.

"As a matter of fact, it does."

"I thought as much." He turned and his eyes fell on Kairma. "Who is this lovely thing?"

Naturi introduced them. Kairma touched her right hand to her brow and said, "It's nice to meet you."

Zacar returned the greeting. "Lo, nice to meet you too. You're the next Vice Miral, aren't you?"

Kairma coughed. "Why yes, I am. How did you know this?"

Zacar's smile was charismatic, and Kairma instantly liked him. "I've lived here for many years. I've been to your weekly services on occasion too. I enjoy hearing what goes on in your village."

Kairma felt a stab of panic. If this man has overheard their services, who also might know about them? Her voice cracked slightly as she asked. "How long have you been *attending* our meetings?"

Zacar patted Collin's horse on the nose. "I started coming to them about six annums ago. It was right after my parents died. I was okay for a while, but then I wanted someone to talk to. I listened for a while and it was clear that you didn't accept strangers, so I kept clear of the village. When Trep came through here a annum ago, I warned him not to interfere with your community." His smile was broad and friendly. "He didn't listen to me." He turned to Kairma, his smile showing a row of strong white teeth. "I watched to see what you would do to him. I tell you, I felt a lot better when you didn't kill him."

Kairma returned his smile. "Since you've overheard our services, you must know now that we are not in a position to turn away healthy strangers." She had felt a similar fondness for Trep when she first met him. At the time, she wrote it off as his being Collin's friend, but now she wondered if it was always like this—meeting strangers.

Zacar nodded. "That brings us to those people out there. Something's wrong. They haven't moved in four days. I was close enough to see there were a couple men who took turns on watch, but the rest of the camp seems oddly sedate. I was thinking about riding out to find out why they're here, but I didn't want to get sick if that's why they're not moving. I saw how sick those poor girls were who came through here with Trep a while ago. Crossing the plains isn't easy. I've seen more than my share of death. Then again, they might just be waiting for reinforcements. Either way, going down there alone didn't sound like a good idea."

Turning to Trep, Kairma said, "We need to find out what's going on down there, and we could really benefit from your knowledge now. You may know who these people are and why they're here. I'm sure they speak like you, as well. I remember it took you some time to understand us."

Trep agreed. "Do y'all want me to ride down there?"

Kairma looked out over the plains. "Not alone. You heard Zacar— that wouldn't be wise. We don't know how many people are there. I think we need more men on our side before we approach them."

Toric stepped up beside Kairma. "If I ride hard, I can be back here with more men by nightfall tomorrow."

"Thank you, Toric. Please tell Isontra what's happening. Don't alarm her, but tell her we found a small group of people camping on the plains. Let her know we suspect they may be sick and may not be strong enough to make it all the way to Survin without my help."

Collin put a protective arm around Kairma. "Someone tried to kill Misha and Lysara. Those could be very dangerous people. Are you sure you want to risk going near them? Maybe you should go back with Toric."

Kairma looked up at Collin, bemused. "When did you become so conservative?"

Collin leaned into her, his lips brushing her ear as he whispered, "When I realized I loved you. Until then, I had nothing to lose."

Kairma pulled away gently, but her heart pounded wildly. "I have to do what I can, and if that means taking a risk—well, I have the whole of Survin to help keep me safe. I want to help them if they're sick, and I can't do that if I go home. Toric can ask Isontra for the Crystal."

Collin held her arm tight. "It's against my better judgment to let you stay, but you don't need the Crystal to help these people." He tapped her forehead lightly. "Everything you need is right here. Toric, please go, we don't have time to waste."

Toric jumped back on his bay mare and galloped off to the west.

Zacar invited the others to have dinner with him, and over the peaceful meal, Kairma broached the subject of Zacar joining the village. "I know you've been here for a long time, but we would welcome you to Survin. I can tell by your height and lack of facial hair, you must have strong Efpec blood."

"I don't know what that means, but my folks were tall like me. That's why we came here. Most folks don't like our kind. My father told me we were searching for the city of the angel." Zacar dished up bowls of hot stew. "One day when you were giving the service, you said something about the angel giving the Crystal to Amanda. Ever since then, I was sure you were the people my father had been searching for all those annums."

Kairma dipped a biscuit into her stew. "You know there are several people among us who'll try to stop us from recruiting you. They might make living in the canyon uncomfortable."

"That's okay with me. I think I'd like to stay here in my cabin, anyway." He waved a large hand around the room. "I like this place, but I wouldn't mind having someone to share it with me."

Collin chewed on a biscuit and nudged Kairma. "I knew we should have brought women with us. What kind of visitors are we? We come expecting hospitality and we didn't even bring him a gift."

Kairma turned to Collin. "We did bring him award-winning apple preserves."

"Yeah, but that ain't the same as bringing women."

Kairma rolled her eyes. "No, but maybe he'd like to choose his own."

Collin winked at her. "Boo, I happen to have excellent taste in women."

Naturi's chair scratched the floor loudly as he got up. "We need to discuss the possibility that those strangers are planning to attack us."

Zacar moved to help clear the table. "I've been watching them pretty close. I don't think there are more than ten people in the group. I think we could handle them if they tried to attack. I'm more worried about getting sick. I watched my parents die shortly after a Madic came through the valley. He was the last of a team of prospectors who were searching for ore. He told us the rest of his team died, but we thought we could help him."

Kairma helped Zacar with the dishes. "I'm sorry to hear about your parents."

"It was a long time ago. It's really nice to have someone to talk to after all these annums."

"That sounds like you've decided to join our family."

Zacar grinned at her. "It's something I've wished for, for a very long time. A man gets a might lonely out here all alone. I've done okay, but the truth is, ever since you let Trep in, I'd hoped we could be friends."

When Toric got back to the village, the sun had just cleared the tops of the tallest pines. He wasted no time in telling Isontra what they had seen on the plains. "We can't really see how many are there, but we think it might be about ten or fifteen. I came to gather more men." He took a ragged breath. "We don't know why they're just waiting out there. It could be that they're waiting for someone. Zacar thinks they might be sick. If that's true, Kairma wants to save them, but she said not to bring the Crystal."

Isontra sipped her terrid slowly and tried to clear her thoughts. "If Narvin led this group of travelers, Kairma could be in serious danger. Take every precaution necessary to ensure the safety of Kairma and

Survin. You'd best take every man you can find. Zedic will go, and take
Siede, Canton, Davis, and Jared."

"We only have six horses and speed is of the essence."

"Take who you can, and please—protect Kairma at all cost."

Toric saluted the Miral. "I will protect her with my life." With those
words he strode from the room in search of any man willing to make the
trip. As it turned out, Jared was just leaving the cleansing center when
Toric walked by, and after a brief explanation, Jared agreed to ride along.
He'd been fascinated by the horses and relished the chance to ride one.

They found Siede asleep. He was dressed and out the door before
Toric could explain all the details. Siede grabbed his pack and almost
ran toward the hospital. "If the person responsible for the poison is out
there on the plains, I'll make him pay for what he did to those poor
girls. What kind of sick man kills with beautiful combs?"

Toric vehemently agreed. "Get in line, son."

When everyone had returned to the hospital, Zedic was just saying
good-bye to Misha. He, too, was looking for revenge. His eyes burned
with reawakened anger as he kissed Misha gently on the forehead. "I'll
be back before you know I'm gone."

Misha smiled. "Take care of yourself out there."

"I will," Zedic said as he followed the others out the door.

The small band of Survinees galloped their horses all the way back to
Zacar's cabin, reaching it a few hours before dawn the following day.
The smell of rain was thick, and heavy clouds covered the rising sun.

Barking from Zacar's dog woke Trep, Naturi, and Collin, who had
been asleep in the tannery. The stone building was spacious, with several
racks for cleaning hides. Zacar was talented when it came to tanning
leather, and even the scraps in the corner were useful as bedding. Toric
and his men dismounted their tired horses and met Kairma and Zacar
at the door.

Siede whistled appreciatively. "You *are* a big man."

Zacar laughed and invited them inside the cabin. "I think Purder may have run off for a few days. He's not one for company."

Siede looked curiously at the tall man. "Purder?"

"He's my cat."

"I find cats pretty much do what they please."

Zacar nodded. "And he's big enough that I don't argue."

Toric estimated the size of the cat by holding up one hand. Siede looked incredulous, but Zacar confirmed the fact that Purder was well over knee high.

Kairma poured hot terrid for the exhausted men while Zacar fried strips of buffalo meat, potatoes, and wild onions. Crossing his arms in front of him on the table, Toric laid his head down. In minutes, the sound of snoring almost shook the table.

Zacar set a plate of food in front of Jared and pointed to Toric. "We cain't do a lot tonight. I'll move him to the back room." Zacar gently nudged Toric. After a little coaxing, Toric stumbled into Zacar's overstuffed bed.

Returning to the dining table, Zacar said, "We only have a few hours before dawn and the Madic camp is at least a three-hour ride from here. If we're going to have the advantage, we need to hit their camp while it's dark. We'll head down there tomorrow night after everyone is rested."

Kairma sat down at the large pine table between Naturi and Collin. "We should try to capture one of their watchmen and find out what we can about them."

Zacar swallowed the meat he had been chewing. "The plains are wide open. It's going to be hard to sneak up and take a man. Might be better if we take the whole group at once."

Naturi rubbed the sleep from his eyes. "The grass down there is high. We should be able to get pretty close if we crawl. I would feel much better if we got closer before we make any solid decision."

Jared stretched his legs and readjusted his position on the hard chair. It had been a long ride from Survin and he wasn't used to riding a horse. His thighs ached and he was sure he'd never walk straight again. "Naturi's right. We need someone to go down and find out what we're up against."

Collin nodded. "We still need the cover of night. They'd spot us the moment we cleared the forest if the sun was up."

Zedic yawned. "I could really use some sleep if I'm expected to put up any kind of fight."

Naturi got up and put his plate by the washtub. "Kairma will stay here. We will find out what we need to know, and if it is necessary for Kairma to heal these men, we will bring them to her."

Kairma stood, eyes flashing angrily. "I will not stay here. I should go with you. You don't know how to evaluate their condition. I'm the one with medical training."

"Kairma, you are assuming they are sick and not plotting something devious. It is not safe. You *will* stay here. Do not argue this point with me. You are much too valuable to risk."

Kairma placed her hands on her hips and glared at Naturi. "But if these people are truly sick, you may not be able to bring them here, and we'll have lost valuable time."

Jared looked over at Kairma. "What makes you believe they're sick? Maybe they're waiting for reinforcements. Could be an ambush too. Just because we can only see a small fire doesn't mean there aren't other men waiting somewhere nearby to attack."

Kairma knew the men were right to be cautious, and her convictions regarding the health of the strangers were probably based more on her desire go with the men than on any tangible evidence. Kairma sat back down slowly. She knew Jared and Naturi were right to keep her away, but she just hated it when Naturi told her what she should or should not do.

She pleaded her case once more, hoping to change their minds. "I need to evaluate the situation and I'll be surrounded by Survin's best men. You know how important it is to save these people if their intentions are not evil, and I can't believe everyone from Peireson Landing wants to hurt us. If they followed you here out of curiosity or a desire to find a new home, we need them."

Jared looked a little puzzled, but Collin nodded curtly.

Naturi's mouth formed a tight line. "That does not change anything. You will not go with us."

Collin touched Kairma's hand; his voice was gentle, almost apologetic. "I agree with Naturi and Jared. We should find out what's going on down there before we put you in the middle of it."

Kairma looked over at Zedic in the hope that he would side with her. However, her brother was sound asleep next to his plate of half-eaten breakfast.

Kairma stood on the porch with the black lab at her feet as the men mounted their horses. The sun was dropping behind the granite hills, and a soft breeze laced with the scent of pine tickled her nose. As much as she would have liked to go with the men, she was safer here at the cabin. Trep said they would be back by tomorrow evening if all went well, but Kairma knew just how often things went as planned.

The eight men rode east with Zacar in the lead. Kairma was just turning to go back inside when she saw Collin break away and head back toward the cabin. Stepping away from the porch, she met him as he jumped off his horse.

His eyes were dark with passion as he grabbed her around the waist and kissed her full on the mouth. She staggered back in surprise, but Collin held on tight. He whispered harshly, "If we aren't back by dawn the day after tomorrow, ride as fast as you can for Survin. Tell your father what happened. He'll raise a posse to come help us. His hands moved up to her shoulders and he looked intently into her ice-blue eyes. "Promise me you won't come after us alone!"

When she didn't answer, he shook her. "Kairma, promise me you'll return home!"

"Okay. I promise."

Collin's palm caressed her cheek. "I know how much you want to come with us, but you're the future of our people whether you want to be or not."

Kairma looked away. "I know. I'll control myself."

Collin smiled and kissed the top of her head. "Thank you." With those words, he turned and raced back to his horse.

Kairma watched him ride away, suddenly realizing Collin had been just as forceful in his desire to keep her safe as Naturi had been. But for some reason, Collin's demand didn't get her back up the way Naturi's had.

As much as she preferred Collin's company, she understood that certain things had been set in motion many annums ago. Certain things were expected of her as the Vice Miral, and she would do whatever was best for her people. She watched the men disappear over the rise. *If I'm going to be mated to Naturi in three weeks, we had best work on our communication skills.*

She walked into the dark cabin and sat down in an overly large chair. Jesse curled up at her feet. Gazing into the low embers in the hearth, she tried in vain to picture her future.

When Collin returned to the group, Naturi's jaw was tight, and a grimace marred his handsome face. Collin looked away to the east, refusing to meet Naturi's glare. Naturi had seen Collin kiss Kairma, and the act appalled him. *How presumptuous of him. I would never force myself on her like that.* He cursed under his breath, "The fool!"

Collin ignored Naturi's scowl. He knew he shouldn't have kissed Kairma like that, but he was afraid he might never see her again. He was well aware of Naturi's claim, but until her Seridar he would kiss Kairma whenever he felt like it, and, as Trep would say, to hell with the pompous Naturi.

Zedic worked his horse between Naturi and Collin. Ever the diplomat, he tried to take their attention off each other. In his most serious tone, Zedic said, "The cloud cover will work to our favor tonight. We should be able to ride fairly close to their camp without being seen. Do you really think they might be sick?"

Collin laughed. *Zedic, one day you won't be there and I'll have to kill him.* At Zedic's puzzled look, Collin shook his head and said, "Zedic, you're a good friend." He spurred his horse ahead. "Let's hope they're sick and not planning an ambush."

Chapter 55

The cover of darkness hid them well, but it also made it nearly impossible to see the Madic camp once they were down on the plains where tall grasses blocked the light of the small campfire. Zacar knew the area quite well because he hunted antelope here often. "The Madics will be next to the river. Once we get a little closer we can send a scout to get a head count."

Toric had been telling Jared about the city. "After seeing the river that feeds the great lake north of Peireson Landing, I have a hard time thinking of this as more than a muddy creek. I can walk across this. It might be a little treacherous in the spring, but the river that flows next to the city is impossible to even swim across. They have the most amazing bridge. It's at least three wagons wide."

Zacar held up a nearly invisible hand. "Keep your voice down. Sound carries a long way. We need to dismount and walk from here." They hobbled the horses by a small ravine. "Snakes really like this long grass, so if you hear the sound of a rattle, stand very still and listen closely for it to move away."

Jared swallowed a hard lump. He really didn't like snakes.

After another thirty minutes of walking, the Survinees heard voices. It sounded like an argument. Crawling on their bellies, they moved up close enough to overhear the Madics.

A small woman with dark hair was arguing with a slightly taller man, her voice carrying clearly in the stillness of the night. "The only reason you're even here is 'cause I wanted Talon to help me. How was I to know he'd tell you and your sister about the gold? What are folks back home gonna think when they find out you and Sinara rode off with me and half a dozen men?"

"Talon's my son. Of course he'd tell me where he was goin' and I don't care what others think. I jess wanna know if you have a plan now."

"Well, it's not my fault everyone got sick. I ain't feelin' the best myself."

The woman lowered her voice. "How much farther is it?"

"I keep tellin' you, I don't know. I don't even know if there *is* a city. Might be just a row of tents or somethin'. They didn't strike me as havin' all that much sophistication. "

"We have to get help soon. Sinara may not make it through another night."

"What the hell do you want me to do?" The man stomped away from the camp.

Jared suggested someone sneak up on the lone man who had left the camp and capture him. "He's at least twenty meters from the others. The woman went into that tent, and it looks like the rest of them are asleep."

Zacar nodded. "Sounds like they are sick. I was afraid of that. I can't tell from here if it's the fever."

Zedic whispered, "I've seen a lot of sick people in my life. I'll check the man who left camp." Zedic could tell by the voice that the man in question wasn't Narvin, but that didn't mean Narvin wasn't among the sleeping men.

Jared nodded. "I'll go with you."

Jared and Zedic crawled through the tall grass. They could see the round-faced man sitting on a stump and playing with something in his pocket. Jared circled behind the man and in an instant he was rolling on the ground, his big hand over the mouth of the smaller Madic.

Zedic helped drag the man back to the others. The Madic's hands were bound and he was gagged, making it a struggle to move quietly back to the ravine where the horses had been left. Once there, Zacar put the prisoner over the back of Belle. About twenty minutes later, the Survinees had moved up the river another mile. Feeling they were a safe distance from the Madic camp, Zedic removed the gag.

They recognized him in the meager starlight. This was the former overseer of Peireson Landing, the man Narvin replaced in the last Choosing. His name was Jaimer, a man often seen hanging on every word Narvin spoke and possibly the source of the poisoned combs.

Trep was quick to pull the gag off Jaimer. "So you worthless pond scum, what brings you here?" Trep spit the words. "Did Narvin send you?"

Jaimer cautiously eyed the men around him. "No need to be upset with me, Trep. Narvin's sittin' back home in his office tower. He thinks he's pretty smart. He mighta been plannin' to visit you all in the spring—wantin' to get his hands on more of the gold and artifacts you have, but Nixon and I got the goods on him." Jaimer tried to get comfortable on the hard ground. He sounded prideful as he regaled his captives with his exploits. "Narvin gave us all the supplies we needed for this trip. Told me I could have the pick of the mines if I followed you and marked a solid trail he could follow come next spring, but I had Nixon mark a new trail."

Zedic's brows knit in confusion and Trep said, "The caves 'round the lake, I believe those are old mines. I think some of 'em were even gold mines. Oh, I know you get your gold down by the river somewhere, but with the right equipment you might get a lot more out of the mines."

Zedic turned back to Jaimer. "So you had someone lead Narvin away from here? He doesn't know how to find us?"

Jaimer nodded. "Nixon was supposed to meet us at the fork once he marked the wrong information for Narvin." He smiled wolfishly, showing a wide gap where a tooth was missing. "He's probably waitin' there now. But Nixon's a liability. He's not very smart, you know.

I continued to follow you and covered our trail real good. We only stopped here 'cause Sinara got so sick, and the trail you cut through the trees is easy enough to follow." He motioned to his pocket. "See there what Narvin gave me. He actually thinks I'm his friend. Won't he be surprised come next spring?"

Trep reached in the coat pocket and pulled out a little satin pouch full of fine white dust containing a fancy gold watch. "What's this?"

"Artuk said Narvin wanted to give a gift for helpin' him out. Nice gift, uh?"

Trep realized then that Jaimer probably wasn't the source of the poison; that left Narvin, his servant Artuk, or the woman Yevve. He shook his head and said, "You're a dead man and don't know it."

Zedic instinctively reached for the watch, thinking to destroy it, but recovered and let Trep slide it back into Jaimer's pocket.

Trep thought for a moment about the implications of the gift. The little cherub-faced man was irritating in his smugness, a puppet of a man, but there was something sinister in his voice. After a moment Trep asked, "Do ya know who'd wanna kill Lysara and Misha? I'm guessin' the hotel fire wasn't an accident."

Jaimer proudly admitted, "The fire was set by me, one of my better flames, I must admit."

Trep couldn't control himself, and both fists pummeled Jaimer in a flurry of anger. Zedic pulled Trep away and threw Jaimer back into the sitting position from which he had fallen. Trep was seething with anger. In his mind, he could still see the frightened faces of the women as he helped them to safety during the early morning fire.

Zedic took over the questioning, allowing Trep a minute to regain his composure. "So why did you burn the hotel?" He didn't tell Jaimer that the sisters had been poisoned with gold combs covered with the same white powder as his prized watch, or that there was a good possibility everyone in the Madic camp had been poisoned as well.

Jaimer spit blood from his cut lip, and the gap where his tooth was missing was even more pronounced. "See, Nixon and I had a plan to blackmail Narvin, but witnesses are bad for business, hence, Deadsville for the strumpets. But I'll be damned if they didn't get away."

Jaimer's smirk hit Trep all wrong, and with one kick Jaimer's head snapped back.

The round-faced man spoke no more.

Zedic grabbed Trep by the shoulders. "Trep, what did you do? We needed this man. We still don't know where the poison came from, or what the girls witnessed. We know this man meant to kill them, but he isn't the source of the poison."

Trep shook as he watched the life leave the little man. He squeezed his temples between his palms and slowed his breathing. "I didn't mean to kill him. I was jess so angry. I'm sorry. I reacted without thinkin'. I don't know what else to say. I'm sorry."

Naturi bent down and took a closer look at Jaimer. "This was not a good man. I think we are best to be rid of him. If the other Madics are anything like this man, we cannot allow Kairma near them."

Jared leaned over to get a better look at the dead man. "I didn't realize they were so small."

Zacar turned in the direction of the Madic camp. "Small or not, they have karracks, the great equalizers."

Zedic knew the Madics might all be dead before the night was over, and ordering someone to die was a lot different from committing the act oneself. When he'd joined the quest to hunt down the outsiders who'd found the temples, he was doing his duty—he was protecting the Crystal. Now, looking at a camp full of sickly men and women, Zedic didn't feel as confident in his duty.

Toric grabbed his karrack and motioned to the others to do the same. "Let's get this done while they are still sleeping."

☙

Trep crawled on his belly behind Zedic, toward the tall cottonwoods that blocked the view of the Madics' horses. Trep had a difficult time keeping his mind on the business at hand because his thoughts kept drifting back to Jaimer's dead eyes. Trep had never killed a man before; that the man had deserved to die didn't ease his guilt. He was sick to his stomach, and he wanted to take back the loss of control that had caused him to kick Jaimer in the head. Trep had never considered himself a violent man. In all the years of bar fights, he had never seriously injured anyone. He most regretted the look on Toric's face. Trep hoped the Survinees wouldn't be sorry for inviting him to be a part of their community. *Who am I tryin' to fool? It's my fault we're crawling out here in the dark of night. If it hadn't been for me, this sleepy little village wouldn't even know what a karrack was. Now look at 'em. Sneaking through the tall grass, seeking out enemies they didn't even know existed before tonight.*

Even in the dark, Collin could see that Trep was troubled by the death. Collin worked his way near the distressed man, and when he'd gotten close enough to Trep, he whispered, "Don't take it so hard, my friend. We probably would've invoked the Law of Fontus anyway."

"Thanks. I 'preciate your concern, but I'll be okay."

"I just hate to see a good man waste precious thoughts on a bad man."

"Y'all are all right, kid." He gave Collin a half-hearted smile. "Best we get movin' before they leave us behind."

As they crept closer, Zacar could make out the outline of a man sitting by the low fire. A karrack lay across his lap and his wide-brimmed straw hat was pulled low over his face. Zacar motioned for Toric and Jared to move around to the south and for Collin and Trep to slide around to the north. As discussed earlier, each two-man team would stand and hold their weapons on the Madics at Zacar's word.

Once everyone was in place, Zacar stood and shouted, "Don't anyone move." He had his karrack pointed at the sleepy watchman. The man attempted to raise his weapon, but one look at the giant man in front of him made him rethink being a hero. He gingerly placed his karrack by the fire and held up his hands.

The sun had set over the hills to the west when Kairma heated up a little leftover stew. While her dinner warmed, she tried to find enough ingredients to make biscuits and gravy for the men, certain they'd be back by morning. As she looked through the small pantry, she began to sense she wasn't alone. The small oil lamp she held threw wobbly shadows on the wall in front of her, making her eyes dart from shape to shape. Steeling her willpower, she went back to the main room. "Is anyone here? Lo? Anyone?"

She looked in the bedroom—nothing. The room was empty, but she could feel the eyes on her. Too scared to look out the window to see if what she was feeling was real, she stood stone-still in the middle of the room for several minutes. She knew the White Ones were very close, surrounding her. The familiar, haunting pain ate at the back of her mind as she bolted the front door and dropped the heavy wood shutters over the windows. She should have asked someone to stay with her.

In the corner by the hearth, the black hound, Jesse, whimpered. Kairma began talking to Jesse because the sound of her voice, shaky as it was, helped to calm her own nerves. "It's okay, girl. Nothing's going to get inside. The men will be back before you know it." Having lost her appetite, she took the stew off the fire and curled up on a blanket next to Jesse. She tried to sleep, but sleep wouldn't come.

The sound of something scraping the wall outside the door sent her heart racing and she wrapped her arms around the still whimpering dog. She wondered where Purder was hiding, and hoped the big cat would come to her rescue the way it had saved Trep a annum ago.

Now something was crawling on the roof. She could hear it moving around up there. It was very quiet, but occasionally it would knock dirt loose from the rafters and she could hear the fine sand hitting the hardwood floor. "Well, Jesse, you think they've come to finish me off this time? You'd think I would have learned from the last encounter, but no, Kairma thinks she's invincible sometimes." She shook her head and Jesse looked up at her. "Yes, I know. She's a foolish girl, a very foolish girl."

Chapter 56

On the plains, Zacar watched several men crawl out of bedrolls as two women came out of the tattered tent. All the Madics' weapons were collected and laid in a pile at Toric's feet. Jared counted five men and the two women. All of them looked pale and undernourished.

A young, thin man with brown hair stepped in front of the women and asked, "What's the meanin' of this? Who are you folks?"

Trep answered. "We'll be wantin' to know the same 'bout y'all now." He waved a hand, indicating the Survinees with him. "These fine folk live in this area. This land here belongs to them, and they wanna know what y'all are doin' out here."

The young man said, "My friend Jaimer asked me if I wanted to own a gold mine. He said he knew where to find one, and if I helped him bring his gear, he'd give me one."

Trep translated for Siede and Jared's sake. Having spent the summer in the city, most of the others had learned enough Madic to figure out what was being said. "I'm 'fraid your friend is dead. It was an accident, but he's dead all the same. He promised you somethin' that wasn't his to give. The mines y'all are talkin' about belong to my friends here. Ain't none of y'all gonna get one."

The young man looked over at the others with him. "This isn't exactly what we had in mind. Guess we need a new plan."

A slightly older man with darker hair and dark eyes came to his side. "We cain't go back to Peireson Landin'. Sinara will never make it."

The younger man shook his head in disgust. "Mother was right not to trust Jaimer. Now I have her out in the middle of nowhere and she's dyin', but that doesn't really change the reason for comin', does it?"

The older man shrugged and turned to Trep. "Name's Talon Durbin. This here's Machek Hipptem, his sister Gyrien." He pointed to a blond girl of fifteen or so who was standing by the tent opening. "The other woman is my mother, Nyrees, sister to Sinara. Sinara's in the tent. She's sick. Don't want to move her if we can help it. Those men there," he pointed to two stout men sitting by the fire, "are Richard Peireson, Patrick Peireson, and the old man over there is Argus Mucceli."

Argus flinched at Talon's words. "I ain't that old, boy."

Trep nodded to each of the men. "I know you boys. Y'all are Acton's sons. Run the Peireson ranch, don't ya? We bought some fine horses from y'all a few weeks ago."

Turning to the men with him, Trep introduced the Survinees. The Madics had a hard time taking their eyes off the giant man, Zacar.

Trep scratched his chin as he studied the youngest man, a boy of about sixteen. Y'all are Conrad's boy? The man who owned the lumber mill?"

"Yeah. After those savages killed my father"—Machek pointed to Naturi and Collin—"Jaimer thought I'd like to come here and pay my respects, so to speak."

Trep brows knitted together. "What are you talkin' 'bout? I thought Conrad was killed by a horse?"

Machek 's jaw tightened and his lip quivered. "Narvin told me one of the savages killed him. Said it was the one who set fire to the livery."

Trep shook his head. "That's a bunch of horse muck. The Survinees didn't start any fires or kill anyone. Why, in seven hells, would Narvin say that? He saw us on the way out of town and didn't say a word 'bout Conrad."

Talon put a hand on Machek's arm, but looked hard at Trep. "We've heard a lot of things about these folk you call the Survinees. Sheriff Bainser said they killed the Dove sisters and burned down their hotel too."

Zedic bristled. "That's a lie! We would never hurt Misha and Lysara. It was Jaimer who burned the hotel! He just admitted to it!"

Talon had a hard time understanding Zedic so Trep explained. "The Dove sisters are safe in Survin. They got really sick while crossin' the plains, but one of the Survinees is a Healer, and the women are better now. Turns out someone gave them a nice parting gift. A set of combs that had been poisoned."

Talon pursed his lips. "Not a nice gift. You say there's a Healer in Survin? Do you think we could get help for Sinara?"

Although Naturi was several inches taller than Talon, the man didn't flinch when Naturi stepped up beside Trep and said, "We are not sure we can trust you. The man you came here with just admitted setting fire to the hotel."

Taking in this latest information, Talon turned to Machek. "She's your mother. What do you want to do?"

"I don't trust them. I think they're lyin' about Jaimer. But they have all the weapons, so it's really up to them, ain't it?"

Talon nodded, squared his shoulders, and faced Naturi. "Your move."

Naturi motioned to Trep to guard the prisoners and asked Toric to join him over by a copse of cottonwoods. Collin followed them and Naturi frowned at him. "I wanted to ask my father's opinion, not yours."

Collin said, "This is a decision that should be made by all of us." His eyes were dark and his thoughts were plain. *You aren't the Comad yet.*

Naturi stopped. "Fine, we will ask the others to join us." He waved the other Survinees over.

Collin nodded, and then turned to Toric. "The red-headed men are Acton Peireson's boys, the ranch hands that taught us to break horses. I don't think they mean us any harm."

Toric looked back over the campsite. "Well, they liked us well enough then, but who knows what ideas they have now. I certainly don't like the company they were keeping."

Stroking his karrack gently, Jared said, "The women are sick. The men aren't in much better shape, and we have all the weapons." Jared's opinion was clear on his face. "We could end this here."

Collin ran a hand through his dark hair thoughtfully. "We need new blood if we can get it. We have tactical advantage, and Kairma would know whether or not the woman might be saved.

Naturi frowned. "They tell us Sinara cannot be moved, but must we risk Kairma by asking her to come here to heal their woman? I do not like this situation."

Zedic caught the end of the discussion. "You already know Kairma's answer to that. I'll go get her. The rest of you can keep an eye on the Madics. We need this resolved before their friend Nixon finds us."

Toric glanced at Naturi, and then at Collin. There was an undeniable tension building between the two young men. Collin, once the image of flippancy, had sobered over the last month, and Toric wondered if it was due to the loss of his parents or the realization he was going to lose Kairma to Naturi in another few weeks. "Well, let's split up the watches," Toric said. "Collin, you and Trep take the first watch. Naturi and I will take over in about three hours. Jared, Siede, Zacar, get some sleep. We'll wake you for your watch."

Collin nodded and went back to the camp to tell the Madics that Zedic was on his way to fetch their Healer.

Chapter 57

Kairma jerked awake. The fire had burned down to red embers and Jesse had slinked off to the door where he was pawing to be let out. "Sorry, girl. I guess I dozed off." She could still sense the presence of the White Ones, but the light of day made her feel a little less vulnerable. Taking a large knife from the cooking area and pulling out her own small blade, Kairma went to the door. "Okay, girl. I guess we can't stay in here forever."

She opened the door slowly, but nothing attacked. Jesse darted past her feet and made a beeline for the fence post. On the west end of the porch, Purder licked the fur of one of his massive paws. The big cat looked over at Kairma with obvious disinterest.

Kairma shook her head. "So where were you all night? We could have used your help, you know." Purder, of course, said nothing as he stretched hugely and slowly slinked back into the trees.

With fear keeping her on edge, Kairma climbed up into the oversized rocking chair without putting down either weapon she held. It was a very long morning as she rocked slowly back and forth. She wondered what the White Ones were waiting for.

Zedic rode hard and arrived back at the cabin before the sun reached its zenith.

Kairma had been watching for their return and her heart ached when she saw Zedic crest the hill across the small valley, riding fast and alone. She ran from the cabin and met him outside the small fenced yard. "Where is everyone? Are they hurt? What happened?"

"They're fine. We captured the Madic camp. There're five men and three women. One woman is really sick, but I think there might be something wrong with all of them. They don't look healthy to me."

"Are they Narvin's men?"

"Not really. This group came here with a man named Jaimer who claimed to be blackmailing Narvin."

Zedic filled Kairma in on all that had been learned about Jaimer and the Madics who were with him.

"I like these men less and less the more I hear about them," she said. "Let's hope Nixon has been able to leave the false directions for Narvin. You said Jaimer had the men cover their tracks. Do you think Nixon will be able to find the camp?"

Zedic followed her into the house to get her supplies. "I don't know. He has two men with him. Jaimer said Nixon was his partner in blackmailing Narvin. Doesn't sound like someone we want as a friend."

Kairma agreed as she grabbed the bag of herbs. But from what Zedic had said, it was likely she would find the strange white poison somewhere in the camp.

Zedic warned her that the Madics weren't friendly and suspected the Survinees of an array of evil deeds. "I think it may take some proof before they believe we weren't involved in the death of several townspeople. Not to mention, they're upset about the death of Jaimer."

Climbing up behind Zedic on the tall palomino, she adjusted her pack and said, "I know we need new blood in Survin, but if these people are bent on revenge, there is really only one alternative."

"I know, but that won't make it any easier to do." Zedic turned the horse eastward and they hurried toward the Madic camp.

At twilight Kairma dismounted and rubbed her sore legs. Riding double had forced them to walk slower and take a few breaks. Looking around the camp, she was astounded by the ingenuity of these people. Their shelters were made of a rough but lightweight canvas that could be collapsed easily for traveling. A large black pot hung on a metal chain above the fire. Three long metal bars came together at the center over the fire and held the chain that held the pot of stewed meat. The dishes and utensils were as intriguing as some of the things she'd discovered in the vault. Trep interrupted her thoughts to introduce her to the Madics. After a formal greeting and a few reassuring words, she was allowed to check the heart rate and temperature of each of the Madics.

As she moved from one Madic to another, she felt a strong sense of anger and fear. She had expected to find them pleasant, like she had found Trep and Zacar at first, but at least one of the men, a young boy, made her very uncomfortable.

Ignoring her feelings as best she could, she concentrated on the symptoms of the illness. Most of the Madics complained of headache and fatigue, and the younger woman complained of stomach cramps. When Kairma examined the older woman they called Sinara, she could tell by the dark circles under her eyes that the illness was much more advanced in her. Sinara was very weak and pale with clammy skin, and although she was extremely thirsty, she had difficulty keeping any food or water down.

Inside Sinara's tent, Kairma's sense of anger disappeared and was replaced by a more understood fear. Examining the older woman, Kairma could sense Sinara's panic intensifying, and she sympathized. However, Kairma couldn't be sure if the woman was afraid of her, or afraid of dying.

Searching the tent for signs of the poison Kairma had found in Misha and Lysara's gifts, she looked through clothing and several small wooden boxes. Sinara eyed her with distrust. "You won't give me the fever, will you? You look like you have it."

Kairma considered her question for a long while before answering. "No, I don't believe I will make you sick. Hopefully, I'll make you well." Carefully picking up a set of ornate glass bottles containing exotic spices, Kairma asked Sinara where they came from.

The unhealthy woman was proud of her gifts. "They were a gift from a friend. Why do you ask?"

Kairma sorted through the words in her head. Sinara's accent was so strong Kairma asked again, "Where did you get these? Have you always had these spices?"

Sinara lay back on her bed. "Narvin gave those to me a month ago." Kairma's eyes shot to the woman at the sound of the name. Sinara went on. "He also gave me some chocolate. It's a very expensive gift. I had one piece, but I was saving the rest for a little celebration when we reached our new home."

Kairma processed the words *new home*. "When did you eat the— what did you call it?—*chocolate*?"

"About a week ago."

"Did you get sick before or after you ate this gift?"

"It was the day after. I remember 'cause that was the day Nixon left us to mark a new trail. Nixon's a good man. Hope he can find his way back out of that awful country. Jaimer sent him off into those barren lands to the east of here."

Kairma nodded. She was picking up the rhythm of the language better now. As she opened the bottles of spices, she asked, "Do you cook with these?"

"Yeah, I do sometimes. Well I did until I got sick. Gyrien's been doin' most the cookin now."

"Does she use these spices?"

"I think so, but you'd have to ask her."

Kairma poured a little spice in her hand and examined it. She couldn't be sure, but it looked like a small amount of white powder was mixed in with the darker spice.

One by one, Kairma poured out the contents of the bottles. Sinara winced and Kairma smiled bleakly. "I'm sorry. I think these might be the cause of your distress. You're very sick and I hope I can help you, but I can't do anything until I can figure out what's making you so sick. I don't want any of you to eat anything you've brought with you, and everything you have must be washed thoroughly. I'll boil some water to make some rose hip and willow terrid for you. If it's the poison I suspect it is, garlic will help clean your body. I'll send Collin and Zedic to find some fresh cloves. What I have with me isn't nearly enough for everyone."

Reaching into her pack, Kairma pulled out some mint leaves and began crushing them in a soft piece of cloth. "I'd like you to hold this under your nose for a bit. It should help with the nausea. We need to get some liquids in you, and if you can't keep the garlic down we'll have to resort to an enema"

Sinara began to sweat and looked up at the young pale girl who was wiping her brow. "Thank you," Sinara said. "Is it true that someone tried to poison the Dove sisters and you were able to save them?"

"Someone gave them beautiful but poisoned combs. It was quite by accident we learned the truth. Although they're still quite ill, I'm certain they're getting better every day. We discovered a gift of maple candies had also been laced with this poison."

Sinara closed her eyes and sighed. "I guess we have a common foe."

Kairma dipped a rag in the cool water and wiped Sinara's arms. "Yes, someone seems intent on hurting us, but having a common adversary does not make us friends."

Sinara cringed. The pale girl was deadly serious.

Kairma began to loosen the woman's clothing. "It would be best if we had you take off your clothing. Poison may be hidden in the fabric you're wearing." Helping the weak woman out of her blouse, Kairma said, "I'll bring these back when I know they're clean. For now I want you to use the blankets we brought with us." Laying the soft leather coverlet over Sinara, Kairma asked, "Why are you here? Do you believe these stories about my people? Do you wish to avenge an evil?"

Sinara's voice was barely a whisper. "If I can believe all I've heard this evening, I think someone from town may have killed my husband. It had first been ruled an accident. They told me a horse kicked him in the head, and I had no reason to not believe the sheriff. The day Trep and your men left town, my son Machek came in tellin' me the livery and hotel fires were caused by your men."

Sinara sat up gingerly and took a sip of the warm terrid Kairma offered her. "Now I'm really confused. You tell me the Dove sisters are safe, and that Jaimer set the hotel fire."

Mixing herbs for a poultice, Kairma nodded. "Jaimer said as much."

Sinara closed her eyes. "I'm not surprised, just angry that I never did anything about it." When Kairma looked up, puzzled, Sinara continued. "Several weeks ago, Conrad told me Narvin wanted to buy the livery stables from the Bowart brothers, but the brothers refused to sell. When the stable burned, I suspected Narvin had a hand in it and told my sister Nyrees about it. That fire had been ruled accidental too."

Sinara was struggling to keep the terrid down so Kairma quickly gave her the poultice of mint. A few minutes later she was able to continue. "I never put it together until now, but a few days after Conrad was killed, Artuk, the taxman, stopped by with a bill. Artuk claimed Conrad owed all this money in back taxes, and since I didn't have that kind of money layin' around, we worked out a deal. If I'd sell my interests in the lumber mill I could keep my house. Machek was heartbroken. He always thought the mill would be his someday." She coughed and spit into the cloth Kairma held for her. "So, a couple weeks later, I was at my sister's. Nyrees lives across the street from the White Dove Hotel. We were sittin' on the front porch 'cause it was too hot to sleep and, I swear I saw Jaimer leave the hotel a few minutes before the fire broke out. I knew Jaimer worked closely with Narvin, but when I mentioned my suspicions to Nyrees, she thought I was bein' silly."

Zedic slipped into the tent with a ceramic bowl of broth and Kairma tested it to see if it was cool enough to drink, and then she thanked him as he left. She turned back to the pale woman on the cot.

Sinara closed her eyes and sighed. "Two days later—the day Machek told me your kin set the fires—Yevve stops by to say hello. She said Narvin was real sorry about the savages killin' Conrad, and he wanted me to have that box of spices and the chocolates. I was very surprised; the man had never given me anythin' before. I asked her why Narvin didn't send Sheriff Bainser after the men who'd done so much damage, and she tells me he's sendin' Jaimer after them. Yevve indicated that Talon was also going, and I wondered if Nyrees knew her son was going to be tracking these dangerous men."

She took a sip of the warm broth Kairma offered her and coughed a few times before going on. "I would never have considered leavin' Peireson Landin' if Machek hadn't demanded to go with Talon to seek revenge for his father's death. He's my little boy; I couldn't let him go alone. I was afraid he'd get himself killed, so I grabbed my daughter and came with him. Of course, when Nyrees heard, she insisted on comin' with us too. I never liked Narvin. The man lies so smoothly that he could make his own mother believe he was another woman's son, but that don't make him a killer." She coughed and spit up some of the broth.

Kairma carefully cleaned her face. After a moment, Kairma said, "Go on please."

Sinara laid back and gathered her strength. "Nyrees and I thought if the land to the west was good for farmin', we might stay. Sold most everythin' we had the day before we left."

Kairma mopped Sinara's clammy brow and said, "The poison may have been insurance that you would never return."

"Looking back on it, it does seem like things worked out the best for a select few. Narvin ended up with the land for his silly garden. Artuk got the lumber mill, and I heard Nixon bought the burned out White Dove Hotel. And since the Peireson boys are here, I'm wonderin' if someone's got his eye on their ranch too."

Kairma's eyes were cold and calculating when she said, "Since Nixon and Jaimer are here, someone else must be watching over their interests in the city."

"I think Yevve planned to take over Lysara's position as city planner. As Narvin's mistress, she's got her hands on everything."

Kairma held the cool cloth to Sinara's head. "I feel it's important that you know what you've walked into. In some ways, you may find us even more disagreeable than Narvin and his friends. We have laws of our own which may make you regret leaving your city."

Kairma looked deep into Sinara's eyes, trying to gauge the woman's reaction to her words. "We will not allow our location to be compromised. Our laws are absolute concerning this secrecy. You will never be allowed to leave this mountain again. Nor will your son or your daughter be allowed to leave. Do you understand what I'm telling you?"

Sinara coughed. "Yeah, but your laws won't affect me. I'm dyin'. Ask my children what they think."

Kairma's smile was sad. "You won't die if I can help it. Once you're well again, you will not be allowed to return to the city."

"I understand. I don't know how much Nixon has to do with all this, but knowin' I was right about Jaimer startin' that fire—I don't mourn his loss a bit. I think I could be comfortable here as long as my children are safe." She swallowed bile that rose in her throat. "Word is out that there are gold and silver mines here, not to mention the gemstones that are everywhere."

Kairma wondered about the rumor as she helped Sinara lay back on the cot. "Think about what I've told you. I'll send your children in so that you may tell them what I've said. Then you need to rest. I'll be back when I have some fresh garlic." Carrying Sinara's clothing, she left the small tent and walked out into the dark night.

The Peireson brothers were talking quietly by the fire with Machek as Kairma approached. They looked up at her curiously because the young woman was so very tall.

Handing Sinara's clothing to Machek, Kairma said, "Would you please put these in that pot of boiling water. The one where your sister is washing blankets? I'll need all of you to boil your clothing as well. I'm hoping to wash away any signs of poison."

Kairma lightly touched Machek's arm. "You can go in and see your mother now. She wants to speak to you and your sister."

Machek grimaced at her touch, but took his mother's clothing to Gyrien. After laying several shirts and pants over a nearby log, the two young people disappeared into their mother's tent.

Kairma sat near the Peireson brothers. She was uncomfortable again, but not particularly afraid. She stirred the fire with a long knurled stick. In an effort to make small talk, she turned to Patrick, the younger of the two men, and said, "Collin tells me you taught him how to fix a horse."

Patrick looked over at Richard. A bewildered look decorated his face. Richard was the one to respond. "'Scuse me?"

A small line appeared at the bridge of Kairma's nose as she tried to think of the right thing to say. "Collin said you helped him fix a horse to accept a rider."

Patrick laughed. "Yeah, we did. Could hardly keep Toric and Collin away from the stables after that." He reached back and picked up a small log and tossed it on the fire. "Both of 'em are good with horses."

"So what brings you here? Sinara tells me Jaimer was supposed to go after Trep and the others for the murder of Conrad Hipptem and the fires in the hotel and livery stable. Are you supposed to be avenging abuses also?"

Richard cleared his throat. "We were told we would be welcomed here. We were supposed to set up a trade route. We never heard about the murder of Conrad. Narvin did mention he thought it was strange that Naturi would ask the Bowart brothers to go to the midsummer dance the night the livery caught on fire, but we didn't think anything about it 'cause we were at the table next to Naturi all night. He never left the dance."

Patrick nodded. "Naturi had a constant line of women waiting to dance with him. He couldn't have set that fire."

Richard said, "It was several days into the ride that Machek told us about the murder of his father. We hadn't heard any of these stories. Jaimer said the Survinees set the hotel on fire, but that was ridiculous. Trep and Lysara were already planning to leave the city. Why would they want to burn her sister's hotel? When the subject of the hotel fire came up, Nixon looked like he wanted to kill Jaimer. I knew then somethin' wasn't right. Nixon has always loved Misha, though he never did nothin' about it.

"Later when we reached the last fork in the river, Jaimer sent Nixon, Chad, and Seth to mark a false trail into the desert east of here in case we were followed. We were supposed to wait for Nixon at the fork, but Jaimer made us move out the next day. He even took pains to cover our trail. It will be a miracle if Nixon can find us."

Kairma shifted slightly on her log seat. "Before he died, Jaimer told Trep that he set fire to the hotel, but I don't know who killed Machek's father."

Richard nodded sagely. "That makes more sense. I can see Jaimer doin' someone's dirty work, and Narvin got a really good deal on the land after the livery fire. Maybe the man got more ambitious after the livery fire and wanted the hotel."

Kairma stirred the coals and looked at each of the men. "We all seem to agree that Jaimer was not a good person. That still doesn't tell me why you're here now and what you plan to do."

Patrick studied his nails in the dim firelight. "Jess followin' bad advice, I think. We were gonna bring lots of new wealth back to the city—be big-time heroes. Thought we were doin' somethin' really good for Peireson Landin'. Town's named after us, you know? I think if we could find one of the gold mines we heard about, we could go home with somethin' anyway."

Kairma took a deep breath and let it out slowly. "I'm afraid you'll never see your homes again. We can't allow knowledge of our colony to leave this place, so we can't let you return. I'm sorry. You'll be given the opportunity to join our colony if you wish, but going home again isn't an option."

Richard sat up straight. "What if we don't want to stay with you?"

Kairma's voice caught in her throat and the words were no more than a whisper. "Then you must be put to death."

"*What*? You cain't be serious? So you are savages, after all!"

"I wish I could tell you why, but at this time I can only give you the choice."

"Join you or die! What kind of choice is that?"

"I'm afraid that was the choice you made when you chose to follow my people home. We'll treat you well. You'll have a home and be allowed to take mates. We would welcome you, but unfortunately we cannot set you free."

"That makes us your prisoners!" Patrick was standing now. Naturi was beside Kairma in a flash, an arrow notched in his bow.

Kairma stood and forced the bow down with her right hand. "Look at it anyway you wish, but you will not leave here. I hope in time you'll understand. You can choose to be happy, and live among us, or ..." She looked away, not having the heart to repeat the words.

Patrick's voice was sharp with controlled rage. "You sent men to our town! You came to us! You, with your jewels and gold!"

Kairma's head jerked up. "Yes, and look at what it cost us."

Richard stood up, wary of Naturi's bow. "I don't see any great loss to you. Who cares if a few people know where you live?"

Kairma's voice returned to its lower tone, but it was not apologetic. "I wish I could explain now. I will tell you when we have returned safely to Survin, but that must wait. We have more important things to consider. You have all been subjected to a powerful poison and that must take precedence."

Kairma turned and looked for Talon, Nyrees, and Argus. They were sleeping. Bad news could wait until morning. Recognizing the symptoms as being the same as the Dove sisters gave Kairma the lead she needed to solve the mystery, but it had taken hours to find the source of the poison, and she was exhausted. Kairma hoped she had arrived in time to save Sinara. The others were not nearly as sick, although in some ways Kairma thought it might have been easier to recruit them if they had been.

Finding Zedic eating by the edge of the camp, Kairma said, "Isontra will be worried. We've been gone a least a day longer than she was expecting."

Zedic swallowed a mouthful of rabbit. "It's been taken care of. Toric left as soon as he heard it was the same poison."

Kairma sat down relieved. "Thank you, Zedic. What would I do without you?"

Zedic thought for a long time, and then said, "Probably get in a lot less trouble."

Kairma laughed for the first time since she'd arrived at the small campsite. "If it weren't for you and Collin, I wouldn't be here at all." She looked around for Collin.

"And you don't think this is trouble?" Zedic followed her eyes. "He went to get the buckboard so we can move Sinara to Zacar's cabin."

"Oh. That's a good idea. Once we have her there safely, I need to go back and meet with the elders. They won't like me bringing home more strangers, Madics, at that."

"That's one meeting I'd like to miss. Have any of the Madics said they would willingly join us?"

Kairma nibbled on a piece of meat Zedic offered her. "Join us or die. What do you think they'll do?"

"Yeah, tough choice. I'm sure they'll tell us they want to be a part of the colony, but at the first chance they get, they'll run faster than this rabbit."

"I'd hate to see them looking like this rabbit. It's up to us to make sure they don't want to leave. I don't want hostages."

"It's not just them. You saw the way Hiram treated Misha and Lysara at the homecoming celebration."

"I think I can convince Grimly to welcome the Madics now. He's softened up a lot since the incident with Kaiden and Rhylee. He also likes the new clothes that came from the city. Never underestimate the power of a bribe."

Zedic handed her another stick bearing roasted rabbit. "That was pretty smart of you, giving that shirt to Grimly instead of letting me give it to Father."

"I have my moments." She chewed on the tough meat. "This could really use some spice. Where's Naturi when I need him?"

Zedic grinned. "I hear Sinara has some spices."

"Not anymore."

Chapter 58

On the edge of the hills, eleven men made camp as the sun slid behind the heavily forested hills. Jules Harman was nobody's fool. Six weeks earlier, in the bar of the Bell Lodge, Jaimer Kokel and Nixon Blong had bragged about secret mission to find the location of the gold and jewels. It didn't take long for Harman to get the information he needed, and even less time to convince Jaimer to double-cross his sponsor.

Harman knew how to take care of himself. He quickly put together a team of investors—ten men who were strong, but not too bright. He didn't risk the chance of one of his own men getting too ambitious. Jaimer left Peireson Landing with only eight men, two old women, and a girl. It was not the kind of group that could challenge a man like Harman.

Following a couple of weeks behind Jaimer, the trail had been easy to find, but recently the trail divided and became more difficult to track. Harman believed that they must be close to the source of the wealth, so he closed the distance between the groups cautiously and found Jaimer's troops stopped at a small river. He estimated Jaimer's camp to be less than a day's ride from where he lounged.

There were no signs of the Survinees the first two days and Harman began to worry that Jaimer was lost. The following morning he saw the eight Survinees in camp and was certain he was close to meeting his objective. Unfortunately the additional men posed a valid threat. Harman would bide his time until he could safely approach Jaimer's group. He had a few questions, but then, once the small group was disposed of, all the mines would belong to him.

❧

Kairma awoke curled up in Zedic's lap. One of his strong arms lay over her shoulder and the warmth of his chest was keeping the morning's chill at bay. He'd been on watch all night and was beginning to doze off. He suddenly jerked awake, startling Kairma.

Stretching, she said, "You need some sleep. I'll wake Naturi."

Zedic yawned hugely. "Fine by me."

Naturi came to relieve Zedic, who gladly crawled into Naturi's recently vacated bedroll, and Kairma went on to wake Talon, Nyrees, and Argus. After a few questions, Argus and Talon told Kairma they'd been planning to stake out a mine and settle in the mountains. When she explained the situation, as delicately as she could, she got the reaction she expected: confusion, and then intense anger, followed by resignation.

Argus yelled, "What do you mean I cain't leave again?"

Kairma replied sharply, "Well, you said you came to stay here. Consider your objective achieved."

"But what good is a gold mine if you cain't take the gold away and sell it?"

"You won't need gold."

"But I want gold. I was gonna be rich. That's why I came here."

Kairma considered the words of Argus. She was confused by their desire to possess gold and didn't understand the meaning of the word *rich*. "These mines you speak of are inhabited, and not by us."

Argus' face crinkled in confusion. "Inhabited?"

"Yes, the White Ones live in the caves. We never enter their homes."

"But your men had gold and jewels. Where did they come from?"

"Ah, the stones. There are a great many temples in the area. Some of these things were left by the gods of Nor for his people."

Argus shook his head in frustration. "This ain't goin' at all like we planned."

From his hiding place, Jules watched the Survinees break down the camp and load the wagons with supplies. He'd seen a few of these tall, copper-skinned people in town last month, but one of the men at the camp was a giant of a man, more than a half head taller than the largest of the Survinees. This wasn't good. Jules would have to figure out a way to separate them. Mounting his small band, Jules made his way through the thick forest to the edge of the valley so he could watch the wagons rumble slowly westward. There wasn't a big hurry. If Jules could discover where they were going he wouldn't need Jaimer.

As the group neared him, Jules was startled to see the Survinees had taken Jaimer's group captive. He could see the extra karracks piled in one of the wagons, meaning that of the sixteen people walking slowly past his hiding place, at least eight were unarmed. Jaimer's people looked weak and tired, and Jules assumed the Survinees had done something to incapacitate them in order to take them prisoner.

About a mile into the narrow valley, the freshly cut trail turned sharply to the south and wound up a steep embankment. Just over the top off the rise sat a roughly built log cabin in a large fenced yard. From the edge of the forest, Jules and his men watched the Survinees help Jaimer's band into the house. Jaimer, Nixon, and two other men who should have been there were not among the captives, and Jules suspected the Survinees may have already killed them. He would have to be cautious in his approach.

Chapter 59

The trip was a strain on Sinara, and there were several times Kairma worried she was pushing the woman too hard. Zacar easily carried the tiny older woman into the house while Gyrien and Nyrees, although feeling quite ill themselves, helped bring in food stores and other supplies. Soon, all the women were comfortably set up in Zacar's spare room. Padded bedrolls on the floor would serve Gyrien and Kairma, though the bed was nearly big enough for all four women.

Gyrien seemed to be the least affected by the poison, possibly recovering faster because she was much younger. She also appeared less frightened by the Survinees—and in fact was openly curious. Once Sinara was resting quietly, Gyrien went out to see if she could help Zacar prepare the evening meal. Zacar showed her where the small pantry was located and Gyrien went to work preparing vegetables for dinner while studying her captors from the corner of her eye.

Kairma sat nearby, in a padded chair by the hearth, with the intention of asking the young girl more questions. But in moments Kairma was sound asleep, only to have her brief nap interrupted when Zedic came in. "I'm sorry to wake you," he said. "I've settled the men in the tanning house. Naturi and Trep are with them now, but someone needs to speak to the elders."

Kairma rubbed the sand of sleep from her eyes, and mumbled, "That would be me." The thought of bouncing around on the buckboard made her cringe, but Zedic was right. She was the appropriate one to prepare the way for the Madics. The hours she'd spent cultivating relationships with many of the elders would benefit her now, but the gods only knew if it would be enough.

ॐ

Outside, Naturi, Trep, Jared, and Siede sat on the porch making small talk as they watched over the tannery. Inside the stone building, while Argus slept in the corner on a bundle of straw, Machek, Talon, and the Peireson brothers discussed the situation hanging over them.

Talon had considered their options and decided to join the Survinees, at least for the time being. "We should take them up on their hospitality now. We need the medicine the girl has. We can make other plans once Sinara is well."

Machek cursed. "I don't like being anyone's prisoner. And you know that's what we are. I don't understand why we ain't allowed to return home." Addressing the Peireson brothers, he said, "You boys weren't lookin' for trouble. Hell, you boys was tryin' to be friends with 'em." Machek paced aggressively back and forth across the tannery. "We only have their word about the fires or my father's murder. I cain't believe the sheriff made up all those stories. Why would he do that? They tell us they want us to become members of their village, but they don't trust us enough to give our weapons back. Why should we trust them?"

Richard picked up a piece of straw and chewed on it. "Don't really even know if your father was murdered. Remember, it was an accident until after the Survinees left Peireson Landin'. Either he was murdered, or he wasn't, but either way one of the stories we been hearin' is a lie. All things considered, I cain't say I like bein' unarmed, and that giant scares me—I never seen a man so big—but till we know more, we best sit tight."

Patrick sat on a low wooden rack. "They could've killed us yesterday. Don't make no sense to heal us only to kill us later. Maybe they need slaves."

Continuing his abject pacing, Machek barked, "I will not be a slave!"

Patrick rubbed the soft stubble of beard on his chin. "I don't pretend to know why anyone would want to poison Sinara, but it does look like we got sick from eatin' her spices. Maybe whoever did this was only after your mother."

"Jess 'cause they said it was poison don't make it true."

Richard spit out the piece of straw. "So you gonna try and go back to Peireson Landin'?"

Machek thought for a while before answering, "I wanna make sure my mother and sister are safe first. That pale girl said she was going to speak with her people. Let's see what they have to offer. I don't wanna be anyone's pet, but ..." He walked over to the doorway and looked out over the fenced yard. "They didn't deny the existence of the mines, and I didn't come all this way to go home empty-handed."

The sun was setting as Kairma and Zedic rode off to the west. Collin quickly followed and once he caught up with them, he pulled the two riders to a stop. "We have to do something about Nixon and the two men with him. I don't want to leave them wandering out on the plains. I'd rather not have any future surprises."

Kairma paled. "I was so worried about what I was going to tell the elders, I completely forgot about Nixon. Someone has to find him and deal with him. Take Jared and Siede with you. See if you can find these men. Trep, Zacar, and Naturi can keep an eye on the Madics here."

"There're eight Madics, and we have to sleep sometime. I can find Nixon and his men by myself."

"*Collin. No one goes out there alone!* Zedic, you go with him then. Make sure he doesn't get in trouble."

Zedic shook his head and rolled his eyes. "Kairma, you just said, 'No one goes out there alone.' Who's going with you?"

Kairma rubbed her forehead in frustration. "Collin, take Jared and Siede, please. They're excellent shots with a bow and sling."

"Okay, but I think Trep would be a better choice. He's been through that country a few times now."

Kairma winced. "Collin, just go find Nixon and his men. I have to get back to Survin."

Zedic looked to the east. "I got a good look at that desert. I've never seen such bad land. Collin, be safe."

Collin nodded as he watched them turn to leave, feeling uneasy for reasons he couldn't describe. He didn't want to let Kairma out of his sight, and although he trusted Zedic to take care of her, something in his gut told him there was a larger danger out there. The tension in the air was thick enough to cut with a knife.

After watching Kairma and Zedic ride away, Collin rode back to the cabin to fetch Jared and Trep. Zacar stood near the gate as Collin pulled his horse to a stop. Siede walked up and took hold of the reins, saying, "I'll tie him up out back of the tannery."

Collin shook his head. "I'll be leaving soon. I'm going to find Nixon. I'll take two men with me."

Zacar said, "I'll keep an eye on the Madics."

Collin dismounted. "There are eight of them. I don't like the odds."

Zacar shrugged. "I know, but really, where do you think they'd go?"

"I'm more afraid of them hurting one of you." Collin stared off toward the tannery where Naturi sat on an old barrel by the door, his feet propped up on the fence and a large bow in his hand.

Zacar followed Collin's gaze. "I think they know what's best. They need rest and good food."

"Don't get too comfortable. We don't know them at all."

"I'll keep the weapons under guard. Now go find their friends."

Collin left Zacar standing by the fence and went to find Jared and

Trep. Jared was anxious to get moving, but Trep suggested they leave in the morning, saying, "A good meal and some much-needed sleep would do us more good than haste, and 'sides, we wouldn't get far before dark. What's got you so all fired up, Cole? You been jumpin' 'round ever since we got back."

"I'm worried, Trep. What if these aren't the only people who followed us? What if there are a lot of people making their way here? We can't fight them all off."

"You're jess borrowin' trouble. This group was sent here for a reason. Most folks got lots better things to do than hike across the country. Y'all ain't the center of the world, ya know."

"I suppose you're right." He grinned a little sheepishly.

"Course I am. Now, let's go eat."

Inside, Nyrees was doing her best to care for Sinara. Kairma had left instructions before she and Zedic left for Survin. The stomach cramps were still keeping Sinara from eating as much as she needed, but she was sitting up now. In the kitchen, Gyrien was stirring a large pot of stew.

When Naturi came in with a load of firewood, he could see through the open doorway where Nyrees was feeding Sinara something that looked like chopped garlic. As he piled the firewood in the corner, Gyrien walked over to the hearth and poured a cup of terrid from a blackened pot. She was so fair and delicate that Naturi couldn't help but stare at her.

Gyrien shyly offered the cup to Naturi. Looking up through long pale lashes, she watched him in return. He sipped the warm liquid and nodded in a slight bow of thanks, causing an unruly lock of thick hair to fall over his brow. Gyrien blushed and went to the bedroom.

Nyrees had witnessed the exchange and warned, "Gyrien, don't do anything foolish. I know he's a looker, but we don't know anything about these folks.

The girl glanced back to the hearth where Naturi sat. "I was wondering if he was married. If we have to stay in their village, it would be nice to get to know him."

"They might not take wives in the same way we do. I've heard stories about savages who use women like farm animals."

"Kairma isn't treated like an animal. The men actually respect her more that they respect each other."

"That's because she's like Doc Winston. She can heal folks. That's not to say other women are treated well in Survin."

Under the watchful eye of her aunt, Gyrien wiped Sinara's brow with a damp cloth while stealing furtive glances at the handsome man in the outer room.

As Kairma and Zedic rode on through the dark, the rest of the men crowded around Zacar's table for the evening meal. Gyrien sat by the hearth to eat, while Nyrees ate in the bedroom with Sinara. Conversation at the large table was stilted, but not unfriendly, as Trep questioned the Madics about the area where they last saw Nixon and his men. Unfortunately, the river and plains had few major landmarks to guide them, so the best they could offer as the location was a fork in the river with the eastern branch heading into the worst-looking desert the men had ever seen.

Zacar asked if the accommodations were comfortable, and Machek had to bite his tongue to keep from saying something he might later regret. Argus answered, "It would be more comfortable if you gave our weapons back."

Zacar leaned back on two legs of his chair. "Sorry, until we know you a little better, we don't know if you can be trusted."

Machek cursed under his breath.

Naturi leaned toward the boy. "Did you have something to say?"

"No. Things are just great." The irony in his voice was thick.

As a subtle reminder, Trep said, "Sinara's looking better. I think she'll recover completely."

Machek nodded. "I guess all good things come at a price."

To Machek's surprise, Trep laughed. "Y'all are awful young to be so cynical."

After a moment, the others began to laugh too, relieving much of the tension in the room.

Trep swallowed a bite of stew, and then looked over to Talon. "Y'all have family at home, a sweetheart or somethin'?"

Talon shook his head. "It's jess my ma and me now. Pa got killed last winter when the ice broke on the river. He was fishin' too far out on the ice."

Trep's voice softened. "Sorry to hear that. I lost my ma when I was a little younger than you."

Argus said, "I lost my wife to the fever. She went to live with the others."

Trep asked, "Ya mean the Worms?"

Argus shot back angrily, "Don't call her a worm! She ain't any different than the pale girl you let take care of Sinara."

Collin looked over at Trep. "Does he think Kairma has an illness like the Worms you told us about?"

Trep shrugged. "She might look pale, but she's strong and the light don't bother her like it does most of the Worms I know 'bout."

Naturi stood abruptly and took his plate to the washtub. "There is nothing wrong with Kairma."

Conversation abruptly moved to the less delicate subjects of hunting and ways of preparing meats, and, as the fire in the oversized hearth burned down, Collin, Trep, and Jared made preparations to leave for the badlands in search of Nixon.

Fingers of light slipped through the trees in the east as Jules watched Collin, Jared, and Trep leave the yard, heading back toward the plains. Things were going well. Two Survinees left at dusk the night before, and three more this morning. Jules calculated there were only three Survinees left to guard Jaimer's group—although one of them was a giant. He sent three of his own men to follow the Survinees who went east and waited for the best time to strike. He still had seven more of his own brutes to take care of the people remaining in the cabin. From the men, he would get information, and from the women—well he'd find a use for them. He thought the young one was pretty enough, and the two older women might make good housekeepers.

Chapter 60

Worry awakened Isontra early that morning. The day before, Toric had filled her in on the condition of the Madic camp, but Isontra was too nervous to sleep. She was tending the hearth fire in the hospital when Kairma and Zedic walked in looking worse for the wear. Isontra noticed Kairma was walking funny and her voice was filled with concern. "What's wrong, dear? Are you hurt?"

Kairma sat down slowly on the side of a cot and rubbed her thighs. "I can't believe I just spent all night on the back of a horse. I'll never walk right again."

Isontra was relived. "Toric tells me the Madics have been poisoned similar to Lysara and Misha. Is that true?"

Kairma stretched her back and yawned. "As far I can tell, it's the same kind of poison. I found what looked like the same white powder in the spices Narvin's assistant had given Sinara. She'd made several meals using the spices, but I think Sinara may have eaten more of the poison. She's far worse than the others."

Isontra poured Kairma and Zedic a cup of hot terrid. Zedic waved it off. "I'm going to check on Misha. I thought she would be here."

Isontra set the pottery cup on the table. "Misha and Lysara are staying in the home Trep is using. They really wanted to get away from here for a while."

Zedic nodded and slipped out the south door. Kairma sipped her

512

hot drink and then said, "We need a council meeting. I have a lot of things I'd like to cover and some people may not be too receptive."

"Your parents will be up soon. Why don't you take a short nap and I'll come get you when we're ready?"

"Thank you, Gramme. I'm really tired." She rolled over and was asleep in a minute. Isontra gently covered her with a light blanket and then went to speak with Tamron and Jettena.

When Kairma awoke her legs were stiff and she had trouble getting out of bed. The cold cup of terrid on the small table by the bed told her she'd slept for several hours. Rubbing her thighs, she hobbled over to the hearth where a pot of hot water hung over a low fire. She dipped a bundle of cloth in the hot water, and after wringing out the extra moisture she sat on a stool placing the hot rags on the inside of her thighs. The heat felt wonderful and Kairma vowed to never ride a horse again.

Jettena came into the large hospital room with a bundle of flowers. Kairma smiled. Her mother always made the meeting space formal yet inviting. Kairma moved to sit at the large, elaborately carved meeting table. Jettena pulled her toward the door. "Oh, no, you don't. You need to change your clothes. You've been wearing these for three days and you slept in them as well. If you want people to listen to you, don't distract them with unnecessary matters like filthy clothes."

Kairma quickly slipped into her room where she found Kinter folding clothes. Entering the room the two girls shared, Kairma asked, "Kinter, can you help me choose something to wear?"

Kinter stopped and looked at her sister. On one hand, Kinter was flattered that Kairma acknowledged her ability to dress properly, but on the other hand, she wasn't sure she wanted Kairma to look good. After a moment of deliberation, Kinter sighed. Thumbing through Kairma's messy shelf of clothing, Kinter said, "You need to look like you're sure of yourself. Take off the scarf. Everyone knows your hair is white. Wearing the scarf just makes you look like you're ashamed of it."

"I am, I think."

"Well, don't let anyone else know, okay? Put on this tan dress and we'll tie the scarf Zedic gave you around your neck, like this." Kinter arranged the scarf so a splash of peach fell gently over Kairma's left shoulder. "There. You look positively majestic."

"Thank you, Kinter. This really means a lot to me."

Kinter harrumphed. "Well, good luck with the meeting. I'll be there in a few minutes."

Kairma paced nervously as the elders came in and took their seats at the long oak table in the corner of the Grand Hall. The meeting table in the great room of the Chancery was reserved for less formal occasions. It was far too small to hold the thirteen people who made up the decision makers of Survin. Jettena's bouquet of snapdragons and violets adorned the oak table along with several pitchers of hot terrid and cool water. A low fire burning in each of the two hearths helped draw out the dampness of the room's stone walls and ceiling.

Kairma glanced at the narrow cots that lined the east wall, empty now that Misha and Lysara had been moved to a home of their own. She was glad she didn't have to move the women in order to have privacy for this meeting. It was possible Misha and Lysara knew the Madics she was intending to bring home and if the outcome of this meeting were negative, she didn't want to upset the two women. If it looked as if the Madics would be accepted, Kairma would have time to find out more about them before bringing them home.

At ninety annums old, Addison was the oldest member of the elders, but her mind was sharp and her bright blue eyes missed nothing. "Kairma, that's a lovely scarf. Was it a gift from the city? I don't recognize the workmanship." Addison was always cordial but never showed anyone what she was thinking until the final vote.

Kairma nodded, held the chair for the fragile woman, and said, "Zedic brought back wonderful fabrics in many colors." She looked over to Zedic, but he was in deep conversation with Hiram. She hoped it was going well. Zedic understood the necessity of winning Hiram's vote.

Mylinda came in with her mother, Martena. Kairma couldn't read their closed faces and briefly wondered if Mylinda blamed her and Isontra for the tragic death of her son, Diakus. She saw a fleeting acknowledgment pass between Isontra and Martena, but was at a loss to understand the reason for it. She hoped Isontra had taken time to brief the elders in the hours while she rested from her long ride home.

Everyone was seated and with a few words Isontra brought the meeting to order. "Thank you for coming on such short notice. We don't often have need for such formalities, but Kairma has some very important data to share with you. We need to make a decision regarding this information immediately."

Kairma moved as gracefully as she could to the end of the long table. All eyes turned to her and she felt the blood rush to her cheeks again. In her mind's eye, she focused on the Crystal, asking it for the strength and the words to convince these powerful members of Survin to side with her on another breach of law. "As you all understand, Survin is a small community. Most of us are first and second generation cousins. There are less than twenty people unmated at present if you don't count those under the age of seven." Kairma clasped her hands behind her back as she had often seen Isontra do, and marveled at how the small gesture hid the nervous twitch in her hands. "As you know, we discovered a group of Madics who followed our men home from the city. There is one extended family and three unrelated men. The family consists of two sisters, each with a son of mating age. Sinara also has a daughter. Two of the other three men are in their late twenties and I would guess Argus is about thirty-five. They're smaller than us, but with the Blood Rite I believe they could survive the harsh winters here and have many children."

Grimly snarled. "I thought these people were trying to kill us. Are we supposed to be friends with them now?"

Kairma looked to Zedic to explain. Standing, he said, "We discovered a man called Jaimer. Nixon, Jaimer's associate, was instructed to make the false trail for anyone who might follow, and Jaimer was supposed to wait for him, but Jaimer double-crossed him. Nixon is now quite possibly lost forever in the badlands to the east."

Kairma cleared her throat. "We have made preparations to intercept Nixon. If he proves to have the same disposition as Jaimer, Collin has instructions to invoke the Law of Fontus immediately. We have taken care of Jaimer." She didn't explain how Jaimer was killed. She only relayed the confessions Jaimer spoke before his death. "We'll have a great ally in Zacar, who has promised to help guard our eastern borders." She looked slowly to each of the elders seated there. "We've been through a lot of changes over the last few annums and I know this is difficult for many of you to accept, but the introduction of the karrack *has* made us stronger. The introduction of the Madics will make us more diverse, and the introduction of their tools and ideas will make us more prosperous."

Isontra rose from her seat and stood beside Kairma. "We want this decision to be unanimous. It's important that Survin sees this final change as not only necessary, but as a blessing."

Grimly conferred with the three most outspoken among the dissenters. Hiram was prepared to stand against the Healers, but Grimly helped sway the older man. "I look around and I see what the Healers are talking about. I've been talking to my granddaughters, Ember and Rose. They have few choices for mates. I think they both wanted to mate with Naturi, but he'll be taken this Harvest Seridar. I never felt comfortable with all this change, but the men did come back, and they did bring some convenient tools with them. My only concern is this man, Narvin." He searched Kairma with his dark gray eyes. "But she seems to be convinced he's not a threat to us."

Martena chewed on a ragged nail. "I never would have thought it, but that young Kairma has grown into quite a Healer. Isontra, you have done more than I'd have thought possible. You should have seen the way Kairma handled things when that bear attacked Rhylee and Kaiden. She might have more wits than we usually give her credit for."

Tristan was nearly as old as Addison, but not as well-preserved. He always had the look of a man about to fall asleep, but he looked up suddenly at the words *bear attack*. "She did a fine job. I helped her as well as I could, you know. Those two were in a fierce mess."

Sabra looked over at Kairma. "Yes, thank you for my son's life. Kaiden is doing quite well." She looked across the table, her wrinkled brown eyes focused on Tamron, but her words were meant for everyone. "I'd like to add a word about inviting strangers to live with us. I was your milk-mother when you were a babe. I raised you as my own son and I've been nothing but proud of the man you've become. I wish your real mother could have been with us, even if that meant giving you up." She looked up at Kairma with a mother's pride. "As my surrogate son, Tamron has given me a strong granddaughter. It pleases me that she is willing to invite these strangers to live with us."

Noah brushed back his thin white hair and added thoughtfully, "I saw Kairma when Efram attacked her in the Gathering House. She held her place real well with him. She came to visit with us after those tragic deaths this summer too. If she says these people are needed, I believe her."

Kairma was uncomfortable with the way they were discussing her abilities as if she wasn't in the room.

Mylinda cleared her throat. Her faced had aged over the summer, a darkness settling in her once laughing brown eyes. "A parent should never have to outlive their child. I was well aware of the flaws in my son, Diakus, but I still loved him as only a mother could. I know he blamed the Healing family for not being able to save his oldest children. It may well have been an irrational grudge, but I understand it more now than I did then. Kairma argued to let Collin leave when his presence may have saved my son." Mylinda's eyes were dark and she kneaded her hands nervously in her lap. "Imagine my surprise when Kairma came to comfort me. At first I wouldn't speak to her, but she never gave up on me." Tears welled up in her eyes. "I know it wasn't Kairma's fault Collin wanted to go to the city. It was my fault. I should have been there for him in his hour of need. I understand now that because he was unhappy, he would have left with or without our blessing and the results would have been the same."

Grimly looked over at the pale girl. "She did an outstanding job at the funeral service for Massie and Diakus, didn't she? I think we should give her our support on this. Agreed?"

Hiram was the last holdout. He felt cornered and grumbled under his breath, "No good will come of this. There are reasons for our laws, and we shouldn't go changing them every few annums."

Martena turned to Hiram. "Well, what's your vote? Everyone else is agreed."

All eyes settled on Hiram, and the room was deathly silent for several minutes. When he finally consented, making the vote unanimous, a wave of relief swept through the air.

Chapter 61

The following morning, Zedic enlisted the help of Efram and Dillon. "Those people from the city are pretty sick. We may have to carry them part of the way."

Efram made a face, and Dillon laughed. "Ever the one to help out, huh, Efram?"

"I do my share. I just had other plans today."

Dillon rolled his eyes. "Sure. You were going to help Alyssum in the field today. I heard the way you were talking to her last night in the Gathering House."

Efram shrugged off Dillon's teasing and went to get his gear for the trip.

Joining the three men as they came through the Grand Hall, Kairma said, "I swore I'd never ride another horse, but I have medicine to give Sinara."

Zedic grinned. "Of course you do. And there isn't anyone here who could administer it for you."

Kairma felt her cheeks flush, but she got on the horse. Before leaving, Kairma suggested the sentry around the canyon be doubled. "I want our newest members to see the futility of trying to escape. Until we know for sure they've accepted our way of life, they must be guarded day and night. I want to make them as comfortable as we can without giving them any ideas about leaving."

After two days of hard riding, they arrived at Zacar's home shortly after midday. The cabin was quiet, and no one answered their calls. Searching the tannery they found signs of a struggle, and Talon lying half buried in straw. Kairma dropped to her knees by his side and checked for a heartbeat, but the coldness of his skin told her the truth. "Zedic, he's dead. Someone killed him."

Efram and Dillon stayed on their horses, but Zedic was beside Kairma in a flash.

Kairma grimaced. "Looks like a knife wound. We better check inside."

Outside, Zedic called to the other men. "Something's wrong. Arm your bows." Zedic loaded his karrack, and then, crawling up the steps onto the porch, he made his way to the door. He kicked out a foot and the door flew open. Nothing moved. The cabin was empty.

Beside the porch, Dillon's eyes were saucers. "Where did they go?"

Zedic studied the trail to the east. "I don't know, Dillon. I think someone may have abducted them. There was quite a struggle."

Efram spit out a long piece of grass he'd been chewing on. "That's silly. Why would they do that?"

Zedic walked over to the tree line. "Talon must have fought with someone in the tannery. Our people are certainly hostages now. If not, they would have stayed here."

Kairma was across the narrow valley. "Hey! I found horse prints here. A lot of horse prints. I'm guessing Nixon's group joined the original group along with a few people we weren't expecting. The tracks lead north."

The three men joined Kairma and began tracking the prints. Efram found a set of tracks going east. "Looks like they split up. Three men went this way. I'll follow them."

Kairma frowned. "I don't want to spilt up. They outnumber us already."

"Your call, sister," Efram said and rejoined the group.

Zedic suggested they go after the smaller group first. "We'll eliminate the weaker threat, take their weapons, and then go after the others."

Kairma agreed, and the four of them headed east through the trees. They had barely covered half a mile before they found the men. Arrows had killed all three Madics. The projectiles were gone, but the wounds were familiar. Efram stood over one of the bodies. "Good shot. Looks like maybe Naturi has learned to hunt after all."

Kairma scanned the trees. "I don't think so." She could feel the presence of the familiar pain. "We might not be alone out here."

The three men searched the shadows, but saw nothing.

Retracing their steps, they started over at the place the trails split. One of the women had torn a piece of her blouse on a wild rose bush and Kairma picked up the tiny scrap of cloth. "They're walking. If we hurry we can catch them."

Dillon looked white. "The sun is setting. We should go back to the cabin."

Zedic shook his head. "We sleep under the stars tonight."

Efram cursed. "Stars and stones, man! You want to end up like those men we just found? We have to get inside before dark."

Kairma dismounted and secured her horse near a thick clump of grass. "We've ridden hard for two days and we can't track them in the dark, so we'd best take advantage of the break."

Following Kairma's lead Zedic hobbled his horse and said, "We'll build a fire and stand watch."

Kairma shook her head. "I don't think we should have a fire. It might attract the wrong attention."

"Kairma, you're crazy." Efram's words rang bitterly in the darkening evening. "We have to have a fire out here. Do you want the White Ones to have us for dinner?"

Kairma stood her ground. "We don't want the Madics to see our fire. If it comes to the White Ones, the fire won't help. You were there when Toric and Grimly went after Naturi. You know they have bows. A fire will only make you a well-lit target."

Zedic stood. "Good thinking. Let's see if there's anything to eat. I wasn't thinking about having many meals on the road when we left home."

The packs had more than enough for a couple of days. Grimly had seen to their packs before they left and had told them how important it was to never leave home without extra food and water.

The night was nearly moonless and the forest was exceedingly dark. As they huddled together in a circle facing outward, they could see the glimmer of a distant light through the trees. Kairma jumped up. "Look, a fire. I think that might be the people we're searching for. I can't tell how far it is, but let's move. Maybe we can recapture our friends."

It wasn't as easy as it sounded, stumbling through the trees in the dark. They often lost sight of the fire and had to back up and take another route through the forest. A sliver of moon was setting before they reached the ridge where their friends were being held captive. They were surprised to see the two women bound by thick cords and tied together around a single tree. Six men were tied in groups of two, and Zacar and Gyrien weren't among the captives. Kairma prayed to Nor that they were still alive and safe. Four unfamiliar, scruffy-looking Madics sat around the fire pit and two others walked the perimeter of the camp.

"Don't move or I'll drop you where—ughggg." The Madic's words were cut off abruptly, and everyone scrambled for cover. Another small man came from the outer edge of the camp, stomping through the trees to see what had alerted his partner.

Kairma could see that the man had Dillon by the neck. The boy was fighting hard as they sprawled on the ground. Crawling over to him, Kairma pulled out her knife, but she was having trouble getting behind them. Before she finished the horrible thought of what she was about to do, an arrow slammed into the Madic's back. The other men from the camp were on their way now.

In one frantic wrench, Kairma pulled Dillon off the ground. "Go! Up there! Hide in those rocks!" She was about to follow him, when she saw Efram go down under the weight of another Madic. She turned to tell Dillon to shoot the man with his bow, but Dillon was gone—his bow was lying on the ground where he'd fought for his life.

Taking the arrow from the dead man's back, Kairma placed it in the bow and drew the string. Her hands were shaking too much. She was going to hit Efram. She wasn't good with a bow— her only training was playful contests with Collin and Zedic. She needed Naturi, but he was tied to Siede fifty feet away. She raised the bow and took aim, but before she could release the shaking arrow, the Madic wrestling with Efram received an arrow in the neck. She had to turn away as blood gushed from the wound, covering Efram with hot red fluid.

Nausea seized her. *Where's Zedic?* Searching the trees and the nearby campsite, Kairma couldn't find him. Two more Madics started from the encampment toward her. She fired the arrow notched in Dillon's bow, hitting the closer man in the leg. It wasn't a fatal wound, but it stopped his advance. The Madic fired at her as she ran through the trees to where Efram was struggling under the dead Madic. Grabbing the arrow lodged in the man's neck, she notching it before swinging around to face the other adversary. Efram was on his feet in time to see Kairma launch an arrow into the shoulder of the man in front of her. As the Madic was hit, he squeezed on the trigger of his karrack, and the noise was deafening. The bullet hit Efram in the foot and he went down like a rock. More karrack firing could be heard on the other side of the camp and Kairma realized Zedic must be there, drawing the Madics away. She was breathing hard and sweat ran into her eyes and matted her hair. In the meager light of the fire, Kairma could see a Madic raise his karrack, aiming it at Zedic's chest. "Zedic! Look out!"

He turned suddenly and the bullet missed her brother. Kairma dropped to her knees, panting in relief. A small, hairy man grabbed her as she knelt near the edge of the camp. She didn't remember running toward Zedic, but she could see him struggling with another Madic not fifteen feet away, across the camp. The rough hand pushed her down on her hands and knees, but as she went down she rolled to the left, pulling her knife from the belt at her waist. Losing his balance, the attacking man rolled with her, and then on top of her. She was average size for a Survinees woman, but had the Madic by more than six inches, and her knife found its way into his chest before Kairma could acknowledge the action.

Still shaking, she staggered to her feet to see a man dragging Efram toward the camp. Her hands and clothes were covered in blood and she thought she was going to be very sick. In a voice as brutal as she could muster, she shouted, "Stop! Let him go!"

The man looked back at Kairma and froze. Efram dropped on his knees in front of his captor—his eyes alight with fear as he looked up at Kairma.

As the man dropped to his knees, Kairma looked across the camp where Zedic stood regally, flanked by twenty or more White Ones. Kairma watched the eyes of everyone turn toward her and then to something beside her. She was afraid to look, but look she did. On either side of her, a line of ten or more White Ones held bows, arrows notched. They weren't aiming them at her, but at the men who had captured her friends.

Kairma walked slowly into the camp and untied Naturi and Siede. Her hands trembled as she freed Sinara and Nyrees. In silence, Siede and Naturi freed the other four men and met Zedic by the edge of the camp. Without knowing why, Kairma understood they were free to go. She started moving toward the rocks where she hoped Dillon had found solace. Almost as an afterthought, Kairma turned back to the camp and put out the fire. As she hurried away, she heard the hiss of arrows in the dark and knew the remaining men would threaten her no more.

Chapter 62

Several miles northeast of Zacar's cabin, Collin and Jared spotted a fire near the river. Hoping it was the men they sought, they hurried past small hills green with prairie sand reed and Canada wild rye. They rode through thick grassland while to the east the land was barren and dead. Tall cottonwoods, willows, and elms lined the river bottom, helping them keep their bearings. As they drew near the fire, it became apparent the small band of men were weary and in need of help. One man looked as if he might already be dead. As Collin, Trep, and Jared approached, the two Madics seated by the fire didn't raise their weapons, but slowly moved them away. A thin man with stringy dark hair stood up slowly. "My name is Seth Rowin," he said, and then he pointed to the slightly taller and stockier man sitting by the fire. "And this is Chad Ontent. We're mighty glad to see you folk. Thought we were destined to wander these plains forever. You seen the rest of our party?"

Collin, Trep, and Jared remained mounted, holding their karracks at the ready. Collin pointed to the man Seth had not introduced. "Is that Nixon?"

"Was Nixon. He died early this mornin'. Have you found Jaimer? I'd like to have a few words with him."

Collin shook his head, his voice grim. "Jaimer's with Nixon now. The rest of your party is about two days' ride from here."

525

Chad slowly climbed to his feet. "Did he get the sickness like Sinara and Nixon?"

Collin looked over at Trep, wondering how much he should tell these men. Trep nodded for Collin to continue. "Jaimer died of a well-deserved broken neck, but Sinara is doing better. Poison in her spices was making her sick. She should be fine in a few weeks."

Seth looked very relieved. "That's good news. I felt so bad when she wanted to bring her two children on this crossin'. I've traveled a bit and the plains ain't no place for women and children."

Collin studied the men before him. "So what do we do with you two?"

"We might make it back to the city before winter sets in if we had our horses. Wolves run 'em off a few days ago."

Collin shook his head. "You won't be going back to the city. You want to bury that man?"

Chad nodded. "I think we should. He wasn't a bad man. He was just mixed up with some really bad folks and this is how they repaid him—strandin' him out in the middle of nowhere."

Collin slipped off his horse and pulled a small shovel from his pack. It was his favorite acquisition from the city. "He was in league with Jaimer. That makes him a bad man in my mind."

Using a sharp, flat rock, Chad helped dig the shallow grave. "I was convinced you folk were truly evil. We heard you was responsible for the fire in the livery and the hotel. While we were lost, and tryin' to save our hides, Nixon told us it was Jaimer's plan to take over all your mines. He told us that Jaimer set the fires too. Claimed Vaden killed Conrad Hipptem and Samuel Mories." He looked over his shoulder at the barren land they had left. "Jaimer was intent on leadin' everyone into that desert. I think he was afraid others would take his mines if given the chance."

Jared helped lower the dead man into the grave. "Is that why you're here, to take over our village, to steal our—what did you call them?—our mines?"

Chad flinched. "I don't want anythin' from you. I just want to go back home again."

Collin stood still, sandy dirt sitting on the shovel he held. "I told you that isn't going to happen."

"What will you do with us?" asked Seth, his dark eyes growing darker.

"We're going to take you with us for now. We'll let the elders sort it out."

Jared was putting out the dying campfire. "We can't hope to cover the signs of this camp and you can see it from quite a distance."

Chad nodded. "We were hopin' someone would find us."

Jared asked, "What about a fire? We could burn all the grass around here and that would hide it."

Trep whirled around. "Are y'all crazy? Have ya ever seen a grass fire? A fire like that would eat up everythin' in sight, includin' most of the trees on y'all's mountain! There's no way to control fire once it's been set."

"So what should we do?"

"We pray no one comes this way before next spring."

Several miles to the west, Naturi and Siede helped carry Efram. The bullet had gone clean through his foot, but the wound looked like it would heal if kept clean so Kairma wiped it with antiseptic and made a bandage from Efram's blood-soaked shirt.

As they made their way back to the cabin, they found Dillon standing in front of the rock outcropping where Kairma told him to hide. His eyes were enormous as he greeted her formally. "You were amazing, Kairma. I saw you take down three of them."

Kairma was still shaking. She didn't feel amazing at the moment. She knew they would all have been killed or captured if the White Ones hadn't come to their aid. *If I weren't nearly as pale as them, would we have been slaughtered as well?* She returned Dillon's greeting and handed his bow back to him. "Thanks for the use of your bow."

Dillon shook his head. "No, you keep it."

Kairma tried to smile, but it looked more like a grimace. "I appreciate the thought, but I really don't need it."

As they walked, Machek asked the question the others were afraid to voice. "Do you command an army of Worms?"

Kairma turned toward his voice and asked, "Worms?"

Machek explained the name to her and asked again if she was their leader.

"No. I've never seen them act like that before. I think they felt the Madics who captured you were the bigger threat." Her mind was racing with possibilities. She didn't understand the motives of the White Ones. They attacked her four annums ago, nearly killing her, yet tonight they let her and her friends go free. Uncomfortable with her lack of understanding, she changed the subject. "What happened? Where is Zacar?"

Naturi, face flushed with shame, but he accepted the blame for not having posted sentries. "Zacar told us he was going out for wood—we used up his reserves. He said there was a good supply of wood on the next ridge and asked if we would be okay without him for the day. We helped him hook up a travois to one of the horses. Gyrien offered to go with him, and Jesse followed. They left about mid-morning. I was in the cabin making something to eat and Siede stayed outside to keep an eye on the others. Our new friends had made no attempt to leave, so we had become complacent in our watch."

Naturi glanced at the small men walking beside him, but the darkness hid their faces. "It was only moments after Zacar and Gyrien left that three men kicked open the cabin door and threatened us with karracks. As they led us from the house, we saw other men escorting Siede and four of the men from Peireson Landing across the yard."

Siede took up the story from there. "We were talking about Survin. Talon wanted to know what I did there." He paused as his throat closed on him. "The boy never had a chance. He was sitting on the rail near the door when the first man came in. The man didn't see Talon at first, because he was looking at the rest of us. Talon jumped him and they wrestled to the ground. Before any of us could intervene, three more men came in with karracks raised. When the other men arrived, the man fighting with Talon killed him, even though Talon had stopped struggling."

Nyrees fell to the ground, sobbing. She had hoped her son escaped when she didn't see him come out of the tannery. Kairma went to comfort her as best she could. "Let's stop for a while. Everyone has been through a lot tonight."

Efram was the most pleased with the idea of stopping. His foot was throbbing painfully, but he didn't want to complain. He had watched Kairma viciously fight the Madics who had threatened their lives only hours before, in stark contrast to the gentle way she now comforted a mother who had just lost her son. He once felt nothing but contempt for her, believing she was abnormal, almost frightening. But tonight she saved his life, not once, but twice. He felt a profound sense of respect, although she was still fearsome to behold.

After a short rest, Kairma went to check Efram's wound. "You don't look so good, Efram—nearly as pale as me."

"I'm fine." Beads of sweat appeared on his forehead and Kairma seriously doubted he was fine. "You need rest. Your body will heal better if you can sleep."

"Can't be expected to walk in my sleep, can I?"

Kairma chewed her lower lip. "I think I have something in my pack."

She sorted through a dozen different leather bags until she found what she was looking for. The herbs helped him sleep as the men took turns carrying him through the night.

A few hours before daylight they reached the cabin and Zacar came to greet them, his forehead knotted with worry. He repeatedly apologized for leaving them without sufficient defense. "Most people don't even know I'm here. I should have thought about the possibility of others being out there. I should never have left you here. I should have at least left Jesse behind—he wouldn't bite, but he would've barked to warn you someone was approaching."

He helped the injured Efram to a bed as he talked. "We returned from our wood gathering just before dark. The place was too quiet. I made Gyrien wait by the edge of the cabin until I knew it was clear." Zacar poured hot terrid for everyone. "Once I knew Gyrien was safe, I went to check the tannery. That's where I found the young boy. I didn't want her to see her cousin until I had a chance to clean up the blood."

Setting plates on the table, Gyrien said, "I was mad that Zacar wouldn't let me see Talon, but he's big—scary big." She looked shyly up at Zacar.

Zacar smiled at the tiny girl, apologized for being so scary, and then continued his account. "By the time Talon was presentable to Gyrien, it was too dark to track the men who killed the boy. So we busied ourselves digging a grave, hoping we could find you come morning."

Zedic said, "Don't worry about it. Some things just take us by surprise."

Kairma stayed in the back room to look after Efram while the others gathered around the table to eat leftover bread and stew. Naturi described how they had been captured, and how Kairma and Zedic had rescued them.

From the other room, Kairma could hear Naturi's tale and felt a little embarrassed that Naturi embellished her actions. Sitting on the bed next to him, Kairma worried. Efram was feverish and sleeping fitfully. Trying to ignore the conversation around the table, she replaced the cold compress on Efram's head.

He mumbled her name and she said, "I'm right here, Efram. I won't let anything happen to you. Get some rest." She thought he might have said, "I'm sorry," before he drifted back to sleep.

The sun was rising in the east as the tired group finished their breakfast and found a place to sleep for a few hours. Once everyone was settled, Zacar set watch at the front gate.

Collin packed up their supplies while Trep and Jared cleaned up the campsite. After Nixon was buried, the small band made their way back into the dark hills of conifers and spruce. It was past midday when they neared Zacar's cabin. Trep rode ahead to let Zacar know they had found Nixon's men.

Zacar met him at the gate looking somber. "Good to see you found the men. Seems you're missin' one. Should I worry?"

Trep shook his head. "Nixon's spendin' time with his friend Jaimer."

Zacar looked wary. "Your doing?"

"No, he was already dead when we got there. The men with him are in rough shape too."

By this time Collin and Jared had reached the gate. They could see that something was bothering the big man, but waited for him to speak. When he did, he asked how they were holding up.

Collin shrugged. "We've been better. Do you think you might have room for us? We've been riding double for too long, and these men"—he indicated Chad and Seth—"are in no shape to ride all night."

Trep smiled at Zacar. "Well, is y'all's hotel open for business?"

Zacar shook his head and rubbed his eyes with one hand. "You know, I lived here alone for years, then Purder finds you with a broken leg, and it's been like a Harvest Celebration here ever since. It's going to be like a tomb here once you've all gone away." A long moment passed before he went on. "Of course you can stay." His words were friendly, but there was an unfamiliar darkness in his face.

Trep waited patiently for Zacar to continue. After a few minutes, Zacar said, "Zedic and Kairma just got back this morning. They've been through a lot. We had a bit of trouble last night."

Collin was off his horse in a flash. "Is she okay?"

"Yes, most everyone is fine. We had some trouble and Talon was killed."

Trep cringed. "Did he try to leave?"

"No," Zacar said. "We had visitors yesterday. I'll let Naturi or Zedic tell you what happened. Kairma plans to move everyone into Survin tomorrow."

Helping Chad off his horse, Collin said, "I guess Kairma was successful in getting the elders to accept the Madics. I hope we're not making a mistake."

Trep was leading the new prisoners to the tannery, but Zacar invited everyone inside. Finding a comfortable place by the hearth, Trep spent the remainder of the afternoon detailing what they had learned about Nixon. In turn, Naturi explained what happened while Trep and Collin were gone.

Sinara was upset when she heard about Nixon's death, but all of the Madics were grateful to Collin and Trep for finding Chad and Seth. When Chad told Machek that Vaden had killed his father, Machek demanded proof, but there was no proof to be found. This was the third story he'd been told, and he didn't know what to believe anymore. He had known Chad for years, and knew he had no reason to lie, but he couldn't be sure about Nixon. Although the Survinees had shown him nothing but kindness, they were holding him captive. So as night fell, Machek made plans to escape, but he never got the chance to leave.

Richard warned him. "You cain't make it back alone. When the time is right, we'll avenge your father, if that's what you need. For now, let's make the best of what we have. That white-haired girl could have left us to die, but she helped us when we were sick, and again last night. I'm not sure why those men captured us, maybe for information, but *they* killed Talon. She could have taken only her own people and left us there."

Argus said, "She wants us to join her village."

Machek stopped struggling against them. "I won't be a slave."

"I don't think that's what they have in mind, but we'll see."

The following day everyone was packed into the wagon or onto horses. Kairma rode beside Efram, who was laid in the back of a wagon and covered with blankets. The ride was rough, but Efram was in no condition to walk. The herbs Kairma gave him were the strongest she could find but he slept uneasily most of the way to Survin.

Chapter 63

Kinter looked up from the hospital bed she was making when Collin and Jared led in two men who were obviously from the plains. They were much shorter than the Survinees and dressed in the traditional city garb Trep wore. Behind them, Trep and Siede led several more Madics into the hospital. Soon the room held nine small people of assorted coloring. Kinter marveled at the fair yellow hair of Gyrien and Chad. It was almost as pale as Kairma's hair.

Walking over to pour a drink of water from a ceramic pitcher, Collin told Kinter what had transpired since they discovered Nixon's men on the plains, but Kinter's mouth dropped open when Dillon told her about the night the other band of Madics attacked. She got confirmation of Dillon's story from Siede and Naturi. Looking at Kairma, she could see her sister's clothing covered with dried blood, as was Efram's buckskin shirt. She watched in awe as Jared and Kairma saw to bedding Efram and Sinara on narrow cots along the east wall of the hospital. While the Madics were made comfortable, Collin and Naturi went to report to the Miral and Comad.

An hour later, the Chancery's great room was deathly quiet as the members of the Healing family took their places around the table.

Isontra sat in the middle of the beautifully carved dining table while Kairma and Kinter sat on either side of her like matching bookends: one light and one dark, but both strong and beautiful. Jettena and Tamron sat at the north end of the long table and Zedic sat at the south end. Toric came in and took a chair next to Zedic, who was allowing his friends to make the report. The table wasn't meant to seat so many and they crowded together, elbows touching. Across from Isontra stood Naturi, Jared, Siede, and Collin. Trep leaned against the west wall. Night had fallen and the oil lamps painted dark shadows about the room. A small fire burned in the hearth, not for warmth as it was late summer, but it was always comforting to have a fire and a large black kettle holding hot water for terrid.

Isontra asked Jared and Siede to move the healthy prisoners to the home across the way. "See to it that they have warm beds and fresh food. We'll assign them homes in the morning."

Collin relayed the information that Nixon and Jaimer had been poisoned. Isontra nodded sagely. "We still don't know who was trying to kill those poor girls or these other men. They must have some connection to each other. Either it was vengeance, or someone in the city wanted to make sure they didn't return." Kairma started to speak, but Isontra held up her hand and asked Trep to come to the table. "Do you believe these men? Do you think others will be misled by their false trail? Unaware of our true location?"

Trep's jaw tightened. "I have no way of knowing. It may have been the truth. Jaimer was awfully proud of the way he'd covered his tracks, and I have no reason to doubt Nixon's men. Jaimer double-crossed Nixon too." Trep studied his hands, not wanting to look at anyone in the ill-lit room.

Kinter rarely spoke at a meeting—it wasn't her place—but the words were out before she could stop them. "Whoever is behind this is too smart for them. He had already poisoned Jaimer and Nixon, meaning he doesn't need them anymore."

Isontra agreed. "Yes, we have to assume whoever sponsored Jaimer's trip has another plan to find us. The only real questions are, when will he come, and with how many men?"

Kairma frowned. "It may have been the men the White Ones killed."

Trep looked up at Isontra and then to the others in the room. "If Yevve's behind the poison, I'm guessin' she just wanted those folks dead. She must have some reason for not wantin' 'em to ever get back to Peireson Landin'. If Narvin or Artuk are the sponsors, they won't want to be away from the city all winter. Actually, I cain't see either of those men comin' all this way. That'd be like you sendin' Kairma to the city. No, it'd be like you goin' yerself." He ran a hand through his hair. "My feelin' is that is that he'd hoped Jaimer would soften us up, and Jules Harman was his backup plan. I think we are out of danger, 'less someone else stumbles on us. Don't think that would happen this late in the year."

Kairma considered Trep's words. "If I sent men on a mission, and they had failed three times, I would go myself."

Zedic was thoughtful. He attempted to speak but paused. Isontra asked him to say what was on his mind and he replied, "I'm worried about what they want from us. If it's just the gold from the mines, we can let them have it. The only thing we really need to protect is the Crystal."

Kairma's already pale face turned an impossible shade of white. Several other people around the table gasped out loud and turned toward Trep. "It's no secret. I've known about the Star for a long time. Before we went to the city, in fact. I never told anyone y'all had it. I know how important it is not to betray its location." He grimaced, and put his head in his hands. "Narvin and several other people, like the assayer and the jeweler, knew you had access to gold and a maybe few artifacts. Narvin collects artifacts. When he saw Collin's ring, I could tell he was impressed. I'm thinkin' he just wants to find more things for his collection. Probably sent Jules to see if you had anything worth takin'."

Isontra folded her hands on the table in front of her. "What is this star you speak of? Is it something different, or is it in fact the Crystal we hold?"

Trep relayed the legend of the Star of Genesis to Isontra. "It's been said that a powerful weapon was made by the Ancient Ones. This weapon could destroy the world a hundred times over. Some people say it already did." He looked around the room. "Some stories say it can make men fly among the stars too." He shook his head slowly. "I don't know if any of that is true, but I suspect the Crystal might be the same weapon mentioned in the ancient legend. Narvin was obsessed with the legend." Trep was beside himself with shame for having befriended this man who would undoubtedly destroy this precious village to possess it. "I cain't believe I trusted him."

Kairma tried to assuage his guilt. She really liked Trep and hated to see him hurting as he was. "We don't believe you brought this on intentionally, and you went to great lengths to dissuade others from coming here. One never knows who one can trust in the end." She reached across the table and touched the hand still hiding his face. "Trust is a funny thing. If you don't trust enough, you'll never find love, and if you trust too much, it can cost you your soul."

Trep thought the words sounded old, like they should have come from Isontra, not the young woman across from him. He looked into Kairma's ice-blue eyes, and then to Isontra's steel gray ones, and lastly to the deep cobalt eyes of Kinter. In each set of eyes he saw forgiveness, acceptance, and, he was sure, a measure of love. It made him hate himself all the more for having hurt them.

Isontra turned to Kairma. "Well, that's part of the story. Tell me what happened in the woods."

Kairma looked at her grandmother shyly. "When we got to the cabin, Talon was dead and we tracked the Madics to the north. We found three strange Madics dead of arrow wounds. I believe the White

Ones killed them, but I don't know why. We tracked the rest of the Madics until after sunset, and then we saw the light from their campfire. I never meant to engage them. We were just tracking them when they attacked us." Her voice began to quiver, and both Naturi and Collin reached for her, but a look from Isontra sent them back to the wall.

"Go on. I understand you were quite brave."

She hadn't felt brave when she wounded the two Madics. The queasiness returned as she told Isontra about killing the man with her knife. No matter how many times she replayed the memory in her mind, she felt sick and was left with a sense of unreality.

After relaying the actions of the White Ones, Isontra put up her hand to keep anyone from speaking. "Kairma, how many times have the White Ones come to you?"

Kairma swallowed a lump in her throat, and her voice was barely above a whisper. "They were there the day Zedic and Collin left to hunt down the Madics, and the day Kinter fell off the cliff, and they came the night I was at Zacar's cabin alone."

Isontra stared at Kairma for a while before speaking. "And then the night you went searching for our captured friends. How odd. For annums we never saw them, almost as if they had left the mountain, but in the last four annums they seem to have become connected to you in some way."

Kairma couldn't help thinking it was her they wanted, but she didn't know why. One thing she had discovered in the woods that night—she wasn't afraid anymore. She had proven to herself she could do the right thing when the time came. She defied the elders when she let Naturi go with Trep and Collin, but it was that very action that brought the new blood, so desperately needed, to Survin. And now, her actions in the woods had saved not only her own people, but the valued new members as well. Kairma could feel the attitudes around her change, or maybe it was only her own attitude that had changed. She was ready for her Seridar. She still had a million things to learn, but she knew she would become the Vice Miral one day.

Epilogue

O ver the next few days the Madics were given homes of their own. Nyrees and Gyrien chose to stay with Sinara, who was still quite sick, and the home they were given was fairly large, having four bedrooms and a covered porch. Machek and the Peireson brothers moved into the not inconsiderable home across the creek from Naturi and Toric, and even though they were each offered homes of their own, Argus, Seth, and Chad wanted to live together as well. As was prearranged, their home was conveniently located near Grimly and next door to Hiram.

Isontra assigned homes and personal sentries to each Madic. "As sentries for our new friends, it will be your responsibility to see that they assimilate with as little difficulty as possible. I want you to bring food to them every day and take them with you when you do your work rotations. I want them to see how the village functions."

Sitting around the dining table with Isontra and Kairma, Toric scratched his head. "I always liked those Peireson brothers. I hope they can find a way to be happy here, but you know they were quite wealthy in the city. Those would be the men I'd choose to work with."

Naturi said, "I think Machek is very unhappy. I cannot be sure, but I believe he still plans to leave here the first chance he gets. There is a real anger that burns in the boy."

Grimly frowned. He really didn't like being assigned to one of the

Madics, but he understood the importance of keeping a close eye on them. Since Grimly was closer in age to Argus, he chose to be his sentry. "Argus seems to have a lot of ideas about raising crops. I didn't think I'd have to spend all day talking about plants."

Isontra laid her long-fingered hand over Grimly's rough hand. "You can always trade with Morgaina if you like. She really enjoys the garden, and since her mate passed away she might like the company."

Grimly grumbled but kept his assignment and, although none of the Madics were left alone, they were no longer treated as prisoners. The Survinees treated them well and taught them as much as they could about life in Survin.

Machek never spoke again about claiming a mine for himself once Collin and Zedic told him the White Ones lived in the caves. The memory of being surrounded by the wraith-like creatures still haunted his dreams. Seeing the Dove sisters healthy and happy went a long way in changing his attitude about the people of Survin. Although Machek still wanted to go back and kill Vaden, his mother convinced him to let that sleeping dog lie.

Naturi and Toric knocked on the door just a short while after dawn, and Machek came to the door rubbing his eyes. "Damned early for company, isn't it?"

Toric strode past the young boy. "Where're the brothers? I've an important matter to discuss with them."

Machek grimaced. "They're asleep like normal folk are at this time of the day."

Toric went to the small kitchen and began preparing breakfast. "I'm going to take a guess that none of you have eaten yet."

Machek rolled his eyes at the older man. "We always eat in our sleep."

Naturi helped his father in the kitchen. "Please wake the others. We have a lot to do today."

Machek grumbled, but went to the back room to wake the other men.

After they'd eaten, Toric led Patrick and Richard to a level pasture area south of the village.

Toric ran a thick hand through his hair. "I was hoping we could build a stable and a corral for training horses. We've seen several wild horses south of here."

Patrick looked at Richard and then turned back to Toric. "Breaking a new two-year-old horse is worlds different from breaking a fully grown wild horse."

Richard shifted nervously. "You ever try to catch a wild horse?"

Toric shook his head. "Collin talked about men riding on horseback the day his sister and brother were killed but he was only about five then so we never put much stock in it until Trep came through here last spring."

"I think we need to work out a plan." Patrick began sketching in the dirt. "We'll build the corral over there and we'll put the barn here. You have hay fields?"

Toric shook his head and Patrick looked back at Richard again. "Okay, horses eat a lot of food. That means finding safe pasture land."

Toric soon realized what he didn't know about horses could fill all the Temples of the Godstones. He listened with great care as the rest of the morning was devoted to plans for creating a viable horse farm.

While Toric worked out the details of the corral with Patrick and Richard, Machek followed Naturi to the home across the creek.

Naturi said, "I need to pick up tools. My duty today is roof repair. Each week we hold a lottery for jobs and you will accompany me while I do mine."

He thought Naturi seemed like a nice man, but Machek had no doubts about the reason he was being forced to follow the tall Survin man around. Just looking up at the cliffs that lined the canyon, he could see several rangers with bows and karracks.

Naturi invited him into the small stone cabin snuggled up against the cliff face. The smell of a cooking fire and tanned leather permeated the home. The place was neat and clean with nicely carved furnishings. Machek couldn't help noticing all the drawings on the pine table in the center of the room. He walked over and saw on top of the stack a picture of the lumber mill his father had owned. Looking at other drawings, he found several more of the mill. The one that struck him personally was the one showing his father guiding a fat log through the spinning blade. Machek's eyes misted and he blinked back tears.

Naturi saw the young man's reaction and understood. "You may have that if you would like. I lost my mother a few annums ago and I spend a lot of time looking at the drawing I have of her."

Machek didn't speak as Naturi explained the other drawings and then said, "I want to build a mill here. We have nothing like this in Survin. We grind wheat and corn by hand to make flour. The mill in your city impressed me. There is no one here that knows how to operate a mill, so I tried to capture as much detail as I could from the mill we toured."

Silence filled the room for several minutes before Naturi spoke again. "I understand you used to work at your father's mill in Peireson Landing."

Machek looked up at Naturi. "Are you askin' me to run your flour mill?"

"I would be very grateful. I need someone to teach us how to operate it, but as Survinees, we will all share the work."

When Machek realized he could have a mill he became excited about the planning. The new mill wouldn't be a grand sawmill like the one his father had owned, but it would be his, so Machek helped Naturi draw plans and work out the details. Because the placement of the mill was the most important consideration, they spent days surveying the area around the canyon and nights buried in sketches at an old pine table in the Gathering House.

As the days passed, Machek became more comfortable in the primitive village and came to think of Naturi as a friend. The various women who always found a moment to stop and talk to the ever-popular Naturi was an added benefit of being his partner.

Chad and Seth grudgingly accepted the terms of living in Survin, confident that given enough time the Survinees would let them leave. But that all changed for Chad the day he was working with Hiram on the drainage canals that fed the gardens. That was the first day Chad saw the tall dark-haired beauty with eyes the color of storm clouds. Alyssum was carrying water from the creek. The soft suede vest she wore did little to hide her bronze, muscular body. Her skirt was long but clung to powerful legs. After staring for a while, he realized what she was carrying. He turned his attention back to the older man he was working beside and asked, "Why do you carry water every day when it would be so much easier to run a clay pipe from the creek to each house?"

Not wanting to look like he was ignorant, Hiram simply said, "Because we don't. We like doing things our way."

Chad had been put in his place and felt foolish. His face was flushed as he looked back at the girl with the brace of water buckets.

Alyssum's heart went out to the startled young man, and she smiled, flashing brilliant perfect teeth. "Don't let my grampe upset you. His bark is far worse than his bite."

Hiram ran a hand over his thin white hair. "You go on child. Don't you get yourself mixed up in men's business now."

Alyssum turned and sashayed away, but not before giving Chad another big smile and a wink full of insinuation.

At the end of the day, most of the Survinees men went to the Gathering House to catch up on the latest gossip and, with the introduction of the Madics, there was plenty to report. The murmur of men's voices carried through the door as Hiram walked in. Crossing the room and taking a seat next to Grimly, he asked about the latest news. Grimly pointed to a table by the large stone hearth where Naturi and Machek sat studying drawings.

Grimly turned to Argus, who sat across the table from him. "Naturi tells me they can build something they call a mill to cut lumber and grind flour.

Argus took a sip of amber wine from the tall ceramic cup he held in his rough hand and nodded sagely. "It would take some time to build since you ain't got a good way to cut wood or move stone, but, yeah, it would be a big improvement over the way things are here. No offense, but you folks ain't even got water piped to your homes. Y'all carry it from the creek every day."

That was the second time that day Hiram had heard someone mention a water pipe. "What's this thing you call a pipe? We have a musical instrument called a pipe, but it has nothing to do with water.

Argus grabbed a few tall cups and, laying them on their sides, he placed them end to end. "See, a pipe is like having several of these cups all attached together. Of course, they wouldn't have bottoms, so water could flow from cup to cup over a long distance, like from the creek to the house."

Grimly grinned. His was mind racing with uses for this thing they called a pipe. The rest of the evening and the next day were spent planning the new water system for Survin.

The next morning was warm, and the smell of the harvest was heavy as Isontra set out the cups of terrid for her granddaughters. The large pine table they used for study was laden with laundry to be folded. Turning the last of the linens onto the table, she suggested a welcome party was in order.

"I want everyone to meet the Madics formally. I think everyone has seen them over the last few days, but a formal welcome will put everyone a little more at ease. I'd also like to thank the men who brought them here safely."

Kairma chewed on her lower lip. "The Harvest Celebration is only a few days away. Do you really want to have two celebrations?"

Isontra folded the blouse on the table in front of her. "This won't be a big event. I'd just like everyone to meet them now that they're a little more comfortable with us. I think it's important to take every opportunity to tell them they're a part of our family now and I'm afraid with everything that goes on at the Harvest Festival, they'd get lost in the activities."

Kairma placed a stack of folded linens on the shelf. "We could have it at the Gathering House, like we did for Misha and Lysara when they first arrived."

"That's exactly what I had in mind. We'll have a bit of a dance and some food. We can hold the reception tomorrow afternoon, right after the Nor Day service. I'm not ready to have the Madics attend the service yet. I want to be sure they understand our way of life a little better before we explain our religion. Tomorrow, at the service, I want everyone to be able to voice their fears or concerns about the Madics without having to say something that might be hurtful in front of those we are trying so hard to assimilate."

Kinter loved parties and was quick to agree. "We can have another baking contest! Radley will play music and I heard Argus plays an instrument similar to my pipes."

Kairma grimaced. "We don't have time to do that much."

"Yes we do. I'll take care of everything." With those words she dashed out the door to spread the news.

Isontra cocked her head toward Kairma. "Well, I suggest you run along and let everyone know about the celebration. You can count on

Kinter to line up the food and entertainment, but it really should be you inviting the guests."

Kairma started through the canyon after taking a few minutes to straighten her buff-colored dress and check her snow-white hair. Things had gone smoothly since bringing the Madics into the village and Kairma was pleasantly surprised. She had expected a lot more opposition from her own people and was grateful the dissension had been kept to a minimum, but what had amazed her the most was how easily the Madics had accepted their own captivity. As she made her way to the first home, the home of Sinara, she hoped she wasn't being naive.

The weekly service was devoted to reports about the Madics. The concerns were mostly limited to the inability to understand the Madic accent. It was uncomfortable to hear the strangers babble on so quickly to each other in their private conversations. Hiram wanted to outlaw the Madic language, but Isontra convinced him that because the Madics were so largely outnumbered by those who spoke the royal language, they would soon find it less and less beneficial to use their own. "They must be just as uncomfortable as we are. Imagine yourself in a foreign place, surrounded by a people much larger and stronger than you. You only understand a few simple commands, but know this is where you are forced to stay for the rest of your life. They gave up their homes to find a new life and this probably isn't exactly what they imagined it would be."

The conversation moved in the direction of the new corral and other projects. Isontra was happy to hear that several people had learned novel and interesting ideas from their newest members. Even Hiram begrudged them the advantages of the water pipe.

Hobbling on wooden crutches, Efram slowly made his way down the trail after the service. Dillon walked beside him and listened as Efram made snide jokes about the Madics. He liked to pick on everything from their diminutive size to their language. His newest name for them was Muddies, referring to the fact they had mixed blood, not the strong and pure blood of the Survinees. When Dillon told him about Machek and his sister, the young Madic girl with the long blond hair, Efram's voice carried down the path to Kairma: "You mean to tell me we have more than one White Witch now?"

Kairma looked back at Efram, and scowled.

Efram laughed. "I'm teasing. You know you're the only real White Witch we'll ever have."

Kairma was hurt, but she couldn't help notice the playfulness in Efram's voice.

At the reception, Kairma draped several tables with the colorful linens Zedic had brought from the city, and Kinter placed flowers on the tables. When the room was set Kinter went to get the guests of honor and Kairma greeted the Survinees as they came into the hall. "Thank you all for coming. This means a lot to us. You'll find food and drinks on the bar. If you have entries for the contest, place them over on those tables." She pointed across the room at a table quickly filling with treats.

Down the valley, a short walk from the Gathering House, Kinter knocked on the wood frame door of the small home where the new Madic women were living and Sinara greeted her at the threshold. "It's nice to see you, Kinter. Are we late?"

"No. I just came to see if you needed my help. I know you still aren't one hundred percent yet." The Madic woman was nervous, but Kinter reassured her by saying, "Everyone is really excited to meet you. I know it's been difficult for you to get out and meet anyone, but you'll be good as new soon, I promise."

Sinara smiled gingerly and allowed Kinter to help her to the Gathering House.

Kinter settled Sinara at a long dark pine table with several of Survin's most respected elders. "Can I get you something to eat?" Kinter asked.

Sinara smiled at the girl and said, "I would love some fruit, but I see there are many people waiting for food. I hate to be a bother. You must have lots of things to do."

Kinter winked. "It's no bother, besides, they never make me stand in line."

Kinter was gliding between the crowded tables with a plate of pan biscuits and fresh fruit when Rose and Ember came in with Gyrien and Nyrees. Seeing the beautiful long dresses the women from the city wore, Kinter was so jealous she couldn't speak. She recovered in time to lead them to their places of honor at the elders' table, where she spent the next several minutes learning everything she could about the wonderfully soft fabric of their gowns.

Several men turned around when the tiny women took their seats. Dillon and Efram had been caught up in an argument about the advantages of the hinge when the room grew quiet. Turning to see what had caused the sudden silence, Efram's eyes locked on to the darkest eyes he'd ever seen. The tiny, fairylike face was crowned with soft waves of sunshine. Her perfect body was draped in the silky lavender fabric decorated with sparkling amethyst jewels that hinted at the fullness of her breasts and her tiny waist. His mouth dropped open.

Reaching over and shutting Efram's mouth for him, Dillon laughed and said, "Meet the new White Witch. If you hadn't slept the whole trip back from Zacar's place, you would have known what to expect."

Gyrien met his eyes and couldn't look away. She had thought Naturi was handsome, but there was something about this man that made her heart race. He was tall and dark like all the men of Survin, but there was a vulnerability about him that intrigued her. She smiled shyly, hoping he would come over and talk to her.

On the other side of the room, Efram's hormones began to dance in a way that embarrassed him. The thought of meeting a woman who didn't know him excited him in a manner he couldn't have voiced. This beautiful woman never saw him when he'd lost his front teeth and looked so silly. She hadn't seen him lose the sling contest to Zedic annum after annum. She didn't know him when he fell into a patch of poison ivy—his skin becoming all blotchy and red because he couldn't stop scratching. What drew him to her more than anything was the fact that he didn't know anything about her—and he wanted desperately to know everything. Without taking his eyes away from hers, he made his way across the room to meet Gyrien.

After several hours of celebrating, Miral Isontra stood on a small stool and cleared her voice. She began to praise the brave young men who had crossed so many dangerous miles to bring home such lavish gifts, and thanked the Peireson brothers for teaching Collin and Toric how to fix a horse. Everyone laughed at the common misnomer. "We have been so very fortunate to have these honored guests, our newest companions, among us," Isontra said. "A week from today is our Harvest Celebration and the beginning of our new annum. We invite you to our service and ask you to join our village." Turning to her granddaughter she reached out her hand. "Kairma, will you do the honors?"

Having finally grown into her long legs, Kairma stepped gracefully up on the stool as Isontra stepped down. Looking around the long room filled with friends and family, she felt a shiver of pride run down her back. All eyes were upon her, and suddenly her shyness returned again. Her voice cracked with emotion as she began the introductions. When Misha stood, Kairma glanced at Zedic, seeing nothing but love in his dark gray eyes. Then, looking around the room at the members of Survin, Kairma could see the Madics had truly found a home with her people. Feeling the love and acceptance of these newcomers was the tonic she longed for, for such a long time. By accepting these small foreign people, the Survinees had at long last accepted her, the peculiar girl with the pale skin and white hair.

After announcing the winner of the baking contest, Kairma led the first dance with her father. A newfound confidence exuded from her smiling blue eyes as she whirled around the room, her long white dress, a scarf the color of sunset draped elegantly over her left shoulder and the soft suede pouch holding the Crystal nestled between her breasts.

"You might as well drop a letter into the world's postal service without an address or signature, as to send that carved mountain into history without identification."

— Gutzon Borglum, 1939
Sculptor of Mount Rushmore

Families of Survin

Calista & Griffin
Parents of Loella & Saffron

Saffron & Grimly
Parents of Massie, Ambrie, Canton, & Davis

Massie	Ambrie	Canton	Davis
Mother of Ellen, Cody & Collin	*Mother of Efram*	*Father of Ember*	*Father of Rose*

Loella & Hamond
Parents of Toric & Rhylee

Toric	Rhylee
Father of Naturi	*Mother of Dillon*

Martena
Mother of Mylinda & Hiram

Mylinda	Hiram
Mother of Diakus	*Father of Karren & Devon*

Diakus	Karren	Devon
Father of Ellen, Cody & Collin	*Mother of Alyssum*	*Mother of Naturi*

Addison
Mother of Sabra & Jacinda

Sabra
Mother of Sharra, Kaiden, & Siede

Sharra & Jerman	Kaiden	Siede
Baby due soon	*Father of Dillon*	

Tristan & Jayden
Parents of Thomas

Thomas & Hestra
Parents of Isontra

Isontra and Petar
Parents of Jettena

Jettena & Tamron
Parents of Zedic, Kairma, Kinter, Tadya, Taren, Tames & Sonty

---

Noah
Father of Loren, Peron & Morgaina

Loren	Morgaina
Father of Jared	*Mother of Dessa & Rossi*

Zacar
Lives outside Survin with his dog, Jesse and his pet mountain lion, Purder

Citizens of Peireson Landing

Pan Aterin	*Jeweler*
Rorey Bainser	*Sheriff*
Lou Bassin	*Assayer*
Nixon Blong	*City Treasurer & homesteader*
Carton Bowart	*Livery owner*
Jake Bowart	*Livery owner*
Lysara Dove	*School teacher & city planner*
Misha Dove	*Hotel Operator, Sister to Lysara*
Nyrees Durbin	*Seamstress & homesteader*
Talon Durbin	*Son of Nyrees & homesteader*
Uri Giman	*Blacksmith*
Jules Harman	*Prospector*
Byran Heston	*Boot maker*
Conrad Hipptem	*Lumber baron*
Sinara Hipptem	*Wife of Conrad & homesteader*
Machek Hipptem	*Son of Conrad & homesteader*
Gyrien Hipptem	*Daughter of Conrad & homesteader*

Jaimer Kokel	*Past Overseer & homesteader*
Tatiance Layesve	*Bank owner*
Artuk Masin	*Tax collector & valet to Narvin*
Tarl Millen	*Hotel employee*
Samuel Mories	*Mercantile owner*
Argus Muceli	*Farmer & homesteader*
Chad Ontent	*Farmer & Homesteader*
Narvin Parns	*Overseer & artifact collector*
Acton Peireson	*Rancher & horse breeder*
Grant Peireson	*Docks owner*
Patrick Peireson	*Son of Acton & homesteader*
Richard Peireson	*Son of Acton & homesteader*
Seth Row	*Field hand & homesteader*
Yevve Stanley	*Narvin's secretary & mistress*
Dianay Suni	*Hotel employee*
Rashad Vaden	*Mercenary*
Trepard Zander	*Archeologist*

About the Author

Michele Poague has written advertising copy, training manuals, and coauthored the guidebook *Creating a Successful Convention*. She currently lives in Denver, Colorado, with her husband, Monte. This is her first novel.

Manufactured By: RR Donnelley
                     Momence, IL USA
                     February, 2011